Praise for Kate Raphael's Palestine Mystery Series

Praise for *Murder Under the Fig Tree*

"Once again, Raphael has delivered a powerful, textured, boldly imagined, and brilliantly executed portrait of Palestine and Israel that is also a wicked pleasure to read. There are no characters in fiction quite like Rania and Chloe. Not to be missed!"

—Carolina de Robertis, author of the international best-seller *The Invisible Mountain*

"*Murder Under the Fig Tree* is a beautifully written and layered novel that takes on the complexities and ambiguities of Palestinian life. It's also a damn good mystery that demonstrates a crime novel can also be fine literature."

—Michael Nava, author of the Lambda award-winning Henry Rios mysteries

"To read this fine novel is to be drawn into both a murder mystery and the lives and day-to-day challenges of two women as disparate as their cultural backgrounds. Exposing the truth of this murder becomes as valuable and necessary to us as it is to them."

—Katherine V. Forrest, Lambda award-winning author of the Kate Delafield mystery series

Praise for *Murder Under the Bridge*

"This riveting story provides a rich portrait of life behind the headlines of the Palestinian-Israeli conflict."

— Ayelet Waldman, best-selling author of *Love and Treasure* and *Kingdom of Olives and Ash: Writers Confront the Occupation*

"Raphael has created a wonderful cast, most especially her Palestinian policewoman, Rania, and a taut, page-turning plot. But the real star here is the setting. When an immigrant is murdered, Rania's investigations take her directly into the treacherous, deadly politics of Israel and Palestine. Authoritatively and vividly rendered, *Murder Under the Bridge* is a compelling read."

> — Karen Joy Fowler, PEN/Faulkner prize winning author of *We Are All Completely Beside Ourselves* and *The Jane Austen Book Club*

"The mix of murder and politics makes for fascinating reading, made even richer by the revealing glimpse of life in the occupied territories."

> — *Booklist*

"Raphael thoroughly captures the tension of life on the West Bank by setting a murder in a location marked by daily violence. Substantial yet humanly flawed female protagonists give depth to both the mystery ... and the political and social turmoil of the region."

> — *Library Journal*, starred review

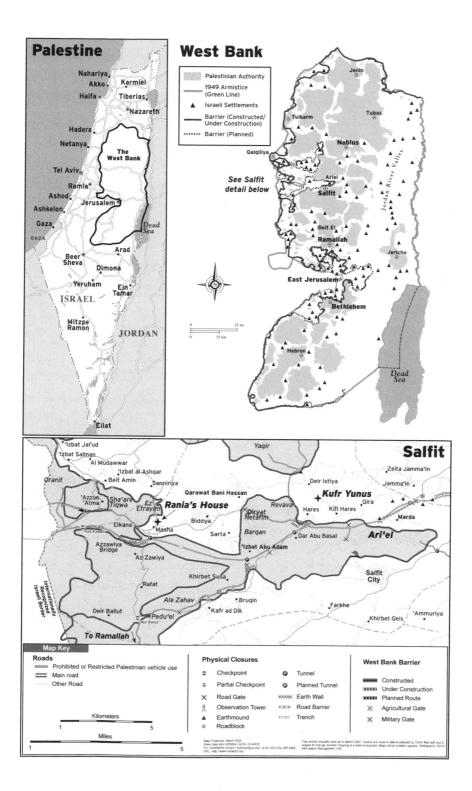

Murder under the Fig Tree

The Palestine Mystery Series:

Murder Under the Bridge

Murder Under the Fig Tree

Murder under the Fig Tree

a palestine mystery

Kate Jessica Raphael

SHE WRITES PRESS

Published 2017
Printed in the United States of America
Print ISBN: 978-1-63152-274-1
E-ISBN: 978-1-63152-275-8
Library of Congress Control Number: 2017941633

For information, address:
She Writes Press
1563 Solano Ave #546
Berkeley, CA 94707

Cover design © Julie Metz, Ltd./metzdesign.com
Formatting by Kiran Spees

She Writes Press is a division of SparkPoint Studio, LLC.

This is a work of fiction. Names, characters, places, and incidents either are the product of the author's imagination or are used fictitiously. Any resemblance to actual persons, living or dead, is entirely coincidental.

For Marilyn

A note about names

Formal Palestinian names have four parts: first name, father's name, grandfather's name, and family name. In official situations, a person might be called by two, three, or all four names. Once someone has a son, they are known by the title *Abu* (father) or *Um* (mother) and the name of the eldest son. Using the honorific is a sign of both respect and affection. Typically, family members and childhood friends call one another by their first names, and everyone else uses the honorific Abu or Um. When I was a human rights monitor in Salfit, we spent a fair amount of our time asking, "Which Um Mohammed do you mean?" and the person might say, "Nawal Um Mohammed," meaning her first name was Nawal, or they might say, "Um Mohammed who lives near the school."

Israelis generally use first names in every situation. Even Palestinians call Israeli police or army commanders by their first names most of the time. This informality does not connote friendship.

The glossary at the end of the book contains most of the Hebrew and Arabic terms I used, as well as a few cultural references that might require clarification.

Chapter 1
March, 2006

"Rania in prison."

Tina's text caught Chloe in mid-glide. She looked around at the skaters, volleyball players, jamming musicians, couples walking with kids licking ice cream cones in their strollers. It was the first clear Sunday in weeks. Golden Gate Park was packed with people thronging to the azalea gardens and the arboretum. A minute ago, she had felt in sync with them all. Suddenly, she was on a different planet. She spun around on her rollerblades and took the hills as fast as her forty-year-old legs would carry her.

Barely a week later, she watched the ground come closer and closer as the plane circled over Ben Gurion Airport. She felt each successively smaller circle gnawing its way into the pit of her stomach. This is a mistake, her brain whispered. They'll never let you in. You should have gone over land, from Jordan or Egypt. Then when they refused you entry, you would have been nearby; maybe you could have appealed, tried again. But, in reality, fifteen miles might as well be fifteen thousand when the Israeli border stood in your way. If she was going to get sent home, she would rather the rendering be swift and brutal. The doors were opening now, and the impatient passengers were shoving toward the steep stairs leading to the tarmac. She let everyone go ahead of her. At least she could give herself a few more minutes.

She parked herself in the mob under the All Others sign and waited, practicing her lines over and over. To her right, Israeli passport holders breezed through the turnstile, joking with the passport control officers in Hebrew.

To distract herself, she imagined Tina pacing around the huge airport lobby, waiting for Chloe to emerge from the secured area. Since getting the news about Rania's arrest, Chloe had been so obsessed with getting her friend out of prison, she had not really considered that she would also be renewing her relationship with Tina. What should her first words be? Would they even still like each other? Theirs had been a whirlwind courtship in the context of a big adventure which had ultimately forced Chloe to leave Palestine. They had spent fewer than ten days in each other's arms, though the intensity had made it seem much longer. Not much to base a relationship on. But Tina had encouraged her to come, so that had to mean something.

To her left, a motley mix of women who resembled her mother and kids who resembled her camp counselors danced a hora under a sign reading Welcome New Olim. The *Olim*, Jews coming to claim the birthright of Israeli citizenship bequeathed to them by Israeli law and the United Nations, stood in the center of the circle, clutching pet carriers and household appliances and looking shell-shocked.

She felt a moment of envy, which she quickly stowed in a tightly locked closet in her mind. Even now, despite all that had happened, if she told the immigration officer she wanted to immigrate to Israel—to "make *Aliyah*," they would whisk her off to a special area reserved for Jews "returning" and help her sign up for government-paid Hebrew classes. In junior high school, she had imagined doing it. She had pictured herself strong in olive fatigues, an Uzi slung over her shoulder, like the two soldier girls just now strolling past her, laughing. She thought one of them glanced her way.

Chloe took deep breaths, or tried to. She should have brought a fashion magazine, as a friend had suggested, to make herself seem harmless. Like that would help. There were agents everywhere whose job was to watch out for people just like her, people who were not what they seemed.

What she seemed to be was a middle-aged American with an unmistakably Jewish countenance and wild dark curls flecked with gray. She wore jeans and a sleeveless T-shirt, like 80 percent of the others in this line. Hers clung to her zaftig middle, creating dark patches where tension was making her sweat. She wished she had a hair dryer, but of course she hadn't even packed one.

She made a game of distinguishing all the languages her fellow tourists were speaking. She picked out snatches of conversation in French, German, and languages she didn't recognize, probably Dutch, Polish, Serbian. Directly in front of her, a group of Christian pilgrims joked in German, all tall, rugged blondness, the crosses around their necks mildly clashing with their grunged-out clothing. If she got in, she would no doubt run into them in the Old City, eating hummus at Abu Shukri's famous shop.

In front of the pilgrims was a South Asian Muslim family, the woman in a lavender headscarf, the father with a long, black beard and white cap. Chloe guessed they were Indian, and the Indian government was a close ally of Israel, so maybe that would help them, but she predicted they would be in for some rigorous questioning. She examined the three children, the oldest not more than five, dancing and hopping around while their mother tried to contain them by clinging to their hands. How would they hold up under the interrogation of the airport authority? she wondered. And if they were taken aside for questioning and background checks, would that help or hurt her own chances? Was there a quota of harassment they had to meet every day? A limited number of people available to conduct strip searches and other invasive procedures? She had no idea. She silently apologized to the Indian family—if that's what they were—for hoping that they would occupy the suspicious slot for this line.

Her turn finally came to walk up to the counter. She watched the Muslim family be herded through an iron door, flanked by two police, one male and one female. One of the kids turned to look back, her pigtails flying out around her head. The policewoman gently but firmly prodded her toward the invisible back room.

Chloe's legs would hardly hold her up. She braced a knee against the bottom of the counter, so the young woman behind it would not see her shaking. She leaned over slightly to make sure the Star of David around her neck dangled into the clerk's line of sight.

"What is the purpose of your trip?" asked the young woman, between chews of gum.

"Visiting friends and family," Chloe replied. Her eyes burned as she tried to keep them from shifting away.

"Family? What family do you have here?"

What should she say? She couldn't name the second cousins she had never even met. The people she considered family were not going to do her any good in this encounter.

"My cousin Nehama," she said. "In Givatayim."

She should have called Nehama and made a plan to say they were cousins. The older woman would surely have agreed. What else had she neglected to do? She had been half-crazed, worrying about Rania, dreaming of Palestine; she had barely gotten it together to find someone to take care of her cat.

As long as the agent didn't ask for Nehama's phone number, it would be okay. If Chloe got to make the call herself, her friend would back her up.

"Nehama what? Her name is Rubin also?"

"No, it's Weiss. She's my mother's first cousin." Might as well lay it on.

"Where does she live?"

"I told you, Givatayim. It's a suburb of Tel Aviv." Of course the woman knew where Givatayim was. She was just testing, to see if Chloe would crack.

"What street?"

"Keren Kayemet."

The young woman chomped noisily on her gum. She swiped the passport's magnetic stripe through the machine, and they both waited impatiently. A flood of information splashed across the blue screen. Chloe couldn't see it, but she imagined she knew what it said, chronicling the trouble she had caused for the Israeli military last time she was here. The woman made faces at it, her hand hovering over the telephone to her right. This is it, Chloe thought. She was going to call the police to come get Chloe and take her into that back room. Chloe instinctively took hold of the Star of David, rubbed it a little for luck. The young woman took her hand off the phone and held the passport with both hands in front of her face.

"How long do you plan to stay?"

"At least until Pesach."

The woman lowered the passport and studied Chloe's face. Chloe concentrated on appearing as middle-aged and nonthreatening as she possibly could. She wished she had gum, so she could chomp like the agent was doing.

Stamp, stamp, stamp. The agent's hand moved rapidly, and now she was holding the passport out to Chloe to take. Improbable as it seemed, her use of the Hebrew name for the Jewish holiday of Passover, coming up in four weeks, had worked like a secret handshake. She was in. Chloe walked away, mentally shaking her head over her dumb luck. In minutes, she was holding Tina's long, lithe body in her arms, burying her nose in her lover's neck.

✷ ✷ ✷

Rania perched on one end of the narrow cot and concentrated on carving into the plaster wall with her hardiest fingernail. When she was done, she counted the tick marks, as if she didn't know them by heart. As if she had not already counted three times today, and it was not even noon. At least, she assumed it was not, because the policewoman had not come to bring her lunch. A lunch she would not want to eat, but probably would, because the boredom was too much to tolerate on an empty stomach.

Here came the young woman now: the one they called Tali, her freckled, copper face glowing with health and rest. From counting the ticks, Rania knew it was Sunday, *Yom il ahad*. Yesterday would have been the regular guards' day off, the Jewish Sabbath. She tried to remember who was here yesterday. She could not conjure up a face. She could not keep the days from blurring one into the other, while she sat here, day after day, looking at these same four walls and wishing wishing wishing herself at home with Khaled and Bassam.

Rania turned her face to the gray wall before the policewoman got to her cell. She would not let the police see her crying for her former life, which seemed so far away now. She could barely remember what Khaled had looked like the day before they took her away. Of course she knew what her own son looked like; she knew his face better than her own, but, at seven, he was changing so fast, becoming more himself every day. Sitting here, she could remember how he had looked as a tiny infant in her arms, as a three-year-old soberly watching her separate the clothes for washing, last month at the party for his cousin's engagement. But she could not remember exactly what he had worn the last day after he came home from school, or if his face had furrowed over his English homework.

"Hakol bseder?" Tali asked as she shoved the tray into the space between the bars. The unappetizing smell of overcooked beef quickly filled the little cell.

The guard didn't wait for an answer, but moved on to the next cell even as the words, Are you okay?, were coming out of her mouth. There was no reason she should wait. Rania had never said a word in reply, in the weeks they had been bringing her the miserable Israeli hummus and the runny, tasteless cheese they served instead of *labneh*. The thought of it made Rania's stomach lurch. They couldn't even make salad right.

"Lo, hakol lo bseder," she said suddenly. The words sounded so strange coming out of her mouth. Not only because she rarely spoke Hebrew, but because she had not heard her own voice in three long weeks. She, who seldom went three minutes without talking. When they had first brought her here, she had worried that she would break under interrogation, just because she loved to talk. She needn't have worried. There had been no interrogations. No one wanted her to talk. They wanted to shut her up.

She was so used to being alone with her own thoughts, she forgot that she had spoken out loud. Now, the startled young woman was back and watching her with annoyance in her eyes. Rania vaguely traced the irritation to the fact that Tali had asked a question she had not registered, unused as she was to conversation.

"Did you say something?" Rania asked.

"You speak Hebrew?" The question sounded vaguely accusatory, as if Rania must have stolen the language.

"Ken, ktzat," yes, a little.

"Ma habeayah?" What's the problem?

What to say? She was not going to tell this Israeli cop that she wanted to see her son or that she wanted to know what was going to happen to her, how long she would be cooped up in this nothing place. She didn't want to give them the satisfaction of knowing they had broken her down, and she couldn't trust them with the knowledge of what was important to her. She thought of her friend Samia, back in the refugee camp in Bethlehem, who had been arrested when they were seventeen. She had been tortured and raped, but she had not named one member of their group.

"Nothing," Rania said in English. "Sorry to bother you."

"No problem." Tali swung away from her, back to the cart of lunch trays she had to deliver.

When she was gone, Rania almost regretted her resolve. It had been nice just to be in the presence of another person, for those few minutes. That tiny bit of interaction had made her feel a little more human. What would it have hurt to have a little conversation with the girl, ask her about her weekend, about the weather, if she had a boyfriend? But, then again, what would it have helped? It would simply have postponed the inevitable agony, when she would be alone again, to sit here trapped with her own thoughts and recriminations.

Ten months ago, Rania had learned dangerous secrets held by two of Israel's top military men. She thought she had outsmarted them, but, all this time, they had been waiting for their chance to lock her away with their secrets. When Hamas won the Palestinian legislative election, the Israelis had rounded up dozens of Palestinian police and others they considered dangerous. She should have been spared; she had been a member of Fatah, President Abbas's party, since she was fifteen. Her enemies, though, had seized the opportunity to put away someone they personally considered dangerous. She had no idea how long they could hold her. If her enemies had anything to say about it, it could be forever.

That thought brought the tears to her eyes again, and she wiped them away with the back of her hand. However long she was going to be here, she would not spend it moping. She stood and stretched up on tiptoe, then bent and touched her toes. Her body felt uncharacteristically stiff, her back aching with inaction. In the normal course of her life, she got lots of exercise, but now she thought maybe she should do some of the calisthenics they used to do in school. She removed the heavy, dark *jilbab*, revealing a red, long-sleeved pullover and black, stretchy pants. She felt ridiculously exposed, though there was no one here to see. She did a few jumping jacks, ran in place for five minutes. While she ran, she hummed one of the marching songs that had played everywhere during the First Intifada.

"Singing is forbidden." Tali was back.

"Why?" Rania was not in the mood to be conciliatory. What more could they do to her?

"Those are the rules."

"If you care about rules, why do you break international law by keeping me here?"

The policewoman walked away, shaking her head. Rania felt surprisingly cheered. In those few minutes, she had recouped a little piece of herself she had been missing since the night they took her away. She would spend the day crafting a campaign of minor resistance.

Chapter 2

As if swept along on a tidal wave, Tina and Chloe followed the crowd to the place where they could catch a shared taxi, called *servees* in Arabic and *sherut* in Hebrew, for Jerusalem. They joined a line of about thirty people who must have had collectively two hundred bags. They clung to carts laden with instrument cases and duffel bags, huge sets of matching, black leather suitcases, ratty backpacks leaking T-shirts, trunks, furniture boxes, and strollers.

A white van with Hebrew writing on the side screeched to a halt next to the curb where they waited. The driver did not get out but opened the doors automatically and yelled at the people to hurry and get in.

Chloe counted the seats. There was room for eleven, plus the driver, but would there be room for all their luggage? She started to count the line by elevens. If seats weren't needed for excess baggage, they would make the next van after this.

Suddenly, a surge of humanity pressed forward, running at the van. The neat line that had formed to wait for the sherut was, apparently, merely a formality. Now that it was here, it was every person for himself. A hunched-over, old woman was using her massive suitcase as a battering ram to clear a path to the door. Chloe and Tina stood aside, mouths agape, watching the van fill up like an inflatable mattress. In seconds, the van was flying out of there, loaded to bursting with people and possessions.

"We're never going to get out of here," Chloe murmured to Tina, as the automatic double doors of the airport opened to eject another fifty or so travelers into the line which, improbably, had formed up again.

The man standing in front of them turned around. He was big and beefy and wore a bright-blue polo shirt. Sweat poured down his bulbous nose.

"This is Israel. You have to push," he said.

"It's Israel to you," Tina said, under her breath.

"What? I didn't hear you."

"That's because I wasn't talking to you."

"Shhh," Chloe whispered, stroking Tina's feathery hair. "Let it go."

"Don't shush me!"

Chloe dropped the handle of her rollaway bag and let it list onto its side. The handle brushed the leg of the man Tina had snapped at, who turned around to glare at them.

"Did I do something to piss you off?" Chloe asked.

"No, sorry." Tina picked up the rollaway. Chloe wished she had reached for her hand instead. "I'm just tired."

That was a plausible explanation. Tina would have had to get up early to make it from Ramallah to Lod in time for Chloe's ten o'clock arrival. Still, how much did she really know about this woman? Their face-to-face relationship probably hadn't comprised more than forty hours—a standard work week. Since Chloe had gone back to the States, what they had been doing could best be described as sexting, supplemented by an occasional phone call or email rant.

When the next van pulled up, Tina was ready. Rolling the suitcase in one hand, she grabbed Chloe's arm with the other and barged through the mush of people. Chloe never quite knew how her bag ended up in the luggage compartment and her body jammed against the window, but somehow it had happened. Seconds later, they were rolling toward Jerusalem.

She gazed out the exhaust-streaked window, reliving the drama of the last time she had traveled this road. She had been in a police van, trying to figure out how to keep them from tossing her unceremoniously onto a plane. That night she had come closer to dying than she ever had before or since. Rania had risked her life and freedom to save Chloe's. Chloe was here to settle that debt.

But she had also come to be with Tina. She turned to face her lover. Tina was leaning back against the seat, her eyes closed. The dimples around her mouth were slack in her smooth, olive skin, and she looked like she belonged in a Modigliani painting. Chloe stretched out her index finger and brushed the other woman's cheek lightly. Tina opened her eyes.

"Sorry mate," she said with a half smile. Her Australian accent made "mate" sound like "mite." "I get you to come all this way, and then I crash out on you."

"That's okay," Chloe said. "How are things at the center?" Tina worked at a counseling center for abused women and their children. Her salary was paid by a fellowship which sent diasporic Palestinians to work in their homeland.

"They're okay," Tina said. "People are worried about money, because of the embargo. And they're worried a little about Hamas, that they will try to restrain what we do in some way. But really, we haven't heard anything from the government in months."

The van rumbled into the outskirts of Jerusalem. Chloe's body tingled awake, from her nose to her toes. She forced open the window, basking in the warm air and ignoring the driver's protest about the air conditioning. She drank in the sight of spindly, dust-scarred olive and lemon trees and strained for the scent of the wild herb called zaatar. Even the military jeeps and the soldiers hitchhiking made her happy. She felt more like she'd come home now than she had when she landed in San Francisco ten months ago. Her time in Palestine, which had ended so abruptly and come so close to disaster, had tested her and taught her who she really was.

She reached for Tina's hand. Tina squeezed hers, but then looked around at the other passengers and pulled her hand away. What was that about? Chloe wondered. She perused the other occupants of the van. She saw no *hijabs*—traditional Muslim headscarves—or other evidence of Palestinians on board. Had Tina changed so much since she had left, that she was concerned about Jewish Israelis judging her sexual orientation? Or was it her feelings about Chloe that had changed? Had Chloe become more attractive in memory than she actually was? She had gained a few pounds during her time back in the States. Was Tina a closet fat-phobe?

For the first time since getting on the plane, Chloe wondered if she had made a huge mistake in rushing over here. She had no real plan for getting Rania out of prison. It was at least as likely that she would land in an Israeli jail herself. But Tina had sent her the text about Rania, and she had encouraged Chloe's plans to return to Palestine. Chloe's typical insecurities must be playing with her head, making her read too much into casual interactions. She determined to take Tina at her word: she was just tired.

"What about Rania?" she asked. "Have you heard anything new?"

Tina shook her head. "No. I called Ahlam yesterday to tell her you were coming. She didn't know anything else."

Chloe had rented an apartment from her friends, Ahlam and Jaber, the last time she had been in Palestine. Chloe and Rania had gotten information that freed Ahlam's son, Fareed, from Israeli prison. That investigation had gotten Chloe thrown out of Palestine ten months ago, and now it had gotten Rania locked up.

"How did Ahlam know about the arrest?"

"I think she read it in the paper."

The van was pulling up to a series of nondescript apartment buildings surrounded by manicured lawns.

"Is this a settlement?" Chloe asked.

"I think so," Tina answered. A family of six climbed over the rest of the passengers to exit the van, the father in long, black coat and high, black hat, the boys' dangling side curls marking them as part of one of the ultra-religious Hasidic sects. They claimed fully half of the luggage piled into the back, and, as the van drove off, Chloe watched out the window as each little boy pulled along a suitcase nearly his size.

The next stop was on Emek Refaim Street, where Jewish hipsters shopped for handmade crafts and sipped coffee in sidewalk cafés. Only a few blocks away on the Bethlehem Road, vans like this one, but older, would be carrying people to the village where Tina's aunt lived and Aida refugee camp, where Rania grew up. Now they were skirting the Old City, its ancient, stone walls as breathtaking as the first day Chloe glimpsed them. The van stopped opposite Jaffa Gate. This would be the end of the official route, the place where West Jerusalem blurred into East. What should they do from here? They could negotiate with the driver to take them close to Damascus Gate, where they could get a car to Ramallah, or they could off-board here and look for a cheaper Arab taxi to go the last three-quarter mile.

"What do you want to do?" Chloe turned to Tina.

"I don't know; what do you think?" Tina never went to West Jerusalem and spoke no Hebrew. She would be expecting Chloe to take charge of this situation.

"L'an atem?" Where are you going? The driver asked impatiently.

"Shaar Shchem," Chloe said, giving the Hebrew name for Damascus Gate. "Kama?" How much?

"Shaar Shchem? Ma yesh lakhem b'Sha'ar Shkhem?"

None of your business why we want to go there, Chloe bit back.

"Come on," she said to Tina. "Let's find another cab."

"Esrim shekel," the driver said before she had gotten both feet onto the ground.

"Forget it." Twenty shekels to go a few blocks? Thirty would get them all the way to Ramallah.

"How much?" Tina asked.

"Twenty. Forget it. He's just screwing with us."

"Offer him fifteen."

"Don't be ridiculous. It shouldn't be more than five."

"I want to go. Offer fifteen."

"Chamesh esrei," Chloe said to the driver. He nodded laconically, ground out his cigarette against the side of the van, and climbed into the driver's seat. Tina nearly threw the money at him as he gunned the engine. When he deposited them on the sidewalk in front of the Faisal Hostel, Chloe almost kissed the ground. The Faisal was the unofficial gateway to the West Bank for international solidarity activists. It was there that Chloe had begun her first adventure in Palestine. She breathed in the heavy aromas of cardamom and burned sugar from the coffee stand, the grease from the falafel place next door, and the warm smell of bread baking down the street. She soaked up the busy to-ing and fro-ing of head-scarved women pulling their kids along to the vegetable and fish markets, the old women sitting cross-legged near the bus station hawking their herbs and fruit, the cries of peddlers warning people to get out of the way of their carts as they plunged into the Old City.

"I'm hungry," she told Tina. "Let's go to Abu Emile's for breakfast." Abu Emile's, where they had eaten the morning after they first made love. She hoped returning to the elegant, cave-like restaurant would rekindle the almost painful closeness they had had that day.

"I have food at my house."

"It could take us an hour to get there."

"Not anymore. We don't have to stop at Qalandia. We can drive straight through."

"I can't leave Jerusalem yet. I just got here. I thought I might never see it again."

"I don't want to go into the Old City. It's crawling with settlers."

"How about the Jerusalem Hotel?" Chloe said. "Just for a cappuccino, and then we'll go home."

"Okay." Tina's face cracked a small smile for the first time since they had left the airport. "Maybe I'll even have a Taybeh."

"Beer at eleven in the morning?"

"Don't be a wowser. I've been up since five. In Melbourne, I'd be ready to quit work for the day."

＊ ＊ ＊

Happily full of a delicious omelet and a satisfactory cup of coffee, savored in the Palestinian chic of the Jerusalem Hotel's screened-in patio, Chloe could enjoy the journey to Ramallah. As Tina had promised, they sailed through the checkpoint and were dropped at the bustling al-Manara, the central square of Palestine's most modern city. Young professionals and students darted into cafés, and patrons overflowed from shops selling sweets or Broaster chicken. In Ramallah on a good day, you could forget that Palestine was an occupied country.

Tina led them to a sunny garden apartment on the edge of the business district, across the street from a hotel that had seen better days. As Tina put the key into the lock, a buxom, middle-aged woman dashed out of the hotel and hurried to greet them.

"Tina, habibti, weyn bakeeti?" Tina, my love, where were you?

"I went to the airport, Um Malik. This is my friend, Chloe. She's going to be staying with me for a little while."

"Miit marhaba, ahlan w sahlan, ahlan w sahlan." Um Malik grabbed Chloe's shoulders and planted two wet kisses on each cheek.

"Ahlan fiiki," welcome to you too, Chloe replied. A hundred greetings, the woman had wished her, when one would do. Um Malik seemed prepared to follow them into the house, but Tina deftly blocked the doorway.

"Chloe's very tired," she told the older woman in Arabic. "She has just come from America."

"Oh, Amreeka," Um Malik bubbled in Arabic. "I love American people. Welcome, welcome."

"Welcome to you," Chloe answered. She wondered how many times the ritual call and response would have to be repeated before she would get to be alone with Tina.

"If you need anything, anything at all, you just tell me. I'm like your mother," Um Malik told Tina.

"Thank you, Um Malik, you're so very kind."

"I'm like your mother, I'm like your mother," to Chloe this time.

Not in the least, Chloe thought. She couldn't even imagine what Ruth Rubin would think of being compared to a hijab-wearing, Arab woman with a giant mole on her nose.

"Shukran," thank you, she said. Apparently that satisfied Um Malik, because she backed out of the gate, mumbling something about needing to get back to the hotel, there was a group arriving from Sweden today. At least, Chloe thought that's what she said, but it could have been any number of other things. Her Arabic, which had never been fluent, was definitely rusty.

"Who is she?" she asked Tina when they were finally alone.

"Our landlady." Chloe's heart leapt up to embrace the word "our." "She and her husband also own the hotel."

The apartment was a single bright room, with a slightly ragged, floral couch, scratched coffee table, and five or six foam mats stacked in the corner to be extricated for sleeping or sitting. The kitchenette at one end comprised a two-burner stove and a first-generation frost-free refrigerator whose constant whirring sound Chloe supposed might, over time, become soothing. A tiny breakfast nook, with a drop-leaf table and two straight chairs of the same vintage as the coffee table, separated the "kitchen" from the main room.

The best thing about the place, from Chloe's perspective, was the venetian blinds which offered some measure of privacy. The worst was that she could hear pretty much every word being uttered by the children in the house upstairs, which didn't bode well for things they might want to do.

"Don't worry," Tina said, reading her mind. "I have a plan."

She picked up two rainbow-striped sleeping mats and opened the door to what appeared to be a closet opposite the kitchen area. Well, it was a closet, but it was a closet Carrie Bradshaw would die for. Only a few dark skirts and multicolored, long-sleeved pastel blouses hung there alongside a gray, wool blazer. Neat stacks of T-shirts, pullovers, and jeans fit on two low shelves, while the two higher ones awaited whatever clothing Chloe might unpack. Tina laid the mattresses side by side, and they fit perfectly. Once they were nestled into the womb-like space, the voices upstairs were reduced to a faint hum. Chloe reached for Tina, who had already taken her jeans off. Lying on her side, in only a tank top and skimpy underpants, she was as gorgeous as Chloe remembered. Chloe reached down to unbutton her jeans, but Tina swatted her hand away. She pushed her lightly onto her back and knelt over her. Her body blocked the light and Chloe saw only a silhouette looming above her. She lay still, concentrating on the remembered gentleness of Tina's hands on her breasts, now moving down to her hips and legs. Chloe dug her fingers into Tina's slender buttocks, and instantly they were moving in sync, like a dance they knew well.

Why had she doubted only an hour ago that Tina still loved her? She could feel the love in each feathery stroke of her fingertips, sending electric currents down her spine and up to her earlobes. She plunged her tongue wetly into Tina's mouth, and they melted together. Like butter and sugar came into her mind, and she giggled. Food was never too far from her thoughts. Tina didn't seem to notice, only intensified her exploration of Chloe's intimate parts, and soon there was no room for thought, but only feelings.

If they made too much noise, Chloe didn't know. She woke five hours later, covered with a light blanket. There was a note on the mattress next to her.

"Shopping for dinner," it read. "Love you lots."

✳ ✳ ✳

Jittery with nervous energy, Tina practically jogged down Rukab Street. What have I done, what have I done? she asked herself over and over, quickening her already frenetic pace. The fringes of her long shoulder bag rose and fell against her hip, like tiny whips, emphasizing that she had screwed up.

"Shit," she said, half-aloud, then glanced around to be sure no one had heard. Which wouldn't matter anyway, she reminded herself, because they wouldn't understand the English.

Being with Chloe had been lovely. She hadn't meant for it to happen so fast. But, when she'd seen Chloe's hesitant, gap-toothed smile and always messy curls, touched her soft skin, she couldn't control herself. And then Chloe had been all about Jerusalem, wanting to sink her teeth into the city, while all Tina could think about was sinking her teeth into that juicy, ample body.

Chloe, of course, had no idea. Her insecurities were so deep, she couldn't imagine how she made Tina's guts dance. She couldn't see herself the way Tina saw her: fierce Fury who could be as fragile as a five-year-old. Tina was going to have to tell her about Yasmina and the Palestinian lesbian group. She'd meant to get it out of the way first thing, over a sober cup of coffee, but, when they sat down at the Jerusalem Hotel, she couldn't burst Chloe's bubble.

She wondered how Chloe would have reacted. Would react, because she was still going to have to do it. But, now, it would be a whole different football game. She could already see the betrayal and confusion clouding Chloe's face. Chloe was always poised for someone to tell her she wasn't worthy. Chloe should be flattered, because Tina couldn't keep her hands off her. But Chloe would never see it that way, especially not after she saw Yasmina.

Yasmina, who was a literal rock star.

Tina turned into the grocery store, throwing random things into her cart. Sardines. Chloe didn't even eat fish. Nutella. Chloe liked it on her toast in the morning. Bananas would go well with the chocolate spread. Hard cheese for grilling. Long-life milk so Chloe could have American coffee in the morning. Almond biscuits. Canned fava beans for *ful*. A couple mealy-looking apples.

One of the things she liked about Chloe was that she didn't try too hard. She didn't imagine that if she stayed long enough or took enough risks or slept with enough Palestinians, she'd become one. Didn't throw Arabic words into her English conversation. She knew who she was and who she wasn't. That gave her a keen sense that she didn't truly belong here, while her upbringing, as a Jew in a small southern American town, had made her hunger for belonging.

Yasmina was going to be a big hurdle. Better wait a while.

Tina hadn't gone off on this walk intending to talk herself out of coming clean. She had thought she would clear her head, figure out what she needed to say, and how to say it. But the streets had a mind of their own. At least, that's what she told herself. If it was the right time, the city would let her know it.

She headed back to the apartment, heard the water from the shower, and got busy putting away the groceries. Soon, Chloe emerged, damp and glistening, from the bathroom and started Tina's innards quivering again.

"Sleep well?" Tina asked, studying the vegetables she had just put away.

"Mmmm," Chloe responded. Crossing the tiny kitchen in two steps, Chloe came up behind Tina and wrapped her arms around her waist, crotch to butt. Tina whirled, vigorously shaking herself loose.

"You can't do that," she snapped, gesturing at the gaping window pane. Tina had opened the blinds to catch the fading sunlight.

Chloe retreated sulkily, and Tina heard her in the living- and bedroom, rummaging through her suitcase. Tina should go and make sure her feelings weren't hurt, but she didn't feel like it. She started pulling vegetables back out of the fridge. She would let her *makluube* do her apologizing for her.

Chapter 3

The days were getting warmer, but the evenings were still cold in Ramallah. Even in his leather jacket, Daoud shivered. The nearer he got to the looming Wall with its high watchtowers, the colder he felt. He zipped the jacket up to his neck.

He hung back for a while, watching people come and go. To his left, people moved easily, returning from Jerusalem to Ramallah without interference. At this hour, people poured out of taxis and teemed through the open gate, stopping to shop at the makeshift roadside stands where you could buy everything from warm bread to bathmats. Old Palestinian cars zoomed through, dust mingling with exhaust. The drivers leaned on the horns when passersby were slow to move aside or when traffic snarled in the narrow intersections. Just beyond, he could see the minarets of Qalandia refugee camp, a quarter mile away, but off-limits to Palestinians without Jerusalem ID.

To his right, cars stretched as far back as he could see, two abreast, with more arriving all the time. They too honked, but only to blow off steam. The new arrivals knew there was nothing the other drivers could do to speed up the checkpoint. He watched as a VW Rabbit with half its fender torn off veered around an orange taxi piled high with luggage on top. The taxi driver stubbornly refused to pull back and let the VW in.

Even this chaotic assembly looked orderly, compared to the crush of bodies pressing toward the turnstile where the pedestrians went through—if they were lucky. Those like him, who had no permit for Jerusalem, could wait for hours only to be turned back, or worse. It was six o'clock and still light out. Next week, the time would change, and then it would be light even later. The longer days were a blessing for the farmers and for people who had a long way to travel to and from work. It was not so good for him, though. Under cover of darkness, he could often still find a way around the checkpoint—a hole in the fence, a place where the Wall was not quite finished, or where the sections had been wedged ever so slightly apart. Six months ago, even in broad daylight, he could always find a way through to Jerusalem. But in the last months, the Israelis had sealed up the Wall around al-Ram and Qalandia, and, now, increasingly, the only ways through were the official ones, which were closed to him.

The two turnstiles, each as heavily fortified as a medieval castle, loomed in front of him like a dare. The old, handwritten signs had recently been replaced with brown, metal placards proclaiming the right line for foreigners and people with blue Jerusalem IDs, the left for Palestinians with green West Bank ID cards.

Daoud would not get through either turnstile legally. He edged closer to the crowd, looking for a young mother he could perhaps befriend. Men and women went through separately, but, if a woman had several small children, and he offered to carry a couple of them through, she might be grateful enough to protest that he was her husband, that one of the babies was sick and they needed to get to a hospital quickly quickly, the soldiers would be impressed with his love for his children and wave him through.

No good candidates for that ruse presented themselves tonight. He looked up at the ugly, concrete Wall looming on both sides. It seemed to grow higher and thicker every time he came, its towers rising ever more menacingly. Not for the first time, he imagined coming here with some sticks of dynamite and lighting the fuses, watching the stone crumble. It would not make any difference. They would build it again the next day, twice as high and twice as deep. But he would not care, because he would be dead and, before he died, he would have known what it was to be free for just one minute.

He shoved the fantasy aside. Bombs and such were not for him. He had considered it, of course, while he was in high school. All the boys in his circle had. A few of them had actually joined the militant resistance, picked up guns, blown themselves up, taking an Israeli settler or soldier or two with them. One of his best friends was in prison now; he had meant to be a bomber, but had been caught on the way to detonate his belt. Probably Daoud would never see him again. He put his friend out of his mind. He could not dwell on such miseries when he was on his way to entertain, to make the audience love him, and be made love to in turn.

He abandoned the turnstiles and instead strode up the line of cars. In between the turnstiles, two soldiers hunkered back to back in a metal booth piled high with sandbags. Each balanced a long rifle on one shoulder, aiming it at the window of the first driver in line, ready to shatter both the window and the driver's head if the car moved prematurely. Daoud leaned against a light post and smoked a cigarette. Four soldiers worked the cars in teams of two. One of the teams was methodical, doing everything just the same with each car, taking this out, then that, asking the same questions of each person. The other team obviously enjoyed mixing it up. They would sometimes look in the trunk, sometimes tell everyone to get out, now take the driver's keys, turn the radio to a Hebrew station and turn it up loud. He needed to avoid those two like rotten meat.

He examined the others, the quiet ones. One was tall and the other short. The tall one had sunken cheeks and a bushy beard; the shorter one was muscular and clean-shaven. His cocoa-colored face was impassive, and he spoke to the people in broken Arabic, using the respectful terms *haj* and *haji* for older people.

When the musc man stretched between searching cars, Daoud cleared his throat. The man looked up at him.

"What do you want?" he asked.

"To go to Jerusalem. To Adloyada."

"Adloyada?" Daoud was sure the soldier knew what Adloyada was. He just wanted to play naïve.

"I have to get there soon. I'm JLo Day-Glo."

A flicker of a smile passed over the young man's lips, but, as quickly, it was gone.

"Do you have a permit?"

"Would I be standing here if I did?"

"Sorry, it's not possible."

"Perhaps we can go there together."

"I'm on duty."

"Gadi," called the taller soldier. "Yalla."

Daoud grimaced. He hated that the Israelis had appropriated the Arabic "let's go" into their stupid language. Gadi, as his partner had called him, might have noticed Daoud's expression or maybe he was just annoyed by Daoud's familiarity. He grabbed Daoud roughly by the arm.

"Come over here," he snarled.

Daoud felt panic welling up inside him. What had he done? He was flirting, sure, but if the guy wasn't interested, he could pretend he didn't understand. Was he a closet case, a homophobe, or both?

"Let me go," he hissed. "I didn't mean anything. Forget it, I'm leaving."

Gadi ignored him, twisting Daoud's wrist so that he yelped. He frog marched him away from the cars to a green metal hut, shoved him inside, and closed the door. The smell of urine and rancid beer assaulted his nose. His stomach churned, and he choked back a little vomit. It was pitch dark, and something squished under his foot. He hoped it was chewing gum or the remains of a chucked-out sandwich. He couldn't breathe. He was going to die in this tin can, and no one would ever know what had become of him. The cell was too short for him to stand without stooping. He put his jacket on the ground and sat on it, folding his long legs up under his knees and hugging them. He didn't like the idea of his prized leather jacket being soiled with whatever might be on this filthy floor, but better the jacket than his pants.

The metal of his jail rattled, making a hollow *thwang*. Latches slid back with a loud creak. Quick, think, what to say? What to offer, what to beg for? He had to get out of here. A slot in the door opened, and a shaft of light pierced the blackness. The harsh glare illuminated a shaft of flesh, Gadi's penis, he assumed. Daoud shifted on the floor until his mouth was in the right place. He said a quick prayer before opening his mouth and taking the prick inside.

He could smell and taste the contempt of the prick's owner. Once again, he almost gagged. He wondered if the soldier had put his gun on the ground, or if he was even now standing with his hand on the trigger. Daoud sucked and sucked and finally felt the squirt in his mouth. He gave a final lick and pulled away. He hoped the soldier could hear him spit the sperm on the ground. Too late, he considered that Gadi wouldn't be the one who had to sit in it. It would be the next poor guy who tried to get through the checkpoint. He should have done it in the corner. How much longer would he be here? He needed to get to Adloyada.

The door flew open. "Come on," Gadi said. Daoud could see no sign in his face of what had just happened. He wondered if it was a nightly occurrence, like drinking coffee. Gadi took his arm, a little less roughly than before, but not gently. He led him to the front of the line of cars and opened the door of a cab.

"Do you have room for one more?" he asked. The cab was full, five adults and two children, but a woman took one of the kids on her lap, and the other passengers good-naturedly shifted around to make room. Gadi waved them through.

Daoud glanced at the two young men sharing the back seat with him. They were nicely dressed for a night out, black slacks and polo shirts. They gave each other a high five. No doubt, they had been anticipating a problem at the checkpoint too. Daoud hugged himself, wondering if the sour smell was coming from the jacket or his own skin, The cab dropped him off at the top of the Mount of Olives. He caught a servees down to Damascus Gate and, from there, walked quickly down HaNevi'im Street and ducked into the small alley called Shushan. When he caught sight of the gray stone oasis, he thrust the memory of Gadi and his moments of panic and humiliation behind him. He opened the door, and a rush of warm air, pungent with beer, wafted to greet him. Mordecai, an elfin, Jewish Israeli with sparse, brown hair, danced over and kissed him on the lips.

"JLo, thank God. You're on in fifteen minutes."

"Don't worry. I'll be ready."

"You had no problems with the checkpoint?"

Daoud hesitated for one second. His friend's eyes had already wandered to the bar, where the bartender was pouring vodka into a row of shotglasses.

"Not too bad," he said.

Chapter 4

The thick, black bars of Rania's cage dropped from the heavens and plunged into the center of the earth. Flat, horizontal bars ran along the top and bottom of a narrow doorway, whose enormous lock required three different keys to unlock. If anyone could ever break out of this cell, it would not be through the door. The gap beneath the door left just enough space for a tray conveying a plate or shallow bowl. They had given her a cup the first day, and she filled it with water from the rusty sink in the corner. When they came with breakfast, she held up the cup, and they poured the coffee through the bars. If she didn't feel like getting up, she didn't get coffee. The preference for coffee first thing in the morning was one thing she had in common with Israelis. Most Palestinians drank tea with breakfast, and coffee was a mid-morning treat, but she had always liked to start the day with bitter coffee grounds between her teeth. Of course, the Israeli coffee was barely worthy of the name.

She thought it was about half an hour until the guard would come with coffee and toast. She got up, splashed water on her face, and tied the hijab around her head in case it was a man who came. Not that she really cared if foreign men saw her hair, but Bassam would care. She rummaged in the small bag of clothes he had sent after a few days, when it became clear that there had not been a mistake, that she would not be getting out soon. He had sent three pairs of socks, one red, one black, one white, almost as if he had anticipated what she was about to do. But then he would have included a green pair.

She took one black sock and went over to the door. She couldn't reach the top bar from the floor, but when she wedged her left foot on top of the lower cross bar, she could just barely reach if she stretched as far as she could. It felt good to stretch. It was awkward trying to tie the sock into a knot around the thick bar while balancing on one foot and stretching up. After three tries, she got it done. She hopped back to the floor and retreated to the bed to admire it. Not much really. Just a little black flag swaying slightly in the warm draft that did not reach into her cell. For the first time since they had brought her here, she was eager for the police to come, to see what they would say.

She exercised to pass the time until breakfast. She stretched, ran in place, and stretched some more. She could barely reach the little windowsill with her fingertips. She tried to hoist herself up, partly to see if there was a view of anything outside, partly just to see if she could do it. She couldn't.

"What are you doing?" Rania turned to see Tali, the breakfast in her hands and exasperation on her freckled face.

"Exercise," Rania said in English. She didn't know the Hebrew word.

"It's forbidden." She used the Arabic word, *mamnuah*. Probably the only Arabic word she knew.

"Everything cannot be forbidden. Why should you forbid me to care for my body?"

"You can exercise, but not with the window."

When Tali arrived with lunch, a white sock dangled next to the black one. Still, she did not react. Rania was a little disappointed, but it was also good, because if Tali had taken them down, Rania might have lost them for good. Of course, there were two of each, but Rania wanted to get at least one full set hung. She battled the temptation to do it all at once. She suspected she would be here a long time. Biding her time was good discipline.

She needed an activity, to pass the time until she could make her next move. She looked around the cell for anything to make into anything else. She found pretty much nothing. Perhaps she should learn Hebrew. Wasn't that what all the political prisoners did? That was why some of the top ex-fighters had ended up in roles that worked most closely with Israelis, after Arafat came back and set up the Palestinian Authority. She didn't really want to know Hebrew. If she ever got out of here, she would be happy never to talk to an Israeli again. But, last year, during the case that had led to her imprisonment, she had wished she had a better command of Hebrew. She had had to rely on others for information she would rather have been able to gather for herself. Most of the top officials in the Palestinian police had occasion to use Hebrew sometimes. If she planned to move up—and she definitely did—she should know Hebrew too.

She started making a mental list of every Hebrew verb she knew and conjugating them. *Hayah.* He was. *He hayta.* She was. *Hem hayu*, they were. *Hu yihyeh*, he will be. *He tihyeh.* She will be.

She did "like," "go," "come," and "bring." Suddenly she couldn't remember any more verbs. What were the first verbs you taught a child in Arabic? What were Khaled's first words? She could not remember. She pushed the thought away before it could take root and drag her down. She was getting up a rhythm. She needed to keep on. Visit, that was a good one. *Zar, bizur.* What was the Hebrew? She had heard it a million times. She could not bring back the word. She needed a dictionary or a textbook. Maybe she could convince Tali to bring her a Hebrew textbook.

She found the last pair of socks, the red one. She separated them and counted to twenty, just to prolong the experience. Then, she hoisted herself up and tied one red sock next to the black one. Black, red, white. It was almost right. But what to do about the green? She looked through the small bag again. No green shirt, no sock, no scarf. She didn't like to wear green; it clashed with her skin tones. She picked through her few toiletries—the toothpaste, no green there, not that it would help. She scanned the cell, poked under the mattress even, to no avail. Her eye caught a flash of green, and, for a second, she thought she had hallucinated it. No, there it was, hanging from the back of the sink, the pair of yellow and green underpants she had been wearing when she was taken.

"That's no use," she said aloud. She wasn't going to hang her underwear on the bars of the cell, even to make a point. Though if she did—she smiled. When she was going to college in Jerusalem and living at home in Aida Camp, she and her friends came up with a trick for getting through the checkpoint easily. They would put sanitary pads on top of whatever else they were carrying. As soon as the soldiers opened the bag, they would shoo them through. In that way, she had smuggled dozens of letters home from wanted men and volumes of banned publications to keep the Intifada spirit strong. Making a Palestinian flag out of her underwear might keep it flying for a while.

She took the panties from their makeshift hook and folded them so that only the green part was showing. But how to keep the fold from coming undone after she hung it up? She rummaged through the tote bag again. She could probably find every object in it in the dark by now. There—the little string of hair ties that Bassam had thought to send. Useful for so many possible purposes. She stretched one between her two thumbs and drew them apart next to her ear. It would make a perfect mini-slingshot, if only she had a stone to throw.

She looped the little band tightly around the oblong of fabric. It was harder to hang than the socks had been, because the fabric was less stretchy, but she managed to nestle it between the black and the red. She pushed the four bits of fabric as close together as they could go and then sat on her bed to appreciate her work. It really did look like a little, misshapen Palestinian flag. Her body felt so light, she imagined she could fly. Fly through the bars and out through these gray catacombs, over the coils and coils of razor wire, to her husband's family compound, where her mother-in-law would be just piling chunks of succulent lamb onto a pyramid of spiced rice. She saw the old woman's veiny hands pouring the thin, white soup into a bone china bowl without spilling a drop. Can I have been here so long that I even miss my mother-in-law? she thought.

For a minute, she could almost smell the delicate seasoning of the meat. Her mouth watered.

"At re'eva?"

She woke with a start. She couldn't believe she was still here. The dream-reverie had seemed so real; she was sure she was free.

"What?" she asked. She was in no mood to speak Hebrew.

"Are you hungry?" Tali repeated in Hebrew. The tray she offered was laden with dull, brown soup, half a cucumber, and a slice of dingy bread. Tears sprang from Rania's eyes at the contrast between what she had conjured for herself and what was available. Then she remembered her Hebrew project.

"Lo, ani lo re'eva." Rania carefully enunciated the foreign words. She got up and walked the seven paces to the locked door of her cell.

"At lo rotzah ochel?" You don't want food? Tali acted like she was going to put the tray back on the cart. Rania reached out for it, her hands through the bars.

"Ani rotzah. Achshav, ani lo re'evah, aval ani ehyeh…" Now I'm not hungry, but I will be… she could not remember the word for later. "Ba'adeen," she said, substituting the Arabic.

"Lo hevanti," I don't understand, Tali said. She passed the tray under the bars.

"Later," Rania said in English. "What is it in Hebrew?"

"Achar kach," Tali said. It was the first time the woman ever smiled at her. But now Rania was tired of speaking Hebrew.

"Perhaps," she said in English, "you could bring me a Hebrew book? So I can study?"

"I don't know," Tali replied in English. "You are not supposed to have anything. No books, no paper. Because you are political."

"Who told you I am political? That is not why I am here." Her mouth rebelled against that statement. She had always been involved in politics; to be Palestinian was political. But that was not what Tali meant. In this context, to be "political" meant you were involved in some kind of armed resistance against the Israelis, or they thought you were.

"Why are you here?" Tali asked.

"I am a policewoman. Last year, I was investigating the death of a young woman, a foreigner. The man who killed her was very high up in the army. He was not punished, and he does not want me to tell what I know."

"They told me you are Hamas."

"I am not Hamas. I am Fatah."

"Tali, bo'ee!" a male voice called from the end of the hall. Tali, ta'ali, Rania translated in her head, and then laughed at the pun.

"Why do you laugh?"

"It is just… he told you to come. Bo'ee. But in Arabic, 'come' is 'ta'ali.' So he would have said 'Tali, ta'ali.'"

"Oh." Tali half-smiled. Rania thought she wasn't sure if she was being made fun of. "I have to go."

Tali had not responded quickly enough, and the male guard had come to see what the holdup was. He towered over Tali, radiating impatience.

"What is that?" he demanded, pointing at the socks dangling from the top of the bars. Rania shrugged. He touched Tali's arm.

"Tell her to take it down," he said in Hebrew.

"Take it down," Tali said in English without enthusiasm.

"I cannot reach it." Rania demonstrated, stretching onto her tiptoes. Her fingers fell well short of the socks.

"How did you put them up there?"

"I did not."

The police looked thoroughly confused. Did they really expect her to admit it? Obviously, she had put them there; who else would have done it? But it seemed not to occur to them that she was capable of lying to them. They both stared at the socks as if they were magic.

The male policeman reached up and grasped the red sock easily. Rania was sure he was going to untie it. Then, his hand moved instead to the green strip, which hung stiffer than the others.

"Tachtonim," he said to Tali, and snickered.

Was he going to order Tali to take it down? She didn't know if he was Tali's boss or her equal. But it wouldn't matter. He could just ask her to do it, and, of course, she would.

"They are yours?" Tali asked Rania. Again, Rania wondered if anyone really expected her to answer. Whether they did or not, she said nothing.

The two police spoke quietly in Hebrew for a minute.

"You won't take it down?" Tali Ta'ali asked in English.

"I told you; I cannot reach it."

Tali translated for the male cop, and they exchanged some more rapid-fire Hebrew. Tali Ta'ali sounded irritated with her colleague. She kept glancing at Rania, and Rania thought she detected a speck of respect in her eyes. But it was probably wishful thinking.

After a long debate, the two cops walked away. The male cop shot Rania a look that said, You'll pay for this.

Chapter 5

Rania ate slowly, dipping the bread into the salty soup and making each bite last one hundred chews. Hard to do with a small piece of soggy bread. She had to concentrate, and concentrating, even on something so stupid, felt good. In between bites, she watched her flag fly in the draft from the hallway. If you had told her a month ago that she could be so happy doing nothing but watching a Palestinian flag made of socks and underwear, she would have said you needed a psychiatrist.

She heard a buzzing in the distance, like flies dancing. She seldom heard anything, except when the guards came to count or bring food. The walls were of the thickest concrete, made to absorb the sounds of torture, she supposed. She didn't know if there were other prisoners on this hall now. Weeks ago, the police had brought two Israeli women down in the middle of the night. She had heard a lot of screaming and cursing and thuds as they were thrown into separate cells on either side of hers. She supposed they had been fighting and put in these cells for punishment. They were gone now.

The buzzing was louder and closer. She got up and stood to one side of the door and then the other, craning to see down the dark hallway. She saw nothing.

Suddenly, boots thundered on cement, accompanied by men shouting. A horde of men, masks covering their faces and long rifles in their hands, raced into view. One of them shouted something in Hebrew. The thundering stopped instantly. The men—at least thirty of them—pivoted as one, training their guns into her cell. She shrank involuntarily, backing into the corner by the sink and making herself smaller than she already was. She wondered what they were looking for. Could someone have placed a bomb here? She couldn't imagine who or why, let alone how.

"Asirah. Bo'ee heyna," a man's voice exploded into the corridor. She couldn't tell who had said, "Prisoner, come here!"

Could he be talking to her? She obviously could not "come" anywhere because her cell door was locked. She stood still.

A shot ran out. Shooting, here? In the narrow hallway, they would kill each other if they didn't watch out. But that familiar smell was not gunpowder; it was tear gas. It was coming into her cell, burning her eyes; they should be more careful about where they aimed it. Another volley and she was down on the ground, retching and gasping. Any other time she had been gassed, she had had somewhere to run, the fields, into the house, but, now, the gas was filling the little cell. She couldn't breathe.

"Stop it!" she shouted in Arabic. They probably wouldn't understand her. Better speak English. But the words didn't want to come. She tried to concentrate, between desperate coughs.

"You are going to kill me with that," she said.

"Come out!" the commander shouted in English. So he must be talking to her. But she still couldn't come out. It didn't make any sense. She wanted to say that, but she couldn't talk. Her lungs were closing up from the gas. She raced to where she had left her clothes and grabbed the first piece to hand, a cotton blouse, and tied it over her nose and mouth. It didn't help much, but it made a little bit of a screen between her and the gas. She inched her way to the gate.

"What are you doing?" she yelled in the direction of the voice that had spoken. A phalanx of human tanks faced her. They wore padded body armor and helmets with gas masks under them. They looked like robots from a science fiction movie. But the guns they held were not science fiction. They were exactly like all the other guns she had faced in her life, the ones that had killed her brother when she was still in high school, in the early weeks of the First Intifada.

"Take those down." The robot in front raised his gun toward her flag.

Was it possible that all this was really a reaction to some colored underclothes hanging from a bar? She burst out laughing, despite the fact that she could barely breathe and tears were running down her face from the gas. She choked on the laughter and the gas and coughed up a mess of spittle. Too bad they were too far away for her to spit it at them. But she wouldn't, really, anyway. She just wished she could. She swallowed it. The gas burned going down her throat.

"I can't take them down," she said. She repeated her performance from earlier, showing how short she was.

"Stand up there," he smacked his gun on the horizontal bar where the lock was.

"I cannot." She lifted her foot, showing him that it wouldn't reach.

"You put them up there. You take them down."

She said nothing. She was not doing it, and that was final.

"Open it," he said in Hebrew to someone behind him.

The male policeman, who had been here before with Tali Ta'ali, stepped out from behind the phalanx of armed men. He wore regular clothes with a gas mask pushed up onto his head. The gas had started to settle. Her bedclothes were probably drenched with it. She would have to check before going to bed.

The policeman rattled his keys finding the right one. He opened the gate. The commander gestured three of the men forward. They clomped into the cell. One tore the blouse from her face and threw it into the toilet. The other two lifted her up like she was a sack of potatoes. One had a hand on her breast; the other grasped each thigh so hard she would have bruises. They held her so that she could easily reach out and untie the socks and panties. She stubbornly held her arms down at her side.

The one holding her breast pinched it hard. She kicked him in the face.

"Ow!" He dropped her, and she fell into the other man. The third one caught her, then threw her to the ground. He knelt on her stomach so hard she thought her organs would collapse on themselves. He slapped her face over and over.

"Whore!" She knew that Hebrew word, because she had heard it so often at the checkpoints. He raised his rifle and swung it at her head. She attempted to raise her arms to protect herself, but one of the other men stomped on her arm. She thought she heard the bone break. She screamed, then she ordered herself to stop. Her father had told her many times about his torture, how the Israeli soldiers had broken his arm, and he had refused to go to the doctor, because he feared they would put him under anesthetic to get information.

She felt the weight lift off of her kidney, and her bladder released a spurt of water down her leg. Her whole body was wet from something: sweat, tears, snot, now urine. She clenched her teeth hard, forbidding herself to show any fear or shame. The tall soldier who had been kneeling on top of her now crouched by her left ear. He leaned down, like a lover about to whisper endearments, and said, in English, too low for anyone else to hear, "Do you want me to kill you?"

She remained mute, counting the pockmarks in the concrete ceiling.

He circled her small neck with his huge, gloved hands. One thumb caressed the indentation in her throat, and her breath shortened, sending waves of panic down her chest.

"I asked you a question," he crooned. He yanked her head up by the hair and banged it lightly on the cement. Forgive me, papa, she said silently, and shook her head a little. It was, apparently, good enough. The crouching man took his hands from her throat and stood up. The one who had stepped on her arm gave her one more kick for good measure, then reached up and easily untied the four little pieces of clothing making the flag. He put the three socks in his pocket, but the panties he turned inside out and tossed onto her face. So much for her idea that they would not be willing to touch them.

Chapter 6

Rania's husband, Bassam, worked at the Palestinian Ministry of Interior. Chloe located the number in Tina's *PASSIA* directory, a book listing every important governmental and nongovernmental office in Palestine. As she dialed, she realized she did not know Bassam's last name. Rania used her father's name, Bakara. She had introduced Bassam only as "my husband."

"Mumkin ahki maa Bassam, Abu Khaled," she asked tentatively, when the operator answered.

"Miin?" Who? The woman sounded impatient.

"Ma'lesh," never mind, Chloe said and hung up.

Maybe the woman just didn't understand her. She couldn't think of another option that wouldn't involve one of those endless games of Palestinian telephone—calling this person who called that person who knew this other person. She would just have to venture down to the ministry and look for him in person. She jotted down the address in the wealthy suburb of al-Bireh and headed to the corner. She had no idea how to get to al-Bireh, but she knew she had to get to the center of town, the Manara. All transit to outlying areas came and went from there. She flagged down an orange collective taxi, hoping it was going downtown.

In what seemed like seconds, she was at the Manara. The circle of lions at the center intersection presided over rows and rows of falafel and sweet shops, shoe stores, jewelry stores, hair salons, outlets for fashionable, Western clothing underneath beige brick office and apartment buildings. Orange vans and yellow taxis vied with cars of all makes and ages for control of the narrow streets. The only thing they had in common was that they all honked their horns and ignored the traffic policeman attempting to establish some order.

Chloe made her way over to a young man pressing out little logs of falafel batter into a vat of bubbling oil.

"Can you tell me how to get to this address?" She showed him the paper where she had written the address of the ministry. Hopefully he could read English.

"You must take a taxi," he said doubtfully. "Do not pay more than six shekels."

The driver tried to charge her twenty. She handed him eight, figuring the extra two were good for a foreigner's tax, and climbed out before he could object. She heard him making some nasty remarks about her mother as he screeched off.

Two policemen hunched over a checkers game in the air-conditioned lobby. The man getting ready to move held a cigarette between his lips, while the other flicked his ashes into a bowl piled perilously with mostly smoked cigarettes.

"Sabah al-kheir," she greeted them. "I want to see Abu Khaled."

"Which Abu Khaled?"

Rats. She had hoped Bassam was the only one. But Khaled was a popular name, especially now that Khaled Mashal had risen to prominence as the power behind the new Hamas government.

"Um, ismo Bassam." His name is Bassam. That should do it. It was unlikely there were two Bassam-Abu Khaleds working in the same ministry. But the men did not appear enlightened.

"Joz Rania Bakara."

"Ah."

She had guessed correctly. Rania was more famous than her husband, even in the ministry where he worked. I wonder how he likes that, she thought as the guard picked up the phone. A minute later, a slender, curly-haired man in a perfectly pressed blue shirt walked toward her with his hand out.

"I am Bassam Aamer," he said in English.

"Marhaba. I am Chloe, Rania's friend from America. I met you the night I left Palestine."

"I remember." Seconds after they entered his modest, windowless office, a secretary appeared with tea. She served it and vanished silently.

"When did you arrive back?" he asked. She was both relieved and disappointed to hear that his English was good. It would have been difficult to have the conversation she needed to have in Arabic, but she was only delaying the inevitable.

"Yesterday," she answered. "I came as soon as I heard Rania was in prison. Can you tell me what happened?"

"They came in the night. Many soldiers. They surrounded our house. They even woke my mother and forced her to stand outside in the rain."

She shook her head sympathetically. What he described was not unusual, but that didn't make it any less appalling.

"I hope she did not get ill."

"No, she is strong. They searched the house with great violence. Khaled was upset and screaming. One of the soldiers came and shook his rifle in my boy's face, threatened to hit him if he did not be quiet."

"Haram," for shame, Chloe said. She remembered the tow-headed tyke who had grabbed her leg the first time she ever met him and begged her to sleep at his house. She wondered what this early experience of the violence of occupation would do to him.

"They found nothing, of course. But when they were finished, after many hours, they told my wife to get her coat and come with them. She insisted they allow her to dress. I thought they would beat her, but the commander agreed. He tried to stay in the room while she dressed, but she forced him to leave."

Chloe detected amusement in his voice as he recounted that part, and she smiled too. Rania with a male soldier trying to watch her get dressed was a nonstarter.

"They put metal handcuffs on her, and shackles on her ankles. They blindfolded her in front of my son. He cried for hours after she was gone," Bassam continued. "We heard nothing for three days. Then, we learned she was at Petah Tikva."

He paused for that to sink in. Petah Tikva was an interrogation center, run by the dreaded Israeli secret police. Bassam well knew the tortures that went on in those centers, having been held there himself during the First Intifada.

"After one week, they moved her to Ramle."

"Well, that's better, right?" Actually, Chloe wasn't sure if it was better. Ramle was a regular prison, not an interrogation center. It was safer, but probably it meant that she was being held under a legal detention order, which would make it harder to get her out. "Did she have a hearing on the detention order?"

"Her lawyer said the judge signed the order, but there was no hearing."

"Has he filed an appeal?"

"Not yet. He is going to."

"What's he waiting for? It's been two weeks already."

Bassam gave his elegant shrug again. "He has a lot of cases. Many others were arrested at the same time."

Chloe tried to remember that, in Palestine, everyone has loved ones in prison. Anyone could be spirited away on an administrative detention order, held without charge for six months, and then another six, and another. But this wasn't anyone; this was Rania, her friend, the only woman detective in the northern West Bank. She and Bassam knew lots of people in powerful positions in the Palestinian Authority. Why wasn't Bassam using their connections to jump to the head of the line?

"Would you give me the lawyer's phone number?" she asked. "I have some Israeli friends who might be able to help. But they will need some information from the lawyer."

She produced the little notebook she had brought from California for this purpose and opened it to the first page. He wrote the name and number in English, fortunately, since she could never remember which Arabic number was which.

"Can Rania have visitors?" Chloe asked.

Bassam's face took on a pained look. "She can have. I tried to get a permit, but I could not."

Chloe nodded. It was rare that men under fifty could get permits to go into Israel, even for life-saving medical procedures.

"Her sister got a permit," Bassam said. "She took Khaled with her. My wife refused to see them."

"Why would she do that? Is she on bad terms with her sister?"

He shook his head vigorously, making his hair flop into his eyes again. Chloe wondered if Rania usually cut it for him. "She told the lawyer she did not want Khaled to see her in prison."

"I guess I can understand that," Chloe said.

"I do not think it is the real reason," he said. "I think she is afraid that if she sees him, she will not be able to be strong."

"You mean, she fears she might give information?" Chloe could not believe that. She had always wondered if she herself would be able to hold up under torture, but she had never doubted her ability to withstand mental pressure. And Rania was much stronger and more determined than she was. She needed to be, to survive the life she had chosen.

"Perhaps." He clearly didn't want to talk about it anymore. He took out his wallet and handed her a business card. "Please call me if you need anything."

"I will call you when I know something," she said with more confidence than she felt.

"Thank you for helping my wife," he said.

"It's the least I can do," Chloe said. "She saved my life last time I was here."

Too late, she realized that Rania might not have told him exactly how close she and Chloe had both come to being shot. But he only shook her hand.

✳ ✳ ✳

Chloe settled on a low stone wall near the ministry and fished out her phone. She dialed the very first number in her address book.

"This is Avi. I am out of the country. Please don't leave a message."

"Shit!" It had never occurred to her that Avi wouldn't be in Israel. She had not been surprised when he did not answer her email—he rarely did. For an accomplished hacker and web designer, he had a surprising distaste for electronic communication. She had counted on his connections and language skills to help her free Rania.

Her second choice answered immediately.

"Chloe!" Nehama's voice could probably be heard wherever Avi was. "When did you get back?"

Chloe quickly explained how and why she had returned. She omitted having used Nehama's name. No need to expose herself for a shameless user.

"Where are they holding her?" Nehama asked when Chloe finished her recitation.

"Neve Tirzah." She gave the official name of the women's prison at Ramle.

"Is she in administrative detention?"

"I don't think so. She was moved there two weeks ago from Petah Tikva. If there was an administrative detention order for her, she would have had a hearing, right?"

"Supposed to be, but you never know. Does she have a lawyer?"

"Yeah, a guy from the Prisoner's Club." She gave Nehama the name Bassam had given her.

"He's very famous," Nehama said. "The best there is."

"He doesn't seem to be in any hurry to get her out."

"He has a lot of cases," Nehama said, just as Bassam had.

"Well, I only care about this one."

"Look," Nehama said. "I have some contacts in the army, from the checkpoint work." Nehama was part of Machsom Watch, a women's group that monitored the many West Bank checkpoints. "I can try to get some information about why they arrested her and if they are planning to charge her. But I don't think I'll be able to get her released."

"Whatever you can find out will be great." Chloe tried to swallow her disappointment. She shouldn't have imagined that one phone call would put her on the road to Rania's freedom. She just couldn't think what else she had in her bag of tricks.

Chapter 7

Rania was curled up in the fetal position on her cot. She could not get comfortable. Her arm was not broken, but it sent agonizing shock waves through her body whenever she moved it. So, she had barely moved from her cot since they finished beating her. She had heard them bring breakfast and lunch and take them away, uneaten, a few hours later. Tali Ta'ali had tried to talk to her once, but she had not responded.

She had not imagined they would react so violently to her little act of rebellion. A small miscalculation to add to the huge one that had landed her here.

She heard the boots on the ground that meant someone was coming to bring more food she did not want. It sounded like Tali's lively gait. She closed her eyes, as if that would protect her from the nauseating smell of boiled chicken. She heard the tray sliding on the cement floor and waited for the footsteps to recede. But they were not receding. Tali was standing at her cell door. She made an effort to still her breathing, so Tali would think she was asleep.

"I brought you something," the girl said in Hebrew.

"I know," Rania said in English, her voice muffled by the mattress. "Leave it."

Maybe she would eat this time after all. She felt woozy from lack of nourishment, but that was sort of helpful for her project of not thinking about what her life was going to be. But the food actually smelled kind of appetizing, so that might mean that she wanted to stay alive. She thought there was some kind of sweet potato on the tray. She would see how she felt once the annoying woman left her alone.

"It will not fit underneath," Tali said, in English this time. "You need to come take it."

Tali was not going to go away, Rania decided. She flipped over gingerly, but not gingerly enough. She yelped with pain before she could stop herself.

"Are you okay?" Tali asked. Rania was sitting up now, and she dragged herself to her feet.

"No, I am not okay," she said. She walked slowly to the bars, holding her right arm to her side with her left hand. "Your friends beat me very badly."

"I am sorry about that." I bet you are, Rania started to say, but she did not. Something in Tali's tone of voice made her think that maybe, just maybe, she really was sorry. She looked at the girl's face more closely than she had ever done before. The heavy freckles were distracting, but, other than that, she was pretty. She did not wear as much makeup as most Israeli policewomen did. It occurred to her that she didn't even know whether Tali was a soldier or a policewoman.

"Are you in the army or the police?" she asked.

"I am both," Tali said. "This is my army service, but I am working in the police."

"Is this what you wanted to do?" Rania asked.

"No. I wanted to be in the border police. The women here are so sad. Sometimes, I cry with them."

Rania considered that. The border police were the worst of the worst in her experience. They roamed around the border areas, which included her village, taunting the young men until they threw stones at their jeeps, and then they shot at them. If that was what Tali would rather be doing, she did not think she wanted to be friendly with her after all. Tali held out a book with a battered spine. Rania reached through the bars with her right arm and again let out a muffled cry.

"Do you want a doctor?" the police-soldier-woman asked.

"No." Of that, Rania was sure. She would not be less brave than her father. But she dropped the right arm carefully to her side and took the book with her left hand. It was heavier than she expected, and she was off-balance because of her injured arm. She dropped the book, and it fell open. She crouched down to retrieve it. It was in Hebrew and Arabic, and when she got closer, she saw it was a textbook.

"Thank you," she said.

"I asked one of the Arab policemen who works here," Tali said. "He brought it from home."

"Tell him I said, 'Shukran,'" Rania said. The thought of a real book to study from cheered her enormously. Something had fallen out of the book. It was her red sock. She looked through the pages and found the other two as well.

"That was nice of you," she said to Tali. She was having to do a lot of attitude adjustment rather rapidly. It was making her head spin.

"Tell me something," Tali said. "Why do you want to make trouble for us?"

Rania was flummoxed. She didn't even really know how to start answering that question. Why wouldn't I? was the obvious answer, but, if she said that, Tali would not understand.

"I do not," she said. "I only wanted to show that I love my country, just like you love yours."

"But it is not the same. You want to kill us."

"How can you say that? It is your people who are always killing mine, not the other way around."

"Let me tell you a story," Tali said. Rania was tired of standing at the bars. She retreated to her cot and sat on the edge, opposite Tali. It was not like they were at eye level even standing up. The Israeli woman had at least six inches on her.

"My grandfather was from Hebron," the policewoman said.

Rania knew what was coming.

"His family was very religious. In 1929, they had just sat down to their Shabbat meal, when Arabs smashed the door with a hatchet and broke into the house. After they broke all the china dishes, they took his small brother out into the yard and cut off his head with a sword. My grandfather would have been killed as well, but he managed to escape to a neighbor's house and hid until the next day."

How did Tali's grandfather feel, Rania wondered, about having escaped and hidden while his little brother was beheaded? If the story was even true. Practically every Israeli she'd ever met claimed a personal connection to that well-documented incident, even those whose ancestors were somewhere in Poland when it had occurred.

"I am also from the Hebron area, which we call al-Khalil," Rania said. "So, you see, we are countrywomen." Tali tipped her chin in acknowledgment.

"I come from a village called Beit Natif," Rania continued. "My family was famous for making tiles. They had many Jewish customers, and some became friends. During the violence of 1936, my family hid two Jewish families in their home for weeks. They lived as members of our family. Then in '48, the Israeli army came to our village. The father of one of the families who had hidden in my grandfather's house? He set the fire that burned Beit Natif to the ground."

"You must be exaggerating," Tali said. "How can you be from that village, if it was burned to the ground?"

Why did she even bother talking to this woman? She was like all Israelis, seeing only what they wanted to see.

"I do not live there," Rania said. "The Jewish National Fund took it and planted a forest. Later they built some Jewish settlements on some of our land. I grew up in a refugee camp about thirty minutes driving from there. But Beit Natif is my village. Someday we will return there and rebuild our home."

"What about the people who live in the settlements?" Tali asked. "If you return, where would they go?"

"Why should I worry about them?" Rania asked. "We were there first."

She saw doubt and fear in Tali's face. She did not want to talk about this anymore. She tried to believe with all her heart that her family and the rest of their people would get their land back some day. But she was not a fool. The evidence of her eyes told her that the Israelis were building more and more every day. It had been years since anyone in Aida had been to Beit Natif. She had no idea what it looked like now.

"Thank you for the book," she said. She looked down at the pages so that Tali would leave. After a few seconds, she heard the boots clicking back down the corridor.

Chapter 8

Chloe could think of only one other person who might have relevant information. She found a cab and headed to Qalandia checkpoint.

By ten thirty in the morning, everyone who was going to work or school had either gotten through or given up. The soldiers lounged against the burlap sandbags that lined the corrugated tin structure, drinking from paper cups and flipping through magazines.

Chloe extracted a green, plastic folder from her back pocket and passed it through the little metal window to a helmeted woman soldier. The woman looked from the folder back to Chloe and did a double take. Chloe was used to that.

"What is it?" the soldier woman asked in English.

"Open it and you'll see," she said.

The soldier reluctantly did so. They always did that, as if suspecting it would explode in their hands. Chloe braced herself for the woman's angry reaction. Of course, she had her real passport on her. She would never get into Neve Tirzah without it. But she always tried to go through checkpoints with a copy in a Palestinian ID folder. It was a tiny act of solidarity with the people who were forced to carry these green folders that confined their movements to ever-tinier enclaves. Just now, a woman with four small kids and at least twenty bulging plastic bags grinned at Chloe as she lined up behind her.

"Hai hawiyyatik?" That's your ID? asked the woman behind her.

"Naam," yes, Chloe responded with a wink. She turned back to the soldier woman, who was still staring down at the passport copy.

"Why do you give me this? Where's your passport?"

"This is what I carry," Chloe said.

"You don't have your passport?"

"This has always been good enough," she lied.

"It's not good enough. Where are you from?"

"The States," Chloe said. Maybe the woman couldn't read English. Maybe she didn't even know for sure it wasn't official ID. That gave Chloe an idea. She pulled her wallet from her backpack and fished out a tattered business card, which she handed to the soldier.

"Go," the woman said, handing the documents back. She pressed the button that released the turnstile. Chloe walked through, chuckling to herself. Avi had helped her make that card last time she was here. It said, "Chloe Rubin, Human Rights Worker," but he had added in Hebrew: "This person is authorized to do important work."

Chloe had never been to Ramle and wasn't really sure how to get there. The simplest way would be to take a servees to Jerusalem, a local bus to the bus station, and then an intercity bus to Ramle. But that would take hours, and, by the time she got there, it might be too late to visit. She studied her Rand McNally map book. Ramle looked to be about thirty miles due north from where she was standing, a short ride on Highway 404 and then a straight shot up Highway 1. Orienting herself in what she hoped was the right direction, she held her hand out, palm down, at a 45-degree angle to her body, trying to make eye contact with the drivers as they whizzed by. Just when she was sure no one was ever going to stop, a middle-aged woman in a beat-up Toyota swerved to the shoulder in a screech of tires.

"Ramle?" Chloe asked. The woman nodded. Chloe climbed into the front seat and in under an hour was within sight of the barbed wire–encircled towers of the prison.

Neve Tirzah was the nearest part of the labyrinthine prison complex. She was relieved to see people lined up at the little barred window marked Visitors. That must mean it was a visiting day. Since Neve Tirzah was the women's prison, most of the visitors were men with children bundled in their arms. Chloe took her place at the end of the line. After ten minutes, she got to hand her passport to a blue-uniformed woman who took it along with Rania's name and disappeared.

The minutes ticked by. She got tired of standing and went to sit on a patch of grass that turned out to be wet. She pulled out the paperback copy of *The Da Vinci Code* she'd picked up at SFO, meaning to read it on the plane. She had wanted mindless entertainment but had been too nervous even for that. She couldn't concentrate on it now either. She read the same page three times. One by one, she watched each set of visitors pass through a gate into a wire cage where they were searched and then shown into a smaller cage where the prisoners paced anxiously. The prisoners wore their own clothes. Their eyes would light up when they saw their visitors come in. They would scoop up their kids into tight hugs, then settle down onto one of the benches and picnic on the food their husbands had brought. Chloe had not thought to bring food for Rania. She examined the contents of her purse. Half a chocolate bar and a package of smoked almonds from the plane would be the sum total of what she had to share with her friend.

Half an hour after the last visitor was ushered back out of the cage, a soft-spoken man with a perfectly round face appeared and asked for her ID. She told him that she had given it to a woman. He looked bemused and went away.

She was wondering if she would ever see her passport again, let alone Rania, when she heard a disembodied voice call "America."

She looked around.

"America. Bo'ee" A hefty policeman stood in the doorway to the cage. Chloe walked over and stood toe to toe, so close she could smell the sweat under his limp blue shirt. She faintly hoped he would move back a foot to get some distance, and she would be able to get one foot in the door.

"What do you want?" he asked.

"I already told three people, to visit Rania Bakara."

"She cannot have visitors."

"That's not true. Her sister visited her." He had not moved an inch. She took another half step closer, until she was nearly standing on his toe. He held his ground.

"Are you her sister?"

"No. But if her sister can visit, I can."

"You have to have special permission to visit security prisoners. Do you have a permit?"

"What kind of permit?"

"Tasrih."

"That just means permit in Arabic. It doesn't tell me anything."

"You need a tasrih to visit her."

"No I don't." She had no idea if she did or not, but she did know that bluffing was nine tenths of the law.

"You cannot visit her because she is in trouble."

"Obviously, that's why I came."

"I mean she is in trouble with us. She makes big trouble for us."

That would be Rania, all right. Chloe stifled a chuckle.

"If you don't let me in, I'll call a lawyer, and she'll call the court, and they'll say you have to. Then you'll get in trouble."

"Wait here." He snapped the gate shut and disappeared into the prison.

Could such a dumb threat possibly work? Or was he going off to get someone to come arrest her? She had lots of time to wonder. Another fifteen minutes crept past before he came back. This time, he spoke to her through the fence, giving her no hope of forcing her way in. She felt her chance slipping away.

"Why do you want to see her?" he asked.

"I am a friend of hers from America. I came all this way to visit her and then found out she was in prison. I can't go back home without seeing her."

"Wait here."

He went away again. Chloe went back to the grass, which had dried in the sun. She took out *The Da Vinci Code*, but couldn't even get herself to open it.

"America. Come."

She looked up. The burly policeman was opening the gate. She almost ran to make it through before he could change his mind. She expected him to tell her to open her purse, as she had seen the other visitors do, but he did not stop. She followed him through the inner cage into the whitewashed stone building, where high ceilings echoed with distant shrieks. It took her eyes a moment to adjust to the dim interior. When they did, she saw what looked like a hospital waiting room, with wooden benches along walls covered with peeling, white paint and penciled graffiti in Hebrew and Arabic. Two heavy chairs faced one another in the middle of the room, like a scene waiting for the actors.

A small woman whose heavy glasses covered half her bruised face entered, flanked by police, one male, one female. A gray *jilbab* cloaked the woman's painfully thin body, a blue headscarf hiding all but a wisp of chestnut hair. Defiance battled intense sadness for domination of her chiseled features.

"Rania!" Chloe ran to her, sweeping her into a hug.

Rania winced and caught her breath sharply. Her wrists were cuffed behind her back, and Chloe told herself that was why Rania didn't hug her back. But no cuffs bound her face, and she didn't offer the traditional three kisses to the cheek. She looked remote and wooden.

"No touching. Come here," ordered Chloe's escort.

He took Rania's arm and led her to a table with chairs on either side. She flinched at his touch, as if he had hurt her. Chloe thought there was something wrong with her right arm. She was leaning to her left, gripping the back of the chair with her white-knuckled left hand. Her right was held at an odd angle. But it was impossible to tell because of the cuffs.

"Can't you take those off?" she asked the policeman.

"No. You have five minutes."

"Would you give us some privacy?" Chloe said. He said something to the other two, and each moved to one wall. Chloe took the empty chair opposite Rania.

"Are you all right?" Leaning forward, Chloe spoke in a low voice.

"You should not have come." Rania turned her head slightly to the right, avoiding eye contact.

Chloe fought the tears burning her eye sockets. Buck up, she told herself. If Rania really felt that way, she would have refused to see her.

"What happened to your face?" she asked.

"Nothing."

"Obviously something did. Did they beat you?"

"Of course. They beat everyone." If anyone else talked to Chloe in that tone, she would snap back at them. She took a deep breath and reminded herself what Rania was going through. If she needed to vent her anger at Chloe, that was probably safer than anything else she could do with it.

"A friend of mine who works with Checkpoint Watch is calling the army to try to find out why they are holding you here," she said.

"We already know why I am here."

"Nehama might be able to get your lawyer access to the evidence against you, so he can appeal the detention order."

"Even if he does, he will lose."

"You don't know that," Chloe said without belief. "Besides, what else can we do?"

"There is nothing you can do. You should go back to America. Otherwise, they will arrest you again."

"There's no reason they would do that," Chloe said, although, of course, everything Rania knew, she also knew. The men who had had Rania arrested had plenty of friends in the Ministry of Interior. Doubtless, they knew by now that Chloe was back in the country.

"If they were so worried about me being here, they would have denied my entry," Chloe said. "Anyway, I'm here, and I'm doing everything I can to get you out."

"You can do nothing. I will not get out." Rania shifted in the chair, grasping the latticed back with her cuffed hands. Chloe knew from her own experiences with handcuffs that holding onto something could relieve the pressure on your wrists.

"Of course you're going to get out. They didn't find anything in your house, right?"

"What would there be for them to find?" They both knew that the only weapon Rania had ever had was buried somewhere in Avi's father's house. Although Palestinian police were permitted to carry weapons, Rania did not.

"So, they will have to let you out. They can't hold you forever."

"Can they not?"

Chloe almost doubted that this bitter, dull-eyed creature was really Rania. "Listen to me. You can't give up. You have to fight and stay strong. We're going to get you out, Bassam and I. We'll find a way."

Rania straightened in her chair and looked straight at Chloe. "You saw Bassam?"

"Yes. He loves you very much."

"Did you see Khaled?"

Mentioning her son's name brought a spark to Rania's face. Chloe wished there was some way she could avoid killing it.

"No," she said. "I met Bassam at his office. He says Khaled is fine, though." She wanted to keep talking about Khaled but could think of nothing more to say. She should have asked Bassam for details about his son. Of course, she had not known she was going to see Rania. She didn't want to let there be silence between them, for fear that the fragile connection would fade away again. "Bassam is thinner, without you to cook for him."

"I'm sure his mother keeps him well-fed." That almost sounded like the old Rania. Chloe laughed too heartily, and the policeman in the corner looked at his watch.

"Time's up," he said.

Chloe didn't think it was worth arguing. "Is there anything you want me to tell Bassam?" she asked quickly.

"Tell him to make sure Khaled wears a clean shirt to school."

"Okay." Chloe suddenly remembered the chocolate and almonds in her purse. She withdrew them, held them out sheepishly and then realized Rania couldn't take them. She walked around and placed them in Rania's left hand, closing the fist around them. She bent and kissed her friend's cheeks, left, right, and left again. On the last one, she felt Rania's lips press her cheek as well. She moved toward the door.

"Chloe," Rania said, so softly she almost didn't hear.

Chloe took a step back toward her, away from the policeman jangling his keys in the iron doorway. "Yes?"

"Will you come again?"

"Of course." As much as it had hurt to leave a minute ago, it hurt more now. With her hands cuffed behind her, Rania had no way to wipe away the tears streaking her swollen face.

Chapter 9

From the Ramle bus station, Chloe caught a sherut to Jerusalem. The driver, a Palestinian with Israeli citizenship, was willing to drop her at Damascus Gate for only five shekels more, and she was back in Ramallah by mid-afternoon. She browsed in the market, bought some spiced nuts that Tina liked, and successfully dodged being dragged into a shop to look at authentic Palestinian crafts made in China.

The unmistakable smell of tomato sauce drew her into a dimly lit restaurant called Enrico's. She ordered a calzone and cappuccino, and tried to get immersed in *The Da Vinci Code*, while the visit with Rania played on a loop in her mind. She wished she could be as confident that she would see Rania outside of prison as that Robert Langdon would find Mary Magdalene's love child with Jesus. The door swung open and a burst of laughter heralded the arrival of a group of young men. They wore tight jeans and skin-tight shirts, some showing gold chains around their necks. They gravitated to a round table in the middle of the room, settling themselves while calling out hellos to other diners and the young woman at the cash register.

"Daoud, when are we going to get married?" the young woman called back.

A young man with a long, heavily embroidered scarf draped around his throat like a feather boa swung around to face her.

"As soon as your parents agree to meet my price."

They all exploded in good-natured laughter, including the cashier.

"You can't marry her; you are going to marry me!" one of the other guys said. He put his arm possessively around Daoud. He was startlingly good-looking, black, wavy hair framing pale, jutting cheekbones.

Chloe wasn't positive she had understood correctly, but she couldn't mistake the word *tjawaz*. She heard "Inti mitjawzi?" Are you married? every day of her life in Palestine. At home, she would think nothing of a group of obviously gay young men goofing around in a restaurant. But this wasn't home.

The young man called Daoud noticed her watching them. She looked down at her book, but too late.

"Where are you from?" he asked loudly in English.

"California," she said.

"West Hollywood?" How did he know about West Hollywood?

"No, San Francisco."

"Aaaaaah!" With the shriek, he jumped up and made for her table, motioning his friends to bring their chairs. Before she knew it, she had a rapt audience.

"I want so much to go to San Francisco!" Daoud said.

"What is San Francisco like?" asked Daoud's would-be fiancé. His long, narrow fingers played the table like a piano, probably unconsciously. "Are the men as beautiful as in the movies?"

Okay, she couldn't be mistaking his meaning.

"I don't know, I don't really notice them, if you know what I mean."

"My sister," Daoud said with a broad smile. "Are you married?"

She was surprised. She thought he had understood, but maybe he hadn't. She doubted news of the San Francisco mayor's short-lived plan to allow same-sex marriages had reached Palestine.

"No."

"Then marry me and take me to San Francisco. Please?"

His friends whooped with laughter. "No, me," said the one with the ponytail.

"I'm the best looking," said the piano player.

"No, Elias," said Daoud. "You have to stay and become the next Ammar Hassan."

"Sah," true, said Elias with an extravagant sigh. Chloe had heard about Ammar Hassan, who had held the nation in thrall two years earlier, when he took second place in the Lebanese television talent competition *Super Star*. He was from a village in the Salfit District, where Rania lived.

"Are you from Salfit?" she asked Elias.

"Yes, from Jemai'in," he named one of the villages in that area.

"My village is also in Salfit. Kufr Yunus," said Daoud.

"I don't know that village," Chloe said.

"That's because it's not even a speck!" said one of the other men, drawing more gales of laughter.

"Do not disrespect my homeland," Daoud said in Arabic. Chloe was gratified that she understood.

The waiter served her calzone. She cut it into six pieces and put it in the middle of the table.

"T'faddalu," she said to them, indicating they should join her.

"No, no, please, you eat," said Pony Tail.

"Really, I invite you."

They might have taken her up on the offer, but her phone rang, and they got up noisily and went back to their own table. Chloe looked at the phone. Nehama, her friend from Machsom Watch. She must have news about Rania's case.

"There's no detention order," Nehama boomed. "She was arrested on the orders of someone high up, that's all my contact could say."

"I already knew that," Chloe said. "Did they say how long she'll be held?"

"They don't know. Whoever ordered her arrested is calling the shots. She'll probably be there until they decide to release her."

"But surely they can't just hold her indefinitely, without even a hearing."

"She'll probably be sent for an administrative detention hearing in a few weeks, but that won't help her. The judge will accept whatever the army says and order her held for six months."

"Six months? So, we need to get her out before they do that."

Nehama was quiet for an unbearably long time. "You have the lawyer's number?" she said finally. "Give it to me. I'll call Rachel, the Israeli lawyer who got you out of prison." And agreed that they could kick me out of the country, Chloe thought uncharitably, as Nehama went on.

"She's very good at getting access to secret evidence. Maybe she can help Rania's lawyer find out what they have on her."

"Okay, thanks," Chloe murmured. She was afraid she didn't sound very grateful. "I'll call you next week and make a date for dinner."

"Good, then." Nehama sounded like her usual, cheerful self. She dealt with such cases every day. To her, Rania was just another unlucky Palestinian.

✳ ✳ ✳

The next morning, Chloe caught a Ramallah-Tulkarem bus which dropped her on the highway near Ariel. The sprawling Jewish settlement, with its rows of identical, red-roofed houses, swimming pools, shopping centers, and university, sits smack in the middle of the West Bank, a teeming monument to the failure of twenty years of peace talks.

The stale, smoky smell of the settlement's police station jolted her back to the day she had spent there a year ago. She recalled in her joints the mingled fear and excitement that had accompanied her first brush with the Israeli authorities. How little she had known then about the true dangers haunting this land. She had barely known Rania then. The Palestinian policewoman had been there that day, but Chloe had not even seen her. Rania had hidden in Benny Lazar's office, listening for evidence that Chloe was an Israeli spy.

Now Chloe was knocking on the door of that same office, hoping she could persuade Benny to get Rania out of Israeli prison. Even as she tapped on the half-open door, Chloe wondered if this was a terrible gamble. Benny liked Rania, and he had seemed to harbor no ill will toward Chloe, but that could all have been part of his act. He was capable of donning a lot of personalities.

"Ken?" Yes? He was looking at her expectantly now, no doubt wondering why this person he barely knew was interrupting his work, only to stand there motionless. Big and bald, he reminded her of Marlon Brando in *Apocalypse Now*.

"Hi," she said. "Remember me?"

Even as she said the words, it hit her that he didn't. Why would he remember some American he talked to for an hour ten months ago?

"I'm a friend of Rania's," she said.

That did it. "How did you get back in?" he asked.

Not the response she was hoping for. Please, she prayed, don't let this mission of mercy end with me being led out of the station in handcuffs.

"Through the airport," she said.

"You didn't have any problems?"

"No, why should I?"

In fact, the agreement under which she had left the country the last time had said that she could return. Nonetheless, he seemed as surprised as she had been that the Israeli government had lived up to its side of the bargain. Could he have her thrown out again? She didn't think so. If someone was supposed to put her on a watch list and hadn't, wasn't that their problem? But she never understood who could do what in this crazy country.

"So, what can I do for you?" Benny asked, his bulging, blue eyes twinkling at her.

He clearly wasn't going to invite her to sit. Well, she wasn't going to stand like a supplicant in front of her lord. The chair directly opposite his desk was host to a pile of manila folders with papers falling out of them every which way. There was another chair off to the right. If she sat in the free chair, she decided, she would be giving up a subtle advantage. Plus, the one with all the papers on it was a vinyl-covered armchair, and the free one was of a hard, metal, folding variety. She carefully transferred the files to the metal chair and plopped down in the armchair.

"I want you to get Rania out of jail," she said.

"Rania's in jail?" His eyes popped out even more. He sounded legitimately surprised.

"Yes. Neve Tirzah. Which I'm sure you already knew."

"How would I know? What did she do?"

"Why do you think she did anything? You know her; she's the most law-abiding person on the planet." Not strictly true, by Israeli standards. Rania had broken any number of Israeli laws in her quest to save Chloe and Fareed. Benny had no direct knowledge of those escapades, as far as she knew. Nonetheless, he looked skeptical. Maybe he knew more than she thought. Or maybe he just understood that it was basically impossible for any Palestinian to live strictly within Israeli law.

"You worked with her on that case last year," Chloe said. "You know why the army wants to keep her quiet."

"If the army took her, it's a security matter. I wouldn't have any influence there."

"That can't be true."

"It is. The army doesn't like the police, especially me."

"You just don't want to help her."

"She wasn't very nice to me."

He was leaning back in his chair, his feet resting on an open desk drawer. She remembered that pose from her interrogation in this room. She understood that his practiced air of relaxation was meant to produce a corresponding lowering of his prey's guard. Just because she wasn't here as a suspect didn't mean she should fall for his tricks.

"There's no reason any Palestinian should be nice to you," she said. "Probably, it's the ones who are that you should worry about."

He seemed to like that. He leaned his chair back precariously on two legs, placing both hands behind his neck.

"What about due process? She hasn't committed any crime," Chloe said. He was an American, born and raised in Minnesota. He must have retained some of what he'd been taught about justice.

"There are lots of Palestinians locked up who didn't commit any crime," he told her, his broad face alive with the joy of having won a point in debate.

How could she have let herself get boxed into such a stupid assertion? She thought of herself as good in an argument, yet she couldn't hold her own with this guy.

"This is Rania we're talking about. She has a seven-year-old son. She's a policewoman, for God's sake. You should at least have a professional courtesy reason for helping her."

He shook his head.

"The days when I ate lunch with Palestinian policemen are over," he said.

✳ ✳ ✳

Daoud checked his watch. His gaze lingered on it for an extra few seconds, admiring the bold, roman numbers on the oversized face and how the black leather band sat on his muscular forearm. He had admired it in the shop, but the shopkeeper had refused to meet his price. Then, his friends had surprised him with it at his engagement party. He hoped they hadn't over-paid, but, even if they had, it was worth it.

He had twenty minutes until his assignation. Not enough time to get any homework done. His mother was resting upstairs, as was her habit in the afternoon, and his sister, Mayisa, was upset, because he had shooed her inside earlier when the boys were throwing stones at the jeeps. She said he was treating her like a baby. Maybe he should go talk to her. He walked down the hall and heard soft voices behind Mayisa's closed door. As he hesitated outside, the voices rose in pitch, one girl telling a story and the others shriek-ing "No!" as she got to the scandalous parts. Never mind that a western audience would fail to find even a hint of scandal in these girls' lives. This was Palestine.

He would talk to Mayisa later. He was not in the mood to deflect the flir-tations of thirteen-year-old girls. If they'd been eighteen-year-old boys, that might be another story. But, of course, that was just a fantasy.

"Mais, I'm going now," Daoud called, using his sister's nickname. "See you at the party."

"Okay," came her less-than-interested response. Good thing she had com-pany. Otherwise, she surely would have asked why he was leaving early.

He'd left his leather jacket in Ramallah, so his mother wouldn't ask where he got it. He pulled a black windbreaker over his crisp, white shirt. The creases in his black pants were perfect, a product of his mother's careful ironing. He'd have to make sure not to get them wrinkled before the party.

He took off up the hill, toward the big, empty mansion a Palestinian-American family had built years ago but never lived in. Before he had walked a few feet, though, he heard some kind of commotion down near the entrance to the village. Shouts and an engine, which might have been a jeep. Soldiers had been in the village earlier, clashing with some kids near the school. Could they be returning? He should go make sure no kids were on the street. He glanced at his watch again. If he headed down to the entrance, he might be late getting to the house, but no matter. The meeting hadn't been his idea.

By the time he reached the village entrance, whatever conflict might have taken place was over. The evening was quiet. He could hear Um Mahmoud's chickens squawking in their coop, and mothers calling their kids to come in for supper. A slight breeze rustled the leaves of Um Mahmoud's olive and fig trees.

Daoud turned to walk toward his destination, humming a popular Arab tune under his breath. Footsteps behind him made him turn, a smile on his face to greet whichever of his neighbors was arriving home. It wasn't a friend, but it was someone he was glad to see. Now, he wouldn't need to make the trek up to the Palestinian American's house, because the person he was supposed to meet was walking toward him.

The meeting was to make an exchange, and he could see that the other person had brought the goods. But they couldn't do it here, on the main village road, right when people were coming home from work. Daoud looked around and gestured for the other person to follow him. The thick, broad leaves of that giant fig tree would just shield them from sight, if they positioned themselves properly. Moving under the tree's canopy, Daoud grasped a branch for balance, then pulled his hand away with a coating of sticky, white sap from the unripe figs. He nearly wiped it on his windbreaker, but picked off a wide leaf instead and swiped at it, as the other person rounded the tree and came into sight.

A few minutes later, Um Mahmoud, about to put spinach soup and lamb stew on the table, heard the unmistakable crack of a gunshot. Or were there two?

Chapter 10

Rania lay on her cot, trying to remember every detail of Khaled's third birthday. They had taken him to Serafi, an amusement park near Nablus. The little airplane ride, where you went around and up and down at the same time, had frightened him and made him cry. Bassam had taken him from her arms, while she continued to fly around, getting a little dizzy, and, when she finally got off, they had bought Khaled a big fluff of pink cotton candy. He had stuffed so much of it in his mouth that he nearly choked. They had never gone back to Serafi. Khaled would probably enjoy it now that he was older, but it was in ruins, a casualty of the tight closure around Nablus. Last time she had passed it, the little airplane cars had been lined up, rusting by the side of the road, like a miniature remnant of World War I.

A loud clanging disrupted her reverie. Tali Ta'ali was unlocking her cell with a giant key. They had not spoken since Tali had brought her the book.

"Bo'ee he'na," the policewoman said.

"Come where?" Rania asked in English.

"Yesh po mishehu." Someone is here.

"Who is it?"

"Lo yodaat." I don't know.

Rania turned her face to the wall. The only people she wanted to see were Bassam, who couldn't get a permit to come, and Khaled, whom she would not allow to see her in chains. Chloe's visit had brought a faint glimmer of hope, but she could not allow herself to believe in it.

"You don't want to come?" Tali's voice sounded a little farther away, like she was already leaving. Rania thought quickly. It might feel noble for a second to refuse to go, but, really, what would it get her? Maybe it was Chloe. If she was back so soon, it must mean she had some information to report.

"Wait," she called in English. "I am coming." At least she would hold onto a little dignity by not conversing in Hebrew, even with Tali Ta'ali.

"Come on then," Tali Ta'ali said in Hebrew. "They are waiting."

Rania put on her sandals and reached for the jilbab hanging on the rail of her bunk. It was still damp, though she had washed it a day ago. In the small sink, she could never wring it out well enough. If it was Chloe who was here to see her, perhaps she could do without it. But there would certainly be men in the halls. She was wearing black, stretchy slacks that showed her legs clearly and a red pullover that hugged her breasts. She pulled on the wet coat, grimacing as the clamminess enveloped her, and tied a hijab over her hair.

She started down the hall while Tali was still locking the cell behind her.

"Wait," Tali said. "Give me your hands."

Rania had momentarily forgotten what humiliation was involved in deciding to receive a visit. Should she turn around and walk back to the bed or acquiesce and be ground into the dirt like a bug?

She didn't have to commit. Tali grabbed her wrists firmly but gently and snapped the cuffs on in front. It didn't hurt her injured arm as much as when they pulled her arms behind her. The policewoman knelt and fastened the shackles around her ankles. Rania shuffled after Tali, holding her head high, telling herself it was totally normal to be bound up like a cow about to be slaughtered for a feast.

She recognized Benny Lazar's booming voice before she saw him in the captain's office. He turned to watch her enter, a broad smile on his open, goofy face.

"Are those necessary?" he asked the captain in Hebrew, gesturing toward the chains.

"Standard procedure," the man answered.

If Benny argued, she would stay. But he merely nodded slightly.

"Take me back," she said to Tali Ta'ali.

The young woman looked at her captain for orders. He looked at Benny.

"What, aren't you happy to see me?" Benny said in English.

"Why are you here?"

"I want to talk to you. Sit down."

Just because she was chained up, he thought he could order her around? He should know her better than that. She stood, shifting uncomfortably from one shackled foot to the other.

"I don't have anything to say to you," she nearly spat in his face.

She turned to leave.

"Mustafa said you would say that."

She hesitated. If her boss had sent him, maybe it meant something. Hold up, she told herself. You know this guy. He'll say anything to get what he wants. God only knew what he might want from her. She couldn't imagine she had any information that would be useful to him. She had been in this prison for less than four weeks, but it seemed she had been locked away forever, and all her knowledge of the outside world had fled.

"I will not talk to any Israelien, ever again," she said. She couldn't stomp out the way she wanted to because of the shackles. She simply turned her back to Benny and gestured with her eyes to Tali that she was ready to go.

"So, don't talk. Listen for a change."

He was telling *her* to listen for a change? That was funny.

"Do you have some coffee?" Benny asked the captain.

The captain, of course, sent Tali to get it. When she returned, she put two cups down on the desk along with a little bowl filled with sugar packets. She left the room, closing the door behind her.

"Do you mind?" Benny said to the captain, who shrugged and left them alone.

Benny emptied four sugars into his cup. The coffee smelled a lot better than the swill they brought her in the morning. In fact, it smelled divine. She told herself she had no choice but to stay and drink coffee with him, but of course that was ridiculous. If she walked out into the hall, someone would materialize fast enough to lock her back into her little cell. She wanted to sit here like a normal person and drink coffee. She wanted to smell something besides half-rotten food and her own body odor and hear something besides her own breathing. She reached her right hand out for the cup, and the left hand was dragged along for the ride. She took the cup in both hands and lifted it to her face. She took only the tiniest of sips, so it would last a long time.

Benny had gulped his in three swallows. She hoped he wasn't going to call for more, which would force her to decide again whether to stay and hear what he had come to tell her or stand on principle and go back to stare at the walls some more. He leaned back, smiling at her. She felt like he could hear her thoughts and remembered that she had thought that in the past, when they were tracking down the murderer of the foreign woman. She fleetingly remembered drinking lemonade in an outdoor café in Tel Aviv, with the sun making her so warm she had taken off her hijab.

This was not right. How dare he come here and act like they were friends?

She slammed the half-full cup down on the desk. Some of the liquid jumped out and splashed onto her sleeve. She dabbed at it ineffectually with her other sleeve. Benny leaned over and plucked a Kleenex from the box on the captain's desk, handing it to her with a flourish.

"I need your help," he said.

"I would rather rot in this jail for the rest of my life than help you," she said, ignoring the absurdity of his needing help from someone who was clearly as helpless as you could get.

"Just hear me out," he said. "A young man has been killed. In Kufr Yunus."

"Who killed him?" she asked in spite of herself.

"We are not sure. No one saw the incident. His body was found under a fig tree near the entrance to the village. People say he had a confrontation with the army earlier in the day."

"In Kufr Yunus?" Kufr Yunus rarely had clashes. It was a tiny village, barely more than a hamlet, and one of only two villages in the Salfit District that did not border any settlements. The army seldom went near there, since it was not on the settler road.

"That's one of the things that doesn't make sense. There are rumors—reasons to think that it could have been a political fight."

"With the army?"

He rolled his eyes. "In the village."

"You're saying Palestinians killed him?"

"You're saying that's not possible?"

"How would I know? I don't even know who he was. I've only been in Kufr Yunus twice in my life. But you tell me he was in a confrontation with the army and, now that he's dead, suddenly Palestinian factions are supposed to have killed him. I've heard that story before."

"So, prove me wrong."

She had been enjoying the argument, and suddenly she remembered where she was.

"How can I prove anything while I'm in here?"

"You can't. I can get you out, if you agree to investigate this thoroughly."

"You want to make me a collaborator." She had feared that as soon as she saw him, and she had known better than to sit down with the devil. He had beguiled her with coffee and repartee. But this had gone far enough.

"Don't be melodramatic. I just want you to find out the truth."

"I found out the truth last time, and look where it got me." The murder of the foreign woman had officially been his case. He had been content to let a Palestinian boy sit in jail for the crime, while knowing that there were powerful Israeli men who had more cause to want the young woman dead. "You want me to tell you some Palestinian killed this young man, so you can get the army out of trouble."

"You think I need you to get the army out of trouble?"

He had a point there. Killing Palestinians was no problem for the army. It was their job.

"Why are you here, then?"

He eyed her half-full coffee cup, and she could tell he wanted to ask if she was going to drink it. She picked it up and drank a few more sips, then put it down again.

"The West Bank is a tinderbox right now. If some group in the village wanted this kid dead, there will be others who knew it. If his family finds out, it could set off a wave of reprisal killings. We can't risk that."

She had to admire his choice of argument. Palestine, in recent months, had come closer to civil war than anyone had ever thought possible. The only thing that had kept them from extinction all these years was their fierce unity. But, since President Arafat had died, that had started to unravel. And since Hamas was elected to lead the government, the United States and Israel had put their money to good use, financing those who wanted to see the new leadership fail.

She herself had no use for Hamas. She had joined the Fatah Youth Organization as soon as she was old enough to join anything. She found it painful to watch her people becoming more and more addicted to religion as the seeds of conservatism took root in the soil of isolation and oppression.

But whatever Rania might feel about Hamas, nothing could be gained by becoming a spy for the Israelis. Benny could say whatever he wanted, but that's what he was trying to do, make her a spy. Whenever anyone got out of jail without serving a full sentence, the rumors clung to them like smoke. If they seemed too interested in anything or too jumpy around old friends, people whispered that they had been turned into traitors. Sometimes they had and sometimes they hadn't, but, always, it was dangerous, not only for them but for their families.

"Forget it," she said. "I don't work for you."

"No, you work for Mustafa. He thinks you should do it."

"Why isn't he here, then?" She knew the answer as she said it. Her boss had been a fighter in the old days, before Arafat returned to Palestine. He had been captured and, like so many of the men of his generation, had spent years in Israeli prison. He might now be part of the Palestinian Authority, but, to the Israelis, he was still a terrorist. He could never get a permit to go into Israel, certainly not to visit a prisoner in military detention.

Still, she wasn't about to take Benny's word for that or anything else. If Captain Mustafa wanted her to get out of jail and work on this case, he would find a way to make it happen. If he didn't, she would stay here and prove herself as tough as he had been.

"I'm not interested," she said. "Go away and don't come back."

Back in her cell, she stripped off the jilbab which had more or less dried from her body heat. Unfortunately, it had taken all her warmth with it. She lay down on the cot, shivering. She had no blanket, only a thin, moldy comforter. She didn't feel as proud of herself as she had when she stormed out of the captain's office. It had seemed so easy then to say, "Forget it, I'll stay here forever." But now that she was confronted with the real possibility of a life inside these four gray walls, she felt like creepy-crawly things were oozing out of her pores. She wondered if Bassam would take a second wife. Would Khaled start to call another woman mother?

∗ ∗ ∗

"You know that Italian place, Enrico's?" Chloe said. She was washing the dinner dishes, and Tina was putting them away. "I met some gay men there the other day."

"How did you know?" Tina scooped the remains of the lentil and rice dish called *mujaddara* into a bowl and covered it with a plate.

"I could just tell. Plus, they were joking around about marrying each other." Chloe ran some warm water into the sticky pot and put it down to soak.

"They could have just been kidding around. But there's starting to be a little bit of an underground gay scene here. There's even a bar in Jerusalem where they have Ramallah Night. Twice a month, these guys from Ramallah perform there."

"Ramallah drag queens?"

"That's right."

"This I have to see." She thought of Daoud, with his gypsy scarf and dramatic flair, and Elias, who was going to be the next Ammar Hassan. Maybe they were performers. "What night do they have it?"

"Wednesdays," Tina said.

"That's tonight! Can we go now?" Chloe said.

She thought Tina was going to argue, but, after a long minute, Tina dropped her dish towel. "Come on, then. We don't want to miss the show."

"What's the name of this place?" Chloe asked after they showed their IDs to the bouncer. It had been a long time since she'd been carded, but the place was so dark, the guy probably couldn't see how old she was.

"Adloyada," Tina said.

"Clever," Chloe said, reaching back to the Hebrew school teachings of her tiny, North Carolina synagogue. The bar stood on Shushan Street, and Shushan was the province in Persia where the Purim story, the Book of

Esther, took place. One of the commandments surrounding the holiday of Purim was to drink *ad d'lo yada*, "until he did not know" the difference between the villain and the hero of the story. Of course, that was exactly how drunk the owner of any bar would want his customers to get. For a gay bar, though, what you "did not know" had a deeper meaning.

Adloyada was also the name for the carnivals held to celebrate Purim, at which people dressed in costume, making it appropriate for a bar that hosted drag shows.

The cozy ambiance inside the bar was a sharp contrast with the last bar she had been in with Tina. That had been a seedy dive in a rough-and-tumble section of Eilat, and they went there an hour after Chloe had nearly been raped. Tina squeezed her hand, and Chloe knew she was reliving the same memory. Nothing bad can happen tonight, her gesture said.

The bar was moderately full, so they did not get a seat on one of the frayed couches that dotted the main room, but they did find a table with a prime view of the stage. It was half a table, actually, which they were sharing with another lesbian couple who was leaning into one another and, more than occasionally, sharing deep kisses.

Chloe and Tina ordered pints of Taybeh and clinked glasses.

"To your triumphant return to Palestine," Tina said. They sipped their beers and ignored the smooching couple until a short, balding man coughed into the microphone.

"May I have your attention please?" he said in English, then repeated it in Hebrew, and, Chloe was pleased to hear, in Arabic.

"Who is he?" she whispered to Tina.

"Mordecai," Tina responded. "He's the owner."

Chloe chuckled to herself. Mordecai was the hero of the Purim story. She wondered if this guy had changed his name to fit the bar.

"I regret to tell you," Mordecai was saying in English, "that there will be no performance tonight." Groans filled the bar. Mordecai tapped on the mike until the grumbles subsided. "I was just informed," he continued, "that Daoud al-Khader, known to most of you as JLo Day-Glo, was killed last night in the West Bank."

Mordecai let the din that followed this announcement go on for a few moments before he signaled for quiet once more. "Some of the guys from Ramallah have gone to pay respects to Daoud's family," he said. "So, in his honor, we will observe solemnity tonight. But," he held up his hand, forestalling a mass exodus, "I invite you all to stay and toast his memory on the house."

Cheers greeted his last statement, though people quickly subdued their friends into more appropriate affect. People began drifting to the bar to claim their free drinks.

"Did you know this Daoud?" Chloe asked Tina. Could it be a coincidence that the flamboyant young man she had met was also named Daoud? It was not an uncommon name, but still.

Tina shook her head. "I don't think so," she said. Chloe turned to the kissy-faced lesbians, who seemed to have decided that mourning demanded a hiatus in making out.

"Did you know him?" she asked the butch one, who looked to be about her age and sported a tattoo that said Peace Now in English. She probably got it in the army, Chloe reflected.

"Not personally," the woman said. "But I saw him perform."

"He did drag?"

"What else?" said the femme, whose long, frizzy hair boasted a shade of red not found in nature.

"Was he tall, with thick wavy hair? Did he wear a leather jacket and a lot of jewelry?" Chloe asked the two of them. They nodded.

"Did you know him, then?" asked Tattoo Woman.

"He asked me to marry him," Chloe said. Suddenly cold, she wished she had brought a sweater.

Chapter 11

"I should have asked him what kind of bullets killed the young man," Rania said out loud. Since her visits from Chloe and Benny, she had taken to talking to herself out loud. In a peculiar way, it made her feel less alone. Only when Tali Ta'ali or one of the others came by did she shut up, so they wouldn't think she was talking to them. Her last conversation with Tali had filled her with sadness when it was over. It had made her think of her grandfather and the village she had never seen. It was too much. She wasn't a history lesson.

She imagined she was sitting in the chair opposite Captain Mustafa's desk, mapping out a strategy for investigating the case. She set her tote bag on the floor in front of the bed and addressed it respectfully.

"First, we need to know exactly how he died," she said. "Were the bullets shot from eye level, which could mean they were fired from inside a jeep or was there a downward trajectory, indicating he was lying on the ground and someone stood over him? Probably no one checked the scene right away to see if there were fresh footprints or tire tracks leading away from the body. It will be too late to do that now. But there must be blood on the ground, and Benny will have a report on the caliber of the bullets. If they are the type used by the army, then we can assume the soldiers killed him."

What is the first rule of investigation? her pretend Captain Mustafa asked.

"Never assume," she answered.

She wished she knew who in the village Benny suspected of wanting the young man dead. Then she would have a nice puzzle to work on. Was he suspected as a traitor? Had he cheated someone or molested someone's daughter? But that type of killing was not committed in secret.

"He was found under a tree," she continued. "Is there a significance to that? Does it matter that it was a fig tree and not an olive?" Unlikely that someone positioned their victim so carefully, but you never knew. She thought about the portion of the Qur'an called At-Tin, the Fig:

By the fig and the olive
And Mount Sinai
And this secure land
We have certainly created man in the best of stature
Then we returned him to the lowest of the lowest ...

Was someone saying that the young man was the lowest of the lowest? That would mean someone who was not righteous. What could make someone not righteous to his neighbors? Many things.

She heard footsteps in the hallway. It didn't sound like Tali Ta'ali. These were heavy boots, and there were more than two of them. She didn't think it was dinner time anyway. She recalled the night they had shot tear gas into her cell and beat her. Were they returning to punish her some more?

"Please, no," she whispered. Her injured arm still throbbed whenever she moved it.

She got up and went to stand by the bars. She would meet whatever was in store face-to-face. Soon, she saw three soldiers and the police captain walking toward her cell. Perhaps they were not coming for her after all. But she had not heard any other prisoners on this hall in a week or more.

"Hinei he," Here she is, the police captain said. He took the heavy ring of keys from his belt, and they jangled menacingly as he located the right one. He opened the door and stood aside to let the soldiers do their will. They strode through the gate, filling the tiny space. Two of them aimed their guns at her heart, their fingers poised near the triggers. Were they going to execute her right here, without even a trial? Israel did not have the death penalty, but it carried out plenty of executions.

She stood straight and as tall as she could make herself, looking into their faces. If they were going to kill her, let their soulless eyes be the last things she saw.

The third soldier, the one whose gun was still slung carelessly over his shoulder, picked up her tote bag.

"Don't handle Captain Mustafa," she said in Arabic.

He turned to look at her, quizzically. "Shelach?" Yours?

A ridiculous question not requiring an answer. Whatever he was going to do with it, he would do whether she answered or not.

"Tekhase et ha'einayim shela." Something about her eyes. She had been studying the Hebrew book, but she had not gotten to "Lekhasot."

One of the gun-wielding soldiers dropped his gun to his side and took the black scarf from his commander's extended hand. He tied it tightly around her eyes, making her glasses dig into her face. She heard a rattling of chains and felt steel shackles being fastened around her ankles, and her wrists were bound tightly behind her back, wrenching her arm again. She gritted her teeth and did not let herself cry out.

They were propelling her somewhere, and she had no choice but to move.

"Where are you taking me?" she demanded in English.

"Shut up," in Hebrew.

"I have a right to know." She stopped walking. A yank on her aching arm got her moving again.

"You have no right to anything." Wasn't that a lesson she had learned thoroughly by now?

"Do you want me to hit her?" one of the other soldiers asked. She didn't understand the answer, but the way they laughed sent shudders through her body.

They walked rapidly for what seemed like a kilometer, and then they were opening doors and pushing her into a jeep. Two of them piled in nearly on top of her. The commander said something to a fourth man who must have been waiting in the driver's seat, and then the doors slammed, and the vehicle leapt forward. She concentrated on breathing. Wherever they were taking her, it couldn't be worse than where she was coming from. At least, she didn't think it could. Her friend Samia, who had been imprisoned during the First Intifada, had been in a big prison camp in the desert, open to the elements, boiling in the summer, wet and freezing in the winter. If they were taking her to a prison camp, at least there would be other women there. Rania would gladly accept physical discomfort to have companionship.

They were stopping now. She tried to recall how long they had been driving. It didn't seem like very long, but her sense of time was all off. They certainly were not in the desert, which was four hours away. Someone opened her door and yanked her out. She hit her head on the way out.

"Hey, be more careful," she said.

"Shut up." The commander didn't seem to have a big vocabulary.

"Do you want me to hit you?" asked the soldier who was now manipulating her cuffs. She knew better than to answer a rhetorical question.

He unlocked the cuffs holding her arms behind her back. She stretched them gingerly. He was kneeling in front of her now, taking off the shackles. She so wished she could kick him in the head, but she couldn't take another beating—yet. In the distance, a donkey brayed. The air was cool and smelled fresh. She had not been outside for over a month. She smelled rosemary, sage, and burning wood. The ground was soft under her feet. It smelled like home.

"Tash'iri et ha'einayim shelakh mekhusot l'od khamesh dakot!" the commander's voice said. She understood "eyes" and "five minutes." The jeep's engine revved with a mighty din and something flew past her head. The jeep swooshed by and was gone. She tore the blindfold from her face.

The first things she saw were her clothes and toiletries, strewn around like snow on the brush. The second was that she was standing in a garbage dump. She knew exactly where she was and wondered if the soldiers had planned this little bit of irony. This was the exact spot where she had found Nadya Kim's body ten months ago, beginning the saga that would land her in prison. The twin minarets of Azzawiya and Mas'ha loomed above her to the left and right. It was mid-evening. A half moon hung low over the horizon.

Garbage had never smelled so sweet to her. She picked her way through Styrofoam cups, half-crushed furniture, and long-abandoned car doors. Some of her clothing had landed in the pools of sludge that flowed down from the hillside settlements of Elkana and Sha'arei Tikva. She left those where they were, to end their days in this de facto landfill, but those that had fallen in the dirt and beneath the scrawny olive trees, she gathered up and put back into the empty bag, which had landed in a ditch. Even the Hebrew textbook was there, spread open on a fallen olive branch. She debated for a minute then put it in the bag. Fortunately, the bag had a shoulder strap. She swung it over her left shoulder and climbed the embankment. Using the spring fires as her guide, she set off toward Mas'ha.

✶ ✶ ✶

Um Bassam was sitting in Rania's favorite chair. The leftovers of a Friday meal, *mansaf* with fresh lamb, bread, salad, olives, and date cookies, still adorned the plastic mat on the floor. Khaled picked up a cookie, and his father wagged a finger at him.

"Khalas," Enough, Bassam said to his son. He was sitting against the wall, reading *Al Hayat*, the newspaper they bought every day.

"Kamaan wahad," One more, Khaled insisted. Her son's blond curls were wild around his cherubic face. She must give him a haircut soon. His black school slacks were a little too short. Trust Bassam not to notice that he had outgrown his clothes. Khaled had a slingshot in the hand that was not holding the cookie. He picked up an olive—rummaged on the plate for a big, juicy one—and placed it carefully in the leather thong. She recognized the slingshot: hers, from her stone-throwing days in the camp. A year ago, she and Bassam had agreed Khaled was too young to play with it. Apparently, she had missed a graduation.

Khaled took aim at his father's head. Bassam didn't seem to notice, or else he didn't mind that he was about to be used for target practice.

"Good evening," she said from the doorway.

Bassam looked up from his newspaper. His lips parted as if to speak, but no sound came out. He got up from the floor, his deep eyes moist, and that slow, lopsided smile she loved spread over the lower part of his face.

"Hamdullila assalaam," he said, giving the ritual greeting to someone who has been released from prison or returned from a journey.

"Allah ysalmak," she replied as custom dictated. "But is that all you can say to your wife, after so long?"

"It is good to have you home," he said with his trademark shrug. He was a little older than he had been in her memories but more striking than ever.

"How did they let you go?" her mother-in-law asked. She did not get up from her chair. Rania tried to believe it was just because of her arthritis. The expression on the old woman's face was not unkind.

"I don't really know," she said. "But I am glad to be here."

"Welcome," Um Bassam replied.

"Welcome to you," Rania said automatically. She waited another moment, to see if her son would say anything. He had not moved. He dumped the olive out of the sling, rolled it in his hand, and repositioned it.

"Khaled," she said softly. "Aren't you going to say hello to me?"

He stood poised, his left thumb holding the olive in the sling and the right pulling the band back by his ear. He looked straight at her face, and she could see tears forming in his slate-colored eyes. His expression softened, and he shifted into a crouch, as if to stand up. Her weight shifted forward of its own volition, planted so that she would not topple over when her son came running and threw his arms around her middle.

He let the olive fly at her head. Fortunately, his aim was terrible. It flew off to the right and landed harmlessly next to the chair where her mother-in-law sat. She plucked it off the cushion and crossed to where her son rocked back and forth on his heels. She crouched down next to him.

"I am sorry I was gone so long," she said. "You know I did not want to be away from you. The Israelis took me to prison."

"Go away. I hate you." He ran for the door. She caught him and strained to pick him up, bearing most of his weight on her good arm. She had lost weight in prison, and he was heavier than he had been. She couldn't hold him if he did not help her. He struggled out of her embrace and ran from the room.

She looked at Bassam for help. She had imagined this moment so many times in the last month, and it had never gone like this. All the tears she had not let herself cry forced their way into her eyes and down her cheeks.

"You refused to see him," her husband said.

"I had to," she sobbed. "Surely he can understand that."

"He is seven." He let that stand between them for a long moment.

"Please go to Khaled," Bassam said to his mother. He wrapped his arms tightly around Rania and half-carried her to their bedroom. She didn't know how long she cried. She woke in her husband's arms and immediately began to cry again. She thought she would never be able to stop.

* * *

Chloe stared at the screen on her mobile phone. Had they recycled Rania's number in the short time she'd been locked up? No, that didn't make sense. Chloe had been out of the country for almost ten months, and her number was here waiting for her when she returned. Bassam must have decided to make use of the minutes left on Rania's SIM card.

"Yes?" she said into the phone.

"Marhaba, Chloe." Greetings.

"Rania! Where are you?"

"In Mas'ha. At home."

"You're out? Hamdullila assalam," Chloe added quickly. She thought that was the right expression. Yes, she remembered people saying it to her after her brief stint in jail.

"Allah ysalmik." Rania's ritual response sounded subdued.

"Are you okay?" Chloe asked.

"Yes. I am tired, but it is good to be home."

"How did you get out?"

"I …well, I am not sure. Benny came to see me."

Chloe's heart jumped for joy. She had done it, then.

"What did he say?"

"He wanted me to look into the death of a boy in one of the villages. I told him I would not, though."

"But you got out anyway?" Maybe it hadn't been Chloe's skills that turned the trick after all. She felt a little less joyful and then scolded herself harshly. The point was that Rania was safely home with her husband and child. It didn't matter how she got there.

"Yes," Rania was saying.

"Who is the boy who was killed?"

"I do not know. But my husband knows his family. We are going to visit them today."

"But you're not going to investigate?"

"No. I do not want to work with Israelis ever again."

Chloe could see why. It had not gotten her anywhere but in prison. "Will you be going back to work?" she asked.

"Of course. I hope," Rania added belatedly.

"I can't wait to see you," Chloe said. "If you can come to Ramallah, I'll take you to this great Italian restaurant I found."

"I would like to try Italian food," Rania said. "I have never eaten it. But you must come here for dinner. My husband likes you so much."

That made Chloe feel warm inside.

"When are you free?" Rania wanted to know.

Good question. She had not thought beyond this moment, Chloe realized. She had no clue what she was going to do next. They agreed to talk in a day or so, and Chloe hung up.

"Do you think she's telling the truth?" Tina asked when Chloe repeated what Rania had told her.

"About what? What are you implying?" Chloe's voice rose involuntarily.

"Why would Benny release her if she refused to work with him? That's not how the Israelis generally work."

"He likes her, and he likes to feel powerful," Chloe said. "And probably he thinks then he will have a favor to hold over her later."

"I hope you're right," Tina said.

Chloe got up and collected the supper dishes, carried them into the kitchen. She was not going to have a conversation about whether Rania could have agreed to become a collaborator. She was just going to give thanks to whatever deity might be out there that her friend was no longer in prison.

Chapter 12

Rania hated visiting the families of martyrs. You were supposed to act happy, because the martyr had gone to his Great Reward and brought honor to his family. But she never felt happy, and she knew the family never did either, and the charade always made her angry. If the young man—or woman, she reminded herself grimly—had carried out a bombing, she was supposed to be proud of them, but she could only think what a waste it was. In a case like this appeared to be, someone shot down like an animal by the army, her fury overcame her, and she wanted to scream and shout, not eat sweets and talk about how blessed his family was.

She plucked a twig from a rose bush and snapped it sharply in two as she and Bassam approached the home of Daoud al-Khader's family. Khaled was home with his grandmother. Rania had managed to have five minutes of conversation with him this morning, bribing him with fries and little pizzas for breakfast, but he was nowhere near forgiving her for her absence.

The front room was full of men, sitting silently in a ring of chairs around the edges. Empty tea cups sat on small, plastic tables placed at three-man intervals. Bassam went to shake hands with Daoud's father, Jamal, a handsome but stern man in his early forties. Next to Jamal was someone Rania was never happy to see. Her former coworker Abdelhakim gave her a long, cool look, his upper lip curling just slightly beneath his carefully trimmed mustache. He had let his hair grow longer, no doubt keeping up with the fashions of Hamas. She would have liked to ask him what he was doing there, but she couldn't speak in this room full of silent men. She nodded slightly in his direction and proceeded through the doorless opening into the next room, where fourteen women sat in virtual darkness.

This room was more like a wide hallway leading to the kitchen, with doors coming off it that were presumably bedrooms. There was not enough space for the chairs to be arranged even in a semicircle, so the women sat in a row against the wall, as if waiting for a lecture to begin—or for a firing squad. Rania was taken aback at her own thought. Before Prison, she did not produce such morbid images.

Daoud's mother would be the one smack in the middle, fingering prayer beads compulsively while the women on either side stroked her arms and shoulders. At least she didn't look happy, though the usual array of dates and chocolate wrappings adorned the plates scattered among the women. Rania bent to kiss the older woman's cheeks once, twice, three times as required.

"Allah yirhamo," God have mercy on him, she said softly. "Um Daoud?" She did not know if Daoud had been the oldest son.

"Um Issa," said the woman, who now acknowledged the ritual greeting by holding out a framed portrait of her martyred son.

"Jamil," beautiful, Rania said. She would have said it even if it wasn't true, but, in this case, she didn't need to pretend.

"He was a perfect son," Um Issa said. "Every weekend, he would come home with sweets for me and presents for his sisters. This is his fiancée," she added, indicating a girl two chairs away. The young woman was about seventeen, with wide, snapping, near-black eyes. No veil covered her shoulder-length brown ringlets, setting her apart from all the other women present. She wore blue jeans and a knit top with three-quarter length sleeves, rather than the traditional jilbab. Rania would not have expected the older women to tolerate such immodesty, but they all seemed very fond of the rebel girl.

"I am Hanan," she said.

"Rania," she responded. A serious-eyed girl with a long braid rose from the stool next to Hanan. She gestured for Rania to take her place and headed into the kitchen

"How long had you been engaged?" Rania asked.

"Two years," Hanan said. "Since I was sixteen."

The marriage was probably arranged, since girls as young as sixteen did

not date in these villages. But Hanan must have considered herself lucky, to
be marrying such a handsome boy.

"Had you set a date for the wedding?"

"No," Hanan said, just as Daoud's mother nodded her head yes.

"They would have been married just before Ramadan," the woman said.

Hanan rolled her eyes. "Daoud wanted to wait," she said. "He thought, if
we married, he might have to leave school. He was studying at the conservatory in Ramallah."

"The Edward Said Conservatory?"

"Yes. He wanted to be an opera singer."

"An opera singer!" This was an unusual family indeed. She didn't know if
there was a single male opera singer anywhere in Palestine. "I didn't know
they even taught opera at the conservatory."

"Yes, he was going to be a great opera singer and travel all over the world,"
Hanan affirmed.

"And are you also a student?" Rania asked.

"I was studying English, but now we have no money, so I had to quit. I am
working at the hospital, in charge of ordering supplies."

There was a thankless task, Rania thought. Navigating the bureaucracy of
the Palestinian Ministry of Health would be a full-time job in itself, even if
you didn't have to then figure out how to get the goods through the Israeli
checkpoints. Hanan must have a real talent for organization, if she was any
good at her job.

"You are very young to have so much responsibility," Rania commented.

Hanan shrugged. "I am only doing it temporarily. The woman who usually does it has gone to have a baby. She will come back after maybe two
years. My cousin Abdelhakim helped me get the job."

"Ah," Rania said.

The girl with the braid returned carrying a thermos, a glass, and a plate of
cookies. She set the glass and the cookies in front of Rania and poured her
tea. Then she went down the line of women, refilling their glasses.

"What happened the day Daoud was killed?" Rania asked.

Heads turned from one end of the row to the other and back again. They
reminded Rania of a row of dominoes toppling over. Was it that the women

had told the story so many times, they were trying to decide whose turn it was? Or were they checking to make sure there wasn't someone present who really knew what happened, before passing on the combination of rumor and fabrication created over the last few days?

She was thinking like a policewoman, she realized, and she probably sounded like one too. No doubt some of the women there knew who she was, though she didn't recognize any of them. They might be subtly warning each other about telling her too much.

"Some soldiers came to the village," said the woman to the left of Daoud's mother. "The shabab," the boys, "threw stones at them, and they fired sound bombs and tear gas. Daoud chased the boys into the school. He argued with the soldiers, and one of them hit him."

"Hit him how?"

"Like this." The woman made a fist and jabbed it toward Daoud's mother, stopping an inch from the other woman's nose.

"You saw this yourself?"

"No, Heba did. My daughter," indicating the girl next to Hanan. She looked about eight and was unmistakably Hanan's sister. Her eyes had the same irrepressible spark.

"What else happened, Heba?" Rania asked. The little girl furrowed her face.

"I heard the soldier say, 'You won't get away with this.'"

"He spoke Arabic?"

After a few seconds, the girl nodded.

"Was he a Druze?" Rania asked. Of all the Palestinians living inside Israel, only the Druze community and a few Bedouins sent their kids to the army.

"No, he was a Yahudi."

Rania was skeptical. Few Jewish Israeli soldiers spoke Arabic well.

"And then what?" she asked Heba.

"The soldiers got into the jeep and drove away."

"At seven o'clock that night," said Hanan's mother, "Um Mahmoud heard two shots."

"Who is Um Mahmoud?" Rania interrupted.

"She lives near the entrance to the village. She and Abu Mahmoud ran out and found Daoud dead. No one was nearby. They said the shots sounded like the guns the Israeli soldiers use."

"Did anyone hear a jeep driving away?"

The women exchanged glances again. Ten heads shook in unison.

"Everyone was startled by the shots," suggested Um Issa. "They were not paying attention to cars."

Rania thought about that. Normally, if you heard shots, you tried to determine whether the jeeps were going into the village or leaving before you ran out to see what had happened.

"I saw the jeep," said the girl at the end farthest from Rania. Rania had to bend nearly double to see her clearly. She wore a gray jilbab and dark-blue hijab. In the dim light, she almost faded away.

"When did you see it? During the day, when the boys threw stones at it?"

"No, that night. When they killed Daoud. I was up on our roof, and I saw the jeep driving in."

A buzz went around the room. Clearly, none of the women had heard this before.

"Why didn't you tell anyone before?" Rania asks.

"I just remembered it now."

Yeah, right, Rania thought. Well, she was not here as a policewoman, so it was none of her business.

"Did Daoud often have problems with the army?" she asked his mother.

"No, he was a good boy."

How many times had she heard that? Whether it was true or not. The best thing about mothers, and the worst, was that they all believed their sons were faultless.

"He worked for peace," said Um Issa. "He went to a camp in Germany, with Israeli students. Abraham's Garden, it's called. Two years in a row he went, with his cousins. The Germans paid for them all."

"Did Daoud have Israeli friends, then?" Rania asked.

Um Issa looked to her neighbors for guidance, which Rania thought spoke for itself. If any of the women knew she was with the police, they would be particularly reluctant to answer yes to a question which could implicate the young man as a collaborator. Even though Daoud was dead, tar on his reputation could damage his entire family.

"Not anymore. When he first came back from the camp, they would call all the time. But since the Intifada, they stopped."

"What about when he went to Ramallah? Many young Israelis go to Ramallah now and then."

"No, he never saw them."

The fact that she was so sure made Rania unsure.

"You said he came home every weekend," she said. "So, he was staying in Ramallah during the week?"

Daoud's mother nodded. "He shared an apartment with some other boys."

"Are any of them here?" She caught herself, but not in time. Her cop side had taken over, following the chain of evidence and witnesses from one to the next, but she had no standing to do that here. Even if Daoud's roommates were in the next room, she could not demand to talk to them, and, anyway, no one had asked her to investigate this death—well, no one she cared to please. As far as she could tell, the Palestinian community was satisfied that the army had killed Daoud, which made him a martyr, and no one was interested in turning up information that might suggest otherwise.

"They came before," Hanan said. "Not today."

That made sense. The closest friends and relatives visited on the first day of mourning. Today, the third day, brought the people who simply wanted to pay respects. Rania tried to think of an excuse to ask the names of Daoud's roommates, so she could track them down and interrogate them. What are you doing? she berated herself. This was not her case. She had not even spoken to her boss yet, because today, Friday, all Palestinian offices were closed. But she would call her boss tomorrow, and if she could tell him something he did not know about this incident, wouldn't that prove she was ready to start work again?

But she only had Benny's word that Captain Mustafa wanted her to investigate this incident, and Benny lied habitually. Even if she were able to establish definitively what happened, it would either prove what everyone already believed, or uncover something far more troubling for Daoud's family and his community.

Still, last year, she had met a young man in the Jenin refugee camp who had gotten a big settlement from the Israeli army after he was shot. They had paid all his medical bills, bought him a fancy wheelchair, and his parents had gotten enough money for a state-of-the art television set. If she could prove the army killed Daoud, his family might get a settlement too.

"Have you talked to a lawyer?" she asked Um Issa.

"A lawyer? For what?"

"To sue the army. For killing Daoud," she added when the woman's expression remained baffled.

"No one can sue the army," said Hanan's mother. Um Issa nodded agreement. Rania stopped talking and sipped her cooled tea. She did not want to get Um Issa's hopes up by telling her about the family in Jenin. She would go see Captain Mustafa tomorrow. She would explain what the women had said and what she wanted to do. Surely he would agree that it was worth investigating, and she was the one to do it. The world suddenly seemed brighter.

She saw all the women looking at her and realized she was smiling too broadly. Doubtless tomorrow, the word would be going around the villages that the policewoman had gone crazy in prison and was acting inappropriately in a house of mourning.

Chapter 13

Rania was about to leave for the city of Salfit the next morning when her phone rang. The digital readout showed, "Mustafa."

"I was just coming to see you," she greeted him.

"I am in Biddya," he said. "I will be there in five minutes."

She set the water on the stove and went out to the porch to wait for him. She ran a rag over the purple plastic chairs, careful to remove every mite of dust. He parked his silver Mercedes in her yard, next to Bassam's BMW.

"Hamdulilla assalaam," he greeted her. Beneath his bushy mustache, his mouth turned up in a rare smile.

"You drove?" she asked, after she had given the ritual reply. It was rare for a Palestinian to risk his car driving over all the Israeli roadblocks between Salfit and Mas'ha. It was safer and faster to take a taxi licensed for the Israeli roads.

"The Israelis removed the roadblocks last week." His always-probing black eyes were scanning her up and down. She thought he was looking for signs of injury or illness, evidence of torture. Should she emphasize her damaged right arm or not let him know she was hurt? Which would prove her more fit for duty?

"I am fine," she answered his unasked question. She shook her arms and legs slightly, to show she had all her functions. Her right arm throbbed.

"You are very thin," he said.

"I did not like the Israeli cuisine." She took a stack of purple plastic stools from the corner of the porch and separated them, hugging them to her stomach for leverage. She positioned two of the stools next to the matching chairs, to use for tea tables.

"Sit, please," she said. "I will bring the tea."

"We can sit inside." He followed her into the house, wiping his feet repeatedly on the red shag mat inside the door. She did not like people to wear shoes in the house, but she would never ask her boss to remove his wingtips.

"T'faddal," welcome, she said. He settled into Bassam's armchair while she went to the back of the house to make tea.

He must have something important to talk to her about, she reflected, as she pinched sprigs of mint into the squat tea glasses. It was shameful for a man to be alone inside with a woman not related to him. If he did not want to sit on the porch, it could only be so that no one could overhear him giving her an assignment. She found a package of crescent-shaped nut cookies in the pantry and arranged them in a circle on a plate. The water was almost boiling. It was hot enough, she decided, impatient to hear what her boss had to say.

He was talking quietly into his mobile phone when she returned. He hung up quickly, but not before she heard him say, "Haiha," here she is. So he had been talking about her to someone. Perhaps she would be working with someone else. She hoped it was not Abdelhakim. She also hoped whatever it was would not interfere with her quest to find out what had happened to Daoud.

She put a glass of tea and the plate of cookies in front of him. He spooned two sugars into his glass, blew on it, and took a few sips, seeming in no hurry to get to whatever had brought him here. As usual in the company of this man whom she revered, she found the silence unbearable.

"I visited the family of Daoud al-Khader yesterday," she said. "They are anxious to know what happened to him."

Okay, so she was more interested in the truth than Hanan or Um Issa seemed to be. Every mother wanted to know how her son died. She pushed away the thought of Khaled's body bloody on the ground. She would be lying there beside him if she had anything to say about it.

"The army killed him," he said with a shrug.

"Perhaps. But no one saw it."

He waved her objection aside. "We don't need to see a donkey to know it brays."

"When Benny came to see me in prison, he suggested that something else might have happened. He said you agreed I should look into it."

"He said that?"

She should have realized Benny Lazar was lying to her. He would say anything to get what he wanted.

"He didn't talk to you?"

"He called, last week. He said he thought he could get you out of prison. Of course, I told him to try. But he told me you refused to take on the investigation."

"I did. I don't want to work with him. But now that I am free and have met the family, I am willing to look into it. I will report to you, not to him."

"I don't know." Mustafa smoothed his mustache with thumb and forefinger. "It might be better to leave it alone."

"But, if I can prove the army killed Daoud, the family might get some compensation."

"There is no compensation for losing a child."

"No, of course not. But his family should get something. After all, he was studying at the conservatory. Perhaps he would have become a famous singer, like Ammar Hassan. Another son of Salfit to become a big international star."

"Not many become like Ammar Hassan."

"We don't know what Daoud could have done. Maybe he could have been even bigger than Ammar Hassan." Might as well spin the dead boy into a folk hero. After all, Ammar Hassan didn't have martyr status.

"His family will get nothing from the army."

"You don't know what they will get until I find out what happened," she insisted. Why was she pushing so hard, when she hadn't even decided she wanted to investigate? At least, it would let him know that she was ready to work. If he didn't want her to work on this case, let him give her another.

"It's too soon. You need to rest, spend some time with your family."

"I rested more than enough in prison."

"Perhaps another child."

She groaned inwardly. Bassam had been bugging her for three years about having a baby, pointing out that Khaled needed a little brother or sister. Had he been talking all over Salfit in her absence—no, likely Ramallah and Jericho too, all over the damn country—about having another baby?

"It's not a time to have more children," she said.

"It's always nice to have children," he said. He practiced what he preached. His four daughters were long grown, with many kids of their own. He had a son not yet in high school, one studying at university, two in the police, and two working in the Gulf. But he also had two wives who did not go out to work.

"Of course, I would like more children, but I want to get back to work first," she said.

He drank the last of his tea then took out a cigar. Most men smoked cigarettes. He was the only one she knew who smoked cigars. Benny smoked them, she recalled. Captain Mustafa had probably picked up the disgusting habit from him.

"I wanted to talk to you about something," he said. "My sister has cancer."

"I'm very sorry," she said. "Your sister Reem?" She had met at least four of his sisters over the years. But Reem was the only one she really knew. She lived in Salfit City and occasionally dropped by her brother's office.

"Yes," he said. "It is in her ovaries. Very bad."

"I'm so sorry," Rania said again, meaning it. She recalled Reem Odeh as a bright, strong woman. Rania's great-aunt had died of ovarian cancer, and it had been a miserable death. "Is there something I can do?"

"I hope so." He puffed on his cigar. She waited impatiently for him to tell her what he wanted. No one in her family or Bassam's was a famous doctor; she didn't have connections with a hospital in Europe or America or even in Jordan. It was not until he had thoroughly polluted her living room with his foul-smelling cigar that he spoke.

"She has permits to go to the hospital in Petah Tikva for treatment. She cannot drive herself, and her husband cannot get a permit to take her. I know you have friends in Israel and from out of the country. Do you think you could ask someone to drive her?"

Rania tried to calm the raging inferno in her skull. Her boss, who knew exactly why she had been imprisoned, didn't even want her for her own skills, just her connections to foreigners and Israelis? You have friends in Israel too, she wanted to say.

Benny claimed to be his friend. Why not ask him? She answered her own question. Benny was not the kind of friend you asked for a favor like this. Even as she struggled with herself, Rania knew she would do it. Chloe would probably be delighted to drive Reem—it was exactly the kind of savior behavior she loved. Rania didn't want to be more beholden to Chloe. She already suspected that, if it were not for the American, she would still be in prison. But there was no one else she could ask. Maybe she would get lucky, and Chloe would not answer. She entered Chloe's number, while the captain continued to puff on his cigar.

Chloe picked up on the second ring.

"I need to ask you something," Rania said, forestalling the other woman's questions about how she was adjusting to life outside.

"Sure, what's up?"

"A friend of mine, well, not mine, exactly, the sister of a friend, needs someone to drive her to the hospital in Israel."

"Well…I'm in Ramallah. It would take me a couple hours to get there."

"No, no, not right now. In a few days."

"Oh. Well, I don't have a car, but I guess I could rent one."

"I thought perhaps your friend Abe would lend you his car."

Abe was the name Avi used when he wanted Palestinians to think he was a foreigner. Though Rania knew he was Israeli, she still used the English name.

"He's out of the country," Chloe said. "I could ask my friend Nehama."

Rania's head was going to explode. She didn't want to wait for Chloe to make more calls. She wanted to satisfy the captain's request, and then maybe he would satisfy hers.

"You can borrow my husband's car," she said. "It's not as good as a yellow-plated car, but with the permit, you should be okay."

"Are you sure?"

"I think so."

"Does it have automatic transmission? I can't really drive a stick shift."

"What do you mean?" Rania knew nothing about cars, except you got in and turned the key.

"When Bassam drives, does he have to press something with his left foot, or only his right?"

"I'm not sure…I think both."

"Okay, it sounds like it's a standard transmission. That's okay; I bet my friend Tina can drive it. When is the appointment?"

Rania realized she had no idea. "You had better talk to Captain Mustafa," she said. "He speaks only Arabic."

"Tamam," okay, Chloe said. Rania handed the phone to the captain. He spoke for a few minutes and then said, "Tayeb," very good, and hung up. Now that he had gotten what he wanted, the captain was out the door in a matter of seconds, mumbling something about calling on her next week to see how she was feeling.

She had not gotten to bring the conversation back around to Daoud. Maybe she could have insisted on having her say, but she had a feeling it would have been useless.

"Why didn't he want to sit outside?" she wondered as she put away the uneaten cookies. Certainly his sister's illness was not a closely guarded secret.

She put the glasses into a bowl of water and added soap. Slowly, she swabbed each with a rag. He hadn't wanted to be seen talking to her. He didn't want her to come back to work. It all added up to one thing. People didn't trust her, because she had gotten out of prison so suddenly. They thought she might be a collaborator.

A soapy glass slipped from her hands and broke into pieces in the sink. When she tried to fish the fragments out, she cut her finger. Instead of finding a bandage to wrap it, she left it sitting in the bowl, enjoying the smart as the water turned deep rose with her blood.

* * *

Bassam may have gotten food on the table every day—Khaled did not look any thinner—but he definitely had not picked up a sponge or cleaning rag in the weeks she had been gone. He was not much of a shopper either. Rania cleared away rotting tomatoes and cucumbers turned to mush and took out her frustrations on a stubborn stain in the refrigerator. Probably, his mother had been preparing all their meals anyway. She scrubbed ferociously, pretending each swipe was at her boss's face.

A series of sharp raps at the front door forced her to close the refrigerator door, leaving the soapy water inside and her rubber gloves on the kitchen table. She had been expecting neighbors to drop by to welcome her home, but, except for Bassam's brothers and their families, and Captain Mustafa with his infuriating request, no one had come yet. She went to answer the door, eager for distraction.

The last person she wanted to see on her doorstep stood there, waiting to be invited in for tea. Well, the last choice would have been an Israeli soldier, but Abdelhakim ran a close second.

"T'faddal," she said, holding the screen door open. He hesitated for a second on the doorstep. Would he opt for the propriety of the porch, or like Captain Mustafa, opt not to be seen with her?

"I will not stay long," he said, wiping his feet carefully on her welcome mat as the captain had done. She glanced down at her own bare feet. A year ago, Abdelhakim would have removed his shoes. He must think his status had risen enough to allow him to sully her floor.

She didn't want to offer him tea, but she also didn't want him spreading rumors that she had forgotten how to behave. She would be under enough suspicion as it was. She went to the kitchen and prepared the tea but neglected to bring out sweets. That would let him know how she felt, in case he was in any doubt.

Her dislike of him was both personal and political. Last year, he had tried to sabotage her work, in order to help his own career. But that was not the most important thing she held against him. Just like her, he came from a long line of PLO fighters. His father and grandfather had been members of Fatah, and he had switched over and campaigned for the Change and Reform Party, the political arm of Hamas. She didn't believe he cared about change or reform. He just wanted to increase his own power. And she had no doubt that, while she had been stuffed away in a concrete box, he had done so.

When she brought out the tea, he was sitting on her flowered couch, flicking ashes into a bowl she had gotten as a wedding present. She plucked it out from under his cigarette and presented the ashtray littered with the remains of the captain's cigar instead.

"How is your son?" he asked.

"Mnih," fine, she said.

"Good. And your husband?" He had just seen Bassam yesterday, at Um Issa's house.

"Fine," she said again. "I am sorry about your cousin's fiancé."

"Yes, a tragedy. So much talent."

"So I hear. What do you think happened?" She couldn't resist asking, even though she would hate to learn that he had information she did not.

"The army," he said. "They had a confrontation with him earlier that day. They returned that night to settle the score."

"Maybe," she said. "But, from what I hear, he was not the type of boy to get into confrontations with the army."

"It is not we who make confrontations," he said. "It is the soldiers who provoke them." Of course she had not meant that the youth caused the conflict with the army. He just wanted to make her feel bad.

"I wanted to discuss something with you," he said, when he finished his tea. Great, maybe he had a sister who needed rides, too.

"Please," she said.

"We want to begin a women's police force," he said. She felt like a light bulb switched on behind her eyes. He had come to bring her back to the police! Perhaps she should have brought cookies after all.

"Go on," she said.

"There are bad things happening in our area," he said. "Girls are staying out late at night, being alone with men, using drugs. There are rumors of girls having sex with men for money. It is not right for men to investigate these offenses. We want to create a special squad of women to deal with them."

Her cheeks were scalding. She must look like she was about to have a stroke.

"That is the most insulting thing I have ever heard," she said.

"I thought you would say something like that. But just listen to me."

"I am listening," she said, though, with the ringing in her ears, it was hard to do so.

"We are not asking you to do this kind of work yourself," he said. "It is just that it is difficult in the police right now. There are so many unemployed men, and, with the Europeans and Americans holding back the funds from the Palestinian Authority, we cannot afford another detective. Abu Ziyad thought that, while you are on leave, you could help to train the new squad."

Abu Ziyad was his boss, the District Coordinating Liaison. The police in this area were under his authority.

"Abu Ziyad suggested me?" she asked. Abu Ziyad had never wanted a woman detective and found Rania far too opinionated. He had tried to get her fired a number of times. She couldn't imagine him choosing her as a role model for the paragons of virtue he would be seeking for his morals enforcement squad.

"It was Captain Mustafa's idea," Abdelhakim clarified. She abruptly took the ashtray and dumped its contents into the teapot. She enjoyed watching the remains of the captain's cigar disintegrate in the urine-colored liquid.

They were all ganging up on her. She was not going to have any choice. If she wanted to work, this was her only option. She didn't wonder why the captain had not brought it up. He knew she would have torn his head off.

"I…I will think about it," she stammered. She stacked their glasses in one hand and picked up the teapot in the other.

"Thank you for coming by," she said. She hoped she didn't sound too sincere.

He had been about to light another cigarette, but he didn't let her abrupt dismissal make him trip. He twirled the cigarette for a second and tucked it back into the pocket of his open-necked, striped shirt.

"Remember me to Abu Khaled," he said on his way to the door.

"I don't want to remember you at all," she mumbled under her breath as the door closed behind him.

Chapter 14

Rania's call had come just in time for Chloe. She was just starting to feel extraneous. That morning, Tina had broached the subject of what Chloe was going to do here.

"How long are you going to stay?" was what she had actually asked.

"Are you sick of me already?" Chloe shot back.

"Not at all. I just thought you might have to get back. You left San Francisco in a hurry."

"True, but it's okay. I wasn't doing that much."

"You don't have to work?"

"Things are still slow in the software industry. I've been doing some consulting, but my last project ended a month or so ago. And you know, I could even work from here if I needed to."

During the Silicon Valley boom, Chloe had signed on with a start-up called Bastille, which went platinum with firewalls in the mid-nineties. If she had gotten out a little sooner, she would have been a multimillionaire, but, as it was, she had a safe cushion between her and the repo man. She maintained a generally frugal lifestyle, except for her penchant for travel.

"So, what are you going to do now?" Tina asked.

"Today, you mean?"

"Well, not specifically. I just meant in general."

"Good question," Chloe said.

Chloe's unemployment had happily coincided with an international call for human rights activists to travel to Palestine. Chloe had answered it at once, but the overdose of testosterone among the group's leaders had gotten too much for her. By then, she had befriended some women in the little village of Azzawiya, which was embroiled in a struggle against land confiscations. Armed with her trusty video camera, she had kept a watchful eye on the Israeli soldiers when they made their periodic forays into the village, searching houses, taking people's kids away for brutal interrogation. In between such incursions, she helped women apply for international development aid to start embroidery cooperatives, and she started a computer class for teenage girls. She had met Rania the day the policewoman discovered the body of Nadya Kim in the fields of Azzawiya, and that set in motion the chain of events which had concluded with Chloe's forced departure from the country.

When she heard that Rania was in prison, Chloe had not thought twice about returning. But now that Rania was back with her husband and son, Chloe had no mission here. She didn't doubt that her friends in Azzawiya would be glad to have her, but she had to acknowledge they had been doing fine without her.

"I thought I might do some interviews with women who were elected to local councils," she said. Two years ago, women's organizations had banded together and demanded a quota of seats on the local councils be set aside for women. Though men and women alike in the rural areas had been skeptical at first, many women had discovered they had a calling to help lead their communities. Women had even been elected deputy mayors in some of the cities.

"You're going to write an article?" Tina asked.

"I might. Maybe even *Ms.* would be interested. But I was thinking of making a video."

"That's a good idea."

"Maybe I'll stay in Azzawiya part of the week and only come down when you're off work," Chloe suggested. She thought too much togetherness might not be good for their relationship.

When the love of her life had walked out two years ago, Chloe had nursed the wounds until they oozed only phantom blood. She had reconciled herself to being alone with her cat for the rest of her life. These ten days in the apartment in Ramallah, she had given herself over to feelings she had thought were buried permanently.

She didn't want Tina to feel suffocated, and she didn't want Tina to be the only thing keeping her in Palestine. Now, she had a good excuse to go up to Salfit, though there was the problem of the stick shift. Maybe she should rent a car after all. Hopefully Avi would be back soon, and she could ask him to find a car she could drive.

* * *

"What did you do today?" Bassam asked after Rania had gotten every last detail of his encounter with a group of students from the American Arab University in Jenin who wanted to set up an art program for kids in the refugee camp. It was an interesting project, and Bassam was a good storyteller. It was the kind of talk she would have enjoyed in years past, taking her mind away from car thefts and family feuds and reminding her of the noble impulses so many Palestinians had in abundance. Now, it just reinforced how meaningful his work was compared to the paltry opportunities presented to her.

"Abdelhakim came by," she said. She didn't even want to dignify Captain Mustafa's request by repeating it. It wasn't that she begrudged him or his sister the help that she was in a position to provide, but it reminded her she had become no more than a vehicle. Vehicle, resounded in her mind. She was going to need to tell Bassam that she had offered Chloe the use of the car. First things first.

"What did he want?" Bassam's voice was neutral. He didn't share her antipathy for Abdelhakim. They had friends in common.

"He came from Abu Ziyad." That should get him on her side. He might trust Abdelhakim, but he hated Abu Ziyad. "They want me to head a women's police force, reporting on women's immodest behavior."

She would have sworn the ghost of a smile crossed his lips. She must have misunderstood it. Her husband could not support this idea.

"What did you tell him?" was all he said.

"I said I would think about it," she said reluctantly. "It is true that women are better at dealing with certain kinds of situations: domestic violence, sexual abuse, this kind of thing. But the idea that we should be interfering in women's private affairs does not sit right with me."

"Is it a private affair, then?" he asked. "If someone violates the morals of our society, that affects all of us. We do not want to end up like America, where women sell sex openly on the streets."

"You cannot think this is a good thing for me to do." Khaled was playing soccer in the courtyard with some of his cousins. She picked out his happy shout from the din outside the open window.

"It would be better for you than sitting around being bored," Bassam said. He pushed his plate toward the center of the table, indicating he was through eating. She took the plates to the kitchen and took down the package of cookies she had bought to feed the well-wishers who had not shown up. While she arranged the rounds in a circle on the plate, she thought about his reaction. It was as if he had already prepared an answer to her objections.

She put the kettle on for tea and went back to the living and dining room.

"Did they discuss this with you already?" she asked, setting the cookie plate in front of him with a satisfying thunk.

"I heard something," he said. He picked up a cookie and took a big bite. "Delicious."

She was supposed to be mollified by being told that she bought cookies well? He had forgotten whom he had married.

"Don't change the subject," she snapped. "You heard it from who?"

"Abdelhakim mentioned it the other day, at the martyr's house," Bassam said. "He asked me what I thought. I told him he needed to talk to you. I didn't want to speak for you."

He was clever, her husband. If he had answered for her, even if he had given the exact same answer she had given herself, she would have destroyed him.

The water would be hot by now. She got up and went back to the kitchen. By the time she had taken the teapot from the dish drainer and measured the tea and the mint, her heart rate had settled to almost normal. She brought the tray with tea, glasses, and sugar to the table.

"I don't think I am going to do it," she said. "I want to work, but this type of work is demeaning." She poured his tea and her own, adding a spoonful and a half of sugar to her glass before relinquishing the sugar bowl. If she had not been angry at him, she would have done his first. Hopefully, he understood.

"It does not need to be," he said, adding two sugars to his glass. He lifted the steaming glass to his lips, but apparently thought better of taking a sip and put it down untasted. "If you make it something useful, you will get the better of them."

"I had not thought of that," she admitted. She reached for a cookie. "But I do not like segregation. We are fighting the segregation Wall and building walls in our own society."

"It is not the same," he said. "The segregation Wall is a way for the Israelis to take our land and make our lives harder. The separation between men and women protects women as well as men."

"Maybe, maybe not," she said. "I have always liked working alongside men."

"There is a time for that," he said, sipping his tea. "But this may be a time to strengthen the individual spheres. It is not like we do not have women and men working together already. Women have been elected to local councils and the legislature in record numbers. Let us see what they can do before we criticize the new government."

Was even her husband questioning his loyalty to Fatah? She did not think that was possible. Perhaps he was right, and they should give the Hamas people a chance to prove themselves.

"Besides," he said, before she could open her mouth. "A training job will be easier to manage if we are blessed with a baby."

"A baby? Who said anything about babies?"

"We have talked about it many times. Khaled is lonely. It is a good time to do it, while you are in-between things."

"I am not in-between. I am unemployed. You are only being paid half of what you are owed. It is a terrible time."

"Don't make it worse than it is. You will be working soon, and the Palestinian Authority will find a way to get the tax money released by Israel before too long. We are not poor. We can manage."

Khaled ran in, flushed from running around. He made a beeline for the plate of cookies, grabbing one with each hand.

"One at a time," she scolded gently. She took one of the cookies from his fist and set it on the tablecloth. She brushed the damp curls off his forehead and kissed the spot where the hair had been. He tolerated her affection, not pulling away but not snuggling up. She made herself let go. He was growing up. One day, she trusted that he would be proud of having a mother who had been in prison. For now, she would let him decide when to forgive her for being gone.

Chapter 15

Before Prison, Rania seldom arrived home before Bassam. She was chronically late to start her family's dinner because of the Israeli roadblocks she had to pass on her way from Salfit City. She had said that so often, she more or less believed it. But, of course, after five years of closure, she knew how long it would take her to reach home. She could have left earlier, but she was usually so engrossed in her work, she didn't even hear everyone else saying goodnight and then was left to hunt for transportation.

Now, her day was a gaping chasm of waiting. Waiting until one o'clock when she could meet Khaled coming home from school—much to his embarrassment. No seven-year-old wanted his mother coming to walk him home from school. She would make up an errand to run in the neighborhood of the school, so she could just happen to run into him on the road. She would spend an hour or two playing with him, and then he would do his homework at the kitchen table while she cooked, and together they would wait for Bassam to arrive home.

Today, she would make vegetables stuffed with rice and minced meat, a dish she seldom had time to make in her real life. She heard the distant squawking of the vegetable truck's loudspeaker: *bandura, filfil, kousa*, tomatoes, peppers, squash. She grabbed her purse and ran outside.

It was so muggy that she started to sweat as soon as she got to the road. The air was fragrant with donkey dung and old grease from the falafel stand. Her neighbor, Um Samer, was waiting for the vegetable truck as well. She wore a tent-like, paisley dress and a filthy white hijab. "You're not working?"

The older woman was clearly fishing for a bit of gossip she could use in a future social encounter. "Not right now," Rania said.

"Mmph."

Um Samer might have pressed the conversation had she not lapsed into a fit of spittle-filled coughing. By the time she had finished coughing up a small ocean of phlegm into the tissue Rania provided, the truck had arrived.

"Hamdullila assalaam," the vegetable peddler greeted Rania.

She did not recognize him, but it didn't surprise her that he knew who she was and where she had been.

"Will you be returning to work?" he asked.

No doubt he too was hoping to increase his stock in gossip, the most coveted currency of the region.

"Insh'alla," she said, God willing, the all-purpose evasion.

Both faces fell, the young man and the old woman, but they let it go.

"What would you like?" He turned to the business at hand. "Tomatoes? Bananas?"

"Bananas from where?" She fingered a bunch. The bananas were firm, and she could smell the sweetness even without lifting it to her nose.

"I don't know." That meant they were from Israel. Most of the tropical produce this close to the Green Line came from Israel. It was cheaper and easier to transport from there than from Jericho. Few of her neighbors cared.

"The squash and cucumbers are from Qalqilya," he offered.

"Kousa," she pointed to the plump zucchini. "Half a box." She filled the other half of the box with bright-orange peppers and huge, aromatic onions.

"Do you need help carrying them?" the young man asked her.

"No, thank you." She staggered under the weight of the box, but consciously straightened her back and made herself walk like someone who was not carrying a quarter of her weight in produce.

In the kitchen, she settled to the task of washing everything carefully, peeling the tomatoes and putting them on the stove to simmer, chopping the onions and the meat, boiling water for the rice. *Mahsheesh* was enough work to keep her mind off what she wished she was doing. She switched on the radio to keep her company.

"…the martyr Daoud al-Khader was gunned down by the Israeli army just two weeks ago in Kufr Yunus," the announcer was saying.

That wrenched her mind back to the subjects she had been trying to avoid—why she was released and what she was going to do. She had been out of prison five days, and Benny had made no effort to contact her. As far as she knew, he had accepted her refusal to investigate the murder of Daoud, and her release had nothing to do with his visit. Abdelhakim's words had confirmed what Captain Mustafa's silence had implied—there was no place for her as a detective right now.

A series of clumps on the stairs prepared her for her mother-in-law's entrance.

"Ahlan w sahlan," welcome, Rania said, kissing the old woman's cheek.

She turned on the gas and lit the burner under the tea kettle while Um Bassam settled herself at the kitchen table. Rania wasn't sure whether she was glad or sorry to have the company. The one-time hostility between the two women had thawed to near affection in the last year, but they loved each other best at a distance. She felt her mother-in-law scrutinizing each small movement she made: scooping the tea leaves into the kettle, pinching sprigs of mint from the window box, spooning the filling into the hollowed-out vegetables.

"Mahsheesh," Um Bassam said. "Bring them here."

"Drink your tea first," Rania suggested, setting the glass of amber liquid on the table along with the sugar bowl.

"It's too hot," Um Bassam replied. She added several spoonfuls of sugar into the glass and set it aside to cool.

Rania didn't want help with her meal. She had counted on the preparation eating up the time before Khaled got home. With her mother-in-law's practiced hands, she would be done in an hour. But refusing the help would jeopardize their fragile détente. Rania placed the heavy pot full of vegetables and the bowl of filling on the table and sat down opposite her mother-in-law. The old woman began working immediately, automatically gathering the right amount of filling in her right hand for the squash or pepper she held in her left. They piled the stuffed ones on the platter between them.

As Rania had feared, the pile of vegetables in the pot dwindled quickly.

"Shu akhbarik?" she asked, what's your news? just for something to say. Her mother-in-law would not have minded sitting silently or listening to the radio together, but Rania was more comfortable with conversation. Especially now, with the long weeks in the solitary prison cell so fresh in her memory, she didn't think she could bear sitting silently with another person in the room.

"Will they let you go back to work?" Um Bassam asked.

"Who do you mean?"

"The Palestinian Authority," the old woman said innocently.

"I hope so," she said. "Why wouldn't they?"

"Nothing is like it was," the old woman said. "There is so little work; many think women should not do men's work."

"What do you think?" Rania asked. Her mother-in-law had always seemed to disapprove of her career but recently had softened her attitude.

"Mmm, who cares what I think? I am just an old woman."

"I wouldn't ask if I didn't care." She wondered if she should tell her mother-in-law about the women's force. But she was pretty sure she knew what the reaction would be, and she didn't want more encouragement for the plan just now. It was appalling enough that she was actually considering it.

"You are unhappy at home," Um Bassam said. "So perhaps you should go to work."

"I would if I could," Rania said irritably. Their hands continued to work in unison, picking up, stuffing, putting down, and reaching for the next. "I think Abu Walid mistrusts me." Abu Walid was the honorific most people used for Captain Mustafa. Only the people who worked for him gave him his title, and only his friends from the PLO called him Mustafa.

"Because you got out of jail so fast."

"So fast? It seemed forever to me."

"Yes. But you know…people talk."

"Have you heard people saying things about me?"

"Someone said an Israeli policeman visited you in prison. The one who arrested the boy from Azzawiya."

"The army arrested him," Rania quibbled.

She noted that she had pounced on that particular bit of trivia, instead of the much more sobering fact that people knew Benny had been to see her in Neve Tirzah. Who had told them, and why?

"You can't believe I gave him information," she protested.

"I don't, no."

"But others do."

"Who knows what they believe? People repeat anything. It doesn't mean they really believe it."

"Bassam wants me to have another baby," Rania blurted out. She was so desperate to change the subject, she forgot she didn't want to discuss this with her mother-in-law.

The old woman's face lit up.

"Yes, a baby would be nice."

"Perhaps. But I would like to be sure of my job first."

"It might be better in a year."

"In a year, I will have been gone so long, they might forget I was ever there. And without my salary, how can we afford two children?"

"You could help in the store."

Rania shuddered at the thought of spending her days counting packs of pins and rewinding bolts of cloth.

"There is not enough work for Marwan and Amir and their sons," she said, referring to her two brothers-in-law.

Bassam's family had owned three dry goods stores, making them relatively wealthy in the eighties, but the closures and the Wall had destroyed much of their business. Just last year, they had finally decided things were not going to get better in the foreseeable future and sold off two of the stores to an engineer who had returned from the Gulf.

The conversation was only making Rania more nervous. She turned up the radio, and they finished stuffing the vegetables without talking. Um Bassam finished sipping her tea at the same time and rose to leave.

"Do you want to eat with us?" Rania asked.

"Maybe."

"Okay, Khaled will come get you," Rania said. Maybe was a polite way of saying yes.

"Insh'alla."

When her mother-in-law was gone, Rania took the stewed tomatoes from the stove, strained them and added some sugar, salt, and lemon juice. She poured the sauce over the vegetables and added a bit of water.

Now the meal was ready to cook. It would need about an hour for the vegetables to get tender. That meant she should turn it on at four o'clock, maybe three thirty. It was barely eleven. Two long hours before Khaled would come home.

She rinsed the cheesecloth she had used to strain the tomatoes and put it in a bleach solution to soak. There was nothing more to do in the house. For the nth time in the last ten days, she asked herself what other women who didn't work did to fill their time.

So often, when she was working long days, she had imagined having time off, being free to spend all day cooking and cleaning. She made a solemn vow never to wish for free time again, once she got her job back. She put on a jilbab and hijab and took her purse. She didn't know where she was going; she just had to go out. She wandered through the village, browsing in shops. She bought a small toy for Khaled, a little airplane that lit up when it flew.

Everywhere she went, people asked, "Will you be returning to work?"

No one asked what they really wanted to know: Why were you arrested, and how were you released?

Maybe that was why she ended up climbing into a shared taxi headed for Kifl Hares, across from the entrance to the massive Israeli settlement of Ariel. She waited until the taxi had disappeared before dashing across the wide street. She stared up the long road that led to the settlement gate. She couldn't see the soldiers who guarded the entrance, but she knew they were watching her, so there was no point in taking off her hijab and trying to pass for Israeli. She didn't want to do that ever again, anyway. This was her land. They had no right to deny her entrance. Experience had taught her that attitude went a long way in convincing Israeli soldiers that you had a right to do whatever you were doing.

She squared her shoulders and lifted her head, walking quickly toward the gate. A noise behind her made her turn around. The bus! Even better. The police station was at the very top of the hill, and she didn't relish walking it in this heat. She didn't give the bus driver a chance to ask her anything, just paid her two shekels and moved to a seat in the very middle of the bus. The driver hesitated, and she held her breath.

Drivers were not allowed to ask for ID, but she had seen plenty of them simply sit and refuse to drive on. This driver didn't need to make that choice; all he had to do was pull up to the gate and say a word to the soldier, who did have the right to ask her for ID. If he did, she didn't know what she would do. If they called in her ID, it could begin a perilous series of events. She could even end up back in prison. On the other hand, maybe they would just look at the ID and decide she was harmless, while, if she refused to give it to them, they would certainly not let her in.

The bus was moving now. She would find out in a few seconds which of her fears was about to be realized.

The driver was talking to the soldier now. She could tell they were talking about her.

She made herself look straight ahead, not down, not watching them. She coaxed her face into a relaxed, bored expression.

"Yesh lach teudot?" the soldier said. Do you have documents? He was still standing at the front of the bus, not near her. Was she supposed to know he was talking to her? The arrogance galled her. But, if she wanted to get in, she couldn't insist on a confrontation. She looked in his direction and met his eyes which were fixed on her.

"Yesh," she said. She opened her purse, reached inside, as if looking for the ID, but didn't pull it out.

"I am going to see Benny Lazar, at the police station," she said in Hebrew.

Please don't call, she begged silently, though she guessed that, if he did, Benny would say to let her in.

"B'seder," okay, the soldier said, not to her but to the driver. He stepped off the bus, and they sailed through the gate.

"I need to see Benny Lazar," she told the young woman at the front desk of the police station. Rania had an urge to take a wet handkerchief to the policewoman's heavy makeup.

"Do you have an appointment?" the woman asked in Hebrew.

"No," Rania replied in English. "But I am sure he wants to see me. Just tell him Rania is here."

"There's an Arab woman here for you," the woman said in Hebrew. She looked disappointed when she hung up.

"You can go up," she said.

Benny's mocking eyes greeted her from behind his desk. Of course, he would not do her the courtesy of getting up, but she didn't care. She hadn't come here for social niceties. Why had she come? She pushed that question aside.

"How did you get out of prison?" he asked.

"As if you didn't know."

He got that look, hurt beyond belief. He was a one-man theater, part of what made him a good detective.

"I don't know what you mean," he said. "Do you want tea?"

"Yes, please." She always liked to make him serve her. If she was going to sit in an Israeli colony, it was her duty to take every crumb she could get.

"One and a half sugars?"

"That's right."

"Baruch!" he bellowed. A dark-skinned, young man appeared in the doorway. She recognized him from the time she had spent here last year.

"Tea with one and a half sugars for my colleague. I'll have a black coffee." Benny ordered. Rania couldn't help being pleased at being called "colleague." It showed just how low she had sunk, to be getting self-worth from an Israeli whom she didn't even like.

"I visited the family of Daoud al-Khader," she said when Baruch had vanished again.

"And?"

"And they are sure the army killed him. Someone claims to have seen a jeep."

"Claims?"

"Someone says she saw a jeep. Why shouldn't I believe her?"

"I don't know. Do you believe her?"

Baruch returned with their drinks. Rania was silent while he cleared off some space on the desk in front of her to put her tea down. She thanked him in Hebrew, and he withdrew again. They didn't serve tea the proper way, in a glass, to hold the steam in. This was in a cup with a handle, already losing its warmth. She picked it up and took a small sip. Typical Israeli tea, bitter and flavorless, with no mint or sage. She put the cup down on the saucer.

"I don't know whether to believe her," she said finally. "She didn't mention the jeep until I specifically asked if anyone had heard one. She said she had forgotten." She drank a few more sips of tea, just to give herself a little time to think. "When the army kills someone in front of you, or near you, everyone talks incessantly about what they saw and heard. You're unlikely to forget something important."

"So you don't believe the army killed him."

"I didn't say that!"

He had been leaning forward, subliminally encouraging her to talk. Now, he leaned way back, propping his feet on an open drawer at the corner of his desk. Even as she fought it, she felt herself relaxing with him. Damn him, she felt like a puppet on a string. But her mind was wrapping itself around a puzzle, and that felt too good to stop.

"If the army wants to kill someone, they don't do it secretly," she said and caught a flash of approval in his face. "Also, it was early evening, in the spring; lots of people would have been outside, but no one else seems to have heard a jeep. Plus, there is the fact that he was involved in peace activities with Israelis, not normally the kind of boy who gets involved in confrontations with the army. But," she adds, "people saw a soldier threatening him that afternoon."

"The army denies that they were in Kufr Yunus that day," he said.

She shook her head. "That part I'm sure of. Many people saw them."

"What did the women say happened?" He picked up a yellow notepad and wrote something.

Rania repeated the story she had been told, trying to remember every detail. She hurried through the part about the children throwing stones at the jeep—she hated giving even that much ammunition to an Israeli policeman, but it gave credibility to the rest of the story. She told him about Daoud chasing the kids into the school and then confronting the soldiers, and how the women said one of the soldiers had hit him. Benny took copious notes. When she finished, he leaned forward again, gesticulating at her with his pen.

He said, "Even *if* this happened…" She cringed at the emphasis on the word "if"—did he think she was lying? Or did he think she was so gullible, she couldn't tell when people were lying to her? "...it doesn't mean they killed him."

"It doesn't mean they didn't."

He made a few more notes, then put the pad down.

"What about his peace activities?"

"I didn't get a lot of information about them. Just some juvenile dialogue projects, I think." She hoped he gleaned the disparagement with which she said "dialogue." Some might use that word for what she was doing here now. She didn't, but she wasn't sure she could explain why not.

"You know what that means."

"You're suggesting he could have been a collaborator?"

"Not necessarily, but some in the village might have suspected him."

She had made the same insinuation to his family yesterday, but that didn't make her more willing to hear it from him.

"That's not what happened," she said.

"Prove it."

There it was, the challenge. She started to say, That's not my job, it's yours. But that wouldn't really be true. His job was to bury the incident as quickly as possible, and allowing Daoud's death to be classified as the execution of a suspected collaborator would serve his purposes admirably. If she wanted to see justice done, she would need to do it herself.

"I'm not working for you," she said.

"No problem. My investigation is over. The army wasn't in the village. The kid was known to fraternize with Israelis, which made him a possible collaborator. No one saw anything. End of story."

She could virtually feel the strings opening her mouth, but it made no difference. What she said was what she had to say.

"If I find out anything, I will tell the captain," she said.

"Good."

He brought the legs of his chair down with a thump and began to rifle through some files on his desk. He made himself so intent on his work that he didn't even look up when she left the room.

Chapter 16

"Mama is sleeping," said Daoud's sister, Mayisa, opening the door to Rania's knock. "Shall I wake her?"

This was good luck. Mayisa might be less suspicious of Rania than her parents would be.

"Don't bother her. Your parents asked me to find out what happened the day Daoud was killed," she said with the confidence of a practiced liar. "If I can prove the army killed him, they might get some compensation from the Israelis."

"What could compensate us for Daoud's death?" Mayisa asked, but she opened the door wider so that Rania could enter.

"Can I see his room?" she asked. Mayisa hesitated. Rania concentrated on making her expression friendly and professional, not pleading.

"I guess it would be okay," the girl said finally. She led the way through the living room to the hallway. Two of the doors Rania could see were open. Past the second one, Rania glimpsed Um Issa, sleeping uncovered on a double bed. She could hear the woman's labored breathing. Mayisa opened the nearest door.

"My brothers sleep here," she said.

There were two sleeping mats on the floor, two desks, and a bureau with four drawers.

"You have only two brothers?" she asked Mayisa.

"I have four, but two of them have their own houses."

"This must be Daoud's side," Rania pointed, and Mayisa nodded. His brother's side looked like a normal teenager's—martyr posters and pictures of soccer players. Above Daoud's bed was a poster of Ammar Hassan, the pop star, and over his desk one of the Palestinian tennis player, Andy Ram. Rania sat down in the desk chair and examined the clutter on top. A well-thumbed biology textbook, an agate marble, a keychain with an olivewood map of Palestine in the national colors. She picked up a narrow-woven strip, a friendship bracelet. She and her girlfriends had traded them in school, but she couldn't remember ever seeing young men wearing them.

"What's this?" she asked Mayisa.

The girl shrugged. "Friendship bracelet."

"Do you know where Daoud got it? Did he buy it for someone, or did someone give it to him?"

"I wouldn't know. He wasn't wearing it, was he? So, what difference does it make?"

Rania didn't know what difference it made. It just seemed unusual. She opened one of the desk drawers. It was filled mainly with old school notebooks and a couple boxes of photos. Some of the photos were family shots, pictures from weddings, vacations in Jericho. Some were formal school pictures, Daoud, Mayisa, two young men who looked enough like Daoud that she was sure they were the brothers. One showed Daoud in the center of a group of Palestinian boys all in a row, arm-in-arm.

"Who are the other boys?" she asked Mayisa.

"You said you're trying to prove the army killed Daoud," Mayisa said. "How is going through his things going to help?"

Damn the girl! Why did she have to be so perceptive?

"I don't know, but it might. First, I need to understand who he was, what he was doing."

"We told you, he was trying to keep the soldiers from shooting the children."

Rania ignored her and went back to looking at the photos. There was a small book of them, each photo encased in cellophane, that was clearly from the camp in Germany. Daoud stood with various groups of boys, all grinning in Abraham's Garden sweatshirts. Two other boys were in nearly all of the pictures—one identifiable as a West Bank Palestinian, the other clearly Israeli.

"Do you know either of these boys?" she asked Mayisa.

For a minute, the girl looked like she might not answer. "That's our cousin, Ahmed. He was Daoud's best friend. I don't know the Yahudi."

"How do you know he is Israeli?" Rania asked, just for fun. Mayisa rolled her eyes.

"May I borrow this?" Rania asked, making to put the little photo album into her purse.

Mayisa chewed her lip. "Maybe I better ask Mama."

"I would hate for you to wake her."

"You'll give it back?"

"Of course, as soon as my investigation is done." She tucked the little book away before the girl could change her mind. There was only one closet. She walked over to it and threw the door open.

"Can you show me which clothes were Daoud's?"

Mayisa pointed to a few white shirts and a single pair of dress slacks. A threadbare school sweater hung next to a windbreaker that was clearly long outgrown.

"This can't be all he had. Where are the rest?"

"Ramallah. In his apartment."

"Do you know where the apartment is in Ramallah?"

"No. I was never there. He said I could visit him there, but my parents wouldn't let me go."

"He couldn't have lived there by himself." Only very wealthy students could afford their own apartments in the cities. Most crammed four or five into a room. "Who did he share with? Ahmed?"

"Yes, Ahmed and their friend, Elias."

"Do you know Ahmed's telephone number?"

"It might be in my mother's phone." Mayisa disappeared for a moment and returned with a standard Jawwal phone, like the ones Rania's brother-in-law, Marwan, sold by the dozen. Rania opened the contacts, and there was Ahmed, first up. She copied down the number.

"What's it like, working for the police?" asked Mayisa, as Rania prepared to leave.

"It depends. Sometimes it's interesting, sometimes it's just a lot of work, like any job. But I like being able to help our people."

"I would like to do something to help our people, too. But I don't think I would like to be in the police."

"What are you interested in, Mayisa?"

"I think I would like to be a nurse."

"My mother is a nurse," Rania said. "It's a good career. Are you good in math and science?"

"Pretty good."

"If you want to be a nurse, you will need to do very well in those subjects. You must work extra hard."

"That's what Daoud said."

"Your brother sounds like a smart boy."

"He was." Mayisa's eyes filled with tears. Rania gently brushed the girl's hair behind her shoulder.

"Honor Daoud's memory by following his advice," she said. Was it her imagination, or did Mayisa close the door behind her extra quickly, as if she didn't want anyone to see that Rania had been in the house?

Chapter 17

Rania was tired and would have liked to go back home and rest before it was time for Khaled to get home. She was unused to working a full day. But she was anxious to speak to Ahmed. Fortunately, he answered his mobile on the third ring and explained how to get to the apartment.

The roads were clear, and, in forty-five minutes, she was walking up the narrow staircase to a gloomy hallway with dirty beige carpets. She knocked on the door of number ten.

She recognized Ahmed immediately. His wide face had not changed much since the photos in Daoud's room were taken, but he had a lazy eye that hadn't shown up in the pictures. His short, dark curls were damp, and he smelled vaguely of soap. He invited her into the living room with a gesture that said he didn't care whether she entered or not but was too polite to keep an older woman standing in the hall.

She sat on the edge of a straight-backed wooden chair. There were more comfortable seats, but she suspected they might have bugs.

"Why do you want to know about Daoud?" he asked. This time, she fluently recited her tale about helping his family get compensation, sounding to herself as if she believed it.

"Why was he in the village that day?" she asked. "Didn't he have class?"

"It was a school holiday," he said. "We all went home for my engagement party."

"You are engaged? Mabrouk," congratulations.

"Thank you."

"When will you marry?"

He shrugged. "When I have saved enough money for a nice house."

With the toll the American and European embargo was taking on the Palestinian economy, she thought that would be quite a while.

"Are you studying at the conservatory also?" she asked.

"Me? No, I am studying English at Birzeit."

"Birzeit! You must be a very good student. I wanted to go there, but I was not accepted."

That was a little lie, to give him a one-up on her. She had been offered a scholarship to Birzeit University, which took only the top students, but it had been the First Intifada, and her parents had not wanted her traveling so far each day.

"I suppose so."

"Why did you choose English?" It certainly wouldn't help him acquire the nice house.

He shrugged, shoulders rippling like a flag in the breeze. "I would like to live in England or America."

"Why do you want to live abroad?" she asked. Coming out of her mouth, the question sounded ridiculous. Every young Palestinian dreamed of a normal life, without checkpoints or soldiers coming in the night.

"It was Daoud's idea," he said. "He wanted all of us to move to America—him, me, Elias, and our wives—and live together in a big compound like the rich Americans have on television."

She smiled. She pictured the young man in the photos, his wide, soulful eyes lit up with plans for transplanting his family and friends to an American television set. Daoud seemed to have lived in brighter colors than anyone around him.

"Do you know when Daoud planned to marry Hanan?"

"No. I don't think they had discussed it yet."

"His mother said they would marry before Ramadan."

He shook his head. "I do not think he would have married before he graduated. He had two more years in school."

"Did he bring other friends here much?"

"Usually, we would all be here together, and sometimes friends would visit." His lazy eye made it seem like he was avoiding her eyes, so she couldn't tell if he actually was.

Rania took out the photo album she had taken from Daoud's room at home. She flipped it open to a picture of Daoud, Ahmed, and the Israeli boy.

"What about this young man? Who is he?"

For the first time, he looked uneasy. "Just some Yahudi at the camp."

"What is his name?"

"I don't remember. I barely knew him."

"You look pretty friendly here."

"It was years ago. The camp was a week, and I never saw him again."

He was lying. But she had no way, and no reason, to make him tell her the truth.

"Why don't you want to talk about this boy?"

"It doesn't matter. I just don't know him. I don't do those things anymore."

"Which things?"

"Normalization." He spat out the English word as if it were a curse.

"Why are you angry?"

"Why shouldn't I be? Look at our lives. We can't go anywhere. We can't go to Jerusalem to pray. My friends are killed for looking at a soldier the wrong way."

She was surprised by his reference to praying in Jerusalem. He didn't strike her as someone who did that much praying.

"Do you each have a room here, or do you all share?" she asked.

"We have two bedrooms," he said. "Daoud and I sleep—slept—in one, and Elias has the other."

"May I see your room?"

He hesitated. She stood up and took a few steps toward the hallway, just to indicate that she wasn't really asking. He shrugged and led the way. When she stepped inside the little room, she thought she knew why he hadn't wanted to show her. The floor was so covered with clothes, she had to pick her way through them to stand in the center. In fact, that seemed to be the only storage system that existed; there was neither bureau nor closet. A few things were folded and stacked in one corner. She imagined this was the clean stash, and the ones strewn around were the dirty ones. Two sleeping mats were semivisible amid the clutter, one partially covered with a light blanket.

"Can you tell which things are Daoud's and which are yours?"

He pointed to the neat stack in the corner. "Those are Daoud's."

"Is that all of them?"

He nodded. She crossed the room and crouched down by the little pile of clothes. She fingered two pairs of jeans, both fairly new, and, she imagined, tight-fitting for someone Daoud's size. A few T-shirts, one well-worn with the logo of Abraham's Garden, another newish with the words Coca-Cola in Arabic, lay atop a cross-colored polo shirt with no logo, a Western style popular in Ramallah.

Next to the pile of clothes stood a silver metal music stand, the kind that folded up. That made sense, given that Daoud had been a musician, but he must not have used it regularly, because it was draped in filmy, bright-colored scarves. He must have been accumulating them as gifts for his sisters. On one corner of the stand hung a leather jacket, similar to the one Bassam had been given when he got out of prison in the nineties. Had Daoud's father or another relative been a fighter?

"Did Daoud buy this for himself?" she asked Ahmed, who was gathering up some of the clothes on the floor.

"I guess," he said.

Expensive item for a student. Daoud must have had some source of income. She plunged her fingers into the pockets. Her fingers touched metal and paper. She pulled out a few coins, an empty cigarette carton, and a small square of pressed cardboard. The little square had English and Hebrew writing on it and a drawing of two people holding hands. She couldn't tell if they were supposed to be men or women. Adloyada, the English said.

She was about to ask Ahmed what it was, but something stopped her. He was still folding up clothes and hadn't seen her take the things from the pocket. She quickly stuffed the little square into her purse. She returned the shekels to the pocket and hung the jacket back on the stand.

"Thank you," she said to Ahmed. "You've been very helpful."

* * *

Rania had just bundled Khaled off to school the next morning when Chloe arrived to borrow the car. Her friend Tina was with her. Rania greeted both of them with kisses on both cheeks.

"Do you want tea or coffee?" she asked.

"Do we have time?" Chloe looked at her friend.

"We are supposed to pick up Reem at ten," Tina said.

Rania checked the clock, although she knew it was just past eight. With the roads open, it should take them only half an hour to reach Salfit.

"You have time."

"Coffee then," Chloe said. Rania half-filled the long-handled brass pot with water and added two heaping tablespoons of sugar. She set the well-used pot on a low flame. While waiting for it to boil, she produced the little cardboard square she had found in Daoud's room yesterday.

"Do you know what this means?" she asked. Chloe took it and held it close to her face, then passed it to her friend.

"Where did you get this?" Tina asked.

"A boy from one of the nearby villages was killed last week, we think by the army. This was in his clothes."

Tina and Chloe exchanged glances.

"What is it?" Rania demanded. "I need to know if it has something to do with why this boy was killed."

More conspiratorial looks passed between the two foreigners.

"Why do you think this is important?" Tina asked.

"I do not know if it is important. It has Hebrew writing on it. This boy was involved in some normalization things. Perhaps…he could have been a traitor."

"It's from a bar, in West Jerusalem but very near East Jerusalem," Chloe said.

"An Israelien bar?"

"It's owned by an Israeli. Israelis go there, and Palestinians too."

"It's a gay bar," Tina said.

"What is gay?"

"It's a word for men who love men, or women who love women."

"But we don't have people like that in Palestine."

Chloe squirmed in her seat. "There are gay people everywhere," she said.

Rania's head was spinning. Something like that among her own people, and she had no idea? They couldn't be right.

"Maybe just one or two," Rania said.

"They say it's 10 percent, ashara bil miyya," said Chloe.

"Who says?"

"People who study such things."

Rania considered it. "I can't believe that. So, you think Daoud was... 'gay'?" She hesitated over the word. "He was engaged."

Chloe shrugged. "I don't know. Most people who go to Adloyada are gay." She picked up the little cardboard square again and fiddled with the layers of paper.

"Rania," she said, "Did you say this guy's name was Daoud?"

"Daoud al-Khader," Rania said. "Do you know him?"

"I met him once," she said.

"At that bar?"

"No, at a restaurant. But I think he performed at Adloyada."

"They have performances? Perhaps he only went there to sing. He was studying to be an opera singer."

Chloe chuckled. "I don't think they exactly sing," she said.

"What do you mean?" Rania said. Why was Chloe being so cryptic? Maybe Chloe was wrong. She was smart, and she tried to be sensitive, but she wasn't Palestinian.

"It's hard to explain," Tina said.

Rania suddenly felt like someone had thrown a bucket of icy water in her face. If men could be in love with other men, presumably women could be in love with other women as well. There was a word for it, *suhaqqiyya*; it wasn't a nice word. She had never called anyone that, but she had heard it whispered about women in the villages who seemed too bold or independent. Could Chloe and Tina...

She turned to the stove, where the sugary water was bubbling away. She stirred in the coffee, held it over the flame, took it off before it boiled over, held it to the flame again, removed it, replaced it, then poured off the liquid into three tiny cups.

"Forgive me," she murmured in Arabic, as the others sipped. "I didn't mean…" But what didn't she mean? She couldn't think of a way to complete the sentence.

"It's okay," Tina said. "We don't have to talk about it if you don't want to. But if you have questions, you can ask us."

"I never thought about this…. If there are…gay…people here, it must be very hard for them."

Chloe smiled, the wide, gap-toothed smile that Rania had first found appealing about her.

"I think it's getting a little easier," she said. "The hardest thing is not being able to talk about it."

Tina touched her friend's arm. "We should go," she said.

Rania was suddenly aware of the tenderness between them.

"Let me get the keys," she said, grateful for an excuse to turn away. She found the extra car keys in the bedroom.

"Why are you investigating Daoud's death?" Chloe asked when Rania returned with the keys. "Have you gone back to work?"

"Not officially, no. But I'm trying to help the family find out what happened. If the army killed him, they might be able to get some compensation, like those people in Jenin."

She was not completely lying, she comforted herself. If the army had killed Daoud, she would give his family the telephone number of the lawyer who had represented the families in Jenin. Chloe did not need to know that the investigation had been Benny's idea. She might inadvertently mention it to someone who would think… She couldn't articulate the difference between what people would think and what she was doing, but there was one.

"When will you go back to work, then?"

"I'm not sure…. They want me to head a women's police unit."

"Wow, that's great," Chloe said. "Isn't it?"

"I don't know. It's kind of a…morals police, I guess you would say."

"Oh, we call it a vice squad," Chloe said. "What exactly would you be doing?"

"I'm not sure. I think they expect us to monitor women's behavior, go talk to girls who are doing improper things with men, that kind of thing."

"That doesn't sound like your type of work."

"No. But I wouldn't necessarily go out as part of the squad. I would be doing the training." Her rationalizing sounded pathetic. The trainer would certainly be as responsible—even more responsible—for the actions of the squad as the women who put the training into practice.

Chloe's face livened up when Rania mentioned training. "That's good, though. If you are the trainer, you can subvert—" She saw that Rania didn't know the word. "You can use their tools to different purposes."

"That's what my husband says."

"Think about this," Tina said. "If you refuse, who knows who they will get? If you do it, you can have a big impact on how the work is done. Things have changed a lot in the last few weeks."

"What do you mean?" Rania leaned forward.

"I work at a counseling center for women whose husbands beat them. In the past, the PA was pretty uninterested in what we did. They gave us our license, we got a little money from the Women's Ministry, and they left us alone. But, in the last month, since the government has been reorganized, men from the Ministry of Interior have been in several times. They wanted to know things about who our clients are, how they find out about us. They looked at our outreach materials and took some back to show their superiors. We are afraid they will want to interfere with our work."

"What will you do?"

"We don't know yet. It depends what they want us to do. We won't give them the names of our clients, and we won't turn women away. But, other than that, we cannot really refuse to cooperate with our own government."

Rania nodded. "My husband works in the Ministry of Interior. I will speak to him about this."

"Thank you." Did Tina already know that? Is that why she had brought it up? Was this another situation of someone pretending to want her opinion, just to get her to talk to someone else? Chloe changed the subject.

"That reminds me," she said, "I want to interview some women who have been elected to local councils. Wasn't your sister-in-law one of them?"

"Yes, Jaleela. I'm sure she would be happy to speak with you. And my other sister-in-law, Dunya, held workshops for women on how to present themselves as candidates. You could interview her, too."

"Definitely. Can you give me their numbers?"

"Reem was elected to council, too, you know," said Rania. "But she has resigned now that she is ill."

"Oh, that's too bad," Chloe said. "But I will interview her anyway, if she's willing."

"We'd better go," Tina said. "Thank you for the coffee."

Chapter 18

"You drive a stick, right?" Chloe handed Tina the car keys.

"You don't?"

"Not well."

"Good thing I'm here then."

Tina started the car and grimaced as the engine putt-putted hesitantly. "This thing is overdue for a tune-up," she said.

"The mechanic's probably in Nablus," Chloe said. "They can't take the car through the checkpoint."

"There are mechanics in Ramallah," Tina said.

"You know how fussy men are about who works on their cars. And this is a BMW."

"So, how do you think he'll feel when she tells him a couple of dykes are driving his car?"

"She won't say 'dyke.' She didn't even know the word 'gay.'"

"No, she'll say suhaqqiyyaat." Tina leaned on the *s* so the derogatory word came out in a hiss.

"I don't think so," Chloe insisted. "She was trying to understand. And she's not that religious."

"She was trying to understand, but that doesn't mean she wants lesbians for friends."

"It doesn't mean she doesn't." Chloe wasn't sure if the defensiveness she felt was for Rania or for their friendship. She reached for the radio. Fortunately, it worked. They drove the rest of the way listening to popular songs and commercials from a changing array of village stations.

Reem's house was a two-story stone building on a wide corner lot. Chickens ran around the backyard, clucking to each other and pecking anything that got in their way. A donkey was tied to the fence by a long tether. At least for the moment, it didn't seem to bother him; he sat with his head on his hooves, eyes closed.

"Ana jaheza," I'm ready, Reem said when she opened the door. She was already wearing her hijab and jilbab. She only needed to grab her purse and lock the door. Chloe was glad they didn't need to go through the ritual of coffee. She was nervous about the checkpoints. She had never traveled on a permit before and didn't know what to expect driving into Israel in a green-plated car.

"Please sit in front," she said to Reem in Arabic, holding the front door for her.

"Thank you," Reem said in English.

Chloe climbed in back, and Tina started the car.

"Let me just make sure I have the permit," Reem said. She spoke perfect English, with only a hint of an accent. She extracted a stapled sheaf of papers and gripped them fiercely. That permit was probably the most valuable thing she owned right now.

"Your English is excellent," Tina said.

"I am an English teacher."

"For which grades?" Chloe asked.

"I teach the girls who are studying for their tawjihi." The *tawjihi* was an exam for students wanting to go to college. The students who chose to take it studied an extra year after high school.

"Are you working now, or are you taking a leave?" Tina asked.

"I will try to work." She sounded apprehensive. Chloe wished Tina hadn't brought up the treatment, but that was silly. Reem wasn't going to forget where they were going.

They were approaching the checkpoint that marked the current border between Israel and the West Bank. Reem swiveled to half-face Chloe.

"This is not the Green Line," she said, referring to the official border between Israel and the West Bank. "Last year, they moved it two kilometers inside. Before the Intifada, we never had to stop at all. We used to go to the sea at Netanya every Friday. I miss the sea."

The line of cars at the checkpoint was not long. Few Palestinians had permission to drive into Israel, and settlers usually did not have to stop at all. Chloe watched one yellow-plated car after another cruise through without slowing more than a few kilometers per hour.

They, of course, could not do that, and Tina didn't even try. If they had been by themselves, maybe they would have done something to show they didn't recognize the legitimacy of the Israeli army in this place, but with Reem's treatment at stake, they would be as obsequious as they needed to be. Tina waited behind the sign that read STOP—CHECKPOINT in Hebrew and Arabic until the bored-looking soldier motioned them forward with a crooked finger. She rolled down the window and presented the permit and all three of their IDs.

"You are Reem Odeh?" The soldier craned his head through the window to look at Reem, who nodded.

"Who are you?" he asked Tina in English, drawing his head back out of the car.

"A friend of hers," Tina said.

"Well, friend, this permit says only her name. What are you doing here?"

"Clearly, I'm driving her."

"Which are you, Chloe or Tina?"

"Can't you tell?" Tina gestured toward the passports he held.

From the back seat, Chloe massaged Tina's neck lightly. She saw Reem notice and dropped her hand quickly.

"I'm Chloe," she said.

"Why do they need you?" asked the soldier.

"They don't. The appointment will be long. I came to keep my friend company while she waits."

"What are you doing in Israel?"

That unanswerable question again. She needed to give an answer that would satisfy, but not encourage follow-up. "Just traveling."

He looked back at the papers, then at Chloe again.

"You know, I don't have to let you through," he said. "The permit is only for her," gesturing to Reem. "She is driving," indicating Tina. "You're not doing anything, so I could make you get out and walk through."

"That's true, but they would have to wait for me on the other side, and that would make our friend late for her appointment, so I will be very grateful if you let me through now."

He actually seemed to consider it, before nodding sagely. "Have a nice day," he said, handing the papers back to Tina.

When they were safely past the checkpoint, all three of them let out a holler.

"Asshole!" Chloe yelled, at the same time "Blooming bastard!" escaped from Tina. Chloe didn't know the epithet Reem used, but she understood "Yahudi" all too well.

* * *

After Chloe and Tina left, Rania puttered around, musing on what she had learned. It didn't bother her to think that they were lovers, though she didn't really understand it. Was being together for them like for her and Bassam? She didn't want to think about the intimate details, but that wasn't just because they were women. During her student days at Bethlehem University, when Palestinians could still go to Tel Aviv, some of her friends liked to go see foreign movies with explicit sex scenes between men and women. She had gone a few times, but she had never enjoyed them.

If it was true that Daoud was sexual with men, it could open up a whole plethora of possible explanations for his murder. Sometimes traitors were accused of being homosexual. She had never believed it, just thought it was another cruel thing to say about someone whose family was already disgraced. But if someone *was* homosexual, and the Israelis found out, they could perhaps use that information to make the person into an informer, and an informer's life was always in danger.

If anyone would know whether Daoud was gay, it would have to be his school friends. She looked at the clock. It was nearly ten. She had three hours until Khaled came home from school. Plenty of time to get to Ramallah and back, if the roads were clear. Just to be safe, she stopped by her mother-in-law's flat on the way out and asked if it would inconvenience her terribly to listen for Khaled to come home.

"I always listen for my grandson," the older woman said.

"Thank you," Rania said and headed out. She couldn't help it, her step was brisk, her mind clear, now that she had a mission.

She had Ahmed's phone number in her phone, but she didn't want to call if she didn't have to; she would rather surprise him. Of course, she ran the substantial risk that he would not be home. In the middle of the day, students were likely at school. But half past ten was not exactly midday for students, if they did not have a long way to travel to school. Hopefully, either Ahmed or the other roommate—Elias?—was the type to lie around until noon.

The servees dropped her in the center of Ramallah. She looked around hesitantly at the streets shooting off the square like spokes in a wheel. She couldn't quite remember where the apartment was, but she was pretty sure it was down Rukab Street, the one with the ice cream place on the corner. She started up that street. She was sure she had passed the juice bar the other day, and that mini-mall up ahead looked familiar, though, in fact, every street in Ramallah had those, and they all looked alike.

"Sabah al-kheir," morning of joy, said a voice behind her elbow. Startled, she wheeled around to face Ahmed.

"Sabah an-noor," morning of light, she responded.

His hair had not seen a comb, and his eyes had the unfocused vulnerability of someone just awakened. Either he was late for something, or there was no food in the apartment. Rania suspected the latter.

"I was about to have some coffee. Would you like to join me?" she asked.

He looked around, as if for a good excuse. "I was only going to the shop," he said.

"Please," she said. "I would like some company." He cocked his head and narrowed his eyes, then rolled his shoulders slightly.

"If you wish," he said. She headed for the first coffee shop she spied, the one with the picture of the Eiffel Tower dangling over the window stuffed with tiers on tiers of artfully piled baklava and date cookies. He hesitated.

"It is better this way," he said, leading her down the block and into an alley, then up a staircase to the mouth of a dark cave. When her eyes adjusted to the dim light, she saw why he had picked this place. At the smart, tiled tables sat several groups of foreigners and Palestinians speaking English. One group of very blond foreigners was speaking a language she didn't recognize. Even the menus were in English. This would be a place where a young Muslim man from a village could sit with a strange, hijab-wearing woman without worrying about shocking his neighbors.

He took a pair of glasses from his shirt pocket and looked at the menu. He took them off when the waiter came and ordered a cheese sandwich and a cappuccino.

"I will have a cappuccino also," Rania said. She was curious to try the drink. These western cafés had come along well after she had married and moved up north.

"You said you're studying English, right?" she said.

He nodded. He was still holding his glasses. He opened and closed the ear pieces a few times. If he would just wear them, his eye wouldn't wander so much. Instinctively, Rania touched her own thick glasses, as if she could subtly influence him. He didn't seem to notice.

"I also studied English, at Al Quds Open," she said. It wasn't exactly a lie. It hadn't been her major, but she had taken classes in English literature. She needed some basis for rapport. "Who are your favorite English writers?"

"I like Hemingway," he said. So much for rapport. She barely remembered anything from Hemingway except endless descriptions of mountains and men trying to act like lions.

The waiter appeared with a tray balanced on one flat palm. He served their coffees with a flourish.

"Cinnamon?" he offered.

"Please," Ahmed said, so she accepted as well. He used a tiny hand grater to grind up a cinnamon stick right on top of the foamy milk and then left the rest of the stick in the side of the cup. Ahmed did not attempt to drink his coffee right away, so Rania let hers sit as well.

"How long had Daoud been engaged to Hanan?" she asked.

"Mmmm, perhaps three months," he said uncertainly. He nibbled at his sandwich, pulling little bits from around the edges and popping them onto his tongue.

She lifted her cup to her lips. The foam was so hot, it burned her tongue, and she didn't manage to get any coffee. The milk tasted awful, like flavorless soup. She put the cup down.

"Was it a love match, or arranged?"

"Hanan is also his cousin, on the other side from me. I think he could not help loving her. She is very beautiful." Not exactly an answer.

"Do you think he wanted to help himself from loving her?"

"I didn't mean that—it's just a figure of speech."

"Did she ever come here to see him? Or did he only see her with their families?"

"She came once. Her parents did not approve, but that weekend they had gone to Jericho. She told them she was visiting a cousin in another village."

"Did she stay at your flat?"

"No, with another girl. A friend of Daoud's."

"Did Daoud have a lot of girls for friends?" she asked.

"Girls. Boys. He had a lot of friends. Everyone loved Daoud."

No need to point out that someone clearly did not love him.

"What did he and Hanan do when she was here? Did they go out?"

"I don't know. Probably they did. I wasn't here that weekend."

"Did he ever take Hanan to Adloyada?"

Ahmed picked up his cappuccino and sipped carefully, sucking the dark liquid out from underneath the foam. So, that's how it was done. She didn't see how she was going to do it and not end up with coffee all down her front.

"Adloyada? What is that?" he asked. His lazy eye got lazier, a tiny vein popping in his forehead.

"Apparently, it is a place in Jerusalem that Daoud was fond of."

"Who told you that?"

"No one. I found something from there in his jacket pocket, in your flat."

"That doesn't mean he went there. He might have picked it up on the street."

"Perhaps. But, if so, why would he have kept it? It wasn't exactly a thing of value."

He didn't answer. He drank some more of his coffee and finished the sandwich.

"I'm not going to make trouble for Daoud's family," she said. "I'm not asking as a policewoman. I only want to help Hanan understand what happened to her fiancé."

"What is to understand?" he said. "The army killed him, just like they killed lots of our friends. Two other friends of ours were killed last year, in demonstrations against the Wall. You didn't come around then, asking questions about where they liked to go."

He had a point. She gave up on being sophisticated and stirred her coffee into the foam with a spoon. She tasted it. It was bitter, but with a little sugar it might be drinkable.

"Was Daoud gay?" she asked. She didn't want to use the derogatory Arabic word, and didn't know what other word to use, so she used the English word. She added two lumps of sugar to her coffee and stirred again, to help it dissolve.

"Laa," no, he said at once. "Who says such a thing?"

"No one," she answered. "But he had something from Adloyada, and people who go to Adloyada are gay, right?"

"I don't know. I told you, I have never been there."

She sipped her coffee. It wasn't that bad.

"Did Daoud ever tell you when he was going there? You were his best friend, after all."

"Once, he said he was meeting someone there. I told him to be careful not to get arrested. A lot of soldiers go there."

"How did you know that if you never went there?"

"A friend of mine goes there sometimes. He told me he saw Daoud talking to one of them once."

"To an Israeli soldier?"

"Yes. But it's not what you're thinking. Daoud was not a traitor."

"I wasn't thinking any such thing," she said.

"Of course you were. Everyone would, if they heard." He stood up and signaled to the waiter for the check. "I'm late," he said.

"Go," she said. "I'll pay the bill."

He hesitated. It was irregular for a young man to let a woman pay for him, but he must have decided that her age made the difference.

"Thanks," he said. She watched him walk out, picking up speed as he went.

The waiter with the gold earring put a hand on his shoulder, but Ahmed instantly shrugged it off. Was he really late or just putting distance between himself and her? She was left with more questions than she came with, but at least she had a direction to pursue.

She drank the rest of her coffee. The milk was soothing, and she was starting to like the cinammony taste.

Chapter 19

Reem introduced herself to the receptionist in English.

"Are you the translator?" the receptionist asked Chloe in Hebrew. Chloe winced.

"No, I'm just a friend," she said in English.

"I do not speak English well." The young woman shook her curly head to punctuate each word. "Please sit down there."

They had just settled themselves in the waiting room when a young man in dark blue scrubs appeared at Reem's elbow.

"I am Dr. Rahman," he said in Arabic. He did not offer her a handshake.

Chloe didn't know why she was surprised that he was Palestinian. One-fifth of the Israeli population was Palestinian Arabs. Despite the discrimination in education and employment, there must be plenty of doctors among them. She suspected the receptionist had scoured the hospital for this one.

"Min weyn inta?" Where are you from? Reem asked.

"Min Gaza," he said. He smiled at the three dropped jaws, ultra-white teeth gleaming in his swarthy face.

"Is it hard to get the permits?" Reem asked.

"No. I have worked here for a long time."

"Aren't you needed in Gaza?" Tina asked.

"There are plenty of doctors in Gaza," said Dr. Rahman. "There is just no money to pay us. I have a large family, and I am the only one who has work."

They followed him to a large room with tasteful seascapes dotting the walls. A nurse settled Reem into a reclining chair, like the BarcaLounger

Chloe had in her living room in San Francisco. There were straight-backed, carpet-covered chairs for her and Tina.

"Do you have any questions?" Dr. Rahman asked.

Reem hesitated. "Will I be sick?" she asked finally.

"Probably not right now," he replied. "The medicine might hurt a little going into your arm, but we will give you something to prevent nausea." Chloe didn't understand the Arabic words for "prevent" or "nausea." She looked at Tina, who translated for her without being asked.

"I am ready," Reem said, as if committing herself for execution. Her skin had gone ashen since they had come into this room. Tina took her free hand and stroked it, as the nurse began to swab a throbbing vein with an alcohol wipe.

Reem settled down once the red liquid was dripping into her arm.

"What is it like where you come from?" she asked Chloe in English.

"We can speak Arabic if it's easier for you," Chloe offered. She didn't think she'd want to speak a foreign language while she was getting an infusion of poison.

"I like to speak English," Reem said.

"Well, San Francisco is very beautiful. Have you ever been to Haifa?" She hoped it wasn't impolite to ask that. Palestinians could no longer go to Israeli cities, but Reem was old enough to remember a time before so many restrictions. Reem nodded. "Many people say that Haifa reminds them of San Francisco. They don't seem that similar to me though. They are both on the water, but San Francisco is cold all the time. The ocean is wild, the shore very rocky with high cliffs. You can walk along the ocean for miles—kilometers. I like to roller-skate there—do you know what that is?"

Reem shook her head. Her eyelids were starting to droop.

"I wear shoes that have wheels, and I can go fast."

"That sounds dangerous," Reem said, sounding far away.

"It is if you go down big hills," Chloe said, "But I try not to. Or, if I do, I don't go that fast. It's very foggy," she continued, "and some days from the top of the cliffs by the ocean, you can just see the outline of the tall buildings downtown rising out of the mist. It looks like a magic kingdom."

Reem's eyes closed and she snored lightly.

"I better not plan on a career as a storyteller," Chloe said.

"It was a bedtime story. I'd love to see you skating around the magic king-dom," Tina responded.

"You should visit sometime."

"Melbourne is beautiful too. You would like it."

"What did you think of Dr. Rahman?" Chloe asked.

"I feel bad about asking why he wasn't working in Gaza. It just slipped out," Tina said thoughtfully. "It's so weird; Gaza seems like a foreign country, and it's not even an hour's drive from here. A woman who works at the center comes from Jabaliya refugee camp in Gaza. She hasn't seen her family in four years."

"Well, I haven't seen mine in two," Chloe said. "But there's no checkpoint between us. Just the Gulf of Political Disunity."

Tina's lips turned up, but her eyes remained sad.

✶ ✶ ✶

"How did it go?" Rania asked when they returned the car.

"Fine, I guess," Tina said.

"She's a lovely woman," Chloe said. "I think it was scary for her, but not too difficult physically. How was your day?"

"It was interesting," Rania said.

"Oh?"

"I met Daoud's cousin in Ramallah. He said that Daoud sometimes met an Israeli soldier at Adloyada."

"Met, as in dated?"

The word "dated" sounded very loud in Chloe's ears. She didn't even know if Rania and Bassam had "dated" or if their marriage had been arranged. She recalled Rania saying they had been in college together, but that didn't neces-sarily mean it wasn't an arranged marriage. Chloe had no idea how Palestinian marriages were arranged. In San Francisco, she had an Indian friend whose parents kept trying to fix her up with men as far away as London.

"I don't know," Rania was saying. "He just said Daoud met this man there. He didn't know, or at least he claimed not to know, anything about him.

Yesterday, I found pictures of Daoud and Ahmed with an Israeli from a peace camp in Germany. I think maybe he was the one he met at that bar."

Chloe was about to ask why she thought it could be the same guy, when Rania said, "Will you go to Adloyada with me?"

Tina's mouth was slightly agape, just as Chloe was sure hers was. "You want to go to Adloyada?" she stammered.

"I need to find out about Daoud's life."

"I don't know—it seems like it would be a hard place for you to talk to people," Chloe said. She hoped Rania didn't ask her to explain why. She didn't want to say, I'm sure no woman has ever walked in there in a hijab. Of course, Rania didn't wear her hijab all the time. She had told Chloe she didn't wear it at work. But Chloe had never seen her outside without it.

"Please, I want to go there," Rania simply said.

"Okay," Chloe said. "When do you want to go?"

"Tomorrow night?"

"I guess that would be okay for us," Chloe looked at Tina for confirmation. "Reem doesn't have to go to the hospital again until Friday, so I'm free."

"I will meet you at Bab el-Amud," Rania said, using the Arabic name for the Damascus Gate.

Chloe agreed, wondering how Rania planned to make it to Jerusalem. There were at least half a dozen checkpoints between here and there. But she didn't imagine anything would stop her friend when she was determined to go somewhere.

Chapter 20

In her college days in Jerusalem, Rania occasionally went to bars. That was during the First Intifada, before people got so religious. She had worn what was fashionable then—tank tops, high heels, short skirts, and makeup. Except for the makeup, she still had all of those things in the back of her closet. She greeted them as long-lost friends. Styles had changed in twenty years. Which was the most contemporary? She chose a black and white leopard-print skirt made out of a stretchy fabric. It was not too short, revealing only a tiny bit of knee. She would be sitting most of the night anyway. A black tank top with little sparkles complemented it perfectly. Medium-heeled sandals, and she was ready. Chloe had said she didn't need to dress up; she could have worn sweatpants and a turtleneck like she usually did under her jilbab. But, if she was going to do something out of character, she wanted to look the part. Or maybe she just wanted to be a different character for the night. It brought back the youthful freedom she had felt in those days of action and promise.

The bar was nothing like she had imagined. The bars she had been to long ago had been elegant, Arab-style lounges, with red, plush carpets and crystal chandeliers dripping hundreds of tiny prisms. This one had sawdust on the floor and scratched faux-wood tables with high stools to perch on. It was so dark she could barely see to walk, and cigarette smoke hung heavy in the still air.

Arab pop music blared over the sound system. As her eyes adjusted, she glanced around. Most of the tables were occupied by people of indeterminate gender. Maybe she would have been able to tell the women from the men if she stared, but she didn't want to be rude. Two young people she was sure were men sat entwined on a love seat that appeared perilously close to collapsing under their weight. Their lips were locked in a passionate kiss. The only place she had ever seen such a display of affection was in foreign movies. She turned away quickly. Her face felt feverish.

She sensed Chloe and Tina being careful not to touch. When Tina found them a table near the bar, they sat on either side of her.

"What would you like to drink?" Tina asked, putting a hand on Rania's shoulder but not Chloe's.

"Red wine," Chloe said. "Do you mind?" she asked Rania belatedly.

"Of course not. I'll have one too."

She had never liked the taste of alcohol, though she had enjoyed the warmth and softness it created in her body. Bassam became very amorous after a few drinks. It was on one such night that they had agreed to marry.

"They have juice and soda," Tina said.

"I will have wine," she said.

"Coming up," Tina said.

She returned with two wine glasses and a tall, dark-colored beer for herself. She also brought a bowl of pistachios.

"Cheers," Tina said, raising her glass. Chloe lifted hers, and they clinked them together. By the time Rania realized she had missed the cue and picked up her glass, the others were already sipping from theirs. She deliberately lifted the glass to her lips and breathed in the sour grape smell. It made her feel slightly nauseated. She set it down untouched and reached instead for a nut.

By the time they had emptied the bowl of nuts, the place was full of people. Most were Israeli, but she heard a smattering of Arabic. She isolated the source of that sound. Five young men huddled around a high, round table crammed with mostly empty beer bottles. Two of them were draped over a third like stoles. The fourth sat in the lap of the fifth. They must have sensed her attention. The one with the two men around his shoulders lifted his glass to her, his upper lip curling slightly.

"I will be right back," she said to her friends and purposefully crossed to the men's table.

"Masa al-kheir," evening of joy, she said.

"Masa an-noor." Evening of light, they murmured.

"Awal marra hon?" one of them asked her. He was asking if it was her first time here.

"Aiwa," yes, she said.

"Ahlan w sahlan," welcome. He made another mock salute.

"Ahlan fiik," she said, as if he had meant it politely. "My friend, Daoud al-Khader, used to come here." She paused, blinked as if fighting back tears. She thought she saw a hint of something—interest? fear?—in the eyes of the boy who had spoken to her. "He told me he had many friends here. Perhaps you were among them?"

"No, sorry," they all agreed after a quick confab of the eyes.

What did she expect? A strange woman showed up asking about their dead friend. They had no idea who she was, but, if they did, they would trust her even less.

"Do you come here often?" she tried.

"Often enough."

"Where from?" No way could they refuse to answer a neutral question that every Palestinian heard any time they met someone new.

"Around."

That was her cue to give up, but her stubborn instincts were kicking in. The more they didn't want to talk to her, the more determined she was to find out what they knew about Daoud. As she was racking her brain for how to prolong the conversation—though you couldn't really dignify this interchange with that name—a series of colored lights flashed, pink, green, orange, blue, and a loud bell clanged four times.

"The show is starting," one of the young men told her. He gestured toward an area she had not noticed before, where a heavy velvet curtain hung. She saw the row of colored lights now and the platform protruding from the bottom of the curtain.

"What kind of show?"

"You will see."

They were clearly not going to make room for her at their table, nor was there any to make. She wandered back to join Chloe and Tina, who were deep in conversation, heads bent across the table like swans. She turned her chair to face the stage, and, as she sat down, the curtain rose. The man at the microphone was not tall and not young. He was dressed from balding head to pigeon toes in silver sequins which shimmered in the multicolored lights, turning him into a walking rainbow.

"Ladies and gentlemen. Boys and girls," he said in English. "Friends. Welcome to Ramallah Night!"

"What does that mean?" Rania whispered to Tina, who was closer to her than Chloe.

"All the performers come from Ramallah," Tina whispered back.

"Of course, we are all still in shock over the death of our dearest JLo," the man on stage continued. A murmur passed through the audience. "And so, here with a special tribute to her memory, please welcome Lena, Tina, and Nina!"

Three women ran onto the stage, holding hands, while the audience thundered approval. The one on the left wore a black evening dress and white gloves under a bouffant hairdo. The one on the right had long black hair and wore a red one-piece suit with something metallic in the material. Rania had never seen anything like it, even on TV. The one in the middle wore a skimpy, spangled tank top above black, stretchy pants. Her straight hair just brushed her shoulders, and her bangs hung almost to her eyelids. She wore massive gold hoop earrings and three gold chains around her neck. They were dark skinned, but didn't look like any Arab women Rania had ever seen.

"These women are from Ramallah?" she asked Tina. The other woman smiled.

"They are men," she whispered. "They are pretending to be American singing stars. It's called a drag show."

"Arab men?"

Tina nodded, but Rania didn't believe it. That an Arab man would get up on stage looking this way—even leaving aside that it was in a bar full of Israelis—was impossible. The music blasted and the women—or men, if Tina knew what she was talking about—shook their hips in a highly provocative way.

"I will survive. I will survive." It seemed like a good anthem for Palestinians.

The dancers twirled and twisted in a rainbow blizzard.

The audience shrieked in appreciation. A hail of shekels clattered onto the stage. One of the women—the one with the bangs—knelt to pick up the money. She put a note to her lips and kissed it, then held it out to the crowd. There was more applause. Rania snuck a glance at the Arab men she had been talking to. They were rapt, eyes fixed on the stage, hollering in Arabic.

Rania felt a pounding behind her eyes, in rhythm with the music. She picked up her wine glass and made herself take a swig. She longed for something to cool her down, but the wine had the opposite effect. Still, the burning sensation it made going down felt almost good, the shock to her system made tangible. She quickly downed half the glass.

"And now, please put your hands together for Sister Leila!"

The woman who took the stage next wore a bright-pink sweater dress accented with something blue and fuzzy around her neck. Black fishnet tights crawled up her narrow, muscular thighs and she balanced on heels higher than any in Rania's closet. A Nancy Ajram song began to play, and the woman gyrated her thin hips just like the Lebanese singing star did.

Rania caught a flash of something familiar near the door and turned to look. Icicles formed in her throat. Her worst fears were about to be realized, and she had no chance to escape.

"Chloe, look," she cried, grabbing her friend's arm. Both women followed her pointing finger.

"What?" Chloe said.

"Soldiers are here." She saw only one soldier, but, where there was one, there were sure to be others.

Chloe made a dismissive half wave. "He's not going to bother us. He just wants to see the show."

Of course, Rania knew soldiers came here. For all she knew, this could be the soldier Daoud had been kissing. He bent down to plant a kiss on the security guard's cheek, his gun sticking out behind him like an awkward tail. She watched him make his way through the throng and, much to her shock, land at the table of young Arab men she had just so unsuccessfully tried to engage. One of them said something to him, and he burst out laughing. He picked up a half-full glass from the table and took a few sips.

She strained to see his face in the dim light. From what she could see, he was definitely not the Israeli in Daoud's pictures.

"Where is the hamam?" Rania asked Tina. Tina gestured toward the opposite corner from where they sat, the one nearest the bar. It was very crowded over there. She didn't know how she would make her way back there or what she would find in the way of a bathroom, but she needed to be alone.

Was she imagining that the soldier watched her walk to the back of the bar? She put it out of her mind. Heavily pierced women and men and people of indeterminate gender sporting skintight leather fashions blocked the door to the single bathroom. So much for a quiet place to think. The music pulsed around them, though, from here, the words were too muffled to make out. She pressed her back against the wall.

She had looked forward to this adventure. Now, her soul was ripping into fragments. She was a liberal, a secular nationalist. Islam was her tradition, but she didn't feel the need to dictate to others how to live. But this—Arab men flirting with Israeli soldiers, performing in front of them like the ones on the stage—could not be right. Yet all these young people, pressed in hip to hip, laughing and singing, were having so much fun. She couldn't say they were hurting anyone.

The MC announced the next performer, and the narrow hallway emptied with a whoosh, leaving Rania staring at a wall of pictures. She leaned forward to study them. Various groups of men and women in poses of love stared out at her, some tender, some teasing. She almost didn't recognize Daoud with eyeliner widening his onyx eyes and long, silver earrings touching his shoulders. But she did recognize the skinny, pock-skinned young man with him—he had just asked her if she was new here. His chin was balanced on Daoud's shoulder, his arm circling the other man's neck. And here was Daoud again—this time in full regalia, page-boy wig and glittering silver dress, holding hands with an Israeli soldier, gun dangling like a third arm at his side. Was it the same soldier she had just seen? She couldn't tell. She searched her memory for the man's features, but her fear had overcome her police training, and she could call up only a fuzzy image. It didn't matter anyway. She could not walk up to a soldier and demand that he talk to her about a dead Palestinian.

It was all so confusing. She had hoped coming here would clarify what she needed to do to find Daoud's killer. Instead, it had opened up ten, twenty, a hundred new possibilities. She couldn't think with the music blaring like that. She pressed her hands over her ears and squeezed her eyes shut.

When she got back to the table, a woman with long, flowing, black hair and snapping, kohl-outlined, dark eyes was sitting in her chair. She turned and half got up when Rania appeared.

"Asfi," sorry, she said in Arabic. "Is this your seat?"

"No, stay," Rania responded.

"Rania, this is my friend Yasmina," Tina said. "We work together."

Did some secret signal flit between the two women? Rania's detective antennae were out of practice. She thought Chloe seemed tense. But maybe Rania was just projecting her own tension onto her friend.

Rania felt a tap on her left shoulder. She looked up to see the soldier standing there, a grim expression in his stone-gray eyes.

"Please come with me," he ordered.

"What's going on?" Chloe was on her feet, and Tina jumped up a second later. Yasmina quickly vanished into the crowd.

"Come." The soldier's grip on Rania's arm would leave a bruise. How would she explain it to Bassam?

Chapter 21

"You can't order us around here. We're not doing anything wrong." Chloe protested all the way to the street.

"What is this about?" Rania demanded. She tried to tell herself Chloe was right, but at the same time knew that, while the foreigners had done nothing wrong, she could go back to prison for six months just for being in Jerusalem. The man with the gun said nothing but propelled Rania forward at a half trot. The others panted behind them.

They turned right from the bar and headed into the lights of Jaffa Road. The main street of West Jerusalem teemed with life on this midweek night. Rania started to relax despite the continuing pressure on her arm reminding her that all these people could not, and would not, protect her from an Israeli soldier determined to make trouble for her.

"Hakol b'seder?" Two border police materialized in front of them, bulletproof vests slung over their gray uniforms.

"Ken, hakol b'seder," it's fine, the soldier said. "I found them near Jaffa Gate. I am taking them to the Russian Compound for questioning."

Rania's heart seized her throat. The border police gave her captor their blessing and moved on. The young man quickened his pace even more. She could see the three spires of the Russian Compound's Trinity Church just in front of them. Nearby, she knew, was the brown stone police station where many had been tortured. I have nothing to hide so I have nothing to fear, she chanted silently, putting one foot rapidly in front of the other to avoid tripping.

"In here," he finally said. This was not the Russian Compound. It was a dark stone structure with no door, barely more than a hut, on the edge of Mamilla Cemetery.

"Sit," he said, releasing her arm. There was no furniture in the little hut. She was not going to sit on the dirt floor.

"You have no right to hold us," Chloe said.

"I am not holding you," he said. He crouched down on his haunches as if to show that he was no threat. The three women remained standing.

"We can go? Then why did you kidnap us from the bar?" Chloe demanded.

"I need to talk to you." He was looking at Rania. "Why were you asking questions about Daoud?"

"I am trying to find out what happened to him."

"Don't you believe that the army killed him?"

"Should I?"

"I don't know," he said slowly. "My name is Lior. I knew Daoud for five years. We were in a summer camp together in Germany."

"Abraham's Garden," she said.

He nodded. "We became friends the first day. Daoud was…he was like a light in a dark room. You could not be sad when he was present."

What a nice thing to say about someone, Rania thought. Bassam was like that.

"Was Daoud gay then, too?" she asked. All three of the others smiled. She felt tears biting behind her eyes. "What did I say?"

"I'm sorry," Chloe said. "It's just…gay isn't really something you become. It's something you learn about yourself."

"I see," Rania said. She didn't have any idea what Chloe was talking about, but this was not the time or place to sort it out.

"Did he know that he was gay at that time?" she amended.

"Yes. He always knew. He was the one who helped me come out."

"Come out?"

"To let myself be who I am. To tell others."

"When you say he helped you, do you mean…?"

He shook his head. "We were not lovers."

Rania didn't know whether to believe him, but she didn't know if it mattered.

"The Palestinian guys at the bar," Lior said, "why were you asking them about Daoud?"

"Why should I tell you?"

"They were afraid that you were with the Palestinian police," he said. She took in a breath too quickly and coughed violently for twenty seconds. Chloe pounded her back until it subsided.

"Sorry," she said. "Why did they think that?"

"I don't know."

"They think the police care so much what bars they go to, that we would send someone to Jerusalem to track them?"

"Then you are with the police?"

She had said "we," she realized. "Not anymore," she said.

"Then why are you asking questions about Daoud?"

"I told his family I would try to find out what happened." That was true. No matter that the family didn't seem that interested in knowing.

"It might be better," he said thoughtfully, "to let them believe he was killed by the army."

"Are you saying he was not? You just said you didn't know." Her police instincts were kicking in.

"I don't know. But I knew Daoud. He would not have gotten into a confrontation with soldiers."

"People saw him arguing with them," she said. "They said he stopped the soldiers from shooting at kids who threw stones."

"Sure, that's like Daoud. He had a big sense of justice. But that they came back and killed him for that? Even you must see that that doesn't make sense."

Though she bristled at the "even you," she had to agree that it would be highly unusual. Unusual, but not unheard of.

"Did you see Daoud the day he died?" she asked. She doubted he would tell her if he had been one of the soldiers Daoud fought with, but she might as well ask.

"No, I was supposed to. We were supposed to meet for coffee in Abu Dis, but he called and said he couldn't make it. He was going home for his cousin's engagement party, and he said he had to go up early. He had a boyfriend up there, and there was some kind of trouble between them."

"He told you he had a boyfriend in Kufr Yunus? Do you know who it was?"

"No. And I don't think he was from Kufr Yunus, but he was from somewhere near there. Before Daoud got the apartment in Ramallah, they would sometimes use my place in Tel Aviv to meet."

"You let them use your place, but you never met the boyfriend?"

"No. Daoud said the guy was from a very religious family, and it would be dangerous for anyone to know he was gay. He wouldn't tell me anything about him, even his first name or what village he came from. But I have an apartment in the city, and I am away at the army all week. So, I figured Daoud might as well use it. I gave him a key."

"That was very nice of you." Would a soldier do such a thing for a Palestinian? It was hard to believe, but so were many things she had learned this week. "Do you think one of the young men I talked to tonight was his boyfriend?"

"Please," Lior said. "I told you I don't know, and I don't. But do not make trouble for those guys. It's hard enough for them as it is."

"I have no interest in making trouble for anyone," she said.

"I'll go now," he said. He straightened up, grimacing from so much time squatting down.

"Wait a second," Chloe stopped him. "You brought us here. My friend can't afford to get stopped by border police walking around West Jerusalem at night. You need to take us back to Damascus Gate and get rid of anyone who tries to ask questions."

"Okay," he said. "I better look like I'm arresting you then," he said to Rania. He reached for her right arm.

"Take the other arm," she said. "One of you already hurt that one."

He twisted her left wrist gently behind her back, and they exited together.

"Wait," she said. "Could you take me to the Bethlehem Road instead?"

"You're not coming with us?" Tina asked. Rania had planned to spend the night at their apartment in Ramallah, but now she craved her parents' house. She needed to think about what she had seen and heard.

"I'm so near Bethlehem; it's a shame to waste a chance to see my parents," Rania said. "They get up early, so I should be there for breakfast." She wasn't exactly dressed for the Camp, but no one would see her at this hour, and she would find some old clothes in her childhood room.

They walked through the now quiet streets of West Jerusalem, past the Citadel and Emek Refaim, to the edge of the Bethlehem Road. Fortunately, she saw a taxi coming toward them and waved it down.

"Do you need money for the cab?" Chloe asked.

"You're sweet, but I can manage," Rania said. Probably she should have let them pay. At this hour, a private cab to Aida would cost her as much as a week's groceries. She would just have to scrimp for a while.

Chapter 22

Rania slept badly. She was unused to drinking alcohol and kept waking up with a vague feeling of unease. She got up at six in the morning and went downstairs, thinking she would make breakfast for her parents. But her mother was already putting the oil in the pan for the potatoes.

"Why are you here?" was her mother's welcome. The kettle was boiling, and Rania busied herself making tea.

"I had an errand in Al Quds," Rania replied. "I finished too late to get transportation back."

"You were working?"

She had not told her parents that the police didn't want her back. Her father was so proud that his daughter was the first woman detective in the whole north. She didn't want to break his heart with her fall from grace, even though it was not her fault. Besides, she had been working. She just wasn't sure who or what she was working for.

"Yes."

"Good," her mother said. "Put some maramiya in the tea."

"Mama, I already put nana." She always drank her tea with mint. She had forgotten that her parents preferred it with sage.

"Put in both. Maramiya is better for the morning."

"You like maramiya better all the time."

"Whose voice is that?!" Her father burst into the kitchen and caught her in a bear hug. She nuzzled her face against his shirt, breathing in the faint smell of lavender her mother put into her olive oil soap. Life felt so uncomplicated here, among people who loved her just as she was.

Though, if that was true, then why was she avoiding telling them she had been laid off?

She moved out of her father's embrace and sank into one of the heavy, upholstered dining room chairs that had been part of her mother's dowry. Every object in this house looked preserved, no different from the day she had walked out of it to her own wedding.

"What's wrong, yaa shatra?" her father asked. She smiled. Only her father could get away with calling her a clever little girl.

"Nothing's wrong, Baba. I'm just tired."

"You are always tired. You work too hard."

"It's hard work. And I want to do it well."

"You have always done everything well."

That's right, she reminded herself. I always did everything well. If I can't go back to the police, I will do something else well.

"Go help your mother," her father instructed. She obediently got up and went to take the plastic cloth her mother was fishing out of one of the myriad built-in cupboards. She spread it on the floor and smoothed out all the air pockets. Her mother placed the heavy tray laden with tea, labneh, fried potatoes, *zaatar*, and bread in the center. Rania went to the kitchen for small tea glasses and poured for her parents.

"You're not having tea?" her father asked.

"I prefer coffee in the morning."

Her mother shook her head. "Make some if you want," she said.

"That's okay, I can wait until later." She nibbled on a fry. "No one makes potatoes like you, Mama."

"Your sister does," her mother answered. "So would you, if you had let me teach you. But no one could ever show you anything."

Rania and her father exchanged half smiles. Perhaps the special bond she had always had with her father was the reason she had ended up working with all men. Was that why she was now reluctant to train a group of women? She stashed that away to think about later. She had never wanted to be one of those women who was threatened by other women.

✶ ✶ ✶

Maybe it was the thought of working with a group of women that led Rania to wander toward her old friend Samia's house after her parents left for work. When Samia answered the door, her hazel eyes didn't quite seem to register who Rania was. But when Rania leaned in to kiss her cheeks, she reciprocated.

"I was afraid you would be at work," Rania said.

"I took the day off. I wasn't feeling well." That would explain why her frizzy, brown hair was oily and uncombed and her pullover looked slept in.

"Can I come in?" It wasn't polite to ask; if someone didn't invite you in, it meant it wasn't a convenient time to visit. But she and Samia had been friends since high school, when they both joined the Fatah Youth Organization in the early days of the First Intifada. They had been among the first girls recruited.

Samia held the door open for her. The house looked like it had not been cleaned in a decade. Ashtrays overflowed on every available surface.

"Samia, what's wrong?" Rania asked.

"It's nothing. Just a headache."

"Have you had it for a year?" Rania couldn't restrain herself. She bustled around the room, picking up trash. She went to the kitchen and rummaged under the sink until she found a bag to put all the garbage in. When she was done with the living room, she started on the petrified vegetables in the refrigerator. Samia watched her from the doorway, but made no move to help her in her industry.

"Samia, tell me what's going on."

"Why do you suddenly care?"

She deserved that. She had not visited in years. She told herself they had drifted apart, but really it was she who had drifted. Samia had never been the same since her torture and imprisonment. Rania had already been married by the time she was released, but she had come back to visit her. Samia had pulled up her shirt and shown her the scars on her breasts, where the soldiers had carved Stars of David with rusty knives. She had shown off the cigarette burns on the inside of her thighs. Now, thinking about the beating she had just gotten in prison, Rania's stomach ached with shame at having run away from Samia's pain.

"Samia," Rania said slowly. She was just starting to piece something together. "Why didn't you ever get married?"

"Why do you ask about that? Who would want to marry me, huh? Look around."

"But you were not always like this. You had more energy than any of us."

"Had. I don't now. I can barely get out of bed sometimes."

"I am sorry. I didn't know."

"You knew. You just didn't want to know."

"It's true, I didn't. But now I do. I was in prison." Rania went to the sink and filled a bowl with soapy water.

"I heard," Samia said. "So, now you feel guilty."

"A little, yes." Rania began swabbing out the refrigerator. Maybe she could wipe away her guilt at the same time.

"The only reason I was not arrested when you were was that our friends protected me," Rania said. "Faisal and Alam, remember them?"

Samia barely nodded. "Faisal was in love with you," she said.

"And Alam with you."

"Just my luck, to attract the one who would end up dead."

"Would you have wanted to marry him?"

"Why not? He was nice looking."

"You never seemed interested." The refrigerator was sparkling white now. At home, she would replace all the food neatly on the shelves. But here, there was nothing to return to it.

"Let me take you shopping," Rania said.

"You don't think I can shop for myself?"

"Of course you can. It doesn't appear that you do."

"I'll shop, I promise. Look at me, I'm not wasting away." Samia had the same curvaceous body she had had as a teenager.

"What I was going to say," Rania started again, "is that when the soldiers would come to arrest the kids who threw stones, Faisal and Alam would grab me and hustle me into the house. They used to tell me I was special, that I had a contribution to make, and it would not be from prison."

"And you see, they were right."

"What I see now is that I was only able to make that contribution because of them. Because they chose me. I always wondered why they protected me more than they did each other. But it never occurred to me to wonder why they didn't protect you."

"I wasn't as special."

"Perhaps you were more special."

"Don't be ridiculous. You don't think that."

"Don't tell me what I think." Rania wandered around the little house until she found a broom. She started at the far corner of the living room, nearest the hallway that led to the bedroom, and swept toward the open front door. "Samia," she asked as she swept, "did you know that women could be in love with each other, and men with men?"

Her friend grabbed the broom from her hand. "What are you saying?" she asked. She punctuated her words with violent sweeps of the broom.

"I was just asking a question."

"How dare you ask me that? You think I am unnatural?"

"I wasn't saying anything about you. I just learned about this the other day, and I am still trying to understand it. You were always the unshockable one, so I thought I could talk about it with you. If you don't want to talk about it, we won't."

They worked together in silence for some moments. Samia swept and Rania put things away as best she could, not knowing where anything went. It would have made sense to switch roles, but Rania didn't dare suggest it for fear that Samia would sink back into whatever stupor Rania had roused her from.

"You know what happened to me in prison," Samia suddenly began talking.

Rania nodded, though the other woman wasn't looking at her.

"The soldiers took special pleasure in raping me, because I was a virgin before they did it the first time. They came to my cell every day for a month. Sometimes two, sometimes three of them, taking turns."

"Haram," for shame, Rania said.

"Then I was moved to the camp in the Naqab. We all slept in a big room with no real roof, just some bars across the top. It was boiling hot in the summer, freezing in the winter."

Rania knew all this too. Why was Samia reliving this history? But at least she was talking and sounded a little less dead.

"The soldiers there did not touch me," Samia went on. "But I had night-mares about them. One night I woke up shaking. I could not stop. Another woman woke up and she got into bed with me. She was someone I did not know well, from another party."

"Jamiya i-Shabia," Rania guessed. The Popular Front for the Liberation of Palestine was the most left-wing of the larger factions making up the Palestinian Liberation Organization.

"Hezb i-Shab," Samia said.

"Oh yes, those Communist girls," Rania said. She congratulated herself for the smile that flickered across Samia's lips.

"She held me all that night," Samia said. "After that, she came to my bed every night. She never did anything improper. She only kissed my cheek and touched my hair. But I loved her. It was the first time—the only time—I really loved anyone. Then she was released, and I never saw her again. When I was released, I went to her village. I learned she was married, with four children, and they had gone to live in Kuwait."

"And then? You never…?"

"No. I never. Because of those soldiers, I cannot be with a man. But I will not let them make me into a freak."

Rania thought about Chloe saying that you don't become gay; it's some-thing you realize about yourself. This could be an exception, she thought. But the truth was that Samia had always been a little different from the other girls in their circle. The boys had treated her as one of them, and Rania had been jealous of that. It had not occurred to her that they were also treating Samia as less than a girl.

"If you love women, it does not make you a freak," Rania said.

"What makes you such an expert all of a sudden?" Samia squinted at her. Rania was happy to hear a bit of her old outrage. It made her seem more alive.

"I'm no expert, I assure you. I told you; I just heard of this a few days ago. I have some friends, a foreign woman and a Palestinian woman from Australia, and I can see that they love each other and are happy. They took me to a bar last night—that's why I am here."

"You left your husband and son to go to a bar?"

"It has to do with my work," Rania said defensively. "Anyway, it was a bar all full of people who are—they call it 'gay.'" She sensed that Samia knew the word. No doubt she had looked on the internet. "The men dress up like women and dance and sing. It seems strange to me, but they are happy. Even some Dafaween go there," using the word for West Bank Palestinians. "If you want to go there, we could go together sometime."

"I am not interested," Samia said. "I am happy being alone. It's better. Who could put up with me, anyway?"

"I don't believe that," Rania said.

"It doesn't matter what you believe," Samia said. "I didn't ask you to come here and try to make my life something different."

She gestured toward the open door. Rania took her meaning.

"I love you," she said softly and kissed her friend twice on both cheeks. "Remember that."

Samia did not answer. But she stood in the doorway and watched Rania walk down the narrow street that led out of the camp.

Chapter 23

Chloe's phone roused her from an unsettling dream, which fled before she could catch it. In the dark closet, she had no idea what time it was. But the phone had a lighted screen, and she jumped out of bed when she saw who was calling.

"Where have you been?" she demanded.

"Germany," Avi's voice said.

"I need you to come to Kufr Yunus with me. Meet me at Hares junction in an hour." Chloe remembered Daoud's friends teasing him that his village was the size of a speck. She had barely managed to find it in her Rand McNally map book, nestled between Hares and Deir Istya, with no direct road from the highway.

"Make it an hour and a half," he said.

That would give her a chance to get breakfast first. Now that she was up, she was hungry. She stumbled into the kitchen. It was almost ten. Tina would have been gone for hours. She must be exhausted, Chloe thought. It had been nearly two when they got home, after leaving Rania on the Bethlehem Road. They had both been wired from their encounter with the soldier, Lior, and had trouble getting to sleep.

Lior's appearance had short-circuited the conversation with that singer, Yasmina. Tina had said they knew each other through work. But Tina had mentioned a number of her coworkers at the women's counseling center, and none of them was named Yasmina. Chloe suddenly felt less sympathetic about Tina's having to get up early. She made coffee and ate her favorite flaky *boureka*, spinach with cheese, before dashing off to meet Avi.

She should call Rania and tell her she had decided to go to Kufr Yunus. She hoped Rania wouldn't be pissed off. Chloe really had no reason to get involved in this investigation, but then Rania's reasons were not that clear either. Chloe felt a kinship with Daoud. Maybe she had only known him for ten minutes, but he had given her the first marriage proposal of this trip to Palestine. She needed to keep busy, and she wanted to see Avi. This was something they could do together, and his artistic skills might come in handy. He worked as an animator, but his passion was making cartoons for anarchist zines.

Rania's phone went straight to voicemail. The policewoman must be somewhere without cell phone service. Chloe made a mental note to try again later and took off to catch a northbound bus.

Avigdor Levav was the scion of what Chloe called an Israeli Mayflower family. He growled at her every time she said it, but only because it was true. Both sides of his family had been in Palestine since the early nineteenth century. His father was known as "Israel's Walter Cronkite" and his mother was a former member of the Knesset.

Avi had rebelled early and often. At sixteen, he had run away to Europe to live in squatter houses and participate in anticapitalist organizing that eventually landed him in a Spanish prison for two weeks and got him permanently barred from the European Union. He had returned to Israel just in time for the Second Intifada and joined the Palestine solidarity movement. He and Chloe had liked each other instantly. Chloe thought of Avi as her Israeli twin—if you could have a twin young enough to be your son.

He was late now, but that wasn't surprising. He was religiously on time for demonstrations but hopelessly casual about time in every other situation. She sat on the roadblock at the entrance to Hares village, trying to get into *The Da Vinci Code*. The people who said Dan Brown books were page-turners had clearly never tried to read him in a war zone. Of course, it didn't help that she was precariously perched on a boulder with jagged spikes that threatened damage in embarrassing places.

She saw a speck in the distance and recognized Avi's loping walk. She walked to meet him halfway.

His curly hair was cropped close to his head, and he had shaved the ridiculous beard that never made him look as much older as he thought. As usual when he came into the West Bank, he had covered the tattoos on one arm with a cotton sock with the foot cut out, rather than just wearing a long-sleeved shirt.

"How did you get into Germany?" she asked as they headed up the dusty road that led through Hares to the interior villages. "I thought you were barred from Europe."

"My non grata–ness has been lifted," he said with a shrug. "Maya has some family there." His girlfriend, Maya, was an immigrant from Ukraine and studied dance at the university in Tel Aviv. She and Avi had been together off and on for years.

"So, it must have felt good to get back there. You lived in Germany for a while, didn't you?"

"Yeah. It was complicated."

It was going to be one of those days. If he had some political problem, he would be chattering away about it nonstop. But, personal problems she would have to drag out of him word by word.

"What happened between you and Maya?"

"Nothing. It was stupid. We ran into my ex."

"Which ex?" In his off times with Maya, Avi always had flings. Girls found his bad boy attitude irresistible.

"Her name's Inge. She was here for a while before you came. She got deported too."

"So, you ran into her in Germany, and Maya didn't want you to see her?" Chloe wondered how much of a coincidence that "running into" was.

"She didn't say that. She just got bitchy and demanding."

"Yeah, and we all know how well you respond to demands."

"Shut up." He was only half-kidding. They were both quiet for several minutes. The only sound Chloe heard was her own labored breathing as they trudged up the hill.

"I told her from the beginning I don't believe in monogamy," he said.

"But you haven't been with anyone else since you've been together," she said.

"True, but that's just because I don't like people very much."

"That probably makes it worse. You don't like people, but you like Inge. So, did you sleep with her?"

"Who are you, my mother?"

"Do you talk to your mother about your sex life?"

"Good point. Of course I slept with her."

"And?"

"She's in Germany. I'm here. She has a boyfriend there. Maya's just being stupid."

"She's not being stupid. She's being human."

"Maybe."

They wound their way through dense groves of olive and fig trees, occasionally greeting farmers pruning trees or herding goats. Stone rooftops and a minaret peeked over the next rise, letting Chloe know they were nearly to their destination. Just before the dirt path gave way to a pitted asphalt road, the groves abruptly ended. Yawning pits dotted freshly leveled dirt, clear signs of bulldozing. Stacks of olive branches littered an area the size of two football fields. Chloe stared in horror.

"I don't understand," she said in a hushed tone. "Why would they bulldoze here? There are no settlements or Israeli roads in this area."

"Punishment," Avi said. "Five settlers reported that stones hit their cars last week on the highway by Hares. The army ordered five hundred trees to be cut down in each of the four villages nearest the spot where it supposedly happened."

"But this is nowhere near the highway. You can't even see it from here."

"Doesn't matter. The kids they arrested confessed—probably after torture—and said kids from several other villages were throwing stones too. But they wouldn't say who they were, so the army punished everyone nearby. You know they don't care if they get the right people or not. That's part of the terror."

The devastation made Chloe want to cry. So many generations of work, destroyed in an afternoon's bulldozing. Perhaps the people had been able to replant the trees somewhere else, but the old trees never did well after replanting. And many people had no other land to plant on.

They walked up the paved road, toward a thicket of spreading fig trees near the entrance to the village. Rania had said Daoud's body was found under a fig tree. Chloe had no way to know which tree was the lethal one.

What else had Rania said? He was found by Um Mahmoud, who lived in the first house in the village. Chloe knocked on the door of the first house she saw, an imposing sandstone two-story with a wrap-around porch, sporting a row of cushioned, wicker chairs. The door was heavy blue metal, befitting a house that got a lot of attention from soldiers. The first house in a village was always popular with the army as a place to start looking for something.

She heard the hollow sound of metal on metal as the latches were pulled back.

"Yes?" The woman who answered the door looked frightened.

"We are not soldiers." Chloe said immediately in Arabic. The woman's face relaxed only slightly.

"My name is Chloe," she persisted. "This is my friend Abe. We are human rights workers, and we would like to talk to you about the death of Daoud al-Khader."

"Come in." The woman was fifty-ish and wore a traditional, long, black coat-dress, heavily embroidered with gold and red threads. She called out to someone to bring tea and settled her guests in the ample living room. Padded arm chairs lined the walls. Chloe settled into one, and Avi left an empty chair between them. The older woman sat on the other side of Chloe. It wasn't the ideal setup for an interview, but it would have to do.

"You are Um Mahmoud?" Chloe figured she might as well confirm the obvious.

"Um Mahmoud, naam," yes.

"I heard that you found Daoud," Chloe began in Arabic. "Can you tell me what you saw, Um Mahmoud?"

"I did not see anything. I heard gunfire." She used the word *slah*, literally just weapons. Chloe glanced at Avi to see that he was following. He gave a tiny nod.

"So, you heard the guns and went to see?" Chloe asked.

"Yes. I waited to hear the jeep leave. But I heard no jeep. I opened my door and saw no one. When I went outside, I saw Daoud."

"And no one else?"

"No."

Chloe wrote it all down. A young woman in jeans and a sweater, a royal-blue silk scarf covering most of her dark hair, brought in a teapot covered with a floral, quilted cozy. She served the foreigners and then Um Mahmoud glasses of steaming tea dashed with sprigs of mint. The tea was so sweet, it reminded Chloe of after-dinner mints.

She wasn't sure what else to ask. She looked at Avi.

"Did you have anything else?" she asked in English.

He shrugged. Chloe wasn't sure if anything Um Mahmoud told them was worth recording in a drawing, but she had dragged Avi here so she should give him something to do. Though she doubted he cared; he should be glad for an excuse to be in the West Bank and away from Maya's sulking.

"My friend is a…" shoot, what was the word for artist? She had looked it up this morning to refresh her memory, but now she was blocking on it. She glanced at Avi. He ought to know, because it was his profession. Just as he opened his lips, it came to her. "Fanoun," they both said at once and all three of them laughed.

"Can you tell him exactly where you saw Daoud, so that he can make a picture?"

"I will show you." Um Mahmoud rose and led them outside. She walked over to the grove of fig trees and pointed to the ground beneath the largest one. The green figs were little and hard on the stout branches. "Here, you can still see his blood."

Chloe knelt, and, indeed, there were brown stains on the rocks that poked up from the soil. She would have to tell Rania. The policewoman would want to come see the stains for herself. Maybe they would tell her something.

"Can you draw this?" Chloe looked up at Avi, to see that he was already taking out his sketchpad and a pencil. He sat on a nearby boulder. It took him a long time. Chloe wondered what to do while he drew.

"How many children?" she asked Um Mahmoud. Women loved best to talk about their children.

"Three girls, four boys."

"Mashalla." A blessing.

"Are you married?" Um Mahmoud asked.

"No."

"How old?"

"Forty-one."

Um Mahmoud looked shocked. Palestinians usually guessed she was thirty. "Why are you not married?"

"I don't want to be."

The older woman laughed. "Ahsan," better, she said.

"Anjad," definitely, Chloe responded.

Avi came to show Um Mahmoud his drawing. He had put in the trees and the house, capturing the precise angle from which she would have seen the body as she approached. "Was he lying this way, or this way?" he asked.

"Hek willa hek?" Chloe translated.

"Zai hek," like this, she indicated, and he went back to his makeshift stool. Out of things to talk about, Chloe knelt again and poked around in the grass. She didn't expect to find anything, but her fingers touched metal. She pushed aside the thick coating of leaves, twigs, and dirt and uncovered a gold-colored shell casing. She rooted around until she came up with another.

"Do you think these are from the gun?" she asked Um Mahmoud. No need to specify which gun she meant.

"Mumkin," could be, Um Mahmoud replied. "I have bullets."

"You took bullets from the ground that night?"

"Yes."

Why was it people never thought to tell you the most important things? Chloe wondered. What had she planned to do with the bullets, if not give them to a human rights worker? But maybe she was waiting for an official visit, from the Israeli group B'Tselem or the Palestinian one, Al-Haq, and didn't want to hand them over to a random foreigner. Couldn't blame her, if that was true.

"Can I see the bullets?" she asked.

"T'faddali," as you please. She led Chloe back to the house. Chloe sat alone in the living room, awkwardly sipping cold tea for a few minutes. Then, Um Mahmoud appeared and put two bullets into her hand. They were dark brown, hard, and cold. She didn't know enough about bullets to know whether they were likely too old to be the ones that killed Daoud or not. At the beginning of the Intifada, in particular, the army had shot hundreds of bullets into villages like this one, sometimes just firing at random on their way through at night to terrorize the population, sometimes shooting at kids who were throwing stones at their jeeps, sometimes going after wanted men. These could have been lying in the soil for years. But, presumably, Um Mahmoud had not spent time hunting in the dirt for them. If she had picked them up just after finding Daoud, chances were they were the right bullets.

"I would like to take these to the Red Cross," she said. "They will be able to see if they match the ones that killed Daoud and if they are the same ones the army uses."

"Welcome," the woman said. "I was going to give them to the human rights, but they did not come." Chloe didn't know which human rights organization she meant, but it didn't matter. She would be the human rights people now.

Avi entered the house and showed Um Mahmoud the finished drawing. She looked pleased.

"Shater," clever boy, she said.

"Shukran," thanks, he answered.

"Can you tell us how to get to the school?" Chloe asked her.

"I will take you."

"It is not necessary. You can just show us the way."

But the woman was already putting on her shoes. The three of them walked up into the village. The school was obviously just letting out. A sea of light-blue polo shirts teemed from one side; a tidal wave of blue and white seersucker dresses rushed in from the other. They met in the middle in a cacophony of teasing and chatter, the universal language that followed the closing school bell everywhere.

Um Mahmoud waved goodbye and headed up the road, probably to shop. Chloe looked around at the ravaging hordes flooding past her and wondered how and where to start. Finally, she caught one girl's sleeve.

"I am looking for the students who saw the soldiers the other day," she said to the startled girl.

The girl's eyes, the color of pale honey, combed her face as if looking for the Mark of Cain or the Kiss of Death. Apparently, she saw neither.

"Ibrahim," she called out. Nothing happened.

"Ibrahim," the girl bellowed, then covered her mouth when she saw not only all the boys but one of the male teachers in the doorway of the boys' school glaring at her.

Ibrahim was a small boy with quick, dark eyes and dimples to die for. Chloe's first impression was that he was eight or nine, but, when he was standing in front of her, she realized he was probably twelve, just short for his age. He spoke to her in perfect English.

"Hello," he said. "How can I be of service?"

Her mouth twitched, but she controlled it. "Where did you learn to speak English so well?"

"My father teaches English at Al Quds Open University."

"Maybe you will do the same."

"No, I am going to be a doctor."

"That's great. You could probably get a scholarship to study medicine in America, if you want to."

"No. I do not like America. Bush," he made a spitting motion.

"I don't like Bush either. Can you tell me, Ibrahim, what happened the day that Daoud was killed? Did you see the soldiers come into the village?"

"Yes. My friend Mohammed and I were just crossing the street when the jeep came up. We ran over there," he looked toward the path leading down to the orchard below and hesitated.

"You went to gather stones?" she asked. He cocked his head for a second, suspicious, then gave a tiny nod.

"Then what happened?"

"We threw stones at the jeep. The soldiers stopped and got out. One of them fired gas. The other shot his gun up to the sky and yelled that we were going to die. Then, Daoud came running up and pushed us into the school yard."

So far that corroborated what Rania had said. "Did you see what happened then?"

"No. Daoud yelled at us to go into the school, and we did."

"When did you come out?"

"Ten, maybe twenty minutes later. Daoud was gone and so was the jeep."

"Ibrahim, this is important. Do you remember what the soldiers looked like?"

He thought. "One of them was short and skinny. The other was taller and not so skinny. One of them had a beard and wore a cap. The other had no beard and no cap."

That wasn't much to go on, but it was something.

"Ibrahim, my friend wants to draw a picture of these soldiers. Could you help him?"

He nodded. Avi took out his pad and leaned on the white stucco wall of the school yard.

"You said one was short. How short? Like this? or like that?" By asking question after question, Avi managed to make a sketch that Ibrahim approved. Ibrahim's friend Mohammed came to look too.

"He had glasses," Mohammed said in Arabic, pointing to the taller soldier.

"He did not." Ibrahim shoved his friend, as if trying to get him away from the picture before he contaminated it with his bad recollection.

"Yes, he did. He just took them off when he shot the gas."

That was possible. A soldier firing tear gas at close range could easily gas himself. He would be better off without glasses to fog up and get coated in gas.

"Do you remember what kind of glasses?" she asked Mohammed.

"Black, with black rims."

"Add sunglasses," she told Avi. "Anything else you remember?" She had learned the hard way that people often held something back until you asked directly.

"Daoud knew one of the soldiers," Mohammed said.

"How do you know?"

"He called him Ron. When he chased us into the school yard, he said, 'Ron, stop.'"

"Did you know which soldier he was talking to?"

"No. But this was the one who was shooting at us." He pointed at the picture of the smaller man with the cap. Avi wrote "Ron?" next to the man's picture.

"That's all?" she asked the two boys. They both nodded.

"Thank you for your help," she said.

"You are very welcome," said Ibrahim in English.

Chapter 24

Rania was gone again. Bassam had barely seen her since she got out of jail. The first night had been like their wedding night again. He had held her while she cried for hours, stroking her back and kissing her hair. He had had to learn the spots where she had been beaten, which he loved twice as much even as he avoided them. He had always been proud of having a wife who was fierce and served their people. That meant accepting that it might be she who suffered and was gone instead of him. But now it was getting old.

Why couldn't she be grateful for the time off from work? She had survived a difficult encounter with the occupation. Everyone needed time to readjust to the world when they returned. She acted like special rules were supposed to apply to her. Of course, people would be suspicious when someone got out of jail all of a sudden without even a hearing. In Rania's case, it was even more complicated, because Abdelhakim was going around saying that an Israeli policeman from Ariel had visited her the day before her release. Bassam knew that Rania would never have agreed to collaborate. He didn't need any investigation by the *muhabarat* to allay his suspicions. But he was her husband. If he was not, he would want her name to be cleared before he trusted her with the secrets of their people. That kind of precaution flowed with the water into homes under occupation.

Meanwhile, they could build their family. Whenever he brought up the subject of a baby, Rania made objections about his insecure salary and the embargo, things that made no sense. His family was well off, even if they were not as wealthy as they had once been. Look at this house. Plenty of room for a dozen kids. Not that he was demanding a dozen. Two or three more would be perfect. He would like a little girl next time. He would call her Sara, after his sister who was killed at the beginning of the First Intifada. She would be just like Rania, eyes alive with fun and mischief. Khaled was dying for a little brother or sister. It was hard to be alone for so long.

His mother's door was ajar. He heard his son's voice as he mounted the stairs.

"Sitti, look," he was saying. His grandmother dutifully raised her eyes to see what he was up to, just in time to meet her son's as he stood in the doorway. He watched his son with gentle admiration. Khaled was good at amusing himself. That went along with being an only child of busy parents. He had constructed a cart with yellow Legos and was piling it with multicolored blocks.

"Fresh tomatoes, peppers, squash, twenty shekels a box," he called out.

The little squares did look like vegetables, Bassam thought, admiring his son's ingenuity.

Khaled pulled a twig off one of the logs by the wood stove.

"Go," he cried and snapped the twig at an imaginary donkey.

Bassam crossed to his son and picked him up in his arms.

"How about letting me be your donkey now?" he said, hoisting his son onto his shoulders. Khaled whipped his back with the twig. Even through his shirt and undershirt, it stung.

"Gently, my son."

"Sorry, Baba." But Khaled flicked the whip again, and it stung just as much.

"Khaled." He put his son down to walk to the rest of the stairs to their flat. "You must be more careful."

"I don't want to," Khaled yelled as he ran into their flat. He picked up a heavy ottoman, bigger around than he was tall, and threw it to the ground. He could not get up much force, since his arms wouldn't even circle the piece, so he did no damage, but Bassam swatted his hand lightly.

"Khalas," stop that, he said sharply.

Khaled responded by kicking the ottoman fiercely. The momentum knocked him to the ground, and he draped himself over the cushioned footrest, beating it with his small fists. Bassam could hear him crying. Well, that was okay. His son could do worse than trying to beat the stuffing out of a piece of furniture, and crying would be good for him. Bassam worried about the toll Rania's absence, physical and emotional, was taking on the boy. When she came home, he would have a talk with her. She couldn't just tear off on rogue investigations, like this one about the boy in Kufr Yunus. She had not even told him she was doing it, but Abdelhakim had said she was running around the villages asking a lot of questions. He had said Bassam should talk to her about it. "People might mistrust her motivations," Abdelhakim had suggested with his supercilious half smile. Bassam didn't completely trust Abdelhakim, because he worked for Abu Ziyad, who was an old family enemy. But Abdelhakim was known as a good man. Bassam would take his advice and talk to his wife about her activities.

He heard her mounting the outside steps. It was about time. He went to open the door. If she had been shopping in Bethlehem, she might need help carrying all the packages inside.

But it was not Rania coming up the stairs. It was her friend, Chloe, who raised a hand in greeting.

"Marhaba, Bassam. Rania hon?"

He shook his head. "I expect she will be home soon," he said. "Please come in." He stood aside to allow her to precede him into the house. He went to the kitchen and put on the kettle for tea. When he returned to the living room, Chloe was standing in the center of the room, presumably waiting to be invited to sit. He gestured to the armchair whose ottoman Khaled had recently been fighting with. His son was nowhere to be seen.

"I'm sorry to bother you," Chloe said a little shyly. "I just wanted to talk to Rania for a few minutes."

"It is no bother," he said. "But my wife has not been home since yesterday. She went to visit her parents in Bethlehem. I expected her home by now, but perhaps the roads are bad."

"Perhaps." Chloe looked doubtful. "Where is Khaled?"

"Probably in his room," Bassam said. "He was upset. He does not like his mother being gone so much."

"I understand," Chloe said. "I'm sure the time she was in prison was hard on him."

"Very," Bassam said. "I worry about him. There is violence in him."

"Violence? What do you mean?"

Bassam told her about the altercation just before she arrived.

"But that sounds very normal," she said. "Kids don't know their own strength. They don't realize they can hurt someone so much bigger than they are."

"That is possible." It was Bassam's turn to look skeptical. "I will see where he has gotten to." He walked down the hall to Khaled's room. His son was not there. He checked his and Rania's bedroom, and he was not there either, nor was he in the bedroom they kept empty for their future children or the little office where their aged computer lived.

"I think he must have run upstairs while we were outside," Bassam said. "I will go check." He mounted the stairs to his mother's apartment, his heart momentarily filled with dread. What if his son was not there? How could someone vanish just like that? But Khaled was there, sitting on the floor and making a fort around himself with pillows from his grandmother's couch. His face was streaked with tears. Bassam took a tissue from the box on the end table and blew his son's nose, which needed it badly.

"He says you hit him," his mother said.

"I did not hit him. Not really. Not the way Baba used to hit me."

"You needed to be hit. You and your brothers were wild, and things were dangerous then."

"Things are not dangerous now? Have you forgotten that, a few weeks ago, soldiers came to our house in the middle of the night and took my wife to jail?"

"It is not the same. If your father had not beaten you, you would be dead by now."

"I'm not so sure." They had had this argument before, but he did not resent his father's discipline. It was what people did then. He picked his son up, smoothing his tousled curls.

"Come on, big boy." Khaled's response was a wail worthy of a torture chamber. He wriggled out of his father's arms and climbed into his pillow fort.

"All right, stay there if you want." Bassam went back to attend to his guest. At least his son was safe here. Let his grandmother ply him with cookies for a while, and hopefully his mother would be home by the time he came downstairs.

He found Chloe studying the pictures on the mantelpiece. She picked up the only one of a woman. "Who is this?"

"That is my sister, Sara. In the First Intifada, soldiers came into our village to arrest some boys they said had thrown stones at the jeeps." He had been one of the boys they were looking for, and, of course, he had thrown the stones. But that was a part of the story he had never told anyone. "They fired gas into the school, and all the students ran out. As we ran out, they fired live bullets at us. Sara was one of five students who were killed that day."

"That's horrible." Chloe studied the photo some more. "So, the boys and girls studied together back then?"

"Not usually, no. But Sara was very good in math, and she planned to become a doctor. My father arranged for her to go to the boys' school half the day, because the girls' school did not emphasize math and science."

"Your father sounds like a very unusual man," Chloe said.

"He was," Bassam said. He went into the kitchen to prepare the tea. "Come, Chloe," he said when he returned. They sat opposite one another, she on the couch, he in an arm chair. He spooned the sugar into glasses and poured the tea. She took a sip.

"Delicious."

A tiny grimace told him she was lying. He did not make tea as well as Rania did. He never understood what she put in it to take away the bitterness. One of the many little secrets women kept from men. When Chloe had managed to finish the tea, she stood up.

"I won't wait any longer," she said. "Please, tell Rania I stopped by."

"No, you must stay for dinner," he said. "I am sure my wife will want to see you. We are so grateful to you for getting her out of prison."

"I really don't think I had much to do with getting her out," Chloe said. "And I'm sure she is sick of me by now."

"Oh, have you seen her recently? She did not mention it."

Chloe looked confused. "You lent us your car the other day, to take Reem, Um Saad, to her appointment."

"Of course." He had the feeling that was not what she had meant, but he could be wrong. Rania had mentioned that Chloe and her friend stopped by to borrow the car, but not that they had stayed to visit.

"In fact," Chloe said, "that was part of what I wanted to talk to Rania about. Reem needs to go to the hospital again tomorrow. Is it possible for us to borrow the car again? I am sorry to ask, but I don't have another one to use."

"Ma'lesh," it's nothing, Bassam replied. "We have a wedding to go to, but it is nearby, in Biddya. If we cannot go with my brother, we can take a taxi. Why do you not spend the night and save yourself the trip from Ramallah?"

"Thank you, but I need to get home." Chloe made to leave.

"Do you want to take the car to Ramallah with you now?" he asked.

"That's very kind," she said. "But I don't trust myself driving to Ramallah. I will see you in the morning. I believe her appointment is at one, so I will be here by eleven."

"See you then," he said.

Chapter 25

When Rania walked through the door, Bassam's silence greeted her like a furnace blast. He was reading the newspaper, while Khaled sat on the floor, creating an elaborate structure of books and old toys. Maybe he would be an architect when he grew up.

"I brought *molochia*," she said, feeling like one of the bad magicians who traveled around entertaining children in the refugee camps. She didn't think her husband would be convinced to "Look over there!" by her promise to cook the spinach he loved, but no one could blame her for trying.

"Where did you go for it, the Naqab?"

"I stopped in Al Quds on the way back from Aida." She had thought she had plenty of time to get back and couldn't resist going through the Jerusalem markets again. It brought back her happy-go-lucky college days. But, by the time she got to the bus station in Ramallah, the north-bound buses were not moving. Something about a roadblock on the way north. She had been stuck there for almost two hours before she found a servees driver willing to go.

"How are your parents?"

"They're fine."

"Why did you go? Is something wrong?" Bassam asked from behind his paper.

"No. Well, I saw Samia."

"Samia? You haven't spoken to her in three years."

"Two. She is very depressed." She unloaded the groceries on the counter and rummaged underneath for a big metal bowl. She filled it with water and dumped the narrow, pointed Egyptian spinach leaves in it to soak.

"You went to Bethlehem because someone you haven't talked to in two years is depressed? I don't understand what you're doing."

"I didn't say that's why I went. I've been trying to find out more about what happened to Daoud al-Khader." She removed the leaves a few handfuls at a time, placing them carefully between two towels and patting them dry. Then, she removed those leaves and began the process with the next batch.

"I heard you were looking into that. Who asked you to?"

"No one asked me to. But I thought if I could prove soldiers killed him, the family could get something from the army."

"Did you tell Mustafa?" he asked.

"I tried," she said. "But all he wanted to talk about was his sister's cancer." She winced at how unsympathetic she sounded.

"It wouldn't hurt you to think of your own family for a while," he said.

"What are you accusing me of?" she demanded. She located the big knife and tested the edge carefully. It could be sharper. She took a pumice stone from the sink and slowly stroked it along the knife's edge.

"I am not accusing. I am just saying that you were away from your son for more than a month, and, now, you are running around doing something no one wants you to do."

"How do you know no one wants me to?" He had said he had heard about her investigation. She could guess from whom.

"Forget it," he said. He went back to his newspaper.

"*Vroom vroom vroom.*" Khaled ran full-tilt at her and rammed her legs with a yellow and black dump truck.

"Ow! There's been a crash! I'm hurt!"

"You were throwing stones! I will bulldoze your whole village."

She turned and stared at her son. How could this be his make-believe? Before Prison, she would have found a way to make a joke. But, now, she could not pretend things were normal. She felt like he was play-acting in the role of her old self.

"Go do your homework, habibi. I need to make dinner. We can play later."

He didn't protest the way he would have before. He had gotten used to not having her around. Maybe she should play with him now and let dinner wait. But, if she did that, Bassam would probably complain that he was hungry. She couldn't please everyone, no matter what she did.

She turned on the radio while she chopped the spinach and started the rich, white soup, simmering on the stove. There was fighting in Gaza between men loyal to Fatah and those belonging to Hamas. The Hamas men who had been shut out of the police while Fatah controlled the government now wanted those well-paid jobs for themselves. The Fatah men were refusing to give up their positions or their weapons.

The report made her anxious. She hated that Palestinians were letting the Israelis and Americans make them fight each other. Their unity was the only thing that had enabled them to hold onto their land for this long time since before the partition in 1947.

"I'm going to Marwan's," Bassam said from the doorway.

"But dinner is almost ready."

"Ma'lesh." Never mind. "I will eat with them."

"But I'm making this for you."

"I will have some when I get home. I heard some news today. I need to discuss it with Marwan."

"What did you hear?"

"The Americans have frozen some bank accounts of the Sulta. If they cannot be convinced to unfreeze them, there may not be enough money to pay salaries next month."

"They froze funds belonging to the Palestinian Authority? How can they do that?"

He shrugged. "They did it."

If she had been going to work every day, she would have come home already knowing this important news, having thought about it and been ready to discuss it with her husband. Now, she depended on him to tell her things that determined her survival. She wiped a plate and flung the towel onto the counter with a satisfying *thwack*.

"Are you going to ask Marwan to take you into the store?"

"No. But I may need to ask him for a loan."

He left without another word. Before Prison, he would have come over to touch her arm, taken at least a sip of the soup she had worked hard to make. When he had clumped down the front stairs, she turned off the soup and went to Khaled's room.

"What shall we play?" she asked.

"Fatah and Hamas," he said. "I am Hamas."

He shoved a plastic ruler into her hand—she supposed it was meant to do for a sword. He sighted down the toy pistol his grandmother had given him for the last Eid. "Bang bang, you're dead."

"How can I play if I'm dead?" she asked.

He made a whooshing motion with his hands. "You are alive again. Come catch me!"

He ran outside, and she followed, careful to stay behind him while seeming to run hard. Last year, he would have wanted to play *jesh w shabab*—army and kids—and he would have wanted to be the Israelis, because they were the strong ones. Now, he wanted to be Hamas because they were the powerful ones. The party she had belonged to since she was fifteen years old was cast in the role of the losers.

"I got you," she cried, as she suddenly swooped down on him, tickling his soft tummy.

"Laa laa!" His words said no no, but his giggle was happy. "I'm a plane!" He stretched his arms wide and zoomed crazily across the yard.

"I'm a bird." She imitated his flight motion without the sound effects.

"I'm a plane, and I kill birds." He engulfed her with his wing arms.

She wrapped her arms around her son. He was at that age where every game ended in murder. She wondered if that was true of kids in every country.

"Are you hungry, habibi?"

"Yes."

"Good, let's go eat."

"Weyn Baba?"

"Baba went to Uncle Marwan's. He will be back later."

They ate the spinach soup with rice, and bread with hummus and salad. After dinner, she looked over his English homework. He had spelled all the words right.

"You are clever," she said. That was as it should be. Both she and Bassam had been good students. "What do you want to be when you grow up?"

She waited for the only answer he had ever given: A policeman, like you.

"An engineer," he said.

"What? Oh, why an engineer?" Engineering was a good career, if that turned out to be what he was suited for. But she felt a throbbing in her throat and turned away from him so he would not see the tears welling in her eyes.

"I want to be an engineer like Yahyya Ayash."

Oh. That kind of engineer. Yahyya Ayash, whose nickname was "The Engineer," had been a Hamas bombmaker from the village next to theirs. After the Israelis killed him, they destroyed his family home, which still lay in ruins.

"Who has been talking to you about Yahyya Ayash?" she asked.

"Teacher Kareem." She would have to speak to Kareem. He shouldn't be teaching seven-year-olds to emulate bombmakers. Yahyya Ayash was the most revered historical figure from their part of Palestine, but the kids were not old enough to grasp the complexity of his contribution.

"An engineer is a good thing to be," she said. "But you don't have to be an engineer like Yahyya Ayash. Engineers build tall buildings and roads and bridges, lots of things to make our people great and strong."

"Hamas makes our people strong."

"What should we read?" she asked. She had had enough of a politics lesson from her child for tonight.

She led Khaled by the hand to the bookshelves. She was pleased when he chose a picture biography of Yasser Arafat.

"Il Ra'is," he said, brushing his hand over the cover photo of Arafat in his classic black and white keffiyeh.

"That's right. Even though he is dead, he is still the President. What party did the President found?"

"Fatah."

"That's right. Go get into your pajamas and brush your teeth, and then we will read about the President."

✳ ✳ ✳

When Khaled was in bed, Rania scrubbed the kitchen counters and the sink until they gleamed. She couldn't make herself put the soup into the fridge but left the covered pot on the stove. Maybe Bassam would still be hungry or would be hungry again when he returned. She heard her mother-in-law's heavy footsteps moving back and forth upstairs, from kitchen to living room, against the hum of the television. Maybe she should turn on the television too, but she doubted there would be anything she wanted to watch.

As she wiped the glass bowls with a piece of cheesecloth, her thoughts turned to Daoud and his Israeli friend, Lior. She had never thought of herself as closed-minded or provincial. She wanted to think it didn't matter to her if Daoud was... "Gay," she made herself say aloud. She thought about Chloe and Tina. She could trust Chloe with her life—already had, on several occasions. Tina seemed like a bright, thoughtful woman. Knowing what they were to each other didn't change that—but it did.

"What are you thinking?"

She hadn't even heard Bassam come in.

"I was wondering when they will let me go back to work."

"It is hard right now. Even the men may not have jobs soon."

"Are you suggesting I should be laid off first, because I'm a woman?"

"Of course not. But you cannot expect them to take you back right now, when things are so insecure."

She said nothing. He had always supported her commitment to her work. She didn't believe he was trying to undermine her. But she was not surprised by his next sentence.

"I hoped maybe you were thinking about the baby."

"There is no baby."

"But there could be."

True. Why was she so reluctant to think about that? She had always assumed she would have more children.

"It wouldn't be smart to have another child if we could both be out of work any day," she said. "You were just talking about borrowing money from your brother."

"You make it sound like children are a burden."

"They are not a burden. But they are a responsibility. It's irresponsible to have them if we cannot support them."

"We will be able to support them. Allah will provide."

"Since when do you believe in Allah like that?"

"I have always had faith," he said.

"Faith, sure, on a spiritual level. I believe Allah protects our people too. But on a practical level, no. Allah does not decide who eats and who starves. We don't believe that the people who are poor are being judged by Allah in some way."

"I never said that."

"You said Allah would provide. That means that if a family does not have enough, it's because Allah is not providing for them."

"Stop changing the subject. I wasn't talking about philosophy or religion; I was talking about us. About having a baby. Why won't you talk about that?"

"I don't know."

He came up behind her and wrapped his arms around her waist. She leaned back against him. It had been a long time since they had been comfortable with each other like this. She nuzzled her shoulders against his chest. His hands crept closer to her sensitive areas, and he planted a kiss in the corner of her neck.

"Now you are the one changing the subject," she said softly.

"Shhh." He turned her to face him, meshed his mouth to hers. She willed her body to respond. She wanted to respond to him. He was her husband, he was her soul mate, he and Khaled were her life. There was nothing she wanted more than to make him happy. She had never looked at another man. But she couldn't turn off her thoughts.

Things were changing so fast. One month, she had a powerful job and was a member of the most powerful faction in the government. The next, she was an unemployed wife of a soon-to-be-unemployed civil servant, and her son was being brainwashed to hate the party to which she had dedicated her life. In the middle of it all, Palestinian men were risking their freedom to dress up like women and dance in front of Israeli men, and her oldest friend had a secret she had never before guessed. She couldn't just forget all that and make love to her husband.

Or could she?

She pushed all the jumbled thoughts out of her mind like wiping a rag over her kitchen counter. She turned in her husband's arms, finding the space between his ribs where her breasts had always fit neatly. She placed her palm against Bassam's chest and felt her pulse synchronize itself to his heartbeat. She swayed in rhythm with his breathing, felt the pressure of his hands on her back and thigh grow more insistent.

"Let's go to bed," she whispered.

Chapter 26

Chloe was nervous and got up early. She moved around quietly, trying not to disturb Tina, who snored softly in their closet. She went next door and insisted on paying Um Malik for four eggs from her chicken coop, ignoring the protests of "I'm like your mother!" She sipped coffee while she fried potatoes and scrambled the eggs with some processed white cheese. When everything was ready, she put it all on a tray and took it into the closet.

"Wake up, sleepyhead," she said softly, shaking Tina's shoulder gently. "I brought you breakfast in bed."

"You're sweet," Tina said, but rolled over on her stomach and pulled the pillow over her head.

"Reem's appointment is at one, and it's going to take a while to get transportation on a Friday. We need to leave in an hour, and I know you're gonna want a shower."

"What are you talking about?" Tina moved the pillow and half-opened her eyes.

"Reem's chemo. I arranged to borrow Bassam's car, but we have to get to Mas'ha to pick it up. We should leave by eight, eight thirty at the latest."

"Chloe, I didn't know the appointment was today. I can't go; I have plans."

"What do you mean, you didn't know? You were there when she made the appointment, just like I was."

"I didn't write it down. I've been so busy; I forgot, and you didn't remind me."

"Didn't know I was your social secretary." Stop being a bitch, Chloe told herself. It's not like you never forgot an appointment. "Can't you change your plans?"

"No, I'm sorry. I'm meeting some friends in Tel Aviv."

"You're going to Israel?" Chloe's arms ached from holding the heavy tray. She put it down on the floor and sat down on her sleeping mat.

"I'm meeting them in Forty-Eight, yes."

"Don't be more Palestinian than thou. I grew up calling it Israel. It'll take a while to get used to the new terminology."

"I *am* more Palestinian than you."

"Tina, I know I am not Palestinian. But that doesn't make me a settler or something. The point isn't what name I use for the place where Tel Aviv is. It's that you're going there, and you always say you hate it, and you didn't tell me. What is it you have to do that's so important?"

"I'm just meeting some friends." Tina got up in one fluid movement and strode over to where her bathrobe hung on an iron hook next to the closet door. Chloe watched her walk, admiring the supple way Tina's back curved into her butt. She felt a stirring in her crotch, which pissed her off. How could she be so aroused by someone who was blowing her off?

"Which friends?" she asked. "From work?"

"No."

"Who, then? I don't get what you're being so secretive about."

"If you really want to know, it's a group for Palestinian lesbians. I got on their e-list a while ago, when I was still in Australia. It used to be just online, but they've started having meetings, and I go to them."

"Palestinian lesbians meet in Tel Aviv?" Why was that what she asked? There were a million things she wanted to know about the group. She had heard rumors of an underground Palestinian lesbian group, but she had no idea Tina was part of it.

"Sometimes they meet in West Jerusalem, but Tel Aviv is safer. No one can risk someone in their family finding out where they're going."

That made sense. Chloe forgot her feeling of betrayal in the hundred questions that flooded her mind.

"What do you talk about?" she asked, nibbling on a fry. She took the breakfast tray into the living room and set it on the coffee table. The breakfast-in-bed thing had been spoiled, but the food was delicious. Tina sat next to her on the couch and poured herself a cup of coffee from the little pot.

"Yum," she said, warming Chloe's heart. Chloe pushed the food toward her lover.

"We talk about everything," Tina said. "Our families, growing up, coming out. It's…I don't know. It's like a miracle. I've never felt so close to any group of people." She caught Chloe's hurt expression. "I said *group* of people."

"I understand," Chloe said. But she couldn't say she did. She had never felt that way. She felt comfortable with other Jewish lesbians but not necessarily more so than with other women. There were things they had in common, but they were the type of things that plenty of women from other cultures shared.

"Does this group have a name?" she asked.

"SAWA," Tina said. "It stands for Sisterhood for Arab Women's Advocacy." It also meant "together" in Arabic, Chloe knew. The word stabbed irrationally at her heart.

"What time's your meeting?" she asked Tina.

"It's at three. And will probably go until after eight."

"A five-hour meeting?"

"It's not just a meeting. We talk, we eat, and then we sometimes go out."

"To a bar?"

"Sometimes. Sometimes to a café or even a play or something. That's why it is best to meet in Tel Aviv on Friday. It's good for the people who live in the West Bank because they have the day off, but West Jerusalem is closed up on Friday night. Tel Aviv is always open."

"I see. So, are you spending the night there or coming home?"

"I don't know. It depends on what time we are finished and whether I'm drunk."

"Where will you stay if you don't come home?"

"Yasmina, one of the women from SAWA, lives in a big house. They have a guest room," Tina went on. "The West Bank women usually stay there."

"Yasmina. She's the one we met the other night."

"That's right."

"You said you work together?"

"Um, well, not exactly. I said I met her through work."

Chloe decided to let it go. Obviously, Tina would not have wanted to say anything about SAWA in front of Rania or, apparently, in front of Chloe.

"I don't see any need to come back if you're not going to be here," Chloe said. "After I drop the car in Mas'ha, I think I'll go visit Jaber and Ahlam."

"Give them my love." Tina and Ahlam both worked with Palestinian feminist organizations. When Chloe had introduced them, they had bonded like instant sisters.

Tina took her cup and plate into the kitchen. Only hers, Chloe noted. Of course, Tina didn't know if Chloe was done eating, but it still seemed symbolic.

"Hey," Chloe called. "Maybe I could write an article about SAWA." Tina appeared in the doorway between kitchen and living room, her green eyes blazing.

"Bloody hell, Chloe, that's exactly why I didn't tell you in the first place."

"What are you getting so upset about? I wouldn't have to use people's names."

"That's not the point."

Tina disappeared into the closet. Chloe cleared the breakfast things and headed for the shower. If she was going to have to manage the stick shift herself, she would really have to get going, because there could be quite a few stalls on the way.

Chapter 27

Friday, the Palestinian Sabbath, was wedding day. There were weddings nearly every week, except during Ramadan, and today was no exception. The wedding Rania and Bassam were invited to was at three o'clock. She told Bassam she would be back by one. He looked annoyed but only said, "Okay, see you then."

Rania had spent many hours talking to grieving family members. Being Palestinian meant being good at funerals. But she had never had an encounter like the one she was about to have with Hanan. What was she going to say to a young woman whose fiancé had been betraying her with another man? Ahmed had insisted that Hanan knew the truth, but that was too much for Rania to believe. How could any woman allow herself to be used in such a way? She pondered this as she walked through the corridors of Salfit Hospital.

If she were sick, she did not think the heavy smell of antiseptic cleaning fluids would make her feel better. As it was, she quickened her steps to put distance between herself and the floors where patients were treated. She took the elevator, which thankfully was working, to the eighth floor, where the administrative offices were housed.

She imagined that this part of the hospital would be a virtual morgue on Friday. She had been quite surprised when Hanan's mother had informed her that her daughter was at work. Medical staff, of course, worked around the clock, but surely Hanan's work was not so essential that it could not wait until Saturday. She found the girl in the windowless office she shared with two other women. At least, she assumed all three desks were occupied by women. Only one other woman was actually in the office, and she and Hanan were deep in conversation that seemed to revolve around the hairbrush in Hanan's hand and the braids she was attempting to sweep into a crown. Rania thought perhaps it was not a work day after all.

"Good day," she said from the doorway. Hanan swiveled her head and looked none too pleased to see her. But she got up and came to the door, bringing the hairbrush with her.

"Can we talk somewhere—" Rania didn't even get to finish the word "privately" before Hanan was signaling to her friend that she would return in a while. She led Rania down a dim hallway to a door which, when opened, revealed a pleasant office with plate-glass windows on two sides.

"The director has gone home," Hanan said. "We can talk in here."

Neither of them wanted to usurp the director's deep, leather-covered chair. Hanan perched on the edge of the shiny, olive-wood desk, and Rania settled into a leather couch that put her head level with the girl's knee. She leaned back to make sure that Hanan's swinging leg did not accidentally catch her in the face.

"I am trying to find out who killed Daoud," Rania began.

"The soldiers killed him."

"We don't know that."

"I know it."

"Do you know something you haven't told me about what happened that day?"

"I don't know anything about what happened. I didn't see it, I told you."

"I spoke to his roommate, Ahmed."

"I know you did." Hanan's half-braided hair made her resemble a cubist painting.

"So, you knew that Daoud was..." Rania hesitated. Ahmed had known the word "gay," but Hanan was not a young man living in Ramallah. The Arabic word for homosexual was *luuti,* derived from the prophet Lot, who lived in a town that was destroyed for its abnormal sexual practices. The word had a highly derogatory connotation.

"Mithli," same, Hanan supplied. "Yes, I knew."

"But you were going to marry him anyway."

"Yes. That way our parents would leave us alone about getting married, and we could do what we wanted. Later, we would have had children, and he would have changed."

"Why do you think he would have changed?"

"Because, all men change when they have children."

Had Bassam changed when Khaled was born? Rania had never thought about it. She felt like she had changed, but not herself, her role in society. Bassam had seemed the same to her before and after, but maybe to others he seemed different, more serious perhaps.

"I loved him," Hanan was saying. "He loved me, too. He would not have allowed me to be unhappy."

"But how could you be happy, married to someone with unnatural desires?"

"I don't see what's unnatural about it," Hanan said. Rania put that in a vault of things to think about later. Did all the young people think this way? She thought of the young Palestinian men at the bar the other night. They had not appeared ashamed or frightened, at least not until she showed up.

"Did you know he performed at a bar in West Jerusalem?"

"Of course. I watched him once. He was wonderful. All of the others only move their lips to the recording, but he sang. He sounded just like the record."

"Hanan, someone told me that Daoud had a boyfriend in one of our villages. Do you know who it was?"

A beat too long passed before the girl said, "No, I don't know. He never said anything to me. I don't believe he had one."

"You are sure? It could be important."

"Why is it important? We know who killed him." She slapped the hairbrush against her palm for emphasis. It made a little red mark. "That soldier threatened him in the afternoon, and, that evening, he came back to kill him."

"You said 'that soldier.' Do you know which soldier it was? Did Daoud know him?"

"I didn't mean anything. My sister told you she saw a soldier hit him. That must be the soldier who killed him."

Rania knew the girl was lying, but there was no point in prolonging the conversation. She got up to go. Just before she got to the doorway, she thought of something.

"Were there soldiers at Adloyada the night you were there?"

Hanan's eyes narrowed. She nodded, almost imperceptibly.

"Did Daoud talk to any of them?"

Another nod.

"Did you hear what they said?"

"No. I was sitting at a table with Elias and Ahmed. We watched Daoud's act. Everyone loved him. They cheered. Then, he went to get changed. I decided to surprise him by going to help him dress." Rania tried not to let her face betray shock. Nice village girls didn't watch their boyfriends get undressed. But then nice village girls didn't go to bars, let alone one like Adloyada.

"I went to the back, where I had seen Daoud go. I asked someone where his dressing room was. He pointed to a door. I opened it. Daoud was there—his shirt was off, but he was still wearing the skirt. There was a soldier there with him. They were kissing. Daoud had his hands—"

Rania gestured that she needn't spell it out. It didn't matter. She knew enough. Ahmed had lied, and Daoud had been involved with an Israeli soldier. Time to get home and prepare for the wedding. But there was one more question she had to ask.

"I'm sorry to make you talk about this," she said to Hanan. "I'm sure it was painful for you. Do you know—did you ever find out that soldier's name? Could it have been Lior?"

"I don't know. I shut the door quickly. I don't think either of them saw me, and I never told Daoud I had seen them."

Rania believed her. She pulled out the photos she had taken from Daoud's room, and opened it to the one in which the Israeli's face was clearest. "Could this have been the soldier you saw?"

Hanan glanced at it quickly and looked away. Rania read her thoughts in the tears that made their way into her opaque, brown eyes. Daoud looked so happy with those boys. Why couldn't he have been as happy with her?

"I only saw him for a second, from the side. I don't think so, but I can't say for sure," the girl said.

Despite the slow Friday transit, Rania was back in Mas'ha before one o'clock. She had plenty of time to make lunch for Khaled, but she didn't feel like it. She stopped at the falafel shop instead. She owed him a treat anyway. She bought ten falafel balls and some fried eggplant.

"We should be more careful about money," Bassam said when she laid the food on the table. "Without your salary and with the PA funds frozen, we might have to do without for a while."

"How can you reproach me for not getting paid, when you keep telling me to forget about work and have a baby?"

"Shhh," he chided her as Khaled raced in, making *zoom zoom* noises with a toy plane. "I wasn't reproaching you about not getting paid," Bassam whispered in her ear.

"Let's eat," she said. She was not going to fight with Bassam today, not after last night. But she didn't want to talk to him either. She wanted to go off and think about Hanan's bombshell. She did the dishes as soon as Khaled was done eating. Fortunately, her son rode off on his bicycle, and Bassam went to smoke on the porch. She went to bathe for the wedding.

Some Palestinian households only had a tub and a cup for pouring water over your head, but she had insisted on a real shower. Her father, who had updated the water system for all of Bethlehem in the seventies, had come up to install it while she and Bassam were on their honeymoon in Jericho. As the warm water coursed over her now, she thought about what she had learned in the last few days. Or, at least, what she had heard, because she had more questions than answers at this point.

Lior had said the person Daoud met at his apartment was Palestinian, but he also said he never met the boy. So, Daoud could have lied to Lior, or Lior could be lying to protect another soldier. Or, of course, Lior could be the boyfriend, and the whole story about lending Daoud the apartment was a lie to throw her off the scent.

Speaking of lies, why had Ahmed lied about going to Adloyada? Was he gay as well, or had he just gone to watch Daoud perform? She would have to have another chat with Ahmed. She didn't relish it.

She stepped out of the shower and into her nicest dress. It was a deep violet with a drop-waist and black and gold embroidery across the chest and on the cuffs. Bassam had brought it for her from Nablus just before the last Eid al-Fitr, the festival that ends Ramadan. She combed her hair and twisted it into a knot at the back of her neck, covering it with a black and gold scarf. She expected Bassam to come in and change his clothes, but he didn't. When she exited the bedroom, he put on his leather jacket and called to Khaled, who was still outside, to come put on his jacket.

"You're going like that?" she asked.

"Why not?" Indeed, he looked fine, his short-sleeved, periwinkle shirt perfectly crisp and gray pants neatly pressed. Still, she suspected he hadn't come into the bedroom to change his shirt because he didn't want to be alone with her.

The wedding was in a hall in Biddya, a short drive from their house. Since Chloe had their car, they rode with Marwan and his family, piled into the back seat with two kids on each lap.

Piercing ululations drew Rania inside. She left Bassam greeting his cousins and walked inside, where women and girls whirled in a furious *dabka*. Old women beat the tablas rhythmically, their gnarled hands flying. There were no men inside except the groom, seated with his bride on thrones on the dais. She did not know either of them. The groom was the son of one of Bassam's endless supply of cousins. The bride looked about sixteen, the groom close to thirty. She recalled that he had been working in the Gulf and had only come home to get married. She wondered if he would be taking his bride back with him or if he planned to live here for a while. With the economy the way it was, she doubted they could stay here for long. She felt sorry for the girl, if she was to be taken far away from her family so young. Maybe that was why she had a pasted-on smile beneath her ornately piled tendrils of hair.

Rania did not feel up to dancing yet. She hoped she would later. She had loved to dabka in her youth; she had been part of a troupe that traveled all over the West Bank for dabka contests. But, right now, she was still tired and confused from the last few days. She found a spot along the wall and allowed her mind to wander along with the music.

There was one other man in the room, she realized. He was putting the final touches on an eight-tiered cake, wielding a pastry tube as delicately as a paint brush. He finished and stepped back to check his handiwork. He moved slowly around the cake, making sure every rosette was the same. He finished and wheeled the trolley containing the cake up to the dais. The drummers beat a final crescendo and silenced their instruments. The girls stopped dancing and melted into the walls, making room for the men who poured into the middle space.

Then, the presentation of gifts began. First, the bride's father came forward and looped several thick gold strands around his daughter's neck. Rania clapped heartily along with the others. By giving the jewelry to his daughter, he gave her power in the relationship. If her husband mistreated or left her, she could take her dowry with her. Then, the groom's father came forward. He presented a gold pocket watch to his son and silver earrings with some type of shimmering stone to the bride. Then came the uncles, mostly bearing pouches stuffed with cash, which they handed to the groom, of course. Bassam stepped forward and handed the groom something. Rania hoped he hadn't gotten overgenerous. After all, they barely knew these people, and he had just been lecturing her about buying falafel.

The men danced the bride and groom over to the cake, and they cut it in the traditional way, hand over hand. They fed each other a piece, and the photographer snapped away. Then, the men began to dance, holding hands in a tight circle. Bassam was not among them. He did not dabka. The women could not dance with the men present. They stood against the walls, clapping and chatting. It seemed Rania had missed her chance. But then, some women she didn't know grabbed her hands and led her, along with a string of other women, to a long, narrow alcove off the main room where they could hear the music. There was no room for a circle, so they made a line and danced. After a little while, she stopped thinking about Ahmed and Lior and Hanan and Daoud and Bassam and Chloe and Tina and just thought about how wonderful it felt to move her body, to be here among her people and not in prison. Someone passed sweet pineapple juice and then nuts and dates and cookies, and, eventually, pieces of wedding cake made it back to where they were.

As suddenly as it had begun, it was over, and everyone quickly gathered their possessions. There must be another wedding coming in. It was often like that on Fridays, one stacked against another. When she reentered the hall, she saw that the thrones were empty. The bride's brothers must already have escorted the couple to their wedding caravan. Rania took her purse and went to find them. People were piling into cars. She looked around for Bassam, but didn't see him. He and Khaled must have gone with Marwan to get the car. As she waited uncertainly, she heard her name and turned.

"Abdelhakim," she said. "I didn't know you would be here." Why was it that the one person she hoped not to run into turned up everywhere she went?

"The bride's brother is my friend from college," he said. "These are their cousins, Yusuf and Elias," he added, indicating the two young men near him.

"Itsharafna," honored to meet you, she said.

"You too," said Yusuf. Elias said nothing.

Yusuf looked to be a few years younger than she, in his early thirties. He had serious brown eyes and a neatly trimmed beard. Elias was probably ten years younger than his brother, taller and thinner. His chiseled features reminded her of the American movie star, Leonardo DiCaprio. She supposed someone that good-looking could get away with sullenness.

"Abdelhakim says you are a policewoman," he said.

"Abdelhakim is kind," she said, thinking that was the last adjective that could ever be attributed to her former coworker. "I *was* a policewoman. Now, I am nothing."

"Hardly nothing," Abdelhakim said. "You are a mother, are you not?"

She blushed hotly. How dare he imply that she put no value on her family? But he was only trying to embarrass her. She wished she hadn't given him the satisfaction.

"Besides," he added, "she is going to be training a women's police force soon."

"I never said that," she said.

"I have confidence in you." Confidence that no other opportunity will come to you, he meant.

"A women's police force," Yusuf said. "Tell me about that."

He sounded genuinely interested. Rania almost wished she had something to tell him.

"I hardly know anything myself," she said. "I think the idea is to train women to intervene when women's behavior, or the behavior of their families," she added, glaring at Abdelhakim, "puts them in danger."

"That is a good idea," Yusuf said. "I think most women would much rather talk to another woman when they have such a problem."

"You really think so?" she asked. "Is it not condescending to imagine that we need our own special police force?" Not to mention that our personal conduct needs policing, she thought but did not say.

"Not at all," Yusuf said. "It is a smart way of handling the complex demands of modernity in a way that respects our culture and its traditions."

"Thank you," she said. "You have given me something to think about."

"Ustaz Horani wins the day," Elias said. He strode away in the direction of the caravan which was assembling behind the bridal car with its long train of tin cans and halo of balloons.

"I do not think your brother likes me," Rania said to Yusuf.

"Don't take it personally," Yusuf said. "He is a temperamental artiste. He cannot be bothered with mere mortals."

She chuckled. "What kind of artist?"

"He studies piano at the conservatory. He is very talented." He was clearly proud of his brother.

"He called you Ustaz. What do you teach?" she asked. Had it been her imagination, or had Elias been in a big hurry to disappear?

"I teach sociology at Al Quds Open University," Yusuf answered. "In fact," he said, "I would like to invite you to speak to my class in the next two weeks. We are doing a unit on the role of police in our society, compared to western societies."

"I would love to do that." Rania said. If she could not do her work, at least she could talk about it. She was starting to feel more like herself already.

"Give me your phone number, and I will call to arrange it." Yusuf was already pushing the buttons on his mobile. She gave him the number.

"Tell me," she said, hoping her tone was casual. "Did your brother have a friend at the conservatory named Daoud al-Khader?"

His face clouded over. "Yes, they were roommates," he said. "Daoud was martyred, you know."

"I know." She saw Marwan's car pulling up at the end of the line of vehicles. Khaled leaned out the window, clutching a green balloon.

"Mama, come on!" he called.

"I must go," she said to Yusuf.

"I will call you tomorrow about the class," he said.

Chapter 28

Chloe almost didn't recognize Reem when she got into the front seat. Her face was drawn and whiter than a corpse's.

"Kiif halik?" How are you? Chloe asked, trying to sound cheerful and not appalled.

"Al-Hamdullilah," Praise God, Reem said. Chloe remembered an American friend who lived in Egypt telling her about a time when she had sprained her ankle on the way to work. When her boss asked her how she was doing, she made the mistake of complaining about her injury, and he simply pointed to the sky, reminding her to give thanks for her blessings.

Chloe was silent as she pulled onto the settler highway. She concentrated on accelerating smoothly, shifting into fourth at the right moment. She wanted to give Reem an opening to talk about what she was going through, but she wasn't sure how to do it.

"You look thin," she said finally.

"I have not been hungry at all."

"Were you sick?" She didn't know if Reem would understand that "sick" was a euphemism for throwing up, but she wasn't going to ask a Palestinian she barely knew if she had been puking her guts out.

"A little. I have been very tired."

"I bet. How many children do you have?"

"Four."

"Wow. How old?"

"The oldest is twenty-one and the youngest is seven." Reem didn't look old enough to have a twenty-one-year-old, but Chloe had learned not to be surprised by that. Reem probably had her first child at sixteen or seventeen. Chloe would have liked to ask, but she didn't want to offend, so she just counted backwards.

"Were you able to work?" She remembered Reem saying that she wanted to work during her treatments.

"We had school only the first week. Last week was a holiday. I went only one day."

Too bad, Chloe thought, that the holiday hadn't come a little later in the process. If Reem was looking this ill already, in a few weeks, she might be too weak to go out at all. She cast about for safe subjects to talk about.

"Do your children like English, too?" she finally asked.

"The oldest, my son, teaches English in our village. My daughter is studying in America."

"Really? Which state?"

"Mi—Michigan?" She pronounced it with the hard *ch*.

"What is she studying?"

"Now she studies English. When her English improves, she will study international relations."

"She must be very smart."

"She is. But my youngest daughter is the smartest of all. She can already speak English better than I do."

"That's saying a lot, because your English is great. Far better than my Arabic," Chloe said.

"Arabic is a very difficult language to learn," Reem said. Her voice sounded strained, and Chloe wondered if she would rather not have to make the effort to chat. But Chloe was too nervous to maintain silence.

"People always say that. But why is it more difficult than other languages? They're all difficult, at least for me."

"Arabic is one of the oldest languages, so it has many more words."

Chloe had heard that before. She found it hard to believe. She had learned at least eight Arabic words for "group," but each one had a corresponding word in English: society, organization, association, committee, community, and so forth. That was true for just about every Arabic word she knew.

They had reached the checkpoint. Chloe presented the permit and their IDs and counted to twenty while the soldier examined them. He handed them back silently and waved them through. Both Reem and she let out deeply held breaths.

"I hope he is there every time we pass," Reem said.

"Amen—insha'alla," Chloe said.

"How is Tina?" Reem asked, after a few moments of quiet.

"She is…fine. She's gone to meet some friends. She has been very busy with work."

"What is her work?"

Chloe thanked the Goddess that her effort to change the subject had worked. "She works at a counseling center for women whose husbands are violent toward them and their children."

"That is good—we need that. She is a good woman, like Um Khaled."

"Yes." Chloe seized the opportunity to stop talking about Tina. "What do women in the villages think about Rania, Um Khaled, being a policewoman?"

Reem said nothing for several moments, and Chloe wondered if she had said something wrong. But, just as she thought she needed to apologize, without knowing what for, Reem spoke.

"All the women love her. Why would they not? She is a very nice person."

All that time to come up with "nice"? "Yes, but she is different from many of the women here in this area."

"They accept that because she is a refugee. She protects our people."

"But maybe women do not understand the way she does it."

"They are a little afraid of her."

"Intimidated."

"I do not know that word."

"Sorry, it means being afraid of someone, usually because we think they are better than we are in some way." See, English has a lot of words too, Chloe wanted to say.

"Say it again?"

"In-ti-mi-da-ted," Chloe repeated slowly.

"Intimidated," Reem said. "I must write it down." She fished in her large purse for a pen and paper. "Can you spell it, please?"

Chloe did. "You're lucky," she said, "that you can read and write in English. I can hardly read Arabic at all, so it takes me longer to remember a word. Writing is a good way to program something into your body memory."

"I can teach you," Reem said.

"I wouldn't want to make more work for you, while you are ill," Chloe said.

"I will enjoy it. You are helping me so much."

"Thank you. I will take you up on that. But there is something else you could help me with too, if you wouldn't mind."

"Anything."

That was such a Palestinian response; Chloe couldn't help but smile. An American would never make such an open-ended promise.

"I want to make a video about some of the women who were elected to the local governments," she said. "I would like to interview you, and also some of the other women on your council. Could you introduce me to some of them and translate for me?"

"Certainly," Reem said.

"How many women were elected to your council?" Chloe asked.

"We were four. Under the quota, we only needed to have two," Reem said proudly.

"And are you all from Fatah?"

"No. Two of us were elected from Hamas." Two of us. Did that mean that Reem was a member of Hamas? Chloe had assumed Reem would be a member of Fatah, because her brother, Rania's boss, was high up in that party. But perhaps Reem's husband was Hamas, or maybe she had joined on her own. Chloe could not think how to ask.

She was spared the need to ask anything for the moment, because she was pulling into the hospital parking lot.

"I can let you off at the front door, if you like," she offered.

"No, I can walk," Reem said.

Chloe found a parking spot and managed to get the car into first, reverse, and neutral in succession without too much grinding of gears. Reem let out a long, shuddering sigh as they walked through the double doors into the gloomy hallway. Chloe reached for her hand and squeezed it.

As soon as Dr. Rahman had situated the IV in her left arm, Reem took out her notebook and a pen. She turned to a blank page and quickly wrote out the Arabic alphabet.

"What letter is this?" she asked Chloe.

"Alef," Chloe responded. That, at least, she knew.

"This one?"

"Ra." That was an easy one to recognize. It was the little circle ones and the ones that were all squiggles and dots that she had trouble telling apart.

They went through the alphabet. Chloe got most of them right, but the order was confusing.

"Now you write them. Copy each letter five times," Reem ordered. Chloe thought she liked her better as a cancer patient than a teacher, but she extracted her own notebook from her pack and diligently copied the letters. When she had finished her assignment, Reem's eyes were closed, and her even breathing told Chloe she was asleep. Chloe opened her novel and let it sit on her lap while she thought.

If Reem was Hamas, would she not want Chloe to drive her if she knew she was Jewish? Chloe had never met anyone from Hamas. Well, that was probably not true. She had never met anyone who *told* her they were from Hamas. If Reem was Hamas, would Chloe still *want* to drive her?

"Do you want something to drink?" A Palestinian woman, with black hair peeking out of her blue scrub cap, was fingering Reem's IV. "She will be done in about half an hour."

"No, thanks," Chloe said. "I'm fine."

"It is nice of you to bring her," the nurse said in English.

"It's nothing."

"It is not nothing." The young woman reached into her pocket and handed Chloe a small packet of Bamba.

"Thank you," Chloe said. The nurse wandered out of the room. Chloe wondered if every Palestinian who worked in the hospital was designated to care for Reem or if Palestinian Israelis made up a disproportionate share of the medical staff. She tore open the cellophane square and popped one of the corn puffs into her mouth. It was basically a peanut butter Cheeto. She was hungrier than she had realized. She tried not to make too much noise with her munching, but Reem didn't seem likely to wake up any time soon.

✴ ✴ ✴

Since it was Friday, Reem's husband and younger children were home when they returned. A Sabbath meal of chicken and rice was already set on the table. Chloe assumed Reem had made it before she left. She had probably been up at six cooking, despite her dragginess. Now she collapsed in an armchair, as if even the drive had drained her.

"You must eat with us," said Reem's husband, Jawad.

"Thank you, but I need to get the car back to Abu Khaled." She had no idea if that was true. Bassam had told her they had a wedding to go to, and she didn't know what time they would be back. But she didn't want to sit here and have a gloomy dinner with a family living through cancer, and she didn't want Reem to have to stay alert and entertain her.

"Please, I insist," Jawad said.

"Thank you, another time," Chloe said.

He accepted the third refusal, which meant he didn't really want her to stay either. Chloe was relieved. She accepted a cup of tea, which he continued to offer long after her three refusals. He left the room to go make the tea.

Chloe shifted uncomfortably on the couch. She liked kids, but she was always awkward around them at first.

"Shu ismik?" she asked the little girl, who sat in an armchair to her right. The girl's hair was dark brown fuzz held back from her face with a faded pink headband.

"Amalia."

"Qaddeesh umrik, Amalia?" How old are you? So far, it was easy to make conversation. These were the questions everyone asked her nonstop.

"Sabah sneen." Seven years old.

"Btihki Inglizi mnih, sah?" You speak English well, right? Chloe remembered Reem saying her youngest spoke the best English in the family.

"I like to speak English very much," the little girl said solemnly.

Directly over the girl's head hung a framed picture of Khaled Mashal, his expression clerically stern. Last year, Yasser Arafat's face had adorned the walls of every Palestinian house. Now, the households were split between those where Arafat still reigned supreme and those that had replaced him with Mashal. It must be true, then, that Reem and Jawad were members of Hamas.

Jawad returned with the tea. He poured for his wife, who roused herself to drink it, and handed a glass to Chloe. It was sweet and liberally flavored with fresh mint. It tasted delicious. While she drank her tea, she repeated a story she had heard from a farmer whom she had helped pick olives. He was invited to the home of an Israeli coworker, he thought, for a meal. When he arrived, they had not made anything, and they explained that they didn't know what he would want to eat, so they had waited. What did he want?

"Oh, nothing, I'm not hungry," he said, confident that they would insist. Indeed, his friend's wife suggested many possibilities. Would he like chicken, cheese, eggs? He repeated that he was not hungry. Then, they shrugged and said, "Okay, if you are sure." And he never got anything to eat!

Reem and Jawad laughed appreciatively. Chloe took her bows and exited stage left. For all the mileage she had gotten out of that story, she reflected as she drove, she should go find that farmer and pay him royalties. She was getting more used to shifting, anticipating the road's bumpy patches and sharp turns with her left foot on the clutch. She didn't stall once on the way to Mas'ha. She should be grateful to Tina. She had always wanted to be able to drive a stick.

She found Rania's house without too much difficulty and pulled the car in-between a tractor missing a wheel and two donkeys grazing. One of the donkeys looked up at her and brayed loudly. Good, if Rania and Bassam were home, they would come out. No one stirred in the house. She waited a few minutes and then knocked on the door. No answer. They must still be at the wedding.

She had had nothing to eat since early morning, except for the little packet of Bamba. She walked up the street until she found a shop where she could buy some bread and hummus and a box of Marawi apricot nectar. But where could she go to eat it? Women were not supposed to eat in public. She could get away with a lot as a foreigner, but she wasn't even living in this village and didn't want to offend their customs. Especially on a Friday in springtime, when so many people were sitting out on their porches. It was too hot to sit in the car. She took her lunch and walked through the town to the edge of the village, where the red roofs of Elkana settlement loomed just past the hulking gray Wall.

Chloe settled on the highest boulder next to the sun-yellow gate to eat her lunch, making sure to face away from the village in case anyone happened to walk by. She took the never-ending *Da Vinci Code* out of her pack. Much as she hated it, she also dreaded the day she finished it, because she didn't have another novel with her. She would have to go to Jerusalem to find an English-language bookstore or borrow one of the dreary, existentialist novels in Avi's collection.

She heard a jeep crunching the stones on the security road across the Fence. She looked up as it screeched to a halt, then went back to her half-hearted reading.

"Come here," boomed the megaphone mounted on top of the jeep. Chloe couldn't see the person it belonged to. She also could not "come here," because the Fence stood in-between them. Presumably they meant for her to get up and come stand next to the gate. She wouldn't. If they wanted her, they could come get her. She diligently looked down at her book, seeing nothing.

"Hey! I'm talking to you." The soldier was out of his jeep now. He was small and rat-faced, his close-cropped, dark hair partially covered by a blue and white crocheted skullcap. Another soldier got out on the driver's side. He was taller and heftier and wore no skullcap. They both looked slightly familiar, but she didn't waste time trying to figure out where she might have seen them. She had seen so many soldiers when she was here before—at checkpoints, home invasions, demonstrations, patrolling the villages. They all looked more or less alike.

"What are you doing here?" the rat-faced soldier asked.

"Waiting for some friends."

"Who?"

"None of your business." At least they spoke English, so she could use the retorts that came readily to mind, though, if they didn't, she could just pretend she didn't know any Hebrew.

"It is our business. You are in a closed military area."

"I am not. I'm in a Palestinian village which is none of your concern."

"See this fence?" He gestured expansively from the concrete Wall to the Fence and the gate. "We built it. It is for our security. The area where you are sitting is part of the security zone. See that sign?" He pointed to a red sign with white letters posted on the Fence about five feet from where Chloe sat. Mortal Danger, it read in English, followed by (she assumed) the same in Arabic and Hebrew. "Whoever Touches or Damages This Fence ENDANGERS HIS LIFE."

"Look, I didn't touch the fence. I am sitting on a rock in a Palestinian village, minding my own business. Which you should learn to do."

She turned away from them and sat facing the village. She made herself read. Robert Langdon was finding out that Sophie was the long-lost descendant of Mary Magdalene and Jesus. About time, Chloe said to herself. Why were people in novels always so dense? Dense! The word roused her from her self-imposed stupor, just as the jeep's engine fired to life.

"Ron!" she yelled, racing back to the gate. For a second, she thought they were going to drive off. Instead, they drove straight toward the gate, stopping only inches from the steel bars. She pressed up against her side of the Fence, lacing her fingers through the wire mesh. The two soldiers jumped out, their fingers caressing the triggers of their guns.

"Who are you?" the short soldier squawked.

"A friend of Daoud's."

"No, you're not," the taller one said.

"Who is Daoud?" asked Rat Face.

The kids had said he was the one who was shooting, and Daoud had called him "Ron." But the tall one had recognized the name Daoud.

"You *are* Ron, right?" she asked the taller guy.

"I don't know you," he said.

"Well, I know you. Daoud talked about you."

"I don't know anyone named Daoud."

"Then why did you say I was not his friend?"

"What's going on?" asked the short soldier.

"Nothing. She's just making trouble. Maybe we should arrest her."

"Do you have your passport?" asked Rat Face.

"That's for me to know and you to find out." She doubted they would come over to this side and arrest her. They probably didn't even have the key. But she had gotten herself in trouble before by thinking she could bluff an Israeli military man. She had almost died because of it. She walked quickly down the road that led into the village. She didn't hear the jeep leave before she was out of earshot.

* * *

When she got back to Rania's compound, Bassam was sitting on the porch with two men who looked just like him. They were laughing and smoking cigars.

"Thank you for letting me use the car," she said, handing him the keys. "Is Rania in the house?"

Bassam nodded. Chloe wished he would get up to tell Rania she was here, but he didn't, so she gathered she was invited to enter the house. Khaled was in the living room, riding his bike through a maze composed of books and toys. He was as adorable as she remembered him.

"Marhaba, Khaled. Ana Chloe," she said. Hello, I'm Chloe.

"Ahleen," hello, he said, not looking up from the course he was navigating.

"Weyn imik?" she asked him.

"Fi matbach." His mother was in the kitchen. Chloe had never been past the living room, but she clearly was not going to get any help finding her way. She wandered through the only doorway and found herself in a hall where the bathroom occupied the central spot. Two closed doors flanked it to the left, but she glimpsed a pantry-laundry room to the right. She correctly surmised that the kitchen must be past that, with a door to the back yard. She found Rania cutting cucumbers and tomatoes into tiny cubes for salad.

"How was the wedding?" Chloe asked.

Rania spun around, startled. She quickly composed her face into a welcoming smile. "It was lovely," she said, after they kissed. "How is Um Saad?"

"She's okay," Chloe said. "Can I talk to you while you cook? I have a couple things to tell you."

"T'faddali." Rania gestured to a plastic armchair next to the small, round table where she was working. Chloe settled into it.

"Can I help?" she asked belatedly. Then, she blushed. Would Rania think she was angling for an invitation to dinner?

"No, thank you. I like to chop things. It helps me think."

"You did seem deep in thought. I'm sorry I interrupted you. What were you thinking about?"

"I met a young man at the wedding, and he asked me to speak to his class at the university about the role of police in our society. I was thinking about what I will tell them."

"How interesting. What will you say?"

"Police in our society are different than in independent societies. In America, for instance, the police protect ordinary citizens from the people who violate your society's laws."

"That's the theory," Chloe said. "But, in reality, the police maintain the social order. So, they enforce the laws against people the government wants to keep at the bottom and protect the people at the top."

"I had not thought of that. What I know about your police comes mostly from television shows."

Chloe recalled that when she had first told Rania she came from San Francisco, Rania had asked if she knew Michael Douglas from *The Streets of San Francisco*.

"Even some of the TV shows depict that reality," Chloe said. "Did you ever see *Hill Street Blues* or *Cagney & Lacey*?" Chloe had no idea what American television was available in Palestine.

"I loved *Cagney & Lacey*," Rania said. "That's why I wanted to be a policewoman!"

"It's not exactly like real life…but some of the episodes were really good. Showed the complexity of race and gender and class."

Rania tilted the cutting board onto a green glass bowl and pushed in the tomatoes and cucumbers. She took an immense bulb of white garlic and broke off three cloves. While she chopped the first one, Chloe peeled the other two.

"Sorry," Chloe said, "you were talking about how it's different in Palestine."

"No need to be sorry. I like talking to you about these things. Understanding your society helps me to better understand my own. But, what I was saying is, in our society, enforcing our laws is secondary to protecting the people against the occupier. Since we do not have an army, the police substitute for that role in many ways. We look for people who may be working on behalf of the Israelis, we make sure that demonstrations in the cities are not attacked by the army, and we help people make peace with their neighbors so that they cannot be so easily turned against one another."

"But don't the police also prevent demonstrations sometimes? I read recently that the PA outlawed Hamas demonstrations just after the elections."

"Yes, because they were an effort to further destabilize the country. We need to show the Americans and Europeans that we are in control, that the situation is calm, so that they will restore the funding they have blocked."

"But then aren't you doing. . . No offense, I'm not trying to tell you how to run your country, but isn't that the same as what American police do? Keeping the people in power at the top?"

Rania scraped the chopped garlic from the cutting board into the salad bowl. "I don't think it is the same. I don't know enough about your country to say, but I believe that the PA has the best interests of my people at heart."

"Even though they won't let you go back to your job?"

"Yes. Although it is hard for me, I understand that decision. They cannot allow someone to work in the police until they are sure that person is not an informer."

"But they asked you to train the women's force, so they must trust you."

"The women's force is not real police. It is a way of enforcing social norms that I'm not even sure should be enforced. It is more like what you are saying your police do." Rania was done with the salad, having squirted a lemon over the vegetables and added salt and pepper. She measured a cup of rice into a saucepan and covered it with water. She set the pot on the stove and lit the flame.

"Do you think if you find out who killed this boy, Daoud, you will get your old job back?" Chloe asked.

"I don't know. I suppose it depends on what I find out. If he was killed because of something related to his being…gay…or being friendly with Israeli soldiers, people would probably rather I left it alone."

"Then, if you don't mind my asking, why don't you?"

"I don't know. I have been asking myself that. I guess because if our society cannot accept the truth, even in a case like this, then we cannot hope to achieve true justice."

"True justice," Chloe mused. "Do you think there is such a thing?"

"There has to be," Rania said. "As a Palestinian, the only thing you can hope for is that there is true justice in the world, which will someday come even to us."

"I find that kind of ideal hard to believe in." Chloe berated herself. If Rania could still believe such a pure form of justice was possible after a month in Israeli prison, who was she to dismiss it?

"Daoud might have been killed by the army after all," Chloe said. That's what I came to tell you. Avi and I went to Kufr Yunus yesterday."

Rania was visibly not pleased.

"I called to tell you," Chloe said. "But you didn't answer your phone."

"I was in Aida, visiting an old friend," Rania said. "There's terrible reception in the camp."

"I wanted Avi to make a picture of the place Daoud's body was found and the soldiers who the kids saw him arguing with. Here they are." She pulled the two drawings from her backpack.

"Your friend draws well," Rania observed, studying the pictures.

"Yes. I saw these soldiers today, just here outside the gate. One of them is named Ron."

"Which one?"

"I am pretty sure it's this one, but the kids told us the other one was shooting at them, and they said Daoud called him Ron when he yelled at him to stop."

"I could show it to Benny," Rania said thoughtfully. "Though who knows what he would do with it. Even if he knew who they were, I doubt he would tell me. But I don't know how else to find out."

"Um Mahmoud gave us some bullets," Chloe said. "She picked them up the night Daoud was killed, but who knows how long they had been there. I'm going to take them to the Red Cross to have them analyzed. There were some blood stains on the rocks where he fell. That's what I wanted to tell you. I figured you'd want to look at them."

"You are right. But I need to see the police report before I go. Otherwise, I won't know what to look for. Give me the drawings. I will make copies and take them to Benny and make him show me his report." Chloe wondered how Rania was going to make Benny do anything, but that wasn't her problem.

Rania took the two drawings out of Chloe's hand. Chloe hated to let them go, but it was Rania's case—insofar as it was a case at all. She had done her duty. She got up to go.

"Won't you eat with us?" Rania asked. Even though the invitation was belated, Chloe didn't think it was pro forma. Too bad she had to refuse. The kitchen was starting to fill up with the pungent smell of chicken. But Chloe didn't eat chicken, and she wasn't hungry, having just eaten.

"Not today, thanks. I need to get to Azzawiya."

"I wanted to ask you about something first." Chloe sat back down.

"The friend I visited in Aida," Rania began. She fidgeted with her sleeves, unrolling the cuffs and rolling them up again. "She is gay." She pronounced the word carefully. Chloe raised her eyebrows. She had been sure that Rania didn't know any gay people. The other day, she had not even seemed to know they existed.

"She just told me yesterday," Rania said, reading her confusion. "Or, in fact, I guessed."

"Once you know about it, it's everywhere," Chloe said with a smile.

Rania did not smile back. Her expression was serious. "She is very sad," Rania said. "I do not know whether that has anything to do with this."

Chloe knew what "this" meant, but it made her smile involuntarily.

"But I would like to know if there is something I can do to help her. I suggested we go to Adloyada together, but she said she did not want to."

"A bar might not be the right thing," Chloe said. "But there is a group for Palestinian lesbians." She saw that Rania did not understand the English word. "Gay women," she amended. "Their group is called SAWA. It's like a support group for gay women. Tina is a member."

"I would really like my friend to know about them," Rania said. She contemplated her sleeve for a long moment. "Perhaps I could call Tina and find out about it?"

"Of course," Chloe said. Maybe she should have asked Tina before telling Rania about the group. But Tina would certainly want to help a Palestinian lesbian. She wrote down the number on the pad Rania produced and stood up once more.

"You are staying at Abu Fareed's house?" Rania asked. Chloe nodded. Rania knew Ahlam and Jaber from Fatah circles.

"We will drive you," Rania said. She stood and untied her apron. "Bassam," she called out. Chloe put out a hand to stop her.

"No, please," she said. "The walk will do me good, really." She kissed her friend's cheeks three times rapidly and left quickly, to let her know she meant it.

* * *

"Why did your friend leave?" Bassam asked when Rania called him for dinner.

"Chloe, you mean?" For some reason, his use of the word *sahibtik* irritated Rania, seeming to imply she had only one friend.

"Chloe, yes. I thought she would stay for dinner."

"She was going to Abu Fareed's."

"Ah." He took three rounds of bread from the plate by the stove and placed one on the open gas flame, turning it over rapidly so it did not burn. "What did you discuss?"

"She and her friend Abe went to Kufr Yunus. They spoke with some of the children who saw Daoud fight with the soldiers and received some bullets from the area where he was killed."

"Not only are you investigating his death without official permission, but you are getting foreigners and Israelis involved?"

He placed the warm bread on the counter and put the next one on the low flame.

"I didn't ask Chloe to go. It was her own idea. She needs something to do with herself also."

"What is she doing here, anyway?"

"How can you ask that? She came to get me out of prison, and she succeeded."

"I thought you did not know why they released you."

She stared at him, hands on hips.

"What are you suggesting?"

"I was not suggesting anything. Just asking a question."

"You told me you liked Chloe."

"I didn't say I didn't like her. I just asked what she is doing here. I never understood why she came to Palestine in the first place."

"You have a tongue. Why don't you ask her?"

"Forget it." He put the plate of warm bread on the table. "Khaled," he called. "Ta'al, n'okel" come, let's eat.

Khaled appeared at once, pulling out his chair with a clatter. Rania suspected if she had called, it would have taken at least three invitations and a trip to the living room. He tore off half a round of bread and started to dip into the hummus with it.

"Khaled," she said. "Use a smaller piece." He looked like he would argue, but then he tore the piece of bread in half again and let half drop onto the table in front of him. She supposed it was a good sign that he did what she asked.

"Chloe told me once that her parents raise money for Israel," she said as her husband and son dug into the salads. She picked up an olive and chewed it thoughtfully. "I think she is trying to make up for what they do."

"Hmm," her husband said. He scooped a handful of mujaddara, mixed rice and lentils, into his mouth. "Do you think she is a spy?"

"Bassam! How can you say that?"

"I am just asking. You cannot be too careful."

Rania looked down at the rice and lentils on her plate. She separated the rice so it looked like a face, with two lentil eyes.

"Khaled, what did you think of the wedding?" she asked.

"It was boring," he said, his mouth full of lentils. "I don't like weddings."

"You didn't like the dancing?"

"I don't like to dance. And there was nothing else to do. I only liked it at the end when they set off explosions." A burst of firecrackers always announced the arrival of the bridal party at the groom's home. Rania sighed.

"Perhaps when you are a little older, you will enjoy dancing," she said. "Your father was a very good dabka dancer once."

"Really, Baba?"

"No, not really. Your mother is just being nice." Bassam smiled at her. They had first met at a high school dabka competition where the boys and girls competed separately. When they had met again, two years later at Bethlehem University, she had not remembered him, but he had reminded her. Her team had won that competition. His had not even made the finals.

"You were better than you thought," she said. She got up to clear the dishes.

"Are you tired?" Bassam asked his son.

"No."

"You should get ready for bed anyway. Tomorrow is a school day."

She had just finished putting the dishes away when her husband reappeared in the kitchen. The quiet in the house told her that her son had yielded to exhaustion.

"I wasn't trying to come between you and your friend," he said. She filled the coffee pot with water and put it on to boil.

"In Bethlehem, I had a whole circle of friends," she said. "You remember. Maysoon, Samia, Abeer, Aya, and I, we were in and out of each other's houses all the time. Then I came here, and nothing was the same. No one understands me."

"You get along well with my sisters," he objected.

"Dunya and Jaleela, yes. They are political, like us. Though their politics—" she laughed. One of his sisters was a Communist, and the other had voted for Hamas in the legislative elections. "But Chloe is an outsider, so we can talk about things that would be hard to discuss with others."

"Such as?" His brow furrowed a little.

"Things like…why she is not married. She says that in America, a lot of women do not get married. I never thought about it, but she seems happy."

"How can someone be happy being alone all the time?"

"She's not alone. She has friends…she lives with another woman, who is single also. They share everything." She had to change the subject, quick. She spooned the coffee into the pot and let it bubble up to the top, stirred it, and set it back over the heat. "Look at your mother. She lives alone, and she is happy enough."

"It's not the same. She has us. She has Khaled here and her other sons and grandchildren right here in the compound."

"Yes, and she has our lives to try to run. But if she didn't, doubtless she would find something else to occupy herself with. She's not going to sit and sulk just because your father died."

"True."

She poured the coffee and they sipped it quietly. She hoped she had not said too much.

Chapter 29

Light streamed in through the big picture windows in Chloe's old flat above Ahlam and Jaber's home. She squirmed on the futon, gauging the sun coming through the branches of the plum tree. She missed this peaceful place. She had no clock or watch, no idea what time it was. She hoped Ahlam had not already left for work. It would be incredibly rude to sleep until mid-morning and slip off without saying goodbye, but Ahlam would never have woken her. She bathed quickly, ran her fingers through her hair, and ran downstairs.

Ahlam was in the living room, dressed for work and pouring tea for Fareed, who flopped in an armchair looking like he had fallen out of bed. He rubbed his eyes and jumped up to greet Chloe.

"Welcome, my sister," he said pumping her hand. His eyes glowed. He owed her his freedom—her and Rania and Avi, and he was a kid who took his debts seriously.

"Fareed. Nice to see you. How is school?" He was studying politics at Al Quds Open University in Salfit.

"Good. There is a new teacher there, Ustaz Yusuf Horani. He is very good, and he is helping me apply for scholarships to American universities."

"You want to go to the States?"

"Only for a while. Many important leaders in our country studied there, like Hanan Ashrawi."

Chloe was impressed that he had chosen a woman as his role model. She should not be surprised; he was Ahlam's son, after all. "Let me know if I can do anything to help."

"Thank you."

Ahlam returned with a breakfast tray—fries, labneh, and *manaqish*, little rounds of bread baked with oil and zataar. She poured more tea for Chloe.

"Eat, Chloe," she said.

"Bless your hands," Chloe said. She broke off a piece of manaqish and dipped it into the creamy, white labneh. Ahlam made a small plate for herself and joined Chloe on the couch.

"How is Um Khaled?" she asked, using Rania's honorific nickname.

"She's fine. It's hard for her because they won't let her go back to work yet. But she might be starting a women's police force." Why had she said that? Rania didn't even want to do the women's force.

"A women's police force for what?" Ahlam asked.

"She isn't sure. Some people want it to be kind of a morals police. You know, prostitution, girls having sex before they're married. She doesn't want to do that."

"I would think not," Ahlam said. She was active in women's affairs, running a network of women's development clubs throughout the region.

"Rania, Um Khaled, is trying to find out what happened to the young man who was killed in Kufr Yunus a couple weeks ago," Chloe said, not wanting to dwell on the women's police force. "You must have heard about that. Daoud al-Khader, I think was his name."

"I knew him," Fareed said. "Some actors from a theater in Jerusalem came to put on a play in Salfit, when we were in high school. Daoud was in it. I was too."

"I didn't know you liked acting."

"As it turns out, I don't." They all laughed. "But Daoud loved it. He was a lot of fun."

"So I hear."

Ahlam stood up and took the breakfast tray toward the kitchen. Chloe got up too and gathered up the tea glasses.

"Will you stay again tonight?" Ahlam asked on her way out of the house.

"No," Chloe said. "I should go back to Ramallah. But I will come again soon."

"You are always welcome," Ahlam said. She kissed Chloe and headed out.

"Fareed, wait," Chloe said to stop the young man from vanishing into his bedroom after his mother was gone.

"Did you need something?"

"I wondered…since you knew Daoud. Did you know anything about who his friends were?"

"Are you asking if I knew he was homosexual?" Fareed used the derogatory Arabic word, luuti.

"I was, yes. I'm sorry if it seems like I'm prying. But someone told us that he had a boyfriend in these villages, and Rania really needs to talk to him. She would be very discreet." She in fact had no idea how discreet Rania planned to be, but she trusted her friend.

"I don't know for sure," he said. "But there was another kid in the play. They seemed very close. I think he came from Jamai'in."

"Do you remember his name?"

Fareed wrinkled his face, as if trying to squeeze the memory to the surface. "I think it was Elias," he said. "He played the piano well."

✶ ✶ ✶

"Marhaba, Tina," Rania said, when Tina answered the phone. "Do you have a minute?"

"Taba'an," of course, Tina replied. "What's going on?"

"Chloe told me you are in a group for Palestinian gay women," Rania said. Pregnant silence met her from the other end. She hoped she had not said something wrong. "I believe it could be very helpful to a friend of mine," she continued.

"I see," Tina said. There was another long pause. "I need to check with the others," Tina said at last. "But it might be possible for your friend to come."

"Oh, no, that is not what I had in mind."

"What, then?" Tina's voice betrayed relief, as well as a bit of impatience.

"I was hoping I could come myself."

"Not to a meeting," Tina said. "We do not allow outsiders at our meetings."

Outsiders, Rania thought, bristling. Tina might have been born here, but she still carried a foreign passport. Who exactly was the outsider here?

"I might be able to get a few of the women to meet with you separately," Tina was saying.

"That would be fine." Better, in fact. She didn't know what they did at their meetings, but she didn't necessarily want to sit through it. She wanted someone to tell her what she could do for Samia.

Tina called back an hour later. "We can meet you on Monday if that is convenient," she said.

"What time?" Rania asked.

"It must be after five, because we all have to work. Is that too late for you?"

"Where are we meeting?"

"It will be easiest to meet in Tel Aviv, at my friend Yasmina's house. I can see if someone could pick you up on the road with a yellow-plated car."

Rania thought about that. It would indeed be easier to get through the checkpoint that way, and she was very jumpy about checkpoints these days. But, if someone saw her on the road, they would wonder where she was going, and she did not want Bassam or anyone else to ask about that.

"Could you pick me up at the bus station in Petah Tikva?" she suggested.

"Fine, see you then."

✳ ✳ ✳

Chloe dropped the bullets off at the offices of the International Committee of the Red Cross in Salfit before going back to Ramallah. When she opened the apartment door, the smells of cardamom, cinnamon, and frying olive oil floated out to greet her. She went into the kitchen. Tina had her back to the door as she fished bits of cauliflower out of the hot oil.

"Mmmm," Chloe said. "Makluube?"

"What else do I make?" Tina turned around, smiling. She looked fetching in a sleeveless, black, girl tee emblazoned with Aussie Chick in white cursive.

"How was your meeting, Aussie chick?" Chloe asked. She told herself sternly to keep the bitterness out of her voice. Tina had a right to have other friends. She had had a life here for a whole year now, during most of which Chloe had been in San Francisco.

"It was good. How is Reem?"

"Fine, as far as I know. The appointment went well. She taught me to write Arabic."

"Oh yeah? Let's see." Chloe fished out the notepad with her carefully copied letters. Tina frowned at them.

"Your handwriting is awful."

"It's awful in English too. I brought some wine." She had stopped for a bottle of merlot in the Christian part of the city. She took it out of her pack. "Want some now?"

"Not yet. But it will be lovely with dinner."

"Shall I make salad?"

"No. I've got it covered. Go take a bath."

"I don't need a bath." Chloe bristled. "I took one at Ahlam's."

"Well, take another one."

Chloe grunted. She didn't want to fight with Tina, but she wasn't going to take a bath just to please her either. She tossed her pack in the living room and lay down on the couch.

"Would you at least go turn the water off, then?" She had not noticed that the bath water was running. Had Tina turned it on for her when she came in? That was sweet, even if she didn't want a bath. She went into the little bathroom. The water was trickling, which was why she hadn't heard it, but the tub was almost full. She dipped a finger in. It was pleasantly warm, for a warm day. Bubbles floated on the surface, and the room was suffused with a smell of eucalyptus. Tina must have brought the bubble bath from Australia. Little tea lights burned at the four corners of the tub and along the edge of the sink.

Chloe stripped her clothes off and wrapped a towel around herself for modesty before venturing into the kitchen. You never knew who might be watching. She didn't see anyone out the window, so she planted a quick kiss on Tina's shoulder before returning to the bathroom to strip off her towel.

✶ ✶ ✶

"Can we go to Adloyada after dinner?" she said over heavenly makluube. She felt refreshed from the tub and from Tina's warmth. Everything seemed right between them. Maybe the time away had done her good after all. "If that guy Lior is there, maybe he knows something about Ron."

"Who is Ron?"

"Oh, I have so much to tell you," Chloe said.

They finished their meal and piled the dishes in the sink to worry about later. They made it to Adloyada before the Saturday night rush began and picked a table near the door. If Lior or any of Daoud's Ramallah friends showed up, Chloe wanted to be able to corner them before they bolted.

By the time they were on their second beer, the place was so full Chloe didn't think a fly would be able to pass through. There was no show, but the DJ spun old English rock and roll mixed with loud, thunking Israeli pop, and the crowd, young and middle-aged, Jewish and Arab, male, female, and everything in-between, danced energetically and drank heartily. The decibel level rose to barely tolerable. There was no sign of Lior or the guys Rania had talked to.

Chloe was about to say "Let's go," when the door opened and a group of soldiers walked in. Chloe looked at their faces closely. She thought she would recognize Lior, but she had been tense, and it had been dark the other night. Soldiers tended to look alike to her, however much she told herself that they were people too. There was something about the green clothing that camouflaged them not only among scrub and olive trees but even among normally dressed civilians.

She studied the soldiers as they filed into the club. Lior was definitely not among them. But Ron was.

He started when he saw her. He moved quickly toward the door, barely saying anything to his friends. Chloe made it to the exit before him.

"Over here," she said. She caught his arm. She didn't know if it was illegal to grab a soldier when he was off-duty, but she was not afraid of this scrawny guy. Even though he had his gun with him, he seemed more or less afraid of his shadow. She led the way around the corner, into the tiny alley called Koresh. She kept hold of Ron's arm, though of course, he could flee at any time. Still, it was an odd role reversal, to be detaining an Israeli soldier. She sat him down on the concrete, second-floor steps of a motel-like office building, and took the step below him so she could trip him if he tried to leave.

"My name is Chloe," she began, hoping she might put him at ease. "I'm an American. I'm trying to help Daoud al-Khader's family find out what happened to him. I know you argued with him in the village that day. I know he called your name and said to stop shooting. But I also know that you were not the one shooting."

"He did not say, 'Stop shooting,'" Ron said.

She looked at him, surprised. She had not expected him to answer. She had just been rambling until she figured out some question to ask.

"He just said, 'Stop.'" Chloe thought back to her conversation with the kids. The boy, Mohammed, had reported that Daoud yelled, "Ron, stop." They had all assumed he meant "stop shooting," but now she realized he could have meant "Stop, I want to talk to you." Which would give his chasing the boys into the school a different meaning as well. He may have meant to protect them, but he also might have wanted them inside so that they would not see him conversing with Israeli soldiers.

"What did he want to talk to you about?"

"What makes you think he wanted to talk to me?"

"Why else did he stop you? You knew him from the club, right? I mean, he performed there regularly, so that makes sense. Were you lovers?"

"No! An Arab guy? Come on. I barely knew him."

"But he knew your name."

Ron picked up a cigarette butt from the stairs. It was a significant bit of a cigarette, obviously discarded by a chain smoker who didn't smoke a cigarette down before lighting the next one. Ron found the seam in the paper and began unrolling the cigarette, laying it out on the step. "My friend Lior was a friend of his. I just knew Daoud to say hi to. That day was the first day I ever talked to him."

"And what did he want?"

He had dismantled the entire cigarette now. He dumped the filter and began rerolling the tobacco into a little roll that resembled a joint. Must be a pot smoker, Chloe thought. "He wanted me to help him get asylum in Israel. He said his brother had threatened to kill him."

"Why would he tell you that, if you didn't even know him?"

"I don't know. Probably because I happened to be there. He seemed scared."

"Did he say why his brother threatened him?"

"He said Issa found out that he was performing at Adloyada." He rolled the little cigarette between the fingers of his left hand. His right rested casually on the butt of his rifle. The only time Chloe had been so close to a lethal weapon was last year, when one had been pointed at her heart.

"So, he asked you to help him get asylum. What did you say?"

"I said I couldn't help him. I don't know anything about getting asylum. I didn't want to talk to him. The guy I was with, Yonatan? He doesn't like gay people."

"Yonatan doesn't know you're gay?"

"No."

"So, you hit Daoud to keep him from outing you to Yonatan?"

"I didn't hit him. He hit me. All I did was push him away, and that's the truth." Ron got up abruptly. "I don't want to talk to you anymore. If you bother me again, I will arrest you and take you to jail." He got up and stepped over her legs, moving quickly up the street. She caught up with him as he was turning the corner onto Shushan.

"I've been in jail, so you don't scare me. What did Yonatan say after Daoud talked to you?"

"He asked how I knew him. I said he was a friend of Lior's."

They were nearly back at the bar. "Did he believe you?"

"None of your business," he said. He showed his gun to the bouncer and entered the bar with a smile. Chloe had to turn all her pockets inside out to get back in.

Chapter 30

"I need the police report."

Benny looked up at Rania from whatever he had been working on. His eyes bulged only as much as they usually did, not the extra bulging they did when he was surprised. The over-made-up policewoman at the front desk must have called to warn him she was on her way up.

"Why don't they stop you at the gate?" he asked. "Do you want some tea?"

"They know how much you want to see me. No, I am in a hurry, and I do not like your tea. Make me a copy of the report, and I'll let you get back to your work."

"You're so kind." He arched an eyebrow at her.

After spending so much time with him last year, she had practiced that one-eyed arch in the mirror. It was very effective at communicating sardonic disdain. She'd never been able to get it down.

"Well?" He made no move to look through the masses of folders covering every square inch of his office. "What have you found out?"

"Did I or did I not tell you I do not work for you?"

"Do you or do you not want to go back to prison?" That eyebrow ticked up again.

Her throat tightened in spite of her assuring herself he was just trying to get her goat. She removed a stack of folders from a chair and plopped down into it. She had meant to get the report out of him before showing him the picture of the soldiers. But he had not-so-subtly reminded her whose weapons were more powerful. She pulled the photocopied drawing out of her purse.

"These are the soldiers who were in the village that day," she said, tossing the picture onto his desk. He pulled it closer and moved his eyeglasses from the top of his head to the bridge of his nose.

"Who drew this?" he asked.

She wondered if there was any reason not to tell him. She didn't want to get Chloe in trouble. But the fact that an Israeli had drawn it, even one with a longer prison record than hers, might make him take it more seriously.

"Chloe's friend, Avi."

"Avi Levav?"

"I don't know his last name." Of course she did. But he knew too. If he had some reason for asking questions he knew the answers to, she must have some reason not to answer them.

He rolled his eyes at her. "Did anyone say which one hit him?"

She didn't know he had heard the hitting story, too. She shook her head. "They say this one shot at the boys," indicating the short one. "But Daoud yelled to this one, 'Ron, stop shooting.'"

"How do you know this is Ron? Surely the children couldn't tell which one he was yelling at."

"Chloe talked to them yesterday at Mas'ha Gate. She said this one knew Daoud."

"That's not much to go on."

"It is more than you have. Can you get me the police report now, please?"

He looked like he wanted to argue some more, but he got up and rifled through the folders on his desk. After looking through the top, bottom, and middle of every pile, he took the top folder from the pile next to his right hand and pulled out several stapled sheets. Could he really have not known that the file was right there? If it was right on top, he must have just been looking at it. She wondered why.

"Baruch!" he called out. His dark-skinned minion appeared and took the paper out of his hand. "One copy," he said in Hebrew.

"How is it being out of prison?" he asked when Baruch had left the room.

The folder he had taken the report out of was pretty thick, she thought. "It is fine. How else would it be? I hope I will never go back there in my life. What else is in that file?"

He chuckled. "You think I am going to share all my secrets with you? Witness statements, mostly."

She stood up and moved to take the folder off his desk. He grabbed it and tossed it into a drawer. That confirmed what she thought: it contained either information about her or about his informants in the village. Or both.

Baruch returned and handed the original and the copy to Benny. Benny handed her the copy and put the original in the drawer.

"Thanks," she said and made her exit. As soon as she was outside the station, she looked at the paper she held. Only then did it occur to her that she wouldn't be able to read it, because it was all in Hebrew.

✶ ✶ ✶

Ten years ago, the trip from Ariel to Salfit would have taken ten minutes through the fields. Now, she had to walk all the way down the hill out of the settlement, half an hour's walk, and wait for a servees which took the settler road to Yasuf. Almost forty-five minutes passed before she was at the police station in Salfit. When she got there, the young woman at the desk told her Captain Mustafa had gone for lunch with Abu Ziyad, the DCL.

She could likely find them at Abu Salaam's *shawarma* shop, but she tried to avoid Abu Ziyad as much as humanly possible. It wasn't easy, because he was close with her boss and probably the most powerful Palestinian official in the district, but it helped that he didn't like her either. Her boss had always defended her, but Abu Ziyad was his oldest friend. They had fought together, back in the old days, when Arafat was in Tunis. One of the captain's gifts was the ability to keep everyone happy.

As far as she knew, Captain Mustafa was the only person in the Salfit police who could read Hebrew. She looked around the little station. Her former coworkers were on the phone or conversing with one another or reading reports. One was reading *Al Hayat*. Some of them had let Khaled play under their desks while she worked, before he was old enough for school. But, now, they seemed to fear that the suspicion which attached to her might be contagious. A few had politely offered "Hamdullila assalaam," when she appeared, but none of them seemed at all interested in finding out what she was doing there. Except Abdelhakim.

"Um Khaled, welcome," he said with a broad smile that managed to seem more like a smirk.

"Abdelhakim." Last she had heard, he had transferred to Abu Ziyad's office, across the street. Now, he was sitting at her desk.

"Can I help you?" As if she were any citizen who came to report the theft of a goat. Trust him to emphasize that she no longer worked here.

"Do you read Hebrew by any chance?"

"Yes." She had asked the question being sure the answer would be no. He was too young to have been in prison during the First Intifada, and she knew he had not been arrested in the Second. She was also pretty sure he had never worked in a settlement.

"My father spoke it," he said, reading her thoughts. "He thought it was important that I learn it."

"And, you see, he was right. Can you translate this for me?" She handed over the police report. He scanned it, and his delicate brow furrowed.

"Where did you get this?"

She hesitated. Um Bassam had said it was Abdelhakim who told everyone Benny visited her in prison. She didn't want to give him more ammunition to spread rumors about her trustworthiness. But if she didn't answer, it would look like she had something to hide.

"From Benny Lazar."

"The Israeli policeman."

"Yes." If she were an informer, would she come here and show him information she had gotten from the Israeli police? The captain and Abu Ziyad were friendlier with Benny than she was. Were they informers? She had a whole dialog with him while he merely glanced coolly at her and looked down at the paper.

"This is about Daoud," he said.

"Yes."

"Why are you looking into his death?"

"The captain asked me to," she said. She was pretty sure if he asked, her old boss would not deny it. "The family wants to sue the army. Surely you had heard that, from Hanan." There, let him feel that he was out of the loop. It seemed to work. He looked back at the report.

"He was found facedown," he said. "No sign of a struggle. It was hard to tell because the night was windy, but it did not appear that the body was dragged or moved postmortem. Injuries consistent with a high-velocity weapon, like an M-16, fired at close range."

"Like an M-16? It does not say for sure?"

"It says similar to an M-16."

"Similar to or like?"

"Who can tell? It's Hebrew. Such an imprecise language." They bonded momentarily over their distaste for Hebrew. "No shells or bullets were recovered. Witnesses reported hearing two gunshots at approximately half past eight in the evening. No one reported hearing a vehicle or footsteps running away."

"Is that all?" It was barely more than she already knew.

"More or less."

"I don't want more or less. I want to know what it says. Exactly." He looked back at the report, and his lips moved slightly.

"There was a gash on his head," he read, "that could have come from striking his head on the rocks. Or it could have been inflicted prior to the shooting."

"I thought you said there was no sign of a struggle."

"That's what it says." She thought about that. Did that mean the Israeli police had a different definition of what a struggle was than she did, or was someone making a determination about which explanation of the gash was more likely? She wished she could have seen the body.

"Can I see that?" she said. He handed the report back to her. She flipped to the last page. There was a grainy photo, but, in the photocopying process, it had become virtually useless. She barely made out the jagged line on his forehead that would have been referred to as the gash. Offhand, she had to guess that he hit his head on the rocks, since he was found facedown. Otherwise, someone would have had to fight with Daoud face-to-face, then somehow shoot him in the back. Unless they fought and Daoud turned to walk or run away, and the person shot him in the back. Or…she thought about the story that the girl named Heba had told her, of Daoud's confrontation with the soldiers earlier. Heba had said that the soldier punched Daoud in the face with his fist. A balled-up fist could not have made a gash like the one she saw in the picture.

"Does it say anything about whether there was pooling blood from the cut on his head?" she asked, shoving the report in front of Abdelhakim once more.

He glanced through it and shook his head.

"Is there anything else I should know?"

"No."

"Thank you very much," she said. She hated having to be indebted to him. Maybe she could use this time of unemployment to study Hebrew. She still had the textbook she had gotten from Tali Ta'ali, but she doubted she would be able to motivate herself.

"Um Khaled," Abdelhakim said as she started to get up.

"Yes?"

"Have you thought any more about Abu Ziyad's request to train the women's police force?"

"No," she said.

"Please do," he said.

She bristled. He had no right to order her around. Of course, he had said please, but he didn't mean it.

"Abu Ziyad is going to want an answer in the next few days."

"Then I will discuss it with Abu Ziyad," she said. "Thank you again."

Chapter 31

The servees dropped Rania at the entrance to Kufr Yunus and rumbled off toward Hares. She waited for the one other disembarking passenger to amble into the village, loaded down with packages from a shopping spree. She was thankful to see no one nearby as she walked to Um Mahmoud's house and took out Avi's drawing. She did not want a group of children following her around asking, "What are you doing?" as she made her investigation. Nor did she need nosy adults asking, "Are you back working for the police?"

She held the drawing in front of her so she could look at it and still see where she was going and paced off thirty feet between the house and the trees. Avi had drawn it very accurately. The huge, lopsided fig tree on the left listed under the weight of unripe figs like a dancer doing a backbend. To the right was a clump of small olive trees, with tufts of scrubby grass and protruding rocks in-between. Just beyond, she could see the spindly almond orchard, branches pointing into the air like the arms of whirling dancers. Straight ahead was the spreading fig tree where Daoud had lain facedown, according to Benny's report.

She knelt in the soft dirt and felt around for any shells or other objects that Chloe and Um Mahmoud might have missed. She did not expect to find any, and she didn't. She brushed away the dirt from the rocks under her fingers, and saw the reddish-brown stains that Chloe had told her about. There was quite a lot of blood, so likely it came from the wound in his chest, where the bullet went through his back, exiting via the heart and nicking the lung for good measure. She saw that not only the rocks but the dirt as well was stained a different brown than the normal shade of the soil. She traced the spatter pattern with her hands. It was right for that kind of wound. So, the boy must have lain like this—she looked around once more to make sure no one was watching and lay on her stomach, carefully bunching her jilbab under the legs to keep it from flying up in a sudden wind. He was much taller than she, so his head would have been about…here. She reached a foot over her head and made a broad circle in the dirt with her finger. Then she clambered up and walked forward to the area she had marked.

She sifted through dirt and cleared off rocks for half an hour, but found no trace of blood in that area. That meant that the gash on Daoud's forehead could not have come from striking his head on the rocks when he fell. She thought about her conversation with Heba, and the one Chloe had reported with all the children. No one had said anything about Daoud having a cut on his head before the confrontation with the soldiers. Of course, no one had asked them, and then too, they might not have noticed. But it seemed likely that the cut was sustained that afternoon—either during that confrontation with the soldiers or sometime between then and when he was killed that night.

She didn't know if it mattered, but she took out her notebook and wrote it down. She took a small tape measure from her bag and carefully noted the distance between the base of the tree and the rocks where the blood stains were. She measured the distance between Um Mahmoud's front door and the fig tree and between the fig and the olives, just as she would have if she were really heading a murder investigation. She doubted her work would ever be useful for anything, but she didn't want to wish she had done it later. If she ended up training the women's police unit, this is what she would tell them, to always take every precaution.

Her phone played the Palestinian folk tune she had chosen when she got her first mobile phone. She looked at the screen. Benny.

"Yes?" she said in English.

"His name is Ron Binyamin," Benny said without preamble. "The other guy is Yonatan Silberman. They're an odd pair. Yonatan is a right-winger, used to go to settler rallies and pick fights with Arabs. Ron is a peacenik. In high school, he went to a camp with Palestinian kids in Germany."

"Abraham's Garden?" Rania asked.

"That's right. How'd you know?"

"Daoud went there too," Rania said. Benny must have learned that as well. If he could get this much information so fast from a drawing and a possible first name, certainly he had the complete dossier on Daoud al-Khader by now.

"No kidding," Benny said. "Quite a coincidence, eh?"

"Don't be ridiculous," she snapped. "They must have known each other."

"You're suggesting he was killed because of something that happened at a dialogue camp years ago?"

"I'm not suggesting anything. I have no idea why he was killed. Does your information say anything about if Ron was…is…" She stopped. She couldn't tell the Israeli police that Daoud was gay. It would give them too much ammunition to make this an honor killing or a religious cleansing.

"If he is what?" Benny sounded impatient. Well, he had called her with this information, so he could wait another minute while she tried to think about the significance.

"Is he married?" she asked. She knew that Israeli youth mostly did not marry until after the army, but she thought the more religious ones married younger.

"No," Benny said. "No wife. No girlfriend either that I know of."

"Okay, thank you," she said. She hung up. Just because he had no known girlfriend didn't mean that Ron was gay. None of this meant anything. But it was interesting. She wandered out to the road to find transportation back to Biddya. She decided to pick up Khaled from school and take him shopping in Nablus for the afternoon. They needed some private time together.

While she waited for a car, she thought about what Benny had told her. If the soldier who shot Daoud had known him from the peace camp, what possible motivation could that have given him to commit murder? She had no idea what went on at such places. Perhaps they talked about their family histories, things that could rekindle old conflicts. She thought about her conversation with Tali in the prison. They had both been so passionate about the histories they had been taught. Two narratives, two old wounds that felt as fresh as the ones Tali's colleagues had inflicted on her the previous evening. Knowing that Tali's grandfather could have been one of those who destroyed her family home did not make her want to kill the other woman. But she couldn't say whether the reverse was true or not.

Idly, she took out the photo of Daoud with Ahmed and the Israeli boy from the camp. The Israeli's pimpled face looked harmless enough. It was hard to see him as a killer, but he would be much older now and probably carried a gun and decided who could go through the checkpoint and who could not. She peered at it more closely. The young Israeli's face—could it be? Maybe she was imagining it. She took out the picture Avi had drawn. She tried to see the tall soldier's face without the beard and sunglasses. It was hard to be sure. The beaky nose was the same, but a lot of Jews had that nose. The cheekbones were similar, but the beard made a difference. Besides, one was a photo and one a drawing. She couldn't be sure. But it didn't really matter. If he was not the one in the photo, it didn't mean he didn't know Daoud from the camp, and, if he did, it didn't mean that was why he killed him. It was all a big jumble.

Her phone rang just as a servees showed up.

"One second, Chloe," she said. She fished out two shekels and handed them to the driver. It didn't seem like much, but she couldn't keep spending so much on transportation. When she was working, she could take this money out of petty cash. Now, with Bassam's job threatened and her own nonexistent, she had to get used to planning her trips more carefully.

"I talked to Ron last night," Chloe said.

"I wish you had called me sooner," Rania said. "I already talked to Benny."

"Sorry. I was out kind of late."

"It's okay." Chloe was undisciplined, Rania thought. She did whatever she wanted and didn't report promptly. But of course, she wasn't a policewoman, and they were not working a case.

"He says Daoud ran up to his jeep and said his brother had threatened to kill him."

"What brother?" Rania took out her notebook and scribbled down what Chloe was saying. With the car jolting up and down over the potholes, she would be lucky to be able to read her own notes.

"He said his name was Issa. Supposedly, Daoud asked Ron to help him get asylum in Israel, because Issa found out he was performing at the club and threatened him. Ron says he barely knew Daoud. I don't believe him."

"Neither do I," Rania agreed. "I am pretty sure he was at the peace camp

with him. There is a photograph of them together—at least, I think it's him."
She quickly ran down for Chloe the details Benny had provided.

"Do you know if Daoud had a brother named Issa, at least?" Chloe asked.

"Um Issa, his mother is called. That means Issa is his oldest brother."

"Ron wouldn't know that unless he knew Daoud pretty well, or else his
story is true," Chloe said. "Do you think it could be?"

"I wish I could say no," Rania said. "But sadly, such things do happen." She
had reached the Qarawa blocks.

"I'll try to talk to Ron again," Chloe said. "But he's probably gone back to
the army today, since it's Sunday. You're more likely to see him than me."

"If I do, I doubt he would talk to me," Rania said. The thought of having a
conversation with an Israeli soldier gave her chills. Before Prison, she hated
what they stood for, but she had not been afraid of them. Now, she trembled
just thinking about being close to one.

"I'll call you back if I find out anything," Chloe said. "What did you say
his last name is?"

Rania told her and said goodbye.

✶ ✶ ✶

"Do you know a guy named Ron Binyamin?" Chloe demanded as soon as Avi
answered his phone.

"I've met him. In a workshop at Neve Shalom."

"You went to a dialogue group?" Neve Shalom-Wahat al-Salam was a
mixed Jewish-Palestinian community in Israel which conducted an array
of peace-building activities. Many Israeli activists got their start there, but
Chloe would have judged it too touchy-feely for Avi.

"Shut up. I was young then."

"You're still young," Chloe said. "Can you get in touch with him?"

"Of course." Dumb question. There was no one in Israel Avi could not get
in touch with, likely including the prime minister.

"Set up a meeting," Chloe instructed. "But don't tell him I'll be there."

Avi called back in five minutes. "He's at Ariel. He gets off duty at three
o'clock. He will meet us at the entrance."

"What did you tell him it was about?"

"Organizing army guys to refuse illegal orders."

"You could just say that on the phone?"

"Sure. You think the government cares about that? People have been trying to do it for years. Besides, they don't think their orders are illegal."

Chloe caught a bus from Ramallah and met Avi at Hares junction. They walked the two kilometers to Ariel. Ron was pacing back and forth between the stone pillars that surrounded the little metal bus stop, his gun looped over his shoulder like an unwieldy purse.

"I am not talking to you," he said when he saw her.

He started to walk up into the settlement. Avi ran after him, putting a brotherly hand on his shoulder. They huddled for a few moments, their lips moving rapidly. Then they came back to the bus stop, Ron dragging slightly behind Avi. Chloe perched on one side of the metal bench inside the shelter, Ron on the other end, leaning into the frame. Avi stood between them, legs apart, like a sentry, or a referee, which was more like his role here.

"He met Daoud at Abraham's Garden," Avi said. "They became friends, and, after they came back, they met frequently at Neve Shalom." He took a pack of cigarettes out of his pocket and offered one to Ron, who accepted. Avi didn't smoke. He must carry cigarettes around for the purpose of putting soldiers at ease.

"They became lovers," Avi said.

"But Daoud had another lover, in one of the villages, right?" Chloe said.

"Yes. But Ron doesn't know his name. Daoud refused to choose. He said he loved them both."

Chloe couldn't quite decide if she was having a conversation with Ron through Avi or talking to Avi about Ron. "Where would they meet?" she asked.

"Sometimes in Tel Aviv, at Lior's apartment." He saw her quizzical look and asked a question in Hebrew. "Other times, they would meet in a house in Kufr Yunus. It is a big house owned by a Palestinian American. He built it in the nineties, during the Oslo years. It was finished only a year or so before the Second Intifada began. He never came to live in it. It sits empty all the time. Daoud's uncle did the electrical wiring, and he had a key. Daoud made a copy of the key and hid it outside the house, and they would meet there."

"How often?" Chloe asked. It was getting to be late afternoon. Cars were zooming by with more frequency as settlers returned from work inside Israel. Ron looked increasingly nervous as the traffic picked up. She had better speed up the questioning. It would be easier to just talk to Ron in English, but he seemed to feel better about talking to Avi in Hebrew. If she changed the arrangement, he might stop talking altogether.

"Once, twice a month," Avi said, after repeating her question for Ron. A flood of words poured out of the younger man. "Daoud was in Ramallah all week and only came home on Thursday night. The last time was the Friday before he died. Ron was on duty, but he said he was sick and had to go back to the base. His friend Yonatan covered for him. He spent the afternoon with Daoud in the house. Just before dark, they heard someone coming into the house. They got up and looked for somewhere to hide, but they did not manage to get away in time. It was Daoud's friend from the village, who had come to look for him. He screamed at Daoud. Daoud told him to go away—at least, that's what Ron believes. They spoke Arabic, and he doesn't know Arabic."

After all those dialogue groups, he didn't know any Arabic? Chloe was constantly amazed by the arrogance of Israelis, even Israeli peace activists. But she supposed she should not be so judgmental. After all, her own Arabic was no great shakes, and she had lived in Palestine for almost a year.

"What did the other guy look like?" she asked. A description wouldn't tell her anything, because she had never met any of Daoud's friends except briefly that day in the restaurant, but if the guy was distinctive enough, Rania might get something out of it.

"Like a movie star," Avi translated. "Like the guy in the film *Titanic*."

"What happened then?" she asked.

"Ron was afraid, so he collected his clothes and ran out of the house half-dressed, wearing only his pants. He put on his shirt in the yard and walked out of the village through the olive groves. Only when he got to the road did he realize that he did not have his gun. He ran back to the house, but Daoud and his friend were still there, fighting."

"Fighting how?" Chloe interjected.

"Arguing, and shoving," Ron said in English, not waiting for Avi to translate.

"So, you didn't go back in?" she asked him directly.

"No. I went back to the base and told Yonatan that a Palestinian had grabbed my rifle on my way back to the base. He found me another one to use," he touched the one hanging down his back. "This is the old type, the Uzi that many of the settlers carry. Yonatan borrowed it from someone in his family. The ones we were issued are M-16s. One day, they will inspect us and find out that I lost my weapon. You have no idea how much trouble I will be in."

"Why didn't he go back to get it?" The two young men consulted for a minute.

"He did not know where the key was," Avi said. "He tried to find it, and he could not. He called Daoud and said he needed to get the gun, and Daoud said he did not have it. He would not say where it was."

"Is that why you killed him?" Chloe asked. Ron looked at her in horror. Avi rolled his eyes, presumably thinking about all the useful ways he could have spent his day.

"Go away," said Ron. "I don't have to talk to you."

He started to walk quickly toward the entrance to the settlement. Her and her big mouth. What, did she think he would just admit it? It had worked for her before, but only because the person she accused intended to kill her.

"Wait," she called. She started to run after him, but the sentry moved out of his box and started toward her, his hand on his rifle. She wasn't interested in any more visits to the Ariel police station. She turned and saw Avi shaking his head, presumably over her ability to screw up every situation.

Chapter 32

"Mama, look!" Khaled ran to the little carousel outside the grocery store. He hopped onto the neck of a giraffe and held out his hand for a shekel, to make it go around. She handed him a coin. He leaned over to drop the coin into the slot, and the little wheel began to turn.

"You ride too, Mama," he called out.

"I'm too big, sweetheart."

"I'm too big, too." He was, in fact. With his feet in the stirrups, his knees were almost under his chin. He was going to be tall, like his father. He seemed relieved when the ride stopped.

"Are you hungry?" she asked.

"No."

"That's too bad. So, you do not want an ice cream?"

"Ice cream! Of course I want ice cream."

"Well, then, come on." They walked through the old city, competing for sidewalk space with merchants pushing heavy, hand-drawn carts loaded with wool blankets or cotton shirts. She bought a fleece blanket printed with lions and tigers for the new bed Bassam had ordered for Khaled's room. He had outgrown his little boy bed and needed a full mattress. She steered her son into a shop where two other families sat drinking milkshakes from tall glasses through long straws.

"What would you like, habibi?" the waiter asked.

"Vanilla ice cream with strawberries and chocolate syrup," he answered.

"Anything for you?" the young man asked.

"Coffee, half-sweet." The ice cream and the coffee came, and mother and son satisfied their cravings in quiet. As Khaled was spooning the last melted ice cream drops from the bottom of the glass, Yusuf and Elias entered the shop. They stopped by her table, and Yusuf greeted her enthusiastically.

"Ustaz Yusuf, this is my son, Khaled," she said.

"Hello, Khaled," the teacher said. "Your mother is a brave and intelligent woman. You are very lucky to have such a mother."

"I know," Khaled said. Rania beamed. She guessed there was nothing like the approbation of men to facilitate a son's approval.

"I was about to call you," Yusuf said. "Can you come on Tuesday to speak to my class?" Today was Sunday, so that would be the day after tomorrow.

"It is not much time to prepare," she said.

"No need to prepare much," he said. "Just talk from your experience. Come at eleven o'clock."

"Okay," she agreed. He wrote the room number, along with his mobile, on a napkin for her. She folded it and put it in her purse.

"Elias," she said. "I need to ask you something about Daoud."

"Why?" the young man said.

"I am trying to find out what happened, to help his family sue the army," she said, ignoring his rudeness. "I wondered, since you were his roommate, if you had noticed whether he had received any injuries in the day or so before he died."

"Injuries?"

"When he died, he had a cut on his head," she explained. "We are trying to ascertain whether he received it at that time or whether it had happened earlier."

"Who is we?" Yusuf asked. He did not look as friendly as he had a minute ago.

"I guess I should have said I," she said with a smile. "But my colleague Abdelhakim went over the police report with me." She wondered what Abdelhakim would tell him, if he asked about where she got the report.

"I never saw any cut on his head," Elias said.

"When did you see him last?" she asked.

"That morning, at the apartment. We were supposed to go together to Ahmed's engagement party, but he said he needed to do something first. So, he went up earlier, by himself."

"Do you know what it was he needed to do?"

"No." The men at the table next to hers paid their bill and left. Yusuf and Elias settled into the vacated chairs as the waiter cleared the dishes.

"Mama, can we go now?" Khaled asked. Rania looked at him guiltily. In her enthusiasm to continue her investigation, she had almost forgotten he was there. She held out a hand to him.

"Come, habibi," she said. "We will buy some fish to cook for dinner." They walked out into the cobblestoned street.

"A moment, Um Khaled?"

She wheeled around, looking for the person who had spoken. A small man with a narrow handlebar mustache was walking toward them. Kareem, Khaled's teacher.

"Ustaz Kareem," she said. "Nice to see you." She had known Kareem since he was in high school, but she wanted Khaled to learn proper respect for teachers, so she addressed him by his title.

"I noticed you talking with those two men," he said quietly.

"Yes?"

"Yusuf is a good man," he said. "But his brother is another matter."

"What are you saying?"

"You should be careful," the young man said. "Someone who has just gotten out of prison should not be too friendly with people who cannot be trusted."

"Why do you think that Elias cannot be trusted?"

"I know certain things," Kareem said. "You should be careful, that's all."

"Thank you for the advice," she said. She took Khaled by the hand and walked quickly away from the shop. She felt the teacher's eyes on them until they turned the corner. She wondered what he meant about Elias and if there was any basis to it. She had a moment's terror that Kareem would take it out on Khaled that his mother seemed too friendly with possible collaborators. But there was nothing she could do about it.

Chapter 33

Chloe felt like she almost had her old Palestinian life back. She had been running around all week doing useful, if self-made, work, and she decided she deserved a day off. She took a longer-than-normal shower, still short by American standards. She started out the door, but dashed back inside when she saw Um Malik coming out of the other side. She didn't know if it was true, but, when she was preparing for her first trip, someone had told her that if you go out with wet hair, people will assume you've just had sex. If only! She found Tina's blow-dryer and made sure her hair was bone dry before venturing out.

She would buy some vegetables, cheese, and pasta to make a nice dinner for Tina and treat herself to lunch at Enrico's. Maybe some of the guys she had seen with Daoud would come back, and she'd be able to ask them about him. Maybe there was a group for gay men, like the one Tina went to for lesbians. If so, they might let her write an article about them for one of the gay papers in the States. Men rarely said no to publicizing themselves.

She grabbed a handful of paper bags, even though she knew it would horrify the merchants she patronized. More than once, she had had to snatch vegetables from someone's hand to keep them from putting it in a new plastic bag.

When she reached the Manara, she browsed in the busy produce market, loading up on delicacies like avocados and spinach. Strawberries were starting to be in season, and she bought so many she would probably have to make jam. She located the good cheese shop with cheddars, goudas, and bries stacked in artful pyramids. Some were local, some from Europe. Some were bright orange, some snowy white. They all looked wonderful. She scooped some grated parmesan into a paper bag. That would go nicely with her pesto. Now, she wanted some grilling cheese and some cheddar for sandwiches. Her cheese dreams were rudely interrupted by her phone's distinctive melody. Reem, said the little screen. Chloe's chest tightened. This could not be good news.

"Hi, Reem," she said. The answering voice was barely audible.

"Chloe, can you come quickly?" Reem croaked. "I think I need to go to the hospital."

"Of course I will come," Chloe said. "But I'm in Ramallah, and I have no car. Wouldn't it be better to call the Red Crescent for an ambulance?"

"Too expensive," she had to strain to hear.

"But, if your life is in danger, you need an ambulance. It could take me hours to find a car and reach Salfit."

"No ambulance," Reem mumbled. "Please come."

"All right, I'm on my way." Chloe hung up, wondering how she could get to Salfit in a hurry. Fortunately, Rania answered on the first ring.

"I need to borrow the car," Chloe said. "Reem's very sick."

"Chloe, I'm sorry," Rania said. "Bassam had to go to Tulkarem for work. He took the car with him."

Rats. What was she going to do now? She had an armful of groceries, no car, and she had somehow become responsible for a possibly dying woman she hardly knew. This day had gone downhill rapidly. She thought of Nehama. Maybe she was doing checkpoint watch in Nablus and could pick up Reem herself. Reem would be unhappy to be passed off to a stranger, especially an Israeli, but it would get her to the hospital much quicker.

"Sorry, I'm in Haifa," Nehama said. "I had to take my mother for dialysis."

"No problem," Chloe said.

Avi was next. She held her breath when he came on the line. If he said no, she would jump in a taxi and damn the cost. Maybe she should do that anyway. But it would be steep.

"Do you want me to come with you?" Avi asked when she explained the situation. She exhaled. At least he didn't say his parents had taken the car to Be'er Sheva.

"Avi, I wish you could, believe me. But I don't know these people. I can't show up with an Israeli without asking." She had been prepared to send Nehama by herself a minute ago. But a young Israeli man was different than a middle-aged woman. "Could you meet me at Zatara and hitch home?"

"Sure, okay." He sounded mildly disappointed.

"You're the best. Half an hour," she said. She was being optimistic. If she was lucky, a Nablus or Tulkarem bus would be getting ready to leave. She trotted the two blocks to the bus station. A Nablus bus was there, although the driver wasn't on it. Once she was sitting on the bus, she called Reem to say she would be there in an hour. Reem sounded calmer.

"I will see you then," she said, enunciating perfectly. Chloe almost wondered if she didn't need to go, but she didn't want to sound unwilling, so she didn't ask. The driver emerged from the terminal, drinking coffee from a thimble-sized paper cup. He tipped his head back to drain the dregs, then crumpled the cup in his hand and tossed it on the ground before climbing into the driver's seat. Usually, Chloe would be furious about the littering, but now she was glad the guy didn't go all over hell-and-gone looking for a garbage can.

She was too tense to read. She looked out the window as the bus slowly wound its way through the Ramallah hills. Only as they picked up speed and turned onto Highway 60 did she think to call Tina and leave a message that she probably wouldn't be home for dinner. She stuffed the cheese and pasta into her backpack. Hopefully, she wouldn't be gone so long that the cheese would spoil.

✶ ✶ ✶

At least Avi's parents' Volvo was an automatic. Chloe bounced along the dirt road between Yasuf and Iskaka and then made the sharp turn onto the paved road that led into Salfit. Only as she spotted the tall Zaytouna Building in the center of the city did she remember that the paper telling her how to get to Reem's house was back at the apartment, in the pocket of her other jeans. It had involved a bunch of turns, and she doubted she would remember, even if she were not so nervous. She called Reem's number.

"Is this…" What was the little girl's name again? She had only met them all very quickly. "Amalia?" Could that be right? *Amalia* meant "operation" in Arabic. It could mean a surgery, but it also meant bombing. Would anyone name their daughter that?

"Yes, it's me."

"Amalia, ana Chloe. Mumkin ahki maa imik?" May I speak to your mother?

"My mother is sleeping," the little girl said in English. Chloe decided she could use English, too.

"I am coming to your house, but I am not sure how to get there," she said, reminding herself to speak slowly. "Is your father home?" Surely Reem's husband would have come home from work if she was so sick.

"Not yet. Where are you?"

"I'm near…what am I near?" Chloe looked around. There were shops all over, but all the signs were in Arabic. She couldn't make out any of the words. "There's a pharmacy," she said, noticing the caduceus over a storefront.

"Which pharmacy?" the little girl asked. Of course, this was not a village, which would only have one pharmacy. She stared up at the signs again, thinking of the minutes ticking away. She needed to get to the house and get Reem into the car and get to the hospital. For all she knew, the woman was unconscious by now, if she had had a bad reaction to the drugs. She looked at the letters. She had spent hours writing them just two days ago. But many of these were in elaborate calligraphy, which was harder to read than normal script. Concentrate, she told herself. Okay, there was a letter she recognized, the *K* sound. That was one of the dot ones next to it, the ones she could never keep straight. One dot on top. That meant *B*—no, that was one dot below. One dot on top was *N. Kn.* The next letter was *Ra. Knr?* She couldn't think of a word that started with those sounds. Wait, it wasn't a *Ra.* It had a broader base so it was the dalit, *D. Knd.* And the next one was the *R.* Only then did she notice the big wooden shoe hanging from the sign. *Kundera,* shoes.

"A pharmacy next to a shoe store," she told Amalia.

"You are right near our house," Amalia said and explained where to turn. When Chloe found the house, the girl was waiting out front, still in her blue and white school uniform.

"Mama's been sleeping since I got home," she said. "It's boring. Now, that you are here, maybe we can play?"

"Amalia, I'd love to, but I came to take your mom to the hospital." Once she was on the right street, she recognized the house. She parked in front and ran up the steps, Amalia lagging behind her. "Is there anyone else home with you?"

"My brother's upstairs, doing his homework." She used the Arabic word, *wajib*. Even a seven-year-old knew some words were not worth learning.

That was good. She wouldn't need to spend extra time finding someone to look after the little kids. She burst into the house. Reem was lying on the living room couch.

"Reem? It's Chloe." Chloe shook her lightly.

"Chloe? Welcome." Reem's eyes fluttered open. "I feel much better."

She looked sick, but not deathly ill. Could it be that Chloe had done all this for nothing? It's not like you had anything important to do, she told herself. But her body was aching from the anxiety of the last two hours. If it was no emergency, Reem could have called her back. Not to mention that Avi's parents would get home and find their car gone.

"Should we go to the hospital anyway?" she asked.

"I do not think it is necessary," Reem said. "I would just like to sleep."

She closed her eyes again.

"Wait a minute," Chloe blurted out. "What should I do?" Did Reem mean for her to turn around and go back to Ramallah?

"Could you look after Amalia for a while?" Reem asked. Her eyes fluttered closed again. Chloe gathered she was meant to spend the night. Momentarily, she wondered if she could really spend the night in a house with pictures of Khaled Mashal on the walls.

"Chloe, come see my dolls." Amalia came running up with a battered Barbie in each hand.

"One minute," Chloe said. "I left some vegetables in the car. I had better bring them inside before they spoil."

"I can help you," the little girl said solemnly. She skipped next to Chloe on the way to the car.

"What is your favorite subject at school?" Chloe asked.

"English!" Amalia said. Chloe opened the trunk and handed Amalia the bag of spinach. She took the heavier one with avocados, strawberries, and cauliflower. Amalia led the way to the little kitchen, which had barely enough space for the refrigerator, stove, and a little round work table. Chloe wedged her purchases in-between the few covered dishes in the fridge. She peeked into one of them. A grayish-brown wedge of lamb peeked out of some soggy rice. Good thing she had shopped.

"Are we having molochia?" Amalia asked, as she put the bag of spinach into the crisper.

"I don't think I can manage that," Chloe said. The girl's face fell. "How about makluube and fries?"

"I like makluube," Amalia said. Chloe hoped she would like the vegetarian version. She wasn't about to cook chicken—not that there was any. If Amalia didn't like it, she could eat fries and bread.

"Shall we play with your dolls now?" she said. Amalia had set up three dolls in a row on the dining room table and was lecturing them.

"In this class, you must speak English," she instructed.

"Ana bidish ahki inglisi," Chloe said, joining the row of students. "Bidi atalam Arabi." I don't want to speak English, I want to learn Arabic.

"Tayeb," fine, said the little teacher. "Shu hada?" What is this? She touched her teeth.

"Snaan," Chloe responded.

"Correct. This?" She indicated her neck.

"Um, I don't know." It hadn't taken long to reach the limits of her knowledge.

"Raqabe," Amalia said.

"Raqabe," Chloe said slowly, hoping she could remember it for twenty-four hours at least. "Raqabe. What else? Wait, I know." She rummaged in her pack until she found what she was looking for.

"Look," she said, presenting a long string of stickers for Amalia's inspection.

"Mulsaqaat!" the little girl squealed. The line of plasticized paper whipped snake-like as she pulled it across the table. She squinted at the stickers, each of which pictured an animal. "Bissa," she said, pointing to the cat.

"Even I know that one," Chloe said with a grin. "Kalb," tapping a dog.

Amalia pointed to the goat and waited for Chloe to supply "Jid."

Amalia giggled profusely.

"That's not right?" Chloe furrowed her brow. She hoped she hadn't said anything totally offensive.

"Jidi," Amalia touched the goat sticker. She crossed the room and took a framed photo from a dark, wooden end table. She brought the photo back to Chloe and handed it to her. The man pictured in close-up had boring, dark eyes surrounded by a thousand tiny lines and a bushy head of white hair. Whoever he was, he reminded Chloe a little of the picture of Mashal in the kitchen.

"Jid," Amalia said.

Ah, Chloe understood. "Abu imik?" she asked. Your mother's father?

"Abu abui," my father's father.

"Aish hon?" Does he live here? Chloe asked.

Amalia shook her head solemnly. "Maat," dead, she said, "The soldiers killed him."

Chloe wondered if she should ask follow-up questions or change the subject. Amalia did not seem distressed, though, so it would be weird to suddenly point to a giraffe and ask its Arabic name.

"When?" she asked.

"A long time ago. Intifada il Uwle." If Jawad's father was killed in First Intifada, that would make it fifteen years before Amalia was born.

"Here, in Salfit?" Chloe asked.

"Over there." Amalia ran to the front door and leapt up to touch a nick in the wooden frame. Chloe walked over to inspect the bullet hole, as she was clearly expected to do.

"Was anyone else killed?" she asked.

"No. But my father got shot in his face." Amalia held four fingers to her cheek. Her other hand clutching the portrait of her grandfather, outstretched, she resembled a tiny actress delivering a melodramatic monologue.

"Can I take your picture?" Chloe asked.

"Andik camera?" You have a camera? The little girl's eyes lit up. She shed her theatrical fervor and became an ordinary kid yelling "Sawrini," take my picture, as Chloe walked through any village in Palestine. Chloe found the camera in her pack and fussed with the settings. By the time she focused it on Amalia, the dramatic intensity she had wanted to capture had disappeared in a toothy smile. She snapped anyway, for form's sake. She didn't see any pictures of Amalia in the room, though there were several of the older boys. If these came out, she would print one and have it framed for Reem.

"Do you want to help me make dinner?" she asked.

"I can peel potatoes," the girl said. An oblique demand for fries, Chloe figured. Fortunately, that was one of the few Palestinian dishes she knew how to make.

Despite the absence of chicken, Jawad had seconds of makluube and pronounced it "zaki," delicious. Her fries met with Amalia's approval, which had become very important to Chloe. Later, Amalia dried the dishes while Chloe washed. When they were done, they sat close together on the couch and Amalia opened her English book so that it straddled their laps.

"Read it," she said.

"It's your book," Chloe said. "You read to me."

"Raja was so excited," Amalia read flawlessly. "Today was the day she would finally get to travel to Al Quds, to the Al Aqsa Mosque."

"What is Al Aqsa?" Chloe asked.

"It is the holiest place in Palestine," Amalia said.

"Have you ever been there?"

"No. The Jews do not allow us to go there."

The back of Chloe's neck prickled at the word "Jews." But what Amalia had said was basically accurate.

"Not all Jews are in the Israeli army," Chloe said. "Did you know that there are Jews who do not even live in Israel?"

"No." Amalia looked down at her book. She turned the pages slowly until she found the picture she was looking for. "These are the Jews." She pointed to two soldiers guarding a staircase in what looked like Jerusalem's Old City. Behind the soldiers, a row of frightened children scurried away, holding hands.

"Those soldiers are Jews," Chloe said. "But they are not the only Jews. I am a Jew, too." She wondered if that was a mistake. If Amalia mentioned it to her parents, would Reem and Jawad feel she had lied to them?

Amalia tilted her head and scrunched up her face. "But where is your gun?"

Chloe laughed. "I don't have a gun. I am not a soldier, see? I am not an Israeli; I am an American Jew."

"I don't care," Amalia said. She closed the book and stood, twirling around. "You are my friend."

It was after eleven, and she was still going strong. Like most Palestinian kids, she did not seem to have a bedtime. But if Chloe was going to play surrogate mom, her surrogate daughter was going to get a good night's sleep.

"You're my friend too," she said. "And friends tell friends when it's time to sleep."

"What does that mean?"

Chloe laughed. "It doesn't mean anything," she said. "Aren't you tired?"

"No."

"I think if you lie down, you will be. It's very late and you have school tomorrow."

She had meant to make a bed for herself on the living room floor, using cushions from the couch. But when Amalia climbed into bed, she rolled all the way into the corner and patted the space next to her. Chloe could not refuse. She just hoped she wouldn't do anything embarrassing, like snore or hog the blanket.

Chapter 34

As Rania prepared breakfast for Khaled and Bassam, she thought about her brief conversation with Kareem. She hoped he would not make trouble for Khaled. She had decided not to mention it to Bassam. She was sure Khaled would let them know if anything untoward happened at school.

If Elias had a bad reputation, why had she not heard about it? Was she that out of the mix? Six months ago, she would have known anything that was vaguely hinted at in any of the Salfit villages. The police station was a hothouse for gossip of every stripe. It had to be. Most information began as gossip.

Bassam took his tea to the living room and sat in his usual armchair with yesterday's paper. She called to Khaled. When he did not answer, she went to his room and found him still in his pajamas, playing with his model train.

"Khaled! Get ready for school or you will be late."

She took his school uniform, dark slacks and light-blue polo shirt, from where she had hung it last night, after washing and pressing it. He remained sitting on the floor.

"*Choo choo choo.* All aboard!" he said in English. At least he was learning some English at school, even if he was also learning to be disobedient.

"Khaled, now," she said. When he did not move, she crossed to where he sat and hoisted him up by the arm. He was like a little rag doll, not fighting her but making her do all the work. She pulled the top of his pajamas over his head and replaced it with the blue shirt. The pants were harder, because she had to lift his legs and that required him to balance on one foot. He toppled to the floor and began sobbing noisily.

"Come on," she said. "You are not hurt. You are being a brat. Do you want to be late and get in trouble at school?"

"I don't care."

"You will care if you cannot be an engineer, because you stayed home and did not study."

That worked better than she would have predicted. He stood up and put his pants on.

"Where are your books?" she asked, and he walked around the room gathering things that appeared to have been scattered by hurricane. She packed them all into his backpack.

"Hurry, you will not have time to eat," she said. He followed her to the kitchen. She set his breakfast on the table. He ate three bites.

"I am full."

"Eat some more. You will be very hungry later." He dipped a little more bread into the zataar. "Khaled. Eat some labneh." Why was he making everything a fight? She managed to get enough food in him that at least she didn't think he would faint from lack of protein. She bustled him off to join the line of kids marching toward the school.

"I think I will come to Ramallah with you," she said suddenly, as Bassam was preparing to leave.

He looked at her quizzically.

"There is someone I need to see," she said. "The roommate of the boy who was killed."

"The martyr from Kufr Yunus?" he asked.

What other boy did he think she might mean? "Daoud al-Khader, yes." Why did everyone persist in calling him "the martyr"? It was as if they were daring her to find out what really happened.

"I still do not understand why you are doing this."

"I told you; I am trying to help his family sue the army."

"If that is so, how will going to Ramallah help you?"

"His roommate was with him in the village, when he fought with the soldiers." It was a bald-faced lie, but he had no right to question her activities.

Besides, she was not sure she believed what Elias had told her about that day. She needed to have a chat with him. She dressed quickly and left the house with her husband.

Once in Ramallah, she made her way to the apartment Elias shared with Ahmed. She wondered if they had gotten another roommate. No one answered the buzzer. She pressed it again, this time holding it down longer. Still no answer. She tried the front door, and it opened easily. What was the point of a buzzer if the door was unlocked? Perhaps the bell did not even work, and that was why they had not responded. She mounted the stairs and knocked smartly on the door.

She was about to conclude that she really had wasted her time when the door opened a crack. Elias stood there, rubbing his eyes.

"Eh? What time is it?" was his not-very-welcoming greeting.

"Close to eight thirty." She tried to make it sound like that was very late. "May I have some coffee?"

"I guess." He opened the door for her. She saw no sign of Ahmed. The living room was not too much of a disaster, barring the heaping ashtrays. There were some dirty dishes on the table, but they were neatly stacked and not crusted with food scraps. She picked them up and headed for the kitchen, which was really part of the living room, separated only by a half wall with windows cut out.

"I can make the coffee, while you dress," she suggested. Being fifteen years his senior, she could act like his mother. He wore a baggy, green T-shirt and sweatpants that looked suspiciously like he had nothing underneath.

"Fine," he mumbled. She put the dishes in the sink and ran a little water to soak them. She easily located the coffee pot next to the sink, but finding the coffee took some effort, as it was hiding behind several days' worth of moldy leftovers in the refrigerator. She set the sugary water on the flame and hunted down the proper glasses.

"Do you want coffee?" she called. Perhaps Ahmed was sleeping in the other bedroom, but she did not care. It was time he was getting up. Elias did not respond. Was he taking a shower? She listened for water, but heard nothing.

She put the long-handled coffee pot on a tray with three glasses. If Ahmed woke up, he could join them. She took the tray into the living room and sat down on the couch. After ten minutes, she decided he had graduated from fastidious to rude. She peeked into the hallway and saw no one. She walked down the hall, past the open bathroom to the bedroom opposite the one Daoud had shared with Ahmed. She knocked on the closed door. No answer. She opened the door a crack, praying Elias wasn't masturbating or something. He was not. In fact, he was not in the room at all. She knocked on the door across the hall. A faint "Naam?" invited her to open the door. Ahmed was in bed, only his eyes visible above the light blanket. Those eyes reflected confusion that turned to alarm when he realized who she was.

"What are you doing here?" he croaked. She forgave him his bad manners, as he had clearly just awakened.

"I am looking for Elias," she responded, trying to act as if it were the most natural thing in the world to be talking to a young man while he lay in bed.

"He is not in here."

"I can see that," she said. She started to back out of the door. She could not figure out where Elias had gone or how he had escaped, but she didn't need to talk to him badly enough to chase him around the streets of Ramallah. Ahmed might not know it yet, but he was today's egg in place of tomorrow's chicken.

"I would like to talk to you," she said.

This young man, unlike his roommate, was too polite to tell her she had no business coming into his home, waking him up, and demanding he talk to her. He said he would be right out, and she withdrew, thoughtfully closing the door behind her. Then, on second thought, she cracked it open. If he was going to abscond out of a second-story window, she wanted at least a possibility of hearing him.

She poured the coffee when he appeared, dressed in jeans and a Kansas City Chiefs T-shirt. The kids all wore strange American T-shirts these days. Either some enterprising Palestinian American had started a company to export leftover American shirts to Palestine or they were being sent over as part of the US economic aid package. The Israelis got F-16 aircraft, the Palestinians got shirts with irrelevant slogans on them.

She poured him a coffee. He sipped it, but without the relish he had shown for the cappuccino.

"Ahmed," she said, "Hanan told me that she was at Adloyada with you and Elias the night she interrupted Daoud with an Israeli soldier."

He sighed and downed his coffee in one gulp. It burned his tongue, she gathered from the quick breaths he sucked in.

"If I had told you, you would have asked who I went there with."

She sipped her coffee, being careful not to make the same mistake he had. It was still very hot.

"So, you lied to protect Elias?"

He nodded. "Elias's father is an imam. His brother, Yusuf, is active in Hamas. It could be dangerous if anyone knew he was gay." He used the same word Hanan had used, *mithli,* meaning "same."

"Were Elias and Daoud…together?" she asked.

"I have no idea," he said. That did not seem likely. They shared an apartment, after all. And it was not her impression that discretion was one of Daoud's virtues. But she left it alone.

"Do you mind my asking…?" It was unlike her not to be able to finish sentences. But he was good at filling in the blanks.

"I am not gay." She tended to believe him. He sounded sincere and didn't look away.

"It did not shock you?" she asked.

"It did at first. But these guys—they're like my brothers."

His friends were lucky that he was so open-minded, she thought. Though just how lucky had Daoud been, after all?

"I'm sorry to have disturbed you," she said. "Please tell Elias it is safe to talk to me."

"Is it?" he asked, as she exited.

She thought about that as she walked out to the street. If Elias had killed Daoud, or even if Ahmed had, what would she do? She had begun this investigation, she realized, assuming that she would prove the army had killed Daoud and then everyone would love her again. Now, she was stirring up a volcano, and she couldn't stop, even though she probably should.

✳ ✳ ✳

At three thirty, Rania set dinner on the table. She had made all Khaled's favorite foods: fried potatoes and cauliflower, salad with tahini dressing, and stuffed zucchini. She left a note on the table for Bassam and went upstairs to tell her mother-in-law she was going out. The old woman didn't bat an eyelid.

At the edge of the fields, she stripped off her hijab and jilbab, revealing her idea of hip Tel Aviv clothing—jeans and a peach-colored T-shirt two sizes too large so that the short sleeves hung down to her elbows. She chose a particularly luscious olive tree bursting with blossoms. She buried her normal clothes at the base of the tree and covered it with loose branches. Then she made her way carefully to the Wall, which, in this place, was a double fence surrounded on either side by trenches and roads.

She walked parallel to the Wall, staying among the trees but always keeping the giant fence in her sight lest she veer off course. At the very last possible minute, she emerged. She looked around once, twice, three times for border police on the military road across the Wall. She saw no dust and heard no engine noises. Here was the place she was looking for. Everyone knew about it, but she had never actually seen it before and it took her several passes to see the small tear in the fence. Whoever had cut it from its posts had carefully bent it back into position so that the soldiers would not notice, and each person who took this perilous route made sure to put it back exactly as they found it. It had been like this for months, and, as far as she knew, the soldiers had never been tipped off. She had better not be the one to mess it up and leave the gap showing, so that they would notice it on patrol.

She slipped through the space, then crouched down and painstakingly reconnected the wires to keep the piece of fence from flapping open in a strong wind. She didn't know if crouching down did anything to hide her, since there was absolutely nothing on either side but wide open space, but it made her feel less vulnerable. She squeezed the wires together as hard as she could and pulled on it to make sure that it was holding, even though she knew that every time you touched the Wall, you increased the likelihood of triggering the sensors. She scampered down into the red dirt ditch and took a minute to breathe, knowing she was momentarily out of sight. Better not to wait until she lost her nerve. This, after all, was the very worst place to be, caught in-between the fences.

She identified the place where the fence was open on the other side before darting across the wide asphalt road. She did not linger in the ditch on the other side. She easily pulled back the bottom of the fence and slid through on her belly. She looked around twice more before she bounded up the embankment, and now she was on the main road, with the bus stop that said Civil Park directly in front of her.

She sank onto the bus stop bench, her heart a bass drum. She felt light-headed from holding her breath. She inhaled deeply, filling her lungs with the air that tasted like freedom to her, even though it would taste like industrial waste to anyone else. Civil Park was home to a massive collection of factories.

The bus came quickly, and she paid her fare without saying a word to the driver. If he spoke to her, she would answer in English, and he would—she fervently hoped—think she was an international. But he did not speak. She took a seat two thirds of the way to the back, next to an old woman with a paisley scarf covering her head. It was not a hijab, she knew, but what the Russians called a babushka, but, still, it felt comforting to sit next to a woman wearing a scarf on her head. Rania took out an English newspaper she had brought for this purpose and pretended to read. She was much too keyed up to take in the words.

In a few minutes, the bus reached the Petah Tikva bus station. She climbed off through the back door and looked around, wondering where she should wait for Tina and her friends. She was a little early; they had said five thirty, and it was about ten past. She settled herself on a bench facing the street, so they would see her, since she had no idea what kind of car they would be driving. She took out her newspaper and really did try to read it. But now her mind kept wandering to the interrogation center only a few kilometers away, where she had spent several days dreading questions that never came.

As if thinking of them had conjured them, soldiers were coming toward her. She folded up her paper and jumped up, looking quickly for a place to hide. But they were not coming to get her. They were just going into the bus station. Probably, they were getting off work from the base where she had been held and going home for the evening. She looked back at her paper.

Fighting was worse in Gaza. The Palestinian Authority had had to lay off more workers because the Americans still had not released the funds they had promised. The call for a boycott of Israel had been taken up by a major church in America, called the Presbyterians. She wondered if it would do any good.

"Where are you from?"

She had not seen the soldiers approaching. There were three of them, hands loosely resting on their guns. They were like sleeping scorpions, seemingly harmless but ready to bite in an instant. She considered her options. Running was not one. One soldier stood on either side of her and the third directly in front. The wooden bench was at her back. She discarded the possibility of telling them she was from Mas'ha, because that would bring questions about permits, which of course she did not have. There were only two choices. She was a Palestinian from Jerusalem, or she was a foreigner.

"I am from America," she said. Her English was good, and she knew a few cities in America. Plus, Americans had the most power in the world.

"Can I see your passport?" The blond soldier asked pleasantly enough, but she did not think it was a simple request.

"I don't have to show you," she said. She did not think that was true. Even Chloe usually produced her passport, or something resembling it, when soldiers asked. But she thought maybe inside Israel, the army could not arrest an international. They would need to get police to come and, by that time, Tina and her friends might have shown up.

"Yes, you do." The blond guy was not taking no for an answer.

She didn't think she would be able to convince him to leave her alone. The only thing to do was get up and walk away, the way she had seen Chloe do, and maybe they would be impressed with her self-confidence and decide she really was American. She stood up.

"Where are you going?" the soldier demanded. He didn't sound quite so casual now.

"My friends are here." Rania started toward the curb, where there was not a car in sight. She had no watch, but she thought it was about time for Tina to arrive. She couldn't count on split-second arrival. She saw a city bus coming up the street. Maybe she should go to the bus stop and get on it and then call Tina and arrange another place to meet. The soldiers were dogging her steps. The blond guy was reaching for her arm. And directly in her path, virtually blocking it, was a uniformed policewoman. Had they called her? Was she going to grab Rania and put handcuffs on her and take her back to prison? Rania took in the woman's face.

Tali Ta'ali.

Their eyes met. Tali's face relaxed in something almost like friendship, that gave way to uncertainty when she noticed the soldiers.

"Ma koreh?" she asked them. What's going on?

"She says she is American," the blond soldier said. Tali's mouth made that little twitching motion. For some reason, Tali had always been amused by her boldness.

"Do you know her?" the soldier was asking now.

"Yes," Tali answered smoothly.

"Is she from America?"

"Yes. I think she is from New York."

"Humph," said the soldier. He turned around and walked next to Tali to the bus station. Rania thought he was hoping for a date. She wished she could thank Tali, but it would have to wait for a better occasion. She stepped to the curb just as Tina and her friend pulled up next to her. She climbed in, thanking Allah that a month ago she had decided to start a conversation with Tali Ta'ali.

Chapter 35

Chloe woke to bright lights and shouting. She leapt to her feet, shaking her limbs to rouse herself quickly. She couldn't work out where she was until she saw Amalia jumping up and down.

"What is it? Jesh?" she said. She always assumed it was the army if she was woken in the middle of the night.

"No. Mama."

"Reem? What is it?" She heard the retching before she saw Reem stagger out of the bathroom, holding her stomach.

"Oh, oh," Reem moaned. She made it a few steps before racing back into the bathroom.

"She is very sick," Jawad said, his face almost as ashen as his wife's. Chloe went to the bathroom door. Reem was shivering as she bent over the toilet.

"Bring some blankets," Chloe said to Jawad. He came carrying a jilbab and hijab instead.

"You must take her to the hospital."

"In Petah Tikva? Now?" Chloe was doubtful. Even with the permit, would they be able to get through the checkpoint at night?

"No, you must go to Nablus."

"I've never driven there. I wouldn't know how to go. Can you come with us?"

"It's better that Amalia goes. If I am with you, they will not let you through the checkpoint." He had a point. But a seven-year-old, even a very put-together one like Amalia, didn't seem like the most reliable guide.

"Shouldn't we call an ambulance?" she asked Jawad.

"No. They will be busy." She knew there was a Red Crescent office nearby, with ambulances sitting at the ready for emergencies like this one. She had sat with them a few nights when Nablus was under curfew, in case they needed to get through the checkpoint. She thought about Reem saying earlier that it was too expensive. That was more likely the reason Jawad was saying no, but she didn't think Reem was about to die so she didn't argue.

"Hurry and get dressed," she told Amalia. The little girl put on her school dress over her pajamas and was ready in five minutes. Chloe put the little stuffed horse in the girl's hands. Jawad thrust a glass of tea at Chloe, and she drank a few sips. Jawad helped Reem into the front seat and Amalia climbed into the back, protesting when Chloe insisted she buckle the seat belt. It might not do much against shooting soldiers, but Chloe knew the risks of her own driving.

Amalia was an able navigator. There was no checkpoint at Zatara, and, in fifteen minutes, they were racing along the road to Huwara. Chloe's stomach clutched as they neared the checkpoint.

She understood that yellow-plated cars did not have to stop. She had seen settlers driving around time and again. This was a yellow-plated car, and they were two women and a child. She didn't see any reason why they needed to stop. She pointed the car to the lane she had seen the settlers use and drove slowly toward the green sign that said, in English, Hebrew, and Arabic, Itamar. Itamar was a settlement, just up this road, famous for its violence. A few weeks ago, a settler from Itamar shot and killed a Palestinian taxi driver who stopped to offer him help with a flat tire.

The checkpoint appeared to be deserted. The fenced-in holding pens, which during the day were crammed with bodies, now looked pacific in emptiness. No light shone from the sandbag-lined guard booths. Only the barely visible coils of razor wire attested to the daily humiliation that dominated this place. They were almost through when Chloe saw shapes racing toward her. They materialized in front of the car, green-clad forms waving frantically. Only when they banged their guns on the windshield did she fully make them out.

She put the car in park and rolled down the window.

"Me atem?" Who are you? demanded the soldier on the left, closest to the driver's side.

"My friend is sick. We're going to the hospital."

"Meayfo?" From where?

"Salfit. Look, I really need to get her to a doctor. I didn't mean to scare you. I didn't think anyone was here."

"We're always here." It was the soldier on the right now, speaking English. "She looks okay to me."

"Well, she isn't."

"Who is that?" He gestured with his gun at Amalia, who cowered in the back seat.

"Her daughter. Please, I'm sorry, you can do whatever you want to me next time I come here, but let us go now." As if to emphasize the urgency, Reem leaned out the window and choked out a foul-smelling mess. When she pulled her head back into the car, there was white foam around her blue lips.

"Get out," the English-speaking soldier ordered.

"What? You can see how sick she is. You can't make us wait here."

"Get out and give me your keys. I need to search the car." The soldier nearer her strode to the window, reaching in to snatch the key from the ignition. Chloe's body made the split-second decision for her. She shifted into drive and gunned the engine. The soldiers fired in unison as she narrowly missed hitting them. She felt the car list to the side as a bullet zoomed through the back windshield and out the front.

Chapter 36

"Get down!" Chloe yelled. Good thing both Reem and Amalia knew English, because she couldn't remember a word of Arabic. She pumped the gas pedal frantically. Why weren't they going faster? The shots were getting a little fainter but were not distant enough. She looked down at the gear shift. She was in second. She shifted to drive, and the car shot forward. A minute later, she heard silence, then the sounds of a jeep firing up. She drove like a stock car racer, thankful for the straight, narrow road.

The jeep was coming closer, and she pumped the accelerator. Chloe heard machine gun fire, but it was so distant she couldn't be sure it was coming from behind her and not from the approaching city. If they made it inside the city gates, they should be okay. She was pretty sure one jeep would not enter Nablus alone at night; there were too many well-armed fighters in the city.

She looked in her rearview mirror. She barely saw the lights of the jeep, but it was definitely advancing. What should she do? She looked to the right and the left and saw nowhere to make a quick turn-off. This was not an area she knew, and, to make it worse, she was unaccustomed to driving. She couldn't engage in some action movie chase scene, much as she would love the story. She could only keep driving and hope the soldiers didn't have too much more speed in their arsenal.

The jeep steadily gained. The lights of the city loomed. She had perhaps three hundred yards to cover, and the jeep was now maybe five hundred behind her. Was the difference enough? She had not taken calculus, so she couldn't do a math problem involving two vehicles traveling at different speeds, especially not while trying to evade the Israeli army. Though she could not really say she was doing much to evade them. She was doing nothing beyond keeping her car in a straight line and her emotions under control. Amalia in the back seat and Reem to her right maintained a deathly silence.

Shots cracked the night. She had never heard a sound so loud or so frightening. Shot after shot rang out. Silence, then more shots; they must have reloaded.

The shots were close, but they were not getting any closer. She looked in her rearview mirror. The jeep had come to a stop, and guns were firing from both windows. She couldn't understand why the jeep was not moving, but she was not going to stop and find out. The dimly lit gates of the city were maybe one hundred yards away.

The jeep spun around, blasting the air with a final, frustrated volley of machine gun fire. As she crossed into the city, she saw a ghostly line of figures move into the road behind her, dancing a little victory dance as they kicked away their impromptu road block. She sent a silent but fervent blessing in their direction, whoever they were.

"Do you know where the hospital is from here?" she asked Amalia.

The little girl shook her head from side to side. Her grown-up-ness had fled with the speed of the bullets. She looked as frightened as anyone Chloe had ever seen. Chloe felt wretched for having been the cause. She had done what she thought was right, but maybe she had been wrong. Would Amalia be scarred for life by the experience? She had no idea. But at least the girl was alive, and so was her mother. Chloe didn't like to think about how narrowly they had missed another outcome.

"Turn here," Reem said, her voice faint but steady.

Chloe made the turn and saw the sign with the circled *H* before her. She careened to a stop in front of the hospital building and helped Reem out of the car.

"Ta'ali," come, she said to Amalia, who obeyed, silently clutching the white horse. She reached for Chloe's free hand, and they entered the hospital together.

It wasn't like an American hospital. The first sight that greeted her was a person-sized list of operations and prices, so no doubt there would be plenty of paperwork and negotiation about the fees later, but now no stern-faced admitting clerk demanded an insurance card. There was no waiting room full of people with tuberculosis and broken arms. White-clad orderlies whisked Reem into an examination room, and, a few minutes later, a nurse came to tell Chloe and Amalia that she was being admitted.

"You did a very good thing bringing her here," the nurse told Chloe. Chloe flushed with joy or maybe relief. If the nurse had said everything was fine and they needn't have come, she didn't know what she would do.

They wheeled Reem into a private room with an IV in her arm. She appeared to be sleeping. The nurse set up a cot and gestured to Chloe to lie down.

"What about Amalia?" Chloe asked.

"Can't you sleep together?" the nurse asked. It was not exactly luxurious, but, right now, Chloe could have slept on a torture rack. She lay on her side on the narrow cot and pulled Amalia in next to her. With the girl's body snuggled against her chest, she slept deeply.

Chapter 37

Rania's head was spinning. The meeting with the lesbian group, SAWA, had been fascinating. There were four of them, not including herself and Tina.

Yasmina, the young woman she had briefly met at Adloyada, was a pop singer, but said what she really wanted to do was rap. She performed regularly with the hip-hop group DAM and was raising money to do a tour with the British-born woman rapper, Shadia Mansour. She had grown up in the Galilee, but her parents did not approve of her singing in public, and so she was living in Jaffa with a group of other women. Her parents, of course, did not know about her sexuality. She seemed to have a special relationship with Tina, and Rania wondered if Chloe knew.

Salaam, who came from Abu Dis in Jerusalem, was only seventeen. She had fallen in love with a girlfriend at fifteen. The cultural norms of village life had made it easy for them to be together during high school; they slept over at each other's homes with no questions asked. Rania guessed she did not share a room with any sisters. But, now, Salaam's parents were pressuring her to let them arrange a marriage for her. She did not know what to do. She had no way to earn a living, and her family could not afford to send her to college.

Rania would need a lot of time to think about what she had learned, but it would have to wait. Right now, fifty eager, young faces gazed up at her, waiting for her to talk to them about the role of the police.

"I am sure you all know of Um Khaled," Yusuf said to the class.

She doubted any of them knew of her, except, of course, Fareed. And

259

Hanan, she realized, sitting in the back. Hanan was no longer a student, she recalled. Yusuf must have invited her specially.

"Um Khaled has done many important things to help our people," Yusuf continued. "And now she is beginning a new women's police unit. Please give her your attention."

Curse Abdelhakim and his mouth. He was determined to box her into a corner where she would have to agree to head the women's force. She wondered if he had suggested this invitation to Yusuf in the first place. She debated saying right out that his announcement was premature. But that was not the way she had planned to start, and she would not be distracted from what she wanted to say. They could get to her future plans later, if necessary.

"Thank you, Ustaz Horani," she began. "You asked me here to talk about the role of the police in our society. But before I tell you what I think, I would like to know what you think. Who can tell me what role the police play in Palestinian life?"

No one responded. She rolled her eyes. When she had been a student, you couldn't keep her hand down. After half a minute's silence, Hanan's hand went up.

"Even though you are not a student, I must call on you, Hanan, because no one else seems to want to answer my question." She smiled at the girl to show the scolding was not aimed at her.

"The police protect us by finding out who among us are traitors." Why did the statement make Rania want to scream? A few months ago, she would probably have given that answer first herself.

"True," she said. "Anything else?"

"You make sure justice is done," said Fareed.

"The police keep peace between the factions," said a young woman whose *niqab* covered her entire face except for a narrow slit across her eyes.

"Right. An increasingly important part of our work, unfortunately. Anything else?"

"If someone violates our laws, the police make them pay for their sin," said a young man with a bushy beard.

"Good, but I want to point out something," Rania said. The young man had given her a perfect entrée into her prepared talk. "Sins are different from crimes. Sin is between the individual and God. The police are concerned only with crimes, which are committed against our people and our society." In the front row, three young women put pen to notepads and began scribbling rapidly.

"The police are concerned not with virtue, but with justice," she went on. Yusuf looked as if he might interrupt her, but he did not.

"Justice, of course, is a virtue," she said, "but it is only one among many. And, at times, other virtues might be at odds with justice. So, that is the role of the police: to look out for what is just and make sure that it does not get neglected in favor of other values in our society, such as the love we all feel for our country or the honor a husband and wife are commanded to give one another. But, at the same time, it is our job to ensure that Palestine remains Palestine and does not adopt a concept of justice that might be appropriate for another country, but not for us." Then she was rolling, contrasting the job of the Palestinian police with that of the American and European police they saw on satellite television.

She finally stopped for breath after fifty minutes. "Are there any questions?" she asked.

A small forest of hands shot up.

"If a girl does not come home at night, what do you think should happen to her?" the girl in the niqab asked.

"I think that is between her parents and her and not a matter for the police," Rania said.

"But," put in a young man in a People's Party T-shirt, "if her father hurts her, then that will be a matter for the police. So, wouldn't it be better for the police to step in right away to ensure that it does not go so far?"

"Those are good questions," she said. "What do you think?"

Then she sat back while the young people argued among themselves. Why was it always girls' behavior that everyone had such strong opinions about? But as long as they were engaged, she had done her job. She noted that the girls were generally more in favor of regulating young women's conduct than the boys. It wasn't surprising. That had been true even back in her youth, before everyone got so religious. And she knew from her college sociology classes that, in most societies, women were the keepers of religion.

The students were still debating when the bell rang for the end of class. Yusuf got up to thank her, but, before he could speak, Fareed stood up.

"Please, one moment," he said, and the students stopped gathering their papers and turned to where he sat in the center of the room. "You all know that last year, I was imprisoned by the Israelis for something I did not do. I owe Um Khaled my freedom and probably also my life. To my sisters here, I say, you cannot do better than to learn from her." There was an appreciative rumble around the room. "If she chooses you for her program, you must work with her."

The class erupted in applause then, and Yusuf merely joined in heartily.

Half a dozen women remained after the others had flocked out. The young woman in the niqab was among them. So was Hanan.

"Where do I sign up?" asked the girl in the niqab.

"I am sorry," Rania said. "Your teacher should not have told you that I am starting the women's squad. I am not sure yet that it is going to happen."

She couldn't see the young woman's face, but the disappointment in her eyes was profound.

"Please," she said. "You must. This is what I was born for."

Rania was suddenly seized by a coughing fit that neatly covered her need to laugh. "What is your name, my sister?" she asked.

"Kawkab," the young woman answered.

"Well, Kawkab, if you want to be in the police, I would be glad to help you apply. You do not need a special women's squad."

"No!" said a woman wearing sandals with four-inch, spike heels under her maroon jilbab. "It is improper for women to police men and men to police women. The spheres are separate, so the law must be separate."

"But we have only one law," said Rania, "for all citizens of Palestine."

"Perhaps, but different laws are relevant to men and women," insisted Hanan.

"That is true," Rania admitted. "But Hanan, what about your job at the hospital?"

"It is boring," Hanan said with a small laugh. "You sounded so happy when you talked about your work. If it can make you so happy, I want to try it. But I do not want to work alongside men."

"Is that how you all feel?" Six heads nodded in unison. "All right," Rania relented. "I do not say necessarily that I will start a separate squad for women, but, if my boss agrees, I will begin a training course for you all. We will meet the night after tomorrow at my house at six o'clock." She wrote down all of their names and phone numbers so she could call them if they did not come.

"You were brilliant," Yusuf said as he walked her out of the building.

"Thank you," Rania said. "I enjoyed it."

"I could tell. You are a natural teacher. You will teach the girls well." Something about the way he said it made her wonder if this had been his goal all along. He had been talking with Abdelhakim when she met him at the wedding. Had it been Abdelhakim who suggested he invite her to speak to his class? She hoped not. Yusuf was much nicer than Abdelhakim.

Chapter 38

The next time Chloe stirred, the nurse was changing Reem's IV. Reem had lost that terrible pallor, but, even from where she lay halfway across the small room, Chloe could still see the bluish tint around her mouth. Reem's eyes were closed, but Chloe couldn't tell if she were sleeping, resting, or semiconscious.

"What happened?" she asked the nurse in Arabic.

The nurse answered in two words, neither of which Chloe understood.

"I didn't understand, I'm afraid," Chloe said in Arabic. "I don't speak Arabic well."

"I speak English very well," the nurse replied. She wore a white hijab with her white pants and white coat. Only her rouged lips broke the monochromatic effect.

"I can hear that you do," Chloe said. "What is wrong with her?"

"A bad infection," the rail-thin nurse replied. She finished her task and left without another word.

"Is Mama going to be okay?" Amalia asked. She was still lying down, combing her horse's mane with her fingers. At least she had not become permanently speechless.

"I think so," Chloe said. "I'm sorry about making the soldiers so angry. I did not think they would shoot at us."

"It was fun!" Amalia said. Her eyes were wide and shiny as silver dollars.

"Don't say that," Chloe said. "We almost got—" She stopped herself. If Amalia didn't know how close she had come to being killed, better not to tell her. "Our car was almost destroyed."

Shortly after she and Amalia had polished off Reem's breakfast, Jawad showed up. Jawad took Chloe's hand in both of his.

"I owe you so much," he said.

"Baba, the soldiers shot us!" Amalia said proudly.

Jawad looked questioningly at Chloe. Great, see how grateful he was about to be.

"They shot *at* us," Chloe said.

"Hamdullila assalaamu," thank God you are all safe, was all he said.

Chloe would never be sure whether she had been reckless or done the right thing. What she did know was that Avi's parents' nearly new Volvo had shattered front and back windshields and at least two bullet holes in its shiny, red exterior. She needed to get to Tel Aviv quickly, because she didn't know how long it was going to take to get it fixed.

She dialed Avi's number, but it went straight to voicemail. His girlfriend Maya answered hers right away.

"Do you know where Avi is?" Chloe said without preamble. "I need his help."

"He's at work. He always turns off his phone when he's working."

"Oh, shoot. That's right; it's Monday." Avi worked twelve hours on Monday and Tuesday, slept most of Wednesday, and saved the rest of his time for activism. Nice work if you could get it.

"Can I help?" Maya asked.

"Maybe you can." Chloe explained her predicament.

"I know where to go," Maya said, laughing. She was always up for an adventure, even a vicarious one. She gave Chloe an address and explained how to get there.

"I'll meet you there," Maya said.

The body shop was in the ritzy suburb of Ramat Gan, naturally. Where else would they be comfortable working on Volvos? It was on a street crowded with like businesses—paint shops, hardware shops, and storefronts offering every variety of automotive necessities—and the requisite number of honking cars. The guy at the counter said they would arrange to have the glass brought over while they fixed the holes in the car. The whole thing would set Chloe back six hundred dollars, far more than it would have cost to take Reem to Nablus in a cab. Good reminder for the next time she prayed would never come.

Being Ramat Gan, the street also had the requisite sidewalk café offering lattes, fourteen types of herbal tea, mint lemonade, and bits of tomato and mozzarella with a tiny strip of basil on half a baguette for the equivalent of eight dollars. Given the din created by the traffic, Chloe opted for an inside table. Maya frowned. She was a Tel Avivit, and a punk musician at that. Her eardrums were permanently desensitized, or maybe cars backfiring sounded like lullabies to her.

Chloe ordered the overpriced Caprese sandwichlet and a mint lemonade. Maya had a tofu salad sandwich, which looked a lot like wallpaper paste on cardboard, and a soy chai.

"How are things between you and Avi?" Chloe asked.

"Fine." Maya sipped her chai and didn't meet Chloe's eyes.

"Are you still upset about Germany?" Chloe figured she might as well pry.

"Sort of."

"Don't be," Chloe said. "Avi loves you."

The younger woman stirred her chai over and over, fastening her eyes on the swirling patterns the spoon made in the milky, tan liquid.

"I wish I could be sure," she said. "Inge has way more political experience than me. She's a lot smarter about all that stuff he cares about, like Gramsci and Bookchin."

"He's here with you," Chloe said. "If he wanted to be with her, he'd be in Germany."

"I guess." Maya turned her violet eyes to the window. Chloe couldn't think what else to say. When you were that age, these relationship hurdles seemed so daunting. She followed Maya's gaze.

And dropped her lemonade glass onto the floor. Sticky, icy liquid poured everywhere, but Chloe continued to stare out at the sidewalk, her eyes glued to the two perfect butts and model-length pairs of legs.

It wasn't just that they matched perfectly: same statuesque height, same slim build, same flowing dark curls, same jeans and skimpy T-shirts. Nor was it just that they strode perfectly in sync with one another, or that their heads were inclined and nearly touching, as if what each woman was saying was the most fascinating thing the other had ever heard. It was that Tina was doing with Yasmina what she would never in a million years have done with Chloe—walking down the streets of Ramat Gan arm in arm. And Chloe was sitting here in a position she had sworn up and down she would never be in again, wondering how she got here and how she was going to get out.

She should have known she didn't stand a chance once the Palestinian dykes were on the scene. She had seen this train wreck a mile off, but there had been nothing she could do about it. Now, her heart was lying smashed on the floor along with her lemonade glass, and she felt the ghost of her old, solitary life creeping back over her like a shroud.

"Can I have the check?" she said to the waiter, who had arrived at their table with a hospital's worth of white towels to mop up the mess.

She pulled out her ATM card and waved it at him while he attempted to contain the spreading disaster.

"What happened?" Maya asked.

"Nothing," Chloe said. She wasn't going to risk having her humiliation whispered all over the Israeli peace movement. "My hand must have been wet. Let's go see if the car's ready."

Chapter 39

When Rania got out of the university building, she realized she was starving and wired from the coffee. She headed for a small café where she often stopped for a snack when she was working in the city. She ordered her usual, falafel and tea, and headed for her usual table in the very back corner, where a woman could eat alone without being too conspicuous.

Too late, she saw that Captain Mustafa and Abu Ziyad were seated at a table, picking at the remains of grilled lamb shawarma.

"Abu Ziyad. Captain."

Abu Ziyad just nodded, his habitual frown deepening.

"Yaa binti," my daughter, the captain said.

Rania felt the warmth of that between her ribs. No matter what Abu Ziyad thought of her or how he and Abdelhakim schemed to put her in her place, she knew Captain Mustafa was on her side. If he didn't defend her vigorously to his boss and friend, it didn't mean he was colluding in their plots against her.

"I was coming to see you as soon as I finished eating," she said to the captain. She hoped his meal with Abu Ziyad was not preparatory to knocking off work for the day.

"Then please, join us," said Abu Ziyad.

Rania hesitated. She would have preferred to talk to Captain Mustafa alone, but she didn't want him to have to choose between her and Abu Ziyad. Even if she suspected he liked her best, she knew whom he needed more. She pulled over an empty chair, as they rearranged to make room for her.

"I was talking to some young women at the university today," she began.

"They are interested in joining the police. I thought I could make a training course for them."

"Then you are agreeing to head the women's force?" said Abu Ziyad.

"I don't know. I would like to know more about it."

"Your role will be to make sure that women are not behaving in ways that get them into trouble," Abu Ziyad said.

"Would be," she corrected.

"I don't understand."

"You said my role will be. But I have not agreed to take the job."

"I see." He saw and he didn't like. What else was new?

"What type of behavior did you have in mind to prevent?" she asked, directing her words to the captain.

"Well," he said, but lapsed into silence, concentrating instead on blowing perfect smoke rings.

"Say a young woman is acting inappropriately with men," Abu Ziyad jumped in. "You would talk to the girl and to her parents, before she becomes pregnant and ruins her life."

"If we do that, her parents will beat her, and maybe her brothers will kill the young men she was with. So, then, the police will have twice as much to do," Rania objected.

"It would also be the policewoman's job to talk to the parents about the proper way to respond," Abu Ziyad replied.

"What if a man is beating his wife?" she said. She had been the go-to person for such cases when she was working under Captain Mustafa before. She had hated them, but at least she agreed that it was probably easier for the woman to talk to another woman. "I assume it would be our responsibility to intervene in that situation, too?" At his nod, she continued, "What would you have us do then?"

"Find out what she had done to provoke him and talk to her about how to avoid it," came the expected response.

Mustafa's walrus mustache twitched. He knew what Rania thought of that approach.

"I need to think about this more," she said. "Abu Ziyad, can you excuse us for a moment? I need to talk to the captain in private." This was extremely rude to say to a man who was both her elder and her superior. It gave her a surreptitious joy.

"Of course." He gulped the half glass of tea in front of him and stood. "I will see you later, Abu Walid," he said to the captain. He did not say goodbye to her, nor she to him. When he was gone, she leaned toward the captain to be sure that no one nearby could hear them.

"I wanted to talk to you about Daoud al-Khader," she said.

"The martyr in Kufr Yunus?"

"Yes. I have been looking into his death. As I told you earlier, I thought if I could prove that the army killed him, it would help his family in their lawsuit. But now," she said slowly, "I am not sure what to think. The gun that killed him came from the army, but I do not necessarily think the soldiers killed him."

"Why not?" He finished his tea and motioned to a passing waiter for a refill.

"Apparently, a soldier lost his gun in the village."

"So, you believe that a Palestinian might have found it and killed the young man with it?"

"This soldier says the gun was left in an empty house belonging to a Palestinian American." His tea arrived. Please, please, don't ask how the soldier got into that house, she prayed. She must have been in Allah's good graces, because he didn't. He put his pack of cigarettes in his breast pocket and, in its place, extracted a cigar. He took out a little instrument and cut off the tip. Then, he focused on lighting it for some minutes.

"We should search the house to see if the gun is there," she said.

"That's going to be difficult," he said. "This is not a police case." His cigar was lit to his satisfaction, and he puffed on it deeply. She leaned back to get as far away as possible from the horrific stench.

"But, surely, if there is a loose gun in the village, we should remove it."

"It would perhaps be easier for Benny to search there. It is against the law for a soldier to lose his gun."

"You would ask the Israeli police to search a village?"

"It's just a thought."

"Forget I brought it up," she said. "Please don't call Benny. I will think of something."

"Mish mushqele," no problem, he said. "When do you think you will decide about the women's squad? Abu Ziyad is anxious to get it started."

"I am meeting with the women the day after tomorrow. After we meet, I will know more."

"Good. I will call you on Thursday for a report."

"A report? As if I am working for you again?"

"Abu Ziyad wants me to follow up with you. He thinks you do not like him." They both grinned at this. She almost felt the old comfort with him, but not quite. "Um Khaled," he added as she swung her purse over her shoulder. "If you need more time to attend to family matters, it is no problem. We can find someone else to train the women."

"What family matters are you referring to?" Her face felt hot.

"Oh, who knows?" He shrugged. "Another child, perhaps."

"Thank you." If her voice had been colder, it could have substituted for ice cream. "I think I can handle it." Not only was she being consigned to a second-rate job, but they were already preparing to take that from her, she thought as she watched him walk back to the police station. She ached to follow him, but she had no place there now.

Chapter 40

Chloe picked up the report on the bullets and shell casings from the Red Cross and took it to Rania's house.

"I made bamiya," Rania said, placing a bowl of rice and steaming vegetables in front of Chloe.

Okra. Chloe's least favorite vegetable. At home, it was the only vegetable aside from beets that she refused to eat. But, here, she could not refuse anything, especially when Rania had made it specially for her. She knew that Chloe didn't eat meat and had probably racked her brain for something to make. You always made chicken and rice for an honored guest.

"Delicious," Chloe said. She managed to get enough down that her hostess would not be offended. Rania studied the report while Chloe ate.

"The bullets matched the shell casings, and both were from an M-16, consistent with those used by the Israeli army. Traces of blood and bone suggest that they shot someone through the heart and exited into the dirt. The condition of the shells indicate that the gun had been fired at eye level, not down into the ground or up into the air. This proves the gun that killed Daoud was from the army," Rania said.

"It doesn't prove a soldier fired it, though," Chloe said.

"No. Tell me again what the soldier said." They had only talked on the phone since her meeting with Ron. Chloe repeated what she could remember about their conversation. As she had before, she omitted the part about why it had ended so abruptly.

"How did he describe the man who interrupted them?" Rania asked.

"Like a movie star."

"Elias," Rania said. "There is no doubt."

"But he denied it, right?"

"He hasn't denied or admitted it. He slipped out the window or something when I went to talk to him."

"You can't force him to talk to you, right?" Chloe said. "I mean, if you are not the police, what power do you have?"

"I have none. But in my experience, if someone has a secret like that, they want to tell someone."

"If he wanted to tell you, why would he have run away?"

"Good question. But his roommate was there. Perhaps if I can find him alone... I know," she burst out. She reached for her mobile phone.

"Ahmed?" she said after dialing. "Can you meet me this afternoon? Oh? What time? No, that is too late. Okay, tayeb, I will call you after that." She was smiling broadly when she hung up.

"Ahmed has class all afternoon. So, he will not be there." She covered the uneaten okra and rice with plates and grabbed her purse.

"But how do you know Elias doesn't have class, too?" Chloe asked as they left the house.

"I do not. But at least if he is home, he will be alone. If he is not, I will go to the conservatory to find him."

Chloe thought her friend was being awfully impulsive, but she had learned it was pointless to try to talk her out of a course of action when she had made up her mind. They walked out to the road and flagged down a servees heading toward Ramallah.

"Is it okay if I tag along?" she asked.

"Tag?"

"Come along," Chloe amended.

"I do not see how it could hurt. You could not make him less interested in talking to me."

That gave Chloe an idea. When they got out of the taxi outside the apartment building, she pulled a necklace out from underneath her shirt. It was a little silver charm, two circles and two crosses intertwined.

"I remember that," Rania said. The first day they had met, it had gotten caught on the corner of Rania's hijab when they kissed goodbye. "Did you say it is something religious?"

"I might have said that, but it isn't," Chloe said. So much had happened since that day. She had had no idea then what Rania would become to her. But, still, she felt a little bad at having lied.

"This," Chloe traced one of the little woman signs with her finger, "is an international symbol for women. I'm not sure where it comes from—the Greeks, I think. The female has a cross, and the male an arrow. Two together like this symbolize two women together—gay women."

As she explained it, she recalled the day Alyssa had bought her the little charm at a women's bookstore in Atlanta, where they had decided on a whim to spend a weekend. Alyssa, her last love before Tina—she wasn't going to think about Tina right now. Fortunately, she didn't have to. Rania was opening the door to the apartment building, not bothering with the buzzer. They climbed the two flights to number ten, and Rania knocked.

"Naam?" came the response.

"Elias? Iftah, lo samaht." Open the door, please. After a second, the door opened.

"T'faddalu," he invited them in.

Chloe recognized Elias immediately. He was the one who joked about marrying Daoud that day in Enrico's. He hadn't seemed too closeted that day. Then, Chloe thought about what Tina had said about SAWA—they needed to meet where they wouldn't run into anyone who knew their families. She supposed Enrico's was a such a place for Elias.

"Could we have some tea?" Rania asked when he did not offer. He went to the kitchen to make it and brought in a nice china teapot on a tray. Chloe leaned over to pour, letting her necklace swing before her into his field of vision.

"Do you mind if we speak English?" she asked. He shook his head. Good. She had a feeling it might be easier for him to discuss the subject at hand in English. Less like talking to a family member.

"Do you remember me?" she asked. "We met at Enrico's a few weeks ago."

"I remember," he said.

"Then you know I understand about you and Daoud." A tiny nod of his head, and he cut his eyes at Rania.

"How long were you and Daoud lovers?" Chloe asked. At her casual use of the word, he looked instinctively at Rania again. The Palestinian woman sipped her tea, her neutral expression testimony to her years of police training.

"Two years," he said. "Since we both began at the conservatory."

"And sometimes you would stay together in Lior's apartment in Tel Aviv and other times at the Palestinian American's house in Kufr Yunus?" Rania said.

"That is right." Elias's long fingers played riffs on the coffee table.

"Why didn't you use your own apartment?" Chloe asked. He gave her a look that she interpreted as, You foreigners don't know anything.

"We lived with Ahmed," he said.

"But Ahmed knew," Rania said.

"He knew we were gay, but that doesn't mean he wanted us making love in his house."

"When did you find out Daoud was also meeting an Israeli soldier at the house?" Rania asked. Elias's eyes narrowed to little slits. He had underestimated Rania, Chloe thought.

"The week before he died, Yom il Jumaa," Friday, Elias said. "We were both home for the weekend, and we met there in the afternoon. His brother found us there together. He yelled at Daoud and said he would kill him."

"How did Issa know you were at the house?" Chloe asked.

"He had heard rumors about Daoud performing at Adloyada. He followed him from his parents' house."

"That's what Daoud told Ron," Chloe said to Rania. "Or at least, Ron said he did."

"Do you know where Issa heard those rumors?" she asked Elias. He shook his head.

"What did you do after Issa found you?" Rania asked.

"I went home, to Jamai'in. Later, I called Daoud but he did not answer. I went to his house, and he was not there, so I went to look for him at the Palestinian American's house. I was afraid that something had happened to him."

"You thought Issa might have killed him right then and there?" Chloe asked.

"Yes. The key was not where we always left it, so I knew that Daoud was still inside. I knocked on the door, and no one answered. I opened the door, and I saw him with the soldier." Tears were starting to well up in his eyes. There was no doubting that he had been in love.

"Ron says he ran out half-dressed into the garden," Chloe said. "And left his gun behind."

"Yes."

"He also says that he saw you and Daoud fighting," said Rania.

"Sure, we fought. He said he was only sleeping with the soldier, because he helped him with the checkpoints. I did not believe him. I remembered him coming home with the leather jacket he had wanted. He said he had bought it, but where would he get that kind of money? I asked if the soldier had given it to him, and he admitted that he had. I left and took the gun with me."

"Why?" Chloe asked.

"I was angry. I wanted the soldier to get in trouble."

"That makes sense," she said. "So, you still have the gun?" She held her breath. If he did, that meant he must have killed Daoud. She stole a glance at Rania. The other woman was drinking tea, looking nonchalant.

"No," he said. "I kept it for a day, but I don't like guns. I didn't like having it in my house. So, before I went back to Ramallah, I took it back to the house."

"Did you and Daoud reconcile?" Rania asked. "You said you had planned to come up together for Ahmed's party."

Elias nodded. His chiseled face softened. "I could not stay mad at Daoud. I went back to the apartment on Saturday. I told Daoud where I had put the gun. We were going to go north together, but then he said he had to meet someone and he would see me at the party."

"Do you know who he was supposed to meet?"

"No. I asked if it was Ron, and he said no. I thought he was lying."

"Where did you put the gun?" Rania asked. Chloe knew where her mind was going.

"Under the bed in the big bedroom," Elias said. "Tuesday afternoon, Daoud called me. He said the gun was not there. He assumed Ron had gotten into the house and taken it, but then he saw him in the village, and

Ron said he did not. Daoud asked me to meet him at the house. When I got there, he accused me of lying. He was talking crazy. He said he was going to leave Palestine. He thought he could win *SuperStar* and move to Italy or America. He was such a big dreamer."

Elias was crying now for real. Rania fished out a Kleenex from her purse and handed it to him.

"He said he was going to tell Hanan at the party that night that he could not marry her. He was going to tell everyone what he was, and, if his family did not support him, he would leave the country. I said he could not do that. We fought," Elias said. "He hit me, and I hit him back. He fell and hit his head on a marble table."

"In the bedroom?" Rania put in suddenly.

"In the living room," Elias said. "I got a towel for him, and he put it up to his head and was trying to stop the bleeding. I was very angry at him and I left. That was the last time I saw him. You have to believe me." He looked at Rania when he said the last.

"I do," she said.

✶ ✶ ✶

"I've got to look in that house," Rania said to Chloe when they were standing on the sidewalk.

"Don't you need a warrant or something?" Chloe asked. She had no idea if the Palestinian police used search warrants.

"Not a warrant, exactly, but we need permission. I am not a policewoman now, so I cannot get the permission."

"Wouldn't you get in trouble if someone found out you searched the house?"

"I will just have to make sure they do not find out."

"Be careful," Chloe said, kissing her friend goodbye.

Chapter 41

If Chloe was not sleeping with anyone, she didn't need to sleep in the closet either. She took her mat and laid it out on the living room floor. She felt chilly, even though the night was warm. She collected all the covers from both mattresses and cuddled up. Nothing like a pillow and a cry to make one want to sleep forever. She woke up, baking in the mid-morning sun. She tossed the covers aside and went to shower. She emerged, comforted by the hot water, and walked into the closet to find some clean clothes.

"Ouch," said a muffled voice from the floor. She had stepped on a leg she had not expected to find there.

"You're home," Chloe said. Tina sat up in bed, rubbing her eyes.

"Of course I'm home. Did I say I wouldn't be?"

"When you didn't come for dinner, I figured you were spending another night in Tel Aviv."

"Another night? I haven't stayed in Tel Aviv since last Friday. You're the one who hasn't been home."

Chloe flipped through her few clean shirts. She had told Rania she would take the report on the bullets to Benny Lazar at Ariel. And, since she would be near Salfit, she would go see how Reem was doing. That meant she needed modest but cool clothing. She picked a long, white blouse—the same one she had worn on her first date with Tina. She wondered if Tina would remember taking it off of her, that magical night in the Austrian Hospice. She half-buttoned the blouse over her Jews Against Israeli Apartheid T-shirt.

"You're saying you didn't stay in Tel Aviv after your SAWA meeting?"

"It wasn't a meeting. It was just a get-together."

"After your get-together, then."

"Of course not. I was with Rania. One of the other women from Ramallah has a car. We drove her to Mas'ha and then came home." Chloe had forgotten that Rania would need to get back home. Tina had stripped off her clothes. Now, she wrapped herself in a bath towel and disappeared into the bathroom. Chloe heard the water raining down as she went to make coffee.

Tina appeared, wearing black jeans and what Chloe thought of as a Ramallah T-shirt—tight, with a scoop neckline. With her hair still pinned atop her head and a little damp, she looked more swan-like than ever.

"How was the meeting—sorry, *get-together*?" Chloe asked.

"Good. Rania asked intelligent questions. I think all the women really liked her."

"Including Yasmina?"

"All of them," Tina said. "What's going on? You're acting weird."

"Don't say *I'm* acting weird."

"What's that supposed to mean?" Tina grabbed a bowl and poured corn flakes into it, ignoring the fact that Chloe was cutting potatoes.

"You took Rania to SAWA, but you won't take me." There, she had said it.

Tina sat at the little table to eat her cereal. "It's not the same."

"Because she's Palestinian. But she's not a dyke. I'm a dyke but not Palestinian. So, what's the difference?"

"Chloe. The difference is that she's trying to find help for a friend who has been deeply troubled for a long time. You just want a cool experience to tell your friends at home about."

Chloe stood with the knife frozen in her hand. She thought, really thought, about what Tina had said. After a long second, she put the knife down and walked over to where Tina sat. She knelt in front of her lover, removed the spoon from her hand and held both of Tina's hands in hers. It wasn't what she had meant to do, but she leaned forward, and Tina met her halfway. Their lips touched. Their mouths locked; their tongues twined.

"Mmmmm," Tina moaned. She reached a hand under Chloe's shirt and teased at the underwire of her bra.

It hit them both at the same moment what they were doing. They rocketed apart as if a truck were speeding toward them. They turned as one to peer outside the window. Chloe didn't see Um Malik or anyone else. Chloe pulled herself up and sat demurely in the chair opposite Tina, as far across the little table as she could get.

"I love you," she said quietly.

"I love you, too." Tina sounded sincere. She also sounded sad.

"Tell me about Yasmina," Chloe said.

Tina did not flinch or look away. "Did Rania tell you?"

That was a blow. Not only was Tina seeing this other woman, but Rania knew about it? Chloe couldn't deal with that double betrayal right now. She tucked it away in her "think about later" drawer.

"No. I saw you together in Ramat Gan."

"Chloe, listen," Tina said. "We were together, what, three weeks? And you were in jail for half of them. I didn't know if you were ever going to come back."

"I never said you should wait for me," Chloe said.

"I know. Shush for a minute. When I told you Rania was in prison, I didn't know you would decide to come back. I was happy when you did, but, even then, I didn't know if you would get in or how long you would stay. Yasmina and I are not a couple. But you have to realize that I live here, full-time. I had a life without you here, just like you have a life in San Francisco without me."

Did she? Chloe wondered. What Tina was saying made sense. For once in her life she wasn't going to indulge in a dramatic gesture that she might regret a minute later.

"Are you having sex?" she asked.

"Why ask that? Does it matter?"

"Yes."

"We haven't. But I'm not going to say that we won't. Our relationship is… different."

"Because you're both Palestinian."

"Yes."

"I understand," Chloe said. The amazing thing was that she actually did. "I'm going to stay with Reem for a while," she said.

"You don't have to," Tina protested.

"I know. But I need to think. I'll be there in case Reem needs to go to the hospital again, and, when she's feeling better, we'll interview women in the villages. I'm sure you can use the space, too." To have sex with Yasmina, she added, but only in her mind.

Chapter 42

The white house belonging to the absentee Palestinian American was unmissable from the road. It towered above its neighbors, not only because of its size but because it was built on the highest hill in the village. It occupied a massive lot, and, as if that were not enough, it was topped by a golden dome reminiscent of Al Aqsa Mosque. Rania got the taxi driver to leave her at the side of the road near the house and climbed up through the brush to the house, rather than going around to the path. As she approached, she saw that the house was surrounded by its courtyard, but white columns surrounded the courtyard, so, instead of a panoramic view, it was as if you were looking out through venetian blinds. What a monstrosity, she thought. Such a pity that someone with so much money should have such terrible taste. But she wasn't here to critique the architecture. She looked around, wondering where Daoud had hidden the key. It would have been easiest to ask Elias, but she had not wanted him to know she was going to search the house. His story was only semibelievable. If he was lying, she would not want him to have time to cover his tracks. Or do something to stop her from going to the house.

She walked around the house three times. The first time, she turned over a heavy bronze turtle on the front porch and put her hand in a watering can in the back yard. The second, she dipped her fingers into the soil of a flowerpot and ran them along the top of the iron door. She opened cupboards that contained water pipes and paraphernalia for smoking *argila*. There were dozens of places a key could be hidden in the courtyard alone. And then there was the garden. A grid search would take days. She was not going to find the key that way. She needed to think like the person who hid it.

Daoud would not have wanted to be seen going into the house, so he would not put the key somewhere that took a long time to get to. That left out digging in the garden or climbing anything or prying up a loose flagstone. She closed her eyes and tried to imagine him mounting these steps, putting his hand...

She was imagining the boy in the photo she had first taken from his mother's house, the one with Ahmed and Ron at Abraham's Garden. Then, he had been a pale, skinny boy, like many others. But that was not who he had been the day he was killed. He had turned into the costumed youth in the pictures she had seen at the bar—rouged cheeks, pouty lips, and long wig. Where would that person have hidden a key?

Now she saw it. Among the treasures scattered around the hideous courtyard was a Japanese doll: a porcelain courtesan, white skin, white robe painted with little flowers, upswept black hair. It reminded her of the pictures of Daoud she had seen in the bar. Rania picked up the statuette and turned it around. There was a hole in the back, where she supposed you were meant to put flowers. She peered in through the hole and there was the key.

The inside of the house was as daunting as she expected it to be. She thought of the Greek myth she had studied in school about the labyrinth where men died because they could not find their way out. She should have brought a string to find her way out of this house-maze.

The entire first floor was presumably what Elias had called the living room, though it was more accurately called a parlor or receiving room, because certainly no living could go on in it, even if anyone had lived in this house at all. All the furniture was hard and dark and cold, from the marble-topped end tables to the hundred or so straight-backed wooden chairs placed exactly four inches apart all the way around the white-walled room. She fought the urge to move one or two of them half an inch, just to drive whoever set them crazy.

There was a small water closet containing just a toilet and sink off the parlor, so that the family need not allow guests into their inner sanctum. Two little decorative hand towels were draped over little metal circles by the sink. A third little towel holder stood empty. This would have held the towel

Daoud used to stanch his blood after Elias knocked him down. Where was the towel? She did not find it in the bathroom.

She ascended the spiral staircase to the second floor. This contained a vast kitchen boasting three stoves and two refrigerators. She opened the refrigerators, more out of curiosity than anything else, and of course found them completely empty—but not turned off. If the Palestinian American decided to come back at a moment's notice, she supposed, he wanted his refrigerator to be at forty degrees for the groceries he would have someone buy to prepare for his arrival. The center island was a cutting board, so every square inch of wall space that was not taken up with the stoves or refrigerators was a cupboard. She opened one after another. One was stacked with pots, one with pans, one with spatulas, wooden spoons, and other utensils. There was a deep drawer displaying every type of knife, and drawer upon drawer of kitchen towels and aprons. When the Palestinian American had banquets, he must hire an army of chefs to come and help his wife.

She moved on to the dining room. More cushioned, dark-wood chairs evenly spaced around a table big enough for twenty. China closets displayed stacks of porcelain dishes, each with a thin band of gold leaf. None of the cabinets were large enough to hold a gun, so she didn't waste time with them. She climbed up to the next level.

This is where the family would live, if they ever lived here. The master bedroom, which occupied half the third floor, was entirely off-white. It had a massive bed as wide as it was long, covered by a cream-colored, satin coverlet over cream-colored, heavy-cotton sheets and a cream-colored fleece blanket with a satin ribbon at the top. Two matching cream-colored bureaus stood against the walls, and, though they were mostly empty, the top drawer of one held a few pieces of cheap jewelry (not cream-colored) and the other a few pairs of boxer shorts (cream-colored, though they may once have been white).

When she pulled back the coverlet, she saw, as anticipated, that this was where Daoud and his friends had done their recreating. Apparently, Daoud had seen no need to change the sheets after his last tryst. She looked under the bed, and, though she could barely see that far, let alone reach to the center of the floor, she was quite sure there was no gun under there. It was not in any of the closets or hidden among the pillows that filled the bottom drawers of each bureau.

The only photo in the master bedroom was an eight-by-twelve family portrait in a silver frame, sitting on a cream-colored night table. She picked it up. The Palestinian American was a florid man with what English novels called a hail-fellow-well-met countenance. His wife's black, likely dyed, hair was uncovered. Her children, three boys and two girls, had the bleached-blond hair Rania associated with America.

Rania was done with the master bedroom, so she made her way to the den where the family obviously watched television and indulged in alcohol consumption. Bottles and bottles of every description were lined up with their labels in alphabetical order behind a wooden bar made of more dark hardwood. The thirty-inch television was hidden behind a rollback door in an entertainment center that held things Rania had only seen in magazines, like a surround sound stereo system. She didn't find a gun behind or among any of the toys in that room nor under the couch or buried in the cushions of the overstuffed chairs.

It did not take her long to search the five children's rooms on the fourth floor because, although there was a plethora of closets, they were all virtually empty. Only the linen closet was stuffed with sheets and towels—cream colored, naturally—but they were all quite neatly stacked and there was no gun shoved in among them.

She was about ready to leave this strange house which felt like it held the ghost of a family. She felt disappointed, though, really, she had not expected to find the gun. If it was not where Elias had put it, there was no reason it would have been somewhere else in the house. She thought about who might have taken it, assuming both Elias and Ron were telling the truth. Issa would be the most likely. Daoud had gotten the key from their uncle, so it stood to reason that Issa might have one as well. Of course, any of their cousins could also have gotten one, but, as far as she knew, they had not threatened to kill anyone who had ended up dead.

She wandered into the little laundry room off the back bathroom (there were three bathrooms on the top floor—one for each of the two girls and one for the three boys to share, she imagined). She opened the washer and the dryer and, not surprisingly, found them empty of lint as well as everything else, including the gun. The hamper was empty except for one small item—a cream-colored towel crusted with dried blood. That part of Elias's story, at least, was true. She smiled, thinking of Daoud, having daubed his forehead until it stopped oozing blood, climbing all these stairs to throw the soiled towel in the hamper rather than leaving it lying on the floor in the parlor. His mother had said he was a good boy. Despite what many people would think if they knew what he'd been up to, Rania thought she agreed.

A rumble of engines outside sent her scurrying to the window. Two Hummers and four jeeps were tearing up the Palestinian American's carefully manicured lawn. Soldiers poured out, dozens of them, and, in an instant, she could tell that the house was surrounded. What were they doing here? Had they come to search for something, and, if so, was it the same thing she was looking for? And why?

Perhaps they just wanted to use the house as a staging ground or to look off the roof. The army often chose the highest house in the village to try to find someone or something hiding among the trees. Or they might be planning to use it for an exercise, a mock search, knowing that it was huge and empty.

Whatever they were doing here, she did not want them to find her. She did not think she was wanted. After all, she had been released from prison; she had not escaped, so the men who had had her arrested must have agreed that she could be freed. Benny knew what she had on them, and they knew he knew, so he would only have needed veiled threats to get their approval. But she could never be sure that they would not put her name right back on the wanted list.

There would not be a way to get out without the soldiers seeing her. Besides, they were already running up the stairs, their boots like a stampede of angry mules. Still holding the bloody cloth, she thought about hiding in one of the kids' empty closets and decided against it. If the soldiers found her hiding in a closet, she was dead or at least in jail. The only hope at this point was to pretend she had every right to be here. She turned the little towel inside out so that the blood stain was not so visible. If they did not look closely, it would look like a dust cloth and that's what she would insist it was.

She stepped out into the hall and walked down the stairs to meet them on their way up. The soldier in front stopped short when he saw her. He lifted his gun, finger on the trigger.

"Who are you?" At least he spoke English.

"I am the housekeeper," she said. "I come once a month when the family is not here. What are you doing here?" she asked. She shouldn't have asked that. A maid would not.

"That is not your business," he said. "Let me see your hawiyya."

She did not recognize his face, but she recognized the blond hair and imperious voice. He was the one who had asked for her ID at the Petah Tikva bus station. She could see him searching his memory for where he knew her from.

"I'm sorry; I did not bring my ID," she said. "I just live down the road." The closest house was half a mile away, so she hoped hoped hoped that he would not send someone with her to get it.

"That's not good," he said. "You're supposed to have it with you all the time."

"Not in my own village," she said. "This is Area B; you are not supposed to be inside." Another mistake. The average Palestinian did not know or care about the intricacies of the Oslo accords. He knew it too.

"Who *are* you?" he hissed.

"I told you," she said.

"You are lying."

She stood stock still. She did not want to lie about whether she was lying. It would become a contest she would not win.

"Maybe I am, and maybe I am not," she said. "But I will tell you this— whoever or whatever you are looking for here, it is not me."

She made herself very small and squeezed past him, gun and all. She walked down the stairs slowly and deliberately. She half-expected someone to grab her, but it didn't happen.

She made her way out of the house, through the line of smoking, gossiping soldiers, and down the path that led into the village. But she did not follow it. Instead, she circled around and came back up to the olive groves on the left-hand side of the house. She went to the tallest tree in the grove. In her youth, she had been good at climbing trees, but, recently, when they picked the olives, she always used a ladder, so she had not had practice. She remembered when she was in prison and had tried to climb up to the window and couldn't. But, there, she had been unable to find a handhold, and this tree had a knobby trunk. She put her right foot on the lowest knob and hoisted herself up. She grabbed the nearest branch and clung on, even when she heard it start to crack. She caught a higher branch with her fingertips, just as the first one gave way. She thought for a terrifying instant that she was going to topple to the ground, where she was almost sure to break her collarbone because of the angle at which she was dangling. But she righted herself and climbed up, choosing her branches more carefully this time. At last, she sat lodged in the top branches of the tree, the heavy foliage providing nice camouflage from which she had a perfect view of the house. Now, she just had to make herself marginally comfortable, so she could wait for the soldiers to come out.

She peered down at the road and saw two men coming from the direction of the house. She wondered how they could have gotten past the soldiers, but, obviously, they had done so. She recognized Abdelhakim's skipping walk and Yusuf's bushy head above his turned-up collar. They crossed the road and found a good place to wait for a servees.

Whatever the soldiers were doing, it took them a long time. She got very stiff sitting in the tree. She would have liked to shift position, but she was afraid she would fall, so she just made herself count, using the days of Khaled's life as she had done in prison. Finally, she saw them trooping out. The guy leading the pack presented a rifle to the blond commander like an offering. When he climbed into the Hummer, Rania could clearly see that he wore a gun slung over his shoulder, just like all the others. The soldiers piled into the Hummers and jeeps and, before long, they were all gone. To her relief, she soon saw the caravan speeding down the highway. They had not gone into the village to look for her.

She scrambled down the tree and headed back to Mas'ha. She wondered if they had found what they were looking for. She didn't see how the gun they came out with could have been in that house.

Chapter 43

As soon as the dinner things were cleared, Rania packed Bassam and Khaled off to Marwan's so she could have the house to herself for the training session. She set out tea and little wafer cookies with chocolate cream in-between. She wanted everything to be nice for the girls, and she realized that she was excited about the meeting.

The college girls, Kawkab, Abeer, Ayat, Noura, and Suheir, came in a bunch, at six on the dot. Hanan showed up a few minutes later.

"Before we begin, I would like you to tell me why you want to be in the police," she said. "Kawkab, why don't you begin?"

"To help our people," Kawkab said.

"Abeer?"

"I need the money," the girl said, "so I do not have to get married right away. The Americans give us money for police. So, it is the only job that we can count on." Rania saw heads bob up and down.

"Ayat, is that why you want to be in the police?"

"It is part of it," Ayat answered in a voice that could barely be heard. "But also, my father used to beat my mother very badly. She had nowhere to go except her family, and they would send her back to him. The police did not help her."

"What do you think the police should do in such a situation?"

"Explain to the woman that she must not anger her husband," said Noura.

"Tell her to kick her husband out!" said Hanan.

Rania smiled at her. "What do you think would happen then?" she asked.

Hanan shrugged. "He probably would not go. But why should she be the one who has to leave, if he is the one who is breaking the law?"

"It's not against the law," said Noura. "Islamic law gives a husband the right to discipline his wife."

"Discipline?" Abeer broke in. "Is she a school child? The Qur'an says husband and wife are equals."

"Each in their own sphere," said Suheir.

"And the house is the wife's sphere," said Hanan. "So, it is she who should set the rules there."

"Enough," Rania says. "It is not Islamic law we are enforcing but the civil law of our country. Who knows what the Palestinian National Assembly has said about domestic violence?"

None of the girls knew.

"That's because there is no law," Rania said. "It is not a crime for a man to beat his wife, unless her injuries are so severe that we can call it attempted murder. But that does not mean that we cannot help her. There are shelters in Bethlehem and Jericho if she is willing to leave, or she might go to her family for a while if they are supportive. And there are counseling centers for battered women and their children in both Nablus and Ramallah.

"Now let us consider another scenario. Imagine that a woman becomes romantically involved with another woman. What do you think the police should do about that?" Part of her listened to her own voice and wondered what the hell she was doing. She was playing with fire, but she could not stop.

"Arrest them," said Noura.

"Why?" Rania asked.

"Because it against our law."

"No, it isn't," Hanan said.

"Who believes Palestinian law forbids homosexuality?" Rania asked. She cringed at the old, unpleasant word, but, if she used one of the new ones she had learned recently, probably no one but Hanan would understand her. The girls looked at one another for guidance before four of the six raised their hands.

"It does not," Hanan said.

"Well, it should," said Noura.

"Love cannot be a crime," Abeer said.

"Our law does not forbid homosexuality. But let's suppose," Rania said, "that the woman's brother finds out about her relationship and kills her. What do you think should happen to him?"

"He should go to jail," said Abeer.

"Why? He was defending his sister's honor," said Noura.

"Hanan, what do you think?" Rania asked. She hadn't known she was going to do it, but she looked steadily at the young woman. Hanan's dropped her lively eyes to the ground.

"I don't want to talk about this anymore," Hanan said. "It is stupid. Something like that would never happen." She gathered up the tea glasses with so much clanking, Rania was afraid she would not have a single glass left.

"Can you help me carry them into the kitchen?" she asked. She heard the others chattering in their wake.

"Hanan," she said when they were out of earshot, "why are you upset?"

"I'm not."

"You are. I would rather you tell me than break my glasses."

"I'm sorry," the girl said, her chin nearly on her chest. Rania put a finger under her chin and looked into her watery eyes.

"You are not the one who should apologize," she said. "I obviously have been thinking about this issue, and I thought it would make a good topic for our discussion. I did not think about how you might feel."

"Tomorrow night, I am getting engaged," Hanan said. "I want you to come to my party."

Rania tried to keep the shock out of both face and voice. "So soon? Who is it?"

"Elias," Hanan says.

"When did this happen?"

"Two days ago. He and his father came to my parents' house, and my father agreed."

"Is this what you want?"

She nodded.

"But you know that Elias is…like Daoud."

Another nod.

"Why, Hanan? Don't you want a husband who loves you?"

"Elias is nice. Gentle."

"I suppose so." Sulky and self-absorbed would have been Rania's assessment. "But there is more to marriage than that."

"It's okay. He will come to love me."

"I don't know, Hanan. I am just learning about these things, but it seems to me that a man like Elias or Daoud cannot change the way that he is."

She had just seen the girls into a taxi when Bassam and Khaled burst into the flat. They must have been upstairs at her mother-in-law's, waiting to hear the front door close.

"Baba got me ice cream!" Khaled crowed.

"You didn't bring me any?"

"It would have melted by now. You were busy such a long time."

"Well, that's true, yaa shater," clever boy. "Why don't you go get ready for bed, and then I'll come read you a story."

"I don't want to go to bed yet. I'm a big boy now."

"Yes, but big boys need to get lots of rest so they can do well in school."

He wandered away, and she thought she had won her point, but, a few seconds later, she heard the computer whirring to life in the little office. She sighed and turned from the sink, drying her hands on her skirt.

"He's impossible," she said to Bassam, who was standing at the dining room table looking at a newspaper.

"He wants to spend time with you," Bassam said. "He hasn't gotten over your being gone."

"How is playing on the computer spending time with me?"

"It's getting your attention."

Point to him. From the piles of children's books strewn around the living room, she picked two at random and went into the office. Khaled was playing Minesweeper, expertly clicking around the bomblets. How had he learned so much suddenly? She could feel him growing away from her. She stood behind him and put a hand on his shoulder.

"Come keep me company for a little while," she said. "I want to see how well you can read."

"All right," he said, not looking away from his game. She tickled the side of his tummy where his shirt was riding up. He squealed with delight. Straining, but trying not to grunt, she lifted him out of the chair and tucked him under her arm, settling into the massive rocking chair which her grandfather had made for a wedding present. He squirmed briefly and then snuggled into her.

"Which book do you want to read?"

He looked at the two on offer, *A Land Called Palestine* and *A Boy's Life*.

"I don't like either of those," he pouted. "They're for little kids." She started to tell him to go get one he liked, but she couldn't stand the thought of him leaving her right now, even for a minute.

"Tell me a story, then," she said, tossing the books to the ground.

He thought, looking quite like his father as he furrowed his small brow. "Once upon a time," he started slowly, "there was a boy named Khaled. He had a mama and a baba and two brothers."

"What were his brothers' names?"

"Mohammed...and Radwan." Radwan was his best friend at school.

"Were they older or younger than Khaled?"

"Younger. Khaled was very big when his brothers were born, and he took care of them when his mother was busy being a policeman."

"Policewoman," she corrected automatically.

"Baba said I might have a little brother soon," the storyteller said.

"Would you like that?"

"Oh yes. All the kids at school have brothers and sisters to play with."

"You have lots of cousins."

"I know, but it's not the same."

She was rocking furiously, she realized. Why did Bassam have to enlist even her son to pressure her? She rose, pulling Khaled up with her.

"Okay, yaa walad, enough stories. Time for bed now." He started to object, but a yawn betrayed him. He was asleep by the time she had finished tucking him into bed. Bassam was waiting for her when she emerged from Khaled's room. He pulled her to him, stroking her hair. She leaned into his kiss, but, when he urged her toward the bedroom, she stood still, lacing her fingers into his.

"You shouldn't get his hopes up about having a brother," she said.

"If it's a sister, he'll be just as happy."

"That's not what I meant."

"I know. But I don't understand what you're waiting for. I want to have more kids."

"So do I, but I just got out of prison. I can't think about this yet. I'm starting the women's police force, and I need to focus on that for a while."

"You didn't even want to do it."

"Well, maybe I was wrong. The girls who came tonight… They were very strong, very excited. They want to make a difference. I can help them."

"Nine months is plenty of time to get them trained." He silenced her with a kiss.

Chapter 44

"Ron is in jail," Avi said as soon as Chloe picked up the phone. It was Friday morning, and she was playing Snakes and Ladders with Amalia. She made a "sorry" gesture to the little girl and walked outside where the signal was better.

"What for?" she asked.

"Killing that kid in Kufr Yunus."

"Daoud? Why do they think he killed him?" And why do they care? she asked silently. When was the last time a soldier was actually arrested for killing a Palestinian?

"Who knows? Who cares?"

"He can't have done it."

"How do you know? You met the guy once."

"Three times, actually. And I think he was really in love." She caught herself. People killed people they claimed to love all the time. Ron had struck her as weak and impressionable, a little power-mad like all soldiers, but not capable of the kind of anger that drove someone to kill. But Avi was right, what did she really know about him?

"How did they catch him?" she asked.

"They found the gun in a house in Kufr Yunus. It matched the bullets you got from Um Mahmoud."

"But he told me he lost his gun," she said.

"I guess they don't believe him. He wants you to visit him," he said.

"He does? Why?"

"How would I know? I'm just the messenger."

The last time Chloe had seen Ron, he had walked away cursing her. The two times before that, he had threatened to take her to jail. If he wanted to talk to her, he must have a good reason.

"Where is he?" she asked.

"Atlit, south of Haifa."

"I can't go today. I'm in Salfit, and Reem has scheduled a bunch of interviews for me with women on the local council this afternoon. Can you take me tomorrow?"

"They might not let us come on Shabbat," he said. "I'll find out and call you back."

She called Rania while she waited for his call. Rania let out a long breath that came out as a little whistle.

"I do not believe he is guilty," she said.

"Neither do I," Chloe said. "But maybe all those stories about him losing the gun were lies."

"I saw the gun," Rania said slowly.

"What do you mean you saw it? Where?"

"Yesterday. I went to the Palestinian American's house, and I searched everywhere. I did not find the gun. But then soldiers came. I hid in a tree and watched them come out."

Chloe smiled to herself. She could picture Rania, in her long jilbab, scrambling up into a tree so she could spy on the army. She wished Rania had called her to go along.

"But you said you saw the gun."

"When the soldiers came out, I saw one soldier hand a gun to the commander of the search. And it was not his own gun, which he had around his neck. I just don't understand how it could have been in the house."

"I wonder why they went there to look for it," Chloe said.

"Yes, and why they tested it against the bullets you found," Rania said.

Chloe's phone beeped, letting her know there was another call coming in. "I'll call you later," she told Rania.

"We can go tomorrow," Avi said. "Take a sherut from Ariel, and I'll pick you up at the bus station."

"Right, then," Chloe said. She had adopted that manner of ending a call from Tina, she realized. She needed to find a new one quick.

* * *

Rania strode into the Ariel police station. Someone might think, seeing her going in and out of the settlement, that she liked it. She didn't. She would rather never enter one again. But she had thought about her options very carefully. She could talk to Captain Mustafa, or she could talk to Benny Lazar. Besides the fact that it was Friday, and the captain would not be working—but she had his mobile number, so she couldn't really use that excuse—she could not imagine how the conversation would go. If she was going to convince him that the soldier had not killed Daoud, she would need to tell him something of what she knew about Elias and Ron and Daoud, and she could not. She hoped she would be able to have this conversation with Benny without revealing secrets that were none of his business, but, if it came down to it, she would rather tell an Israeli, even a settlement policeman she could not stand, what she had learned than tell her boss.

She ignored the receptionist and walked up to his office as usual. As usual, he did the eyebrow thing.

"Congratulations," he said. "It's done. Ron Binyamin killed Daoud al-Khader."

"He did not," she said. The eyebrow went up again. "And there is no need to congratulate me, because I had nothing to do with his arrest."

"The army found his gun on a tip from the muhabarat," Benny said. "I assumed it came from you." He leaned his chair back perilously on the back legs and balanced his socked feet on the edge of his desk.

"It did not." She thought feverishly. It made no sense. Why would the muhabarat, the Palestinian secret police, have information about an Israeli soldier's weapon? One thing she had seen yesterday seemed like a possible connection. Abdelhakim had been in the area, and he was close to Abu Ziyad, who had ties to the muhabarat. Could he have been involved in setting up the search? Could he have planted the gun? And how much of any of this should she say to Benny?

"The soldier did not have his gun," she said.

"What do you mean?"

"That soldier, Ron, left his gun in that house," she said. "But then someone else took it."

"Who took it?"

"That I cannot tell you. I will not tell you," she said when he beetled his eyes at her. "But that person said he lost it too."

"A lot of losing going on," Benny said. He scribbled something on a yellow notepad in front of him. She couldn't tell if he was making notes or just doodling. Especially since Hebrew writing looked like doodling to her anyway.

"The most important thing is," she said, "that I searched that house top to bottom just before the army got there. And the gun was not in that house."

"What are you saying? You think the army planted it?"

"It's possible." A lot of things were possible, and none of them made much sense to her. Why would the army want to frame one of their own for killing Daoud?

"How did they know the gun belonged to Ron?" she asked.

"Every gun issued by the army has a serial number," he said.

"And how did they know to test it against the bullets Chloe gave you?"

He shrugged. "They read the same reports you did. He had been in the village. He had fought with the kid who was killed. Why are you asking so many questions? Just be happy it turned out to be the army this time."

"It was the army last time too."

"Touché." He took his feet off the desk and stood up. He gathered up the top layer of papers on his desk—including, she noted, the top sheet from the pad he had been doodling on while they talked—and put them into a briefcase.

"It's Friday afternoon," he said when she looked at the clock. He ushered her out and locked the door. "I'm going home, drinking a couple beers, and tomorrow I'm going to play matkas."

"What is that?"

"A game where big men try to hit a little ball."

Did he make it sound filthy on purpose? "Have a nice time," she said.

She sped up and bounded down the steps before him. If any Palestinians happened to be coming into the police station, to report that settlers had killed their sheep or whatever, she did not want to be seen leaving with him. There were enough rumors about her already.

Chapter 45

The last thing Rania felt like doing was celebrating Hanan's engagement to Elias.

She was dead tired, she had a lot on her mind, and she was irritated that the girl refused to take her advice. Nonetheless, she, Bassam, and Khaled dutifully joined the throng of well-wishers crowding into Hanan's parents' house in Kufr Yunus.

The house was not large. The modest living room was crowded with women and girls, while men lounged in the courtyard, drinking tea and smoking argila. Rania saw small plates that had clearly once contained sweets but now held only a few orphaned nuts and blobs of honey. Khaled ran to join a group of children playing with balloons near the chicken coop. A stooped man in a long white robe greeted Bassam with an arm slapped around his shoulder. In a second, they were deep in conversation. Rania silently said farewell to the men in her life and started for the women's room where dreary gossip about nothing awaited her.

She stopped in the doorway between the two worlds and watched Hanan's little sisters painting her hands and forearms with the mud-like henna. Hanan was unusually subdued, but the chattering women sitting around the edges in their flowing, white headscarves did not seem to notice. Hanan wore a white bridal dress straight out of a Lebanese magazine, with a strapless bodice that angled from her right shoulder to just above her left breast. Later, Elias would sit next to her for the ritual part of the evening, but now he was tucked away somewhere among his brothers and cousins. Rania had not noticed him. She picked out Ahmed by his height,

300

surrounded by a cloud of argila smoke. Where Ahmed was, she had no doubt Elias was near.

"Um Khaled, good evening."

She turned to see Yusuf on the porch. "Mabrouk," congratulations, "on your brother's engagement."

"Mabrouk to you," he said. "I hear the Israeli soldier who killed Daoud has been arrested." She wondered how the news had traveled so quickly, but the riddle did not persist for long. Abdelhakim materialized next to him, along with a young man she knew but could not place.

"This is Issa, Abu Wael," Yusuf said. Daoud's brother. She had never met him, but the resemblance was striking. For a second, she could not help thinking about how Issa would look in a long wig with rouge on his cheeks.

"Tsharafna, Abu Wael," she said. She wasn't sure whether she should congratulate him on his cousin's engagement or express condolences for the loss of his brother. It seemed safer just to say it was nice to meet him. He nodded.

"How is your mother?" she asked.

"She is well, thanks. Still grieving, of course. But she is pleased that the soldier has been apprehended. Yusuf tells me you are responsible for that. You must come to visit, so that my mother can thank you herself. Perhaps now we can sue the army."

"I am not convinced the Israeli soldier killed your brother," she said on a whim. This was not the place where she had meant to have this conversation, but he was here, and the subject had come up. His mouth turned down a little.

"Why do you say that? I understood that it was you who matched the bullets from the soldier's gun to Daoud's wounds."

"It was not really me," she said. "My friend, an American, took the bullets that were found by Um Mahmoud to the Red Cross in Salfit. They did the tests."

"No matter," he said. "We owe you gratitude nonetheless." He seemed content to return to his original premise, that she was the hero of the hour. The fact that he did not ask why she thought the soldier had not killed his brother made her deeply suspicious.

"Have you known Yusuf and Abdelhakim for a long time?" she asked.

"Yes, we were all in college together."

"At Al Quds Open?"

"An Najah," he said. "Abdelhakim and I majored in Islamic Studies. Yusuf was only interested in politics." He grinned at his friend. Apparently, this was an old bone of contention.

"Abu Wael, could you come with me for a moment?" she said. "I do not see my son, and I am afraid he may have climbed a tree or something. I would not be able to get him down."

"Of course," he said. "I will get my friends to come as well." He started to gesture to Abdelhakim and Yusuf.

"Oh, that is not necessary," she said. "Whatever he has gotten into, I am sure he will not be difficult to extract."

He hesitated. She smiled to herself, wondering if he feared she would try to seduce him. She forestalled his decision by striding down the steps. He followed her. She knew exactly where Khaled was, of course, but it was true she could not see him because he was at this moment at the bottom of a pile of children fighting over a half-deflated soccer ball. She walked by them, checking momentarily to see that her son's head was not being smooshed under anyone's foot or knee.

"What does your son look like?" Issa asked.

"He is seven years old and has light curly hair and a wonderful smile," she said. She smiled, picturing him as she described him. "I saw him running this way a few minutes ago," she said, taking off in the opposite direction from where her son was playing.

He followed, with only a doubtful glance backward.

Shouts exploded from the children, and they were all up and running now, chasing the ball and each other. She saw Khaled's little legs carrying him toward the front of the house, and she quickly disappeared around the back, so that Issa would not catch sight of the distinctive blond curls.

"Abu Wael," she said, as soon as they were far enough away from the nearest party-goers. "I need to ask you something."

He looked at her doubtfully, clearly suspecting a trick, and she hastened on.

"Did you threaten your brother's life because he was gay?" She used the word she had learned from Tina, mithli. He looked confused.

"I do not understand," he said.

"Because he loved other men rather than women," she said. She could have made life easier simply by saying luuti, but her mouth seemed to have a mind of its own.

"That is not true. How can you say that?" His face was the color of ripe purple grapes.

"Elias told me you found them together in the Palestinian American's house," she said. This was not how she had meant for this conversation to go. She had not thought it out. If somehow the story Elias had told her was not true, she had just revealed a damaging secret about him on the night of his engagement party. But then Elias would have only himself to blame.

"I do not know what you are talking about," Issa said. "My brother was not homosexual. I have never been in that house."

He wheeled and walked quickly toward the front of the house. She rushed after him, catching up just before he turned the corner.

"I am going to find out the truth," she said. "If you don't tell me, someone else will."

"You are a curse," he hissed at her.

By the time she got back to the courtyard, he was huddled with Abdelhakim and Yusuf, talking hard. All three of them glared at her as she entered the house. She had no doubt he was telling them she was a horrible, wretched woman out to destroy his brother's reputation. She assumed and prayed he would not tell them what she had said about Elias. She shook her head at her own idiocy.

Their voices carried just slightly, and, as she crossed the threshold into the living room, she thought she heard the words "American" and "weapon."

Chapter 46

Chloe was half-sure that the guards at Military Prison Six would tell her she couldn't visit. That had happened every time she had gone to visit anyone in Israeli custody. But, this time, they merely took her ID and told her to follow them.

"Can my friend come, too?" she asked. She remembered how easily she had blown her last conversation with Ron. It might help to have Avi as a go-between again. But the guard shook his head.

"One at a time," he said.

"Go," Avi said. He took a paperback copy of *Brave New World* out of his back pocket and looked around for somewhere to wait. Chloe felt mildly shamed. She was still carrying *The Da Vinci Code* in her backpack.

She followed the guard through a series of gates and tunnels before arriving at a dungeon-y cavern where Ron Binyamin was waiting, his legs in shackles and his hands cuffed in front of him. She remembered meeting Rania with her hands cuffed behind her. Soldiers charged with murder, she thought, were given a slight privilege over Palestinians charged with knowing too much.

They sat opposite one another across a table of gray-green metal, in metal chairs bolted to the floor. As if anyone would try to steal them. Or perhaps it was to prevent anyone from trying to move closer to one another, despite the presence of four armed guards in the four corners of the room. The long table had chairs for ten pairs of visitors, but she and Ron were alone in the room. She did not know if that was because he was considered high security and kept in isolation or simply because no one else had visitors right now.

She wanted to ask him, but it didn't seem like the right question to get started with. She decided on a neutral "How are you?" instead.

"Okay," he said.

Silence. He had asked to see her, so what was he being so reticent for?

"I was surprised you wanted to see me," she said. "The last time we met, you didn't seem anxious to talk to me." That was an understatement if she'd ever uttered one.

"I need you to make them believe me. I did not kill Daoud."

"I don't know how I can make them believe that," she said. "Seems like an Israeli—"

"No. It's that Palestinian policewoman. Lior said you are friends with her. You have to convince her I didn't do it."

"I hate to tell you this, but Rania had nothing to do with you being arrested. She doesn't even believe you killed him."

A modicum of fear penetrated his pocked face. He looked like he had not slept in a week.

"Tell me what happened," she said. She hated to think that this young man was putting his hopes for freedom in her hands. She had been able to do precious little for herself when she was in prison, and it had taken a lot of luck to get Rania out. She knew nothing about how the Israeli army dealt with its own miscreants.

"I told you, I lost my gun," he said. "On that Tuesday, I went to look for it."

"I thought you didn't know where the key to the house was," Chloe said.

"I didn't. I don't. But I thought maybe I would be able to figure it out. I don't know; if I had to, I would have broken a window."

"But your friend, Yonatan, was with you. Why didn't you go by yourself?"

"We were on duty. He said there was going to be an inspection the next day, and, if I didn't have my gun, I would be in trouble. I told him I knew where it was."

He was licking his lips compulsively, looking rather like a german shepherd. "Can we get some water over here?" she asked one of the guards. He shook his head.

"You said Yonatan didn't even know you were gay, so what did you tell him you were doing at the house?"

"Smoking marijuana. I told him Daoud got great stuff in Ramallah, which was true, actually. I told him we met at the house to get stoned and some other soldiers came, and I got scared and ran out without my gun."

"Good story," Chloe said. She was warming up to him a little.

"We were looking at the house, trying to find a way to get in, and Daoud came out. I told him I needed the gun, and he said it wasn't there. I didn't believe him. I thought he had hidden it. I told him to let me in to see. He refused. Yonatan said, 'Let's turn this dirty Arab in. Tell the SHABAK he stole your gun, and they will make him tell where it is.' He got in the jeep and started it up. I had to go with him, to stop him."

"And Daoud ran after you," Chloe finished.

"Yes."

"Why did you think he had hidden the gun?" she asked.

"He used to say he was going to. He thought if I lost it, I would have to leave the army. I said it would ruin my life, and he said he would ruin my life to save my soul."

"Sweet." Was it possible that Daoud had done that after all? That he had hidden the gun somewhere and someone had unearthed it? No, that didn't fit with what Elias had said—unless Elias was the one who had found and used it. "You didn't want to leave the army?"

"I wanted to. Believe me, I did. But I couldn't do it to my family. The army is everything to them. My father lost his foot in the Six-Day War."

"Okay, so you didn't find the gun, and you fought with Daoud in the village. What then?"

"Nothing. We left. The next day, I said I was sick and stayed home, so I missed the inspection. I was sure I would be able to make Daoud give me the gun before the next one. But then I learned he was dead and…everything. Three days ago, there was another inspection."

"Why didn't you miss that one?" she asked.

"We didn't know about that one in advance. They sprang it on us; they do that sometimes." Quite a coincidence, Chloe thought. But who would have set it up, and why? She leaned forward to encourage him to continue. "They asked me what happened to my gun, and I said Palestinians took it. They asked where, and I said near Mas'ha. I don't know why they searched that house."

"They got a tip," Chloe said. "From the muhabarat." He looked bemused at that. He scratched at an old pockmark until it bled.

"They arrested me right away for losing my gun," he said. "It's the worst thing you can do." He hesitated, maybe conscious that he was saying the army rated the loss of a gun worse than killing a Palestinian. But Chloe already knew that.

"Yesterday, they came and said they had found the gun, and they were charging me with killing Daoud. I can't believe this is happening." His eyes were starting to fill up. She felt bad for him, in spite of herself. In spite of the fact that he had threatened to arrest her twice. But, the fact was, she didn't see how she could help him. She opened her mouth to tell him that.

"I'll see what I can do," her mouth said instead. "Try not to worry. It will all work out."

He looked a little more cheerful as she left, which only made her feel worse. Two of the guards accompanied her as she wound her way back through the network of wire cages and barbed wire–lined passageways to where Avi was embroiled in the World State. Once he had gotten them onto the southbound highway, she called Rania's number. It rang twice, and she was just thinking it would go to voicemail, when Rania answered.

"Chloe!" The single word was more panic-stricken than Chloe had ever heard.

"What's wrong?" Chloe asked. Her pulse throbbed in her temple.

"Khaled is missing," her friend said, and burst into sobs.

Chapter 47

If Hanan insisted on marrying Elias, Rania would need a present. That's why she announced to Bassam on Saturday that she was going to take Khaled to Nablus after school. It was a furlough day for his ministry, her husband said, so he would join them. He looked happy. At the party the night before, he had talked with colleagues who were highly placed in the Foreign Ministry. They thought that a deal with the Europeans would be struck soon, a deal that would get euros flowing to the Palestinian Authority again. When they arrived home, they had made love for the second night in a row. A family outing was just what they needed to get their lives back on track.

They went together to pick up Khaled from school. Bassam heard that the checkpoint was not too bad, so they drove their own car into Nablus for the first time in over a year. That meant they could buy whatever they wanted. She loaded up on vegetables and fruit from the produce market, even though she would have to carry the heavy bags around while she looked at possible gifts, because she did not want to miss the produce vendors, who often went home early. She bought bananas and mangos from Jericho. Inside the walls of the Old City, she hurried them through the street where enormous cow and sheep carcasses hung from every doorway, sending rivers of blood down the cobblestones. She covered her face with her hijab, feeling sorry for her husband and son that they had nothing to block out the stench.

In the fish market, Bassam said that his mother had asked him to bring back some haddock. He went to check out the stalls, to see who had the freshest catch at the cheapest price. The phone reception in the Old City was almost nonexistent, so they arranged to meet in half an hour at the ice cream shop where she and Khaled had gone a week ago. She took Khaled by the hand, and they went to the store that featured hand-blown Nablus glass. Khaled got bored as she picked up heavy decanters and delicate bud vases, candelabra and fluted bowls, sometimes inquiring about prices.

"Mama," he complained, "I want to ride on the elephant."

"Habibi, you're too big," she reminded him. "You tried last week, and you did not enjoy it, remember?"

"I want to," he whined.

"Fine, suit yourself." She handed him a shekel. "I will be right there," she called after him. The carousel was just across the street. She made her choice—two long-stemmed goblets marbled in shades of green and blue. She haggled with the shopkeeper until he agreed to a price that was still high, but she liked the symbolism of two colors swirling into one. Maybe even an odd couple like Hanan and Elias could be fused by tradition into a happy family. She counted out the money while the shopkeeper wrapped the glass in layers of white tissue paper. She took her purchase and went outside. The carousel was still going around and around. Khaled was not on it.

He must have gone into the store to look at the candy. She peeked down its narrow aisles, overflowing with candies and cookies. She did not see him. She went to the counter, where the cashier was adding up a woman's purchases on a long strip of paper.

"Excuse me," she interrupted. The cashier looked up, annoyed. He was doing the math in his head, and now he would have to start over. "My son," she said, attempting to keep the rising panic out of her voice. "He is seven years old, curly light hair. He was riding the carousel, but he is gone now. Have you seen him?"

Both the cashier and his customer shook their heads. "Sorry," the cashier added.

Rania felt their judgment piercing her back as she left the store. What a terrible mother, to let her son wander loose in Nablus.

She ran up and down the crowded street, pushing people out of her way. She looked in every store. In the barber shop, she even insisted on checking behind the curtain that hid the various hair products and cleaning supplies.

It was just the kind of place an adventurous child would like to play. But Khaled was not there.

Half an hour had passed, and it was past time to meet Bassam. She dragged her feet along the cobblestones. She felt her throat tighten when she saw him, sitting at the window table and checking his watch. She had half-hoped he would not be there, and she would have a few more minutes before she had to tell him that she had messed everything up again. But this was worse than anything else she had ever done. Worse than making him wait for dinner because she was so focused on an investigation she did not notice that it was time to go home, worse than staying all day in Bethlehem and not calling to say she would be late, worse even than getting arrested and being in prison for a month. This he could never forgive, and she could not blame him because she could not forgive it either.

She burst into tears as soon as she got to the table.

"Habibti," he said, dear one. Although they were in public, he got up and put his arms around her. It was okay; she was his wife, and she was upset. They were a modern couple. The tears poured out of her so fast she could not speak. Then, he noticed she was alone.

"I don't know where he went," she said before he could ask. "He wanted to ride the carousel. I was looking at the glass. I went to get him, and he was gone. It was only a minute, really. I have been looking for him for almost an hour," she exaggerated, lest he imagine that she had not been diligent in her search.

"We will find him," he said. He took her hand and led her out of the shop. She could not believe he did not berate her. He did not even seem like he wanted to. His face was full of concern but not reproach.

They ducked into shop after shop. Up one alley and down another, past the plaque commemorating the murder of a family by an Israeli tank in 2002, past the mosque and the old prison built by the British, and finally they reached the police station. Just then, she recognized the little folk tune of her phone's ring, deep within her purse. Bassam went into the station to start the process of getting the police to look for their son, while she excavated the ringing instrument. She prayed it would not stop before she found it. She managed to answer just before it would have gone to voicemail. She did not have time to see who was calling, but she was sure it was someone who had found Khaled. Funny, she didn't even think he had her phone number. She must have given it to him one time, for some reason, and he, smart boy that he was, had kept it in the pocket of his school pants.

It was Chloe. She, of course, did not know anything about Khaled; she did not even know that Rania was in Nablus. She was calling to report on her visit with the Israeli soldier. Rania blurted out her news.

"I'm coming," Chloe said. "I am near Haifa, so it will take me a long time, but I will call you when I get there."

"No, that's not necessary," Rania said. "I am sure we will find him before that." If we don't, she said silently, I will slit my wrists.

"Why don't I call you when we're near Tulkarem," Chloe said. "And if you still have not found him, I will come help you look." She hung up, murmuring platitudes about how it was going to be all right. Rania walked into the police station. Bassam was there, speaking to three uniformed officers. They all looked much too young, she decided. They could not be more than rookie patrolmen. She would insist on talking to someone higher up.

"They have something to tell us," Bassam said. He looked very worried.

"What is it?" Why was he keeping her in suspense? She couldn't wait a second longer.

"Come this way," said one of the policemen. He was smooth-skinned and had eyes like pools of molten chocolate and was not quite as young as she had thought. She followed him and Bassam through a heavy metal door riddled with bullet holes from numerous Israeli incursions. For a police station, it didn't look that bad. She had seen doors that looked like swiss cheese.

"We had a phone call," said the young officer, who said his name was Majid. He sat behind a desk, and they sat in chairs facing him, like recalcitrant students sent to the headmaster.

"Who from?" She realized she was sitting as if she was ready to dart out after whoever it was as soon as he said the name. She planted her feet on the floor and looked straight into his chocolate eyes.

"I don't know exactly who. But they said they have your son, and he is fine." He hastened to say that part. She tried to take comfort in it.

"Did they say why they took him?" Bassam asked. A very reasonable question, to which she was sure she knew the answer.

"They said that your wife," he said, looking at her, "should stop asking questions about things that do not concern her. They took the boy to demonstrate that they are serious."

"That's criminal," she said. "You have to find them immediately and arrest them."

"I agree," he said. "But first we must make sure that your son comes to no harm."

"What do we do?" asked Bassam. He was so calm in a crisis; she wanted to strangle him.

"They said you should go to Al Yasmeen Hotel," said Majid. "They will contact you there."

"Contact us how?" she asked.

"I do not know. But I am sure they will find a way. Do you know who they might be?"

She thought about what to say. There were many people who were upset about her investigation. If she knew who had reason to take Khaled, she assumed she would know who killed Daoud and would not need to ask questions people didn't want her to ask. She did not want to cast aspersions on innocent people. But there was one person who knew Nablus and perhaps had the most to lose.

"There is a young man named Issa al-Khader," she said. "He is from Kufr Yunus, and he went to school at An Najah. His brother was recently killed, and I am trying to find out who killed him."

"I would think he would want to know," Majid said, small wrinkles appearing at the corners of his eyes.

"Yes, but things are not always as they seem."

"I will send someone to speak to him." Majid made a note on the pad in front of him.

"We will go now," Bassam said. He got up and held out his hand for her to follow. She stuck her feet to the floor and her behind to the chair.

"What are you going to do?" she asked Majid, "while we are sitting drinking mint lemonade at Al Yasmeen?" She could not imagine spending the afternoon at the quiet luxury hotel, while her son was being tortured—or more likely overfed on milk and cookies—in an undisclosed location. Kidnapping in Palestine was often a matter of enforced hospitality, not the fingers-cut-off variety. But it didn't make it any easier on the ones who waited for word.

"There is not that much we can do right now." He emphasized the last two words. "Nablus is a big city, and he could be anywhere. We cannot go house to house. But we have our ears to the ground. We have people asking all over the city, and I am sure we will know something in an hour or two."

"An hour or two?" Her voice went up plaintively at the last word. In two hours, she would have no hair left on her head.

"It can take some time," Majid said. "But, really, there is no need to worry. I am sure he is fine, and he will be returned to you before long. Go to Al Yasmeen now. If they try to contact you, you must be there." That was true. She rose to go.

"Where did the call come from?" she asked. "Surely you could trace them that way."

"It was not from a telephone," he said. "It came from a Skype account, but the owner of the account is in Finland and has never been in Palestine." Smart of them to choose a Finnish account, she thought. Any Muslim country, and people might start imagining an Al Qaeda connection. She doubted there were ten Muslims in Finland. She followed her husband out of the police station, and they raced through the streets of the Old City to the hotel just outside the walls. Rania couldn't stop herself from looking into every store they passed, trying to catch a glimpse of her son's blondish curls, even though she understood the futility of it.

After an hour of sitting on the deep-cushioned, wicker chairs in the lobby of Al Yasmeen, she gave up and called Captain Mustafa.

"I am not sure what I can do," he said. "If the Nablus police are handling it, we must let them do their job. But," he forestalled her protests, "I will call Abu Ziyad and see what he thinks. Perhaps we can offer some assistance." She thanked him. She didn't know what she had expected. At least it was something to hang a little hope on.

Her phone rang. Al Yasmeen had intermittent service. She went out onto the terrace to take Chloe's call. The city looked calm and lovely from that vantage point.

"Could you call the international press?" she asked.

"I suppose I could," Chloe said. "But, I don't know, is it a good idea? I mean, I really don't know anything about kidnapping, but, at home, I think they usually say to let the police handle it."

"I think you should call them," Rania said.

"I'll talk about it with Avi," Chloe said. "He knows people who have been kidnapped."

"Tayeb," very good, Rania said. She was frustrated that people were being so deliberate, but her own tendency to leap before looking had created this situation in the first place. She could not blame her friends for wanting to be sure they would not make things worse. They knew, if they did, the fact that she had suggested the course of action in the first place would not protect them from her anger.

"Avi thinks we should just call Al Jazeera," Chloe reported a few minutes later. "The Western press will misconstrue it." Rania did not know what "misconstrue" was, but she wasn't the least bit interested in an English lesson right now.

"Please," she said. It was a generic plea, carrying a host of requests. Please get my son back soon. Please don't let him be hurt, emotionally or physically. Please don't let my husband be angry that I jeopardized our family once more. But she knew that Chloe would understand it as Please call Al Jazeera, which in fact was the only one of Rania's requests she had any power to grant.

The Al Jazeera reporter showed up in twenty minutes. She wore a smart, navy-blue pleated skirt, falling just to mid-calf, and a blue and red plaid blouse, accented with a red scarf around her neck. Her soft, brown hair flipped under just below her chin. She wore a little makeup, just a touch of red on her lips and a tiny bit of foundation covering a blemish or two.

"I am Dunya," she introduced herself.

"My sister's name is Dunya," Bassam said with his lopsided smile.

"Greetings, yaa akh," my brother, Dunya said. "You are the father?"

"Yes. Where are you from?" he asked.

"Kuwait. But I am Palestinian. Is this the mother?" The father. The mother. The reporter. The hotel manager. All neatly arranged into a nice, cozy scene for the viewers, who would turn on their television sets at five o'clock, or look on aljazeera.net on their computers, and hear about the tragedy of the boy snatched from the carousel in Nablus where, no doubt, Dunya and her crew had stopped to shoot a little tape for background use.

Dunya gathered them in front of the fireplace, taking care to get the argila smokers over her left shoulder, and signaled to her camera people to point their lenses at her.

"In the lobby of this elegant hotel on the outskirts of Nablus's Old City," she intoned, "a drama is playing out with a seven-year-old child at its center." She went on like that for a few minutes, and then stuck her microphone in Bassam's face. Naturally, she would turn to the father first.

"My wife can say more about the reasons for this attack on our family," he said simply and turned to her.

Rania had had a bit of time, since Chloe's call, to think about what she wanted to say. Well, not what she wanted to say—which was that if the kidnappers didn't bring her son back this instant without a hair on his head having been harmed, she would personally cut off each one of their testicles and stuff them into their mouths and watch them choke—but what she thought was right to say. She took a deep breath to make sure that she did not come across as hysterical, but as sincere and worried, someone deserving of compassion from everyone seeing her, including, she fervently hoped, the people who were holding her child.

"I do not know what the people who took my son hope to accomplish," she said. "I am not a militant. I am not a politician. I am a policewoman, but I am on leave, so I have no power to help or hurt anyone in our country." The word *baladna*, our country, could also mean our village. That should remind whoever had Khaled that they were one people, deeply connected. Khaled was their son as much as hers.

"Whatever quarrel you have with me," she said directly to the men she could not see, "it is wrong to frighten a small child in order to express it. Please, return my son, and I promise that whatever it is you want, I will do it if I possibly can." They had said she should stop asking questions about things that did not concern her. The death of Daoud did concern her, so she wasn't lying in saying she would meet their demand.

Chapter 48

Dunya was happy with her. Rania had been passionate but articulate. Dunya nodded to the camera people, and they began unplugging their long electrical cords and winding their long cables between their hands, tossing them from one to the other over and over again. Just past the television people, Rania saw Abdelhakim dashing in with Ustaz Kareem. Kareem noticed them first.

"What brings you here?"

"Abu Ziyad called me," Abdelhakim answered, though she had spoken to Kareem. "I ran into Ustaz Kareem and told him where I was going, and he asked to come along."

"Khaled is my pupil, after all," said the teacher. Dunya heard that and said something to the camera guys. They started unwinding their cables again. Her eyes were starry over the prospect of interviewing Khaled's teacher. She stuck her mike in Kareem's face. Rania did not get close enough to know what Kareem said. She heard the word *shater*, clever child, and of course that was true, but doubtless he omitted the part where he had suggested that the shater's mother was a collaborator.

Dunya went off to edit her tape, and the hotel manager appeared with a third pot of tea and some *borekas* to nibble on. Rania was not at all hungry—and she was surrounded by bags of fruit and vegetables if she had been—but the young men enjoyed the snacks. Rania wanted to ask them if they knew where Issa was, but she didn't know how she would explain why she was asking, so she just sat and watched them chat among themselves.

Half an hour later, Chloe walked in just in time to see the Al Jazeera report on the large screen. Rania got up to kiss her friend. The American's presence was comforting or as comforting as anything could be, given that she wanted to chew her fingernails off their cuticles. Bassam shook Chloe's hand warmly.

"This is the American who got my wife released from prison," he told the younger men.

"Perhaps it would have been safer to leave her there," Chloe said with a smile. She flushed after that, belatedly realizing this might not be the best time for a joke.

Chloe might be the only person in Palestine with less tact than herself, Rania thought. But Bassam chuckled and said that was true.

"How is Tina?" Rania asked, when Chloe was settled with a cup of tea and the last half boreka.

"Honestly, I'm not sure," Chloe said. It was Rania's turn to blush. Come to think of it, the last times she and Chloe had spoken, Tina's name had not come up. She knew Chloe had been staying in Salfit, and she hoped nothing was wrong between them.

A rush of air caused her to turn toward the door. Yusuf walked in and came immediately to join their group.

"I just saw the report on Al Jazeera," he said. He sounded out of breath, as if he had run the whole way from Jamai'in.

"Did you come from your village?" she asked him.

"No, I was in Nablus, visiting some friends," he said. "I came as soon as I heard."

"That was kind of you," she said.

"Will you excuse us a moment?" he said and drew Abdelhakim and Kareem outside to the terrace. She watched them take out cigarettes—she thought very religious Muslims did not smoke. But these were young people; who knew what they did? They talked intently for ten minutes or more. Then, Abdelhakim came back alone.

"Yusuf thinks he might know where Khaled is," he said.

"Tell me." She was already getting up, gathering her bags, to go wherever he pointed her.

"Stay here," he said. "It is only a slight possibility. We will go there and let you know as soon as we find out anything."

"But where is it?" she demanded. "How does he know?"

"He does not know. He only suspects. He thinks his brother might have something to do with it."

"His brother Elias?" Who else would it be? But she could not imagine Elias having the organizational skills or gumption to mastermind a kidnapping in Nablus, and, besides, he had been busy getting engaged to Hanan all week. She was sure he had been partying late last night.

"Yes. We will be in touch." Abdelhakim left, and he and his friends walked down the stairs that led to the Old City. She fought the need to run after them and demand to be taken along. Instead she puzzled over Elias some more. She did not like him, but this did not seem like his style. How would he know whom to contact to pull it off? Of course, he was a student, and even the Said Conservatory must have some militant groups. But Issa, who had studied here at An Najah, seemed a more likely candidate.

Daoud was the key. Somewhere among all the information she had gathered was the critical piece she had missed, that would unravel the whole mystery. She needed to find it. She thought back over everything that had occurred since she had gotten out of prison. She tried to recall every interview, every gesture of Hanan, Elias, Issa, Yusuf, even Benny and Captain Mustafa. Someone had slipped somewhere. She must be getting close, or they would not have snatched her child.

Bassam was talking quietly with Chloe. Chloe was nodding and smiling, showing her crooked, gapped teeth. Rania struggled to pay attention to what they were saying. Something about Bassam's work, and the women that Chloe had interviewed in Salfit. They wanted to start a cooperative, she gathered, to help women in their village sell their crafts. Chloe was asking what they would need to do to get a license from the Ministry of Interior, which was part of Bassam's job.

"Look." Chloe grabbed her hand and pointed to the doorway.

Yusuf and Kareem each had Khaled by one hand. He looked rested, and he was hopping a little as he came to where she had jumped up. She grabbed him in her arms and hugged as hard as she could. She lifted him like a bag of feathers, and he put his arms around her neck. He was carrying a stuffed black dog with long, floppy ears that tickled her skin.

She handed him to his father and gazed at him, poring over his face as if she needed to learn it for a very important final exam.

"Where did you get that?" she asked, touching the dog.

"Ustaz Kareem gave it to me," he said proudly. He wagged the dog up and down vigorously.

"Show your mother the dog," Yusuf said. Khaled obediently handed it to her.

She took Yusuf aside. "Was he where you thought he might be?" she asked.

He shook his head. "No. The police found him. We just happened to be nearby, and Kareem said we would bring him to you. We thought it would be reassuring for Khaled, since Kareem is his teacher."

"I'm sure you were right," she said. "I must thank him."

She went back to the little group.

"Are you hungry, habibi?" she asked her son.

"Yes, very."

"Perhaps we can order something from the restaurant here," she suggested, looking at Bassam for approval.

"I am sick of this place," he said. "Let's go into the Old City and find a place to get shawarma. Then, we can get the ice cream we promised you," he said to Khaled. Khaled jumped up and down enthusiastically.

"Come with us," she said to Chloe.

"I should be getting home," Chloe said. It was after eight and quite dark. Her friend Avi had brought her to the gates of the city and gone back to Tel Aviv. It would be hard to find transportation to Ramallah at this hour.

"Nonsense," Bassam said. "You will stay with us tonight."

"Please," Rania said. "We really want you to."

"Naami andna," sleep at our house, Khaled put in.

Chloe grinned. "Can't say no to that," she said.

"Will you eat with us?" Rania asked the young men. She really did not want to have dinner with Abdelhakim, but he and his friends had brought her son back to her, after all.

"No, thank you, Um Khaled," said Yusuf. "It is late." The others nodded in agreement. She breathed a sigh of relief.

"Let's go find some yummy shawarma," she said to Khaled. "And a falafel for Chloe, because she doesn't eat meat."

"Why don't you eat meat?" Khaled asked Chloe.

"Ana nabatiya," I'm a vegetarian, Chloe said.

"What's a vegetarian?" Khaled asked.

"A person who doesn't eat meat," Chloe responded with a shrug.

Chapter 49

It took a while to get the details. Chloe could tell Rania's mother side was holding her cop instincts in check. Rania barely ate, but she drank four glasses of tea, waiting for Khaled to wolf down his shawarma before she asked a single question.

"Why did you get off the carousel?" Rania asked at last, betraying only the tiniest trace of annoyance.

"Two girls came up to me. They said that the jesh had taken you away, and they would take me to Baba."

Chloe wondered how the child thought Israeli soldiers could have dragged his mother out of the shop without him seeing them, but it was not her place to ask. The kidnappers were clever to use women. Not only would a child be more inclined to trust them, but they would be more or less indescribable. Black jilbab and white headscarf. The police could stop girls and women from here to Jordan and never find them.

"Did you walk a long way?" Rania asked. The empty apartment where Khaled had been found was only a few blocks from where he had been taken. Her friend must be trying to determine if he had been moved there from elsewhere or if the women had taken a circuitous route to get there.

"No," said Khaled.

"What happened then?" his mother asked. She nibbled on a french fry.

Khaled leaned his head to the side as he tried to recall. His eyes were looking heavy. Chloe thought, if he had been home, he would fall into bed just about now.

"One of them played with me for a while," he said. "The other one asked if I was hungry. I said I was, so she got me some milk and cookies."

Khaled's Arabic was easy for Chloe to understand. She supposed she could be proud of having attained a seven-year-old's conversational level.

"Then, I was sleepy, so she put a mattress down on the floor, and I went to sleep," the child went on. "When I woke up, they were gone."

Sleeping pills in the milk, Chloe thought. No wonder he had seemed so relaxed and was now so droopy.

The policeman named Majid joined them for *knaffe* and coffee. Chloe did not like the knaffe, the sticky, cheesy sweet that Nablus was famous for, and joined Khaled for chocolate ice cream instead.

"We asked all around the building," said the dashing young officer. "Neighbors saw the two girls go in with the child and come out about half an hour later. No one else went in or out. They could not give any details about the girls and did not know which way they went."

"That seems impossible," Rania objected.

"If they persuaded everyone to lie for them," Majid said, "then they are part of a very powerful group. We have a few leads we will follow up on in the next days. But you have your son back, so, if I were you, I would go on with your lives and be more careful in the future."

Rania's opened her mouth to say something and closed it, her cheeks scarlet. The policeman had basically said that Rania was a bad mother, and it was her fault. Chloe wanted to say something in defense of her friend, but she couldn't think how to say it in Arabic. She clasped Rania's hand under the table and felt it trembling.

"How did you know where he was?" she asked the policeman.

"Someone called us," he said.

"Skype again?" Bassam asked. Rania remained silent and sulking.

Majid nodded. "Another account, this time from Hong Kong."

Khaled was asleep by the time they got home. Chloe, being bigger and a little stronger than Rania, carried him into the house and tucked him in bed. He was still clutching the little stuffed dog, but it fell out of his hand on the way into the bedroom. When she returned to the living room, Rania was sitting in an armchair, crying fiercely with her head against the shaggy little toy.

"You can't let what that cop said bother you," Chloe said, although she didn't really imagine that it was Majid's voice as much as her own that Rania was hearing over and over. "You are a great mother."

"I am not. I never think about my family first. Everything is about me. My job, my satisfaction. I was bored; that is why I took on this investigation."

"You couldn't have known," Chloe tried again. She sat on the arm of Rania's chair, stroking her friend's hair. Bassam had come into the room after parking the car. He stood in the doorway, making no move to join them. Chloe felt very much in the way, but she couldn't go anywhere else. The living room was where she was to sleep. If Rania and Bassam wanted to be alone, they would have to make the move. Bassam looked at them for a long moment and left the room.

Rania sat up, swiping impatiently at her eyes with the back of her hand. It was almost like she didn't feel she had a right to cry. Chloe thought back to the day she had visited Rania in prison. She had made the same gesture. Rania turned the little dog around and around in her hands. "Maybe I should just stop," she said. "The Israeli soldier is in prison. If I tell everyone he killed Daoud, they will forget all about it and leave us alone."

Chloe was silent. She wondered why she disliked that idea so much. It wasn't really that she cared so much about Ron. She had thawed toward him some during her visit, but, basically, he was a weasel. He might be privately critical of the norms of his family, his friends, and his country, but he wouldn't stand up to them. If he had not killed anyone, it wasn't because he was not willing to. Nothing too bad would happen to him. No Israeli soldier went to jail for long for killing a Palestinian.

It was more what she felt the suggestion said about Rania. The last few times she had seen her friend in the throes of solving a mystery, she had been the sharp, headstrong policewoman Chloe had first met under the Azzawiya bridge. Chloe could almost see that person receding, and a fearful, self-doubting woman taking her place. To let an innocent person be imprisoned, even an innocent person who was not so innocent, was inconsistent with the Rania she knew.

Rania was examining the little dog. Her fingers found a little tear in the back seam. Typical, Chloe thought, recalling that one of the first words in her Arabic conversation book was *harbaan*, meaning damaged or out of order.

"What's that?" she asked. Something stuck out of the little hole in the fabric, like a scrap of paper. Rania pulled it out. It was, in fact, a little folded piece of paper.

Rania unfolded it. She showed it to Chloe. There were two lines, written in Arabic with a black, felt-tipped pen.

"What does it say?" she asked.

"If you do not stop what you are doing, he will not be returned so quickly next time," Rania read.

Chapter 50

Chloe woke at six. She heard Rania moving around the kitchen and knew her friend had not slept much, if at all. She wished she had that problem. It took a virtual earthquake to keep her from sleeping or eating, which she always took as indicators of her severe shallowness as a human being. She sternly forbade herself even to think about turning over and burying her face in the pillow against the streaming sun. Instead, she sat up on the thin mattress, held the cover with one hand while she awkwardly pulled on her jeans with the other, lest Khaled or Bassam burst into the open room while she was dressing.

"Sabah al khcir," she said as she entered the kitchen, trying for a light tone.

"Sabah an-noor," Rania responded. "Nimti kwa'is?" Did you sleep well?

Would it be rude to answer truthfully, that she had slept like a log, knowing that the other woman had not? "Yes," she said in English. Much as she liked to practice Arabic, she did not feel like doing it right now, and it was a useless waste of energy to do it with someone who spoke English almost like a native.

"What are you going to do today?" Rania asked.

That was the question Chloe had been dreading. She really had nowhere to go. Reem was feeling fine, at least until her next appointment, which was in three days. She had gone back to work, and, though she would not say so, she did not need or want Chloe hanging around, being another mouth to feed. Amalia would miss her, Chloe knew, but they would see each other soon enough, when she brought Reem home from her treatment. She would spend the night again then, in case Reem had another late-night emergency. Hopefully, if that happened, she wouldn't get any more bullet holes in anyone's car.

She could stay at Avi's, of course, but she thought he and Maya needed some time together too. Which made her think about her own relationship, and whether she was ready to face a sudden death playoff for Tina. She didn't think so.

She put off the decision at least until after breakfast and went to help set the tea things on the breakfast tray.

"Mama, Mama," Khaled burst into the kitchen, his energy not at all dampened by yesterday's brush with—well, with whatever it had been. He was carrying the little, floppy-eared dog, which he must have retrieved from the living room floor.

"Good morning, habibi." His mother bussed him on the cheek and quickly turned back to the potatoes she was frying. Chloe saw a tear escape from the corner of her eye.

"How were your dreams?" Chloe asked him in Arabic, mainly to see if she could say it in a way that he would understand.

"Good," he said. "I dreamed Mama and I were riding on a giraffe, and Baba brought us ice cream." She thought he said "giraffe," though he could have said *jerafa*, bulldozer.

"Khaled," Rania asked, placing a plate of fries and labneh on the kitchen table, "you said that Ustaz Kareem gave you the dog, right?"

"That's right," Khaled answered. He sat at the table and reached for the hot potatoes. Chloe waited for Rania to join them before plowing into the bread, labneh, and zaatar. She heard Bassam moving around in the hall between the bedrooms and bathroom.

"Did he buy it on the way to the hotel, or did he have it when you first saw him?" Rania asked.

Chloe held her breath, following Rania's train of thought. None of the young men had been carrying anything when they arrived at Al Yasmeen. If Kareem had bought the toy in the *suq* on the way back to the hotel, then one of the three of them had to have written that note.

"He gave it to me as soon as I saw him," Khaled said.

That made it a little more interesting. It still seemed likely that one of them had bought the toy and put the note in it, but it was also possible that someone had handed it to them. In either case, there was something they had conveniently left out of their narrative the previous evening.

"I am going to have to talk to Yusuf," Rania said to Chloe in English.

Chloe didn't ask why him and not one of the others. She knew how Rania felt about Abdelhakim, ever since he had tried to sabotage her work last spring. Kareem would be in school, teaching Khaled, and Rania would not want to make unnecessary trouble with her son's teacher.

They got Khaled bundled off to school and sat down for another glass of tea with Bassam. He stroked his chin and looked unhappy when she said she was going to call Yusuf in a little while.

"Let it rest," he said. "Don't you even care that you are endangering our child?"

"Of course I do," she protested. "But I am so close."

"Close to what?" he asked. He stirred the sugar into his tea emphatically. "Everyone is content. The soldier is in jail. If you leave it alone, the family may be able to get their money. You said that was what you wanted to achieve."

Rania put her hands on top of her head and tugged gently at her uncovered hair. Chloe felt like she was trying to yank the conflicting feelings out of her head.

"If the soldier goes to jail for a crime he did not commit, where is the justice?" Rania said.

"Ya'anni, there is no justice in this land," Bassam replied. He finished his tea in a gulp and walked out. A few minutes later, he waved silently to them on his way out of the house.

Chloe thought about that exchange as she went to brush her teeth. She had always believed she cared about an absolute form of justice as deeply as anyone on the planet. But Rania was a breed apart. It made her an ideal detective. It didn't necessarily make her an ideal wife.

✴ ✴ ✴

Rania's phone rang. It was Captain Mustafa. "Naam?" she greeted him.

"How are you?" he asked.

"I am well," she said. "Thank you for your help."

"I did not really do anything," he said. "But I am glad it worked out." Worked out. That was an odd way to put it.

"I spoke to the Nablus police," he said. "They will continue trying to find out who is behind it."

"They must talk to the young man from Jemai'in," she said.

"Who?"

"Elias Horani," she said. "Yusuf's brother. Yusuf said he thought his brother might know something about it."

"I did not hear that," he said. "I will tell Captain Majid." She had not known Majid's title was captain, same as her boss's. He seemed awfully young for so much responsibility.

"I have one more question," she said, forestalling his goodbyes. "Benny said the army searched the Palestinian American's house on a tip from the muhabarat. Do you know where the muhabarat got the information?"

"No, I did not hear anything about that," he said. "I will see if Abu Ziyad knows." She thanked him and hung up. She gathered up the breakfast dishes and set a pot of water on the stove to wash them with. Chloe emerged from the bathroom as she was waiting for the water to get hot.

"I guess I should be going," the American said. "What are you up to today?"

"I have an appointment in Ramallah," Rania said.

"Oh. What kind of appointment?"

"Just someone I need to see." Chloe's eyebrows shot up—both eyebrows, not one, like when Benny did it.

"I just thought it might have something to do with Daoud," Chloe said. "I didn't mean to pry."

"You are not prying. I just cannot talk about it right now. But," she said on a sudden impulse, "I have something to discuss with you. Can you come to Ramallah with me and, after my appointment, have lunch with me? There is a very nice café I went to once, with Daoud's cousin, Ahmed. I would like to go back there."

"Well," Chloe said, "I was not planning to go to Ramallah. Can't we discuss whatever it is now?" Rania sensed there was some reason her friend did not want to go to Ramallah. But she insisted.

"I do not have time," Rania hedged. "I would rather get together later. And I would like company on the trip."

"Sure." Chloe shrugged. "I don't know if I am going to stay in Ramallah, but I can hang out there for a while."

They had nearly reached Ramallah when Captain Mustafa called back.

"Yes?" Rania answered. The reception was bad and the car was noisy. But she heard the words "Abdelhakim," "muhabarat" and "Abu Ziyad," and understood that the tip that brought to soldiers to the Palestinian-American house had come from Abdelhakim via Abu Ziyad. Just as she had figured. The only questions were, had Abdelhakim planted the gun himself or was he passing on a message from one of his friends and, if the latter, which one? He and Yusuf had been in the area the day of the search, she reflected, but she did not see how they could have put the gun in the house just then. It must have been somewhere she had missed.

Chapter 51

Rania had become adept at sneaking into Jerusalem. She had given herself two extra hours to make the crossing, in case one, or even two, of the usual crossing points had soldiers lurking around. She made it on the first try, so she was very early for her appointment. She thought she was going to the Jerusalem Hotel for a coffee, but instead she found herself wandering into the Old City and standing in line for the Al Aqsa Mosque.

After guaranteeing the *Waqf* men who searched her things that she was not menstruating, she entered the sanctuary. She had been here quite a few times in her youth, before Jerusalem was closed to West Bank Palestinians and before she had lost interest in religion as anything but a way of being connected to her people. She was struck again by the beauty, almost the magic, of the place. Foreigners only knew the golden dome that presided over the city, but the hand-painted ceiling mosaic and the Italian marble that made the walls were its true glories.

She passed under the graceful arches and followed the sea of headscarves to the women's chapel in the western corner. She removed her shoes and stood watching the women prostrate themselves to pray. She had not brought a mat, of course. She walked around the edge of the room and there found what she was seeking: a little bin full of ragged prayer mats. She took one and walked hesitantly up the center aisle. She laid out her mat on the soft, red carpet and knelt, then bent from the waist and placed her hands down by her sides. She felt a twinge in her middle and momentarily thought she was going to be sick. She ignored it, and the feeling subsided. She barely remembered how to do it. But when her head touched the ground, the tension she had been carrying since her release from prison dissolved like a sugar cube in hot tea.

"Allah Most Merciful," she prayed. "Show me my path."

When she stood up, she felt a rush of well-being, as if a space had opened in her lungs and the love of God, or of her community, which might be the same thing, had rushed in to fill it. She was no longer afraid of what she might learn at the appointment she was now in danger of being late for.

She took a servees to the Shuafat refugee camp and asked someone for directions to the medical clinic. She had chosen this camp precisely because she had never been there and knew no one who lived here, though now it seemed a silly precaution. She entered the little storefront, tucked between the fitness club and the pharmacy, and gave her name to the receptionist. Half an hour later, she had the information she had been dreading, which she now accepted with a calm serenity, if not the excitement the nurse was expecting.

"How far along am I?" she asked.

"Perhaps two months," the nurse said. As Rania suspected, she had already been pregnant when she was in prison. She shuddered to imagine that she could have given birth in there, shackled to a dirty bed with soldiers watching her spread her legs and push the baby out. Then she wondered, could all the men who were nagging her about having a baby see something in her that she herself had not? If so, it would not be the first time.

She bounded into the street to find a servees to Ramallah, where she would have a lovely lunch with Chloe. Tonight, she would give Bassam the good news.

✳ ✳ ✳

It felt strange to be in Ramallah but unable to call Tina. For so long, Chloe had dreamed of them being in the same city. How quickly it had fallen apart, once her dreams had become reality. But that was usually the case with dreams. She had come here on a noble impulse, to get Rania out of jail, and she had succeeded. She wouldn't undo it if she could.

She tried to shop for presents for her friends at home. She looked at

T-shirts printed with English slogans—why would you bring those as souvenirs from Palestine?—and Chinese knickknacks. Water pipes always seemed like a good idea, but, in fact, no one she gave them to ever used them. It would be better to buy things in the Old City in Nablus or the market in Tulkarem, where you could get real crafts for a fair price. Or, better yet, she would call one of the Salfit women Reem had introduced her to and arrange a private showing of the crafts they made to sell in their hoped-for cooperative.

She passed a travel agency with signs proclaiming Amsterdam—800 NIS, London—1200 NIS, Riyadh—600 NIS, Tokyo—4000 NIS. If she had seen a sign for San Francisco, she might have gone in. As it was, she passed it by. Tina had said she still loved her. Maybe something could be salvaged. The bigger question was what she was going to do. She couldn't just float around, looking for people who might need rides to the hospital or help getting a relative out of jail. She would work on her video, maybe write an article about women in the Palestinian government, but that wasn't a full-time job.

She was passing the building on al-Irsal Street where Addameer, the prisoner support group, had its offices. She had gone there a year ago, when she was trying to get Fareed released. Why not? she thought. What do you have to lose? She took the elevator to the group's seventh floor offices.

"I was wondering," she said to the receptionist in passable Arabic, "if you might need any computer help."

Half an hour later, she walked out with a disk containing the files from their website, which she had agreed to redesign. After her lunch with Rania, she would call Tina and see if it was okay for her to go back to the apartment and start her work. When she stepped into the art café called Ziryab, Rania was already sitting at a table near the little gas fire, reading an Arabic newspaper.

"You look happy," Chloe said.

"I am," Rania said. "I am pregnant."

"That's wonderful," Chloe said. She had thought Rania wasn't so sure she wanted another kid right now. But, if her friend was happy, she was happy for her.

The waiter appeared to take their order. "I will have a cappuccino and an omelet," Rania said. "And some fries. I am very hungry," she added to Chloe.

"Sounds good," Chloe said. "I'll have the same. So, what did you want to talk to me about?" she asked when the waiter had gone to place their orders.

"It is not important," Rania said.

Chloe felt her face fall. Silence sat between them for some seconds.

"I had planned to ask you," Rania said, playing with the fringes of her headscarf, "if you knew how to end an unwanted pregnancy."

Chloe's mouth dropped open, and she snapped it shut, her teeth clacking against one another. "I don't, at least, not here," she said. "Though I'm sure I could have found out. What…what changed your mind?"

The waiter brought their coffees and Rania stirred two sugars into hers.

"I went to the mosque," she said. She cradled the cup in both hands, though the café was warm and they were seated by the fire. "Somehow, it all became clear to me. I have been thinking that I needed to choose between my work and my family. But when I knelt down to pray, I saw that I can have everything I want."

"That's great," Chloe said. She wanted to ask if Rania normally drank coffee while she was pregnant, but she decided that would be crossing the intimacy line. Khaled was perfectly healthy, so Rania clearly knew how to take care of herself during pregnancy. One espresso was not going to hurt the baby.

"I had thought maybe…" Chloe said, then stopped.

Rania looked up from her drink, which she had been studying as if to learn its secrets. "…you wanted to tell me about Tina and her friend Yasmina."

Rania looked startled, then abashed. "I was not sure there was anything to tell," she said.

"Did it seem to you," Chloe asked, the words coming one by one like stray olives at the end of picking season, "that they were more…natural…together than Tina and I are?"

Rania looked down at her coffee. She swirled it in her hand, making the froth jiggle. She lifted it to her lips but did not really drink. "Honestly, no," she said at last. "They spoke Arabic together, and perhaps they spoke less. But that may not mean they are more comfortable together. It could mean they have less to say."

Chloe thought about that. She remembered the conversation she and

Tina had had about Rania. She is Palestinian but not lesbian; I am lesbian but not Palestinian, Chloe had said then. She had thought that since Yasmina was both, she would be a more perfect fit for Tina, who was both as well. Now she thought, Yasmina is Palestinian but not Western; I am Western but not Palestinian. She thought about how difficult it must be for Tina to find one person who could comprehend her complex identity. But could Chloe share Tina with another woman? Would that be better or worse than living without her?

The waiter put steaming plates of eggs and fries before them. It had been hours since their breakfast. Chloe realized how hungry she was. She ate half the fries on her plate before she slowed down. Rania was taking one bite every few minutes. Chloe wondered if she had a little morning sickness—or afternoon sickness, since it was nearly one.

"I've been thinking about something," Chloe said. Rania looked down at the food on her plate, no doubt wondering what uncomfortable subject Chloe was going to bring up next. "Why did Yusuf think that Elias might be involved in Khaled's kidnapping?" she said. She hoped it was not a mistake to bring up the kidnapping. But Rania seemed intrigued.

"I did not ask him," she said. "I was so thankful to have my son back, I forgot."

"Do you think Elias killed Daoud?" Chloe asked.

"I do not know what to think," Rania said. "I thought he told us the truth. But he told us Issa found them together, and Issa says that he did not. One of them is obviously lying. After yesterday, I am not sure who to trust."

They ate in silence for a few minutes more. "I must call Yusuf and ask him about this," Rania said suddenly. She rummaged in her purse and pulled out a folded napkin. When she unfolded it, it revealed some smudged writing. Upside down, Chloe could not begin to read the Arabic, but she could see that it contained numbers. Rania took out her mobile phone and started to punch in the numbers. She stopped after four digits.

"Elias," she said and jumped up. She fumbled in her purse for her wallet and extracted a twenty shekel note. She signaled frantically for the waiter.

"What's going on?" Chloe asked. She swatted Rania's hand away from the waiter, who had arrived at their table, and thrust at him a fifty of her own.

"I must warn him," Rania said. She was speeding out of the café, and Chloe had no choice but to run after her.

"I don't understand," she said breathlessly, when she caught up to her friend. Rania was about to jump into a taxi. Chloe climbed in after her, nearly landing on top of her.

"This note," Rania waved the little piece of paper she had taken from the stuffed dog in Chloe's face. She must have been carrying it in her purse. She took it out of her friend's hand. She couldn't read it; it was in Arabic. She sounded out the words letter by letter, but for what? She knew what it said.

"I believe the person who wrote this note," Rania said, "also wrote this one." She handed Chloe the napkin with Yusuf's phone number. "Yusuf wrote this to tell me how to get to his class," Rania explained. "And that means he wrote this one as well."

"I understand," Chloe said, though she did not exactly. "But why then are we going to Elias's house?" She assumed that was where they were headed.

"I told Captain Mustafa that Yusuf had implicated his brother," Rania said. "The police may come to arrest him. I am sad to say it, but our interrogation methods can sometimes be unpleasant."

Chapter 52

It took only a few minutes to cover the short distance to Daoud's old apartment. Rania ran inside and tore up the stairs two at a time. She heard Chloe running up behind her, huffing and puffing. She turned to tell her friend to wait outside, but the voices coming from the apartment made her turn back and quicken her pace.

She reached the door and started to throw it open, but then stopped. Men were shouting, but it did not sound like police arresting anyone.

"I protected you!" Elias was yelling. "I told them it was Issa who found us."

"And I protected you," Yusuf screamed back. "I told Issa to make Daoud leave you alone. He told me he would take care of it. But then he said he could not do it."

"You killed the man I loved." Elias again.

"It was his fault," Yusuf responded. "When I met him that afternoon, I gave him a choice—leave you alone or I would kill him. He said he would rather die than lose you. So, I gave him his wish." His voice had dropped to a normal, almost reflective level. "What else could I do?" he asked. "He would have ruined your life."

"It was not him," Elias said. "It is me. I am mithli."

"Do not say such things. You will marry Hanan and forget about this foolishness."

"I will not. It is not fair to Hanan. And it is not fair to me."

"Fair?" Rania heard a crash and someone yelped in pain. It sounded like someone was throwing furniture. If she didn't enter now, she might find the door barricaded before she could. She flung open the door.

"Are you being fair?" Yusuf shouted at his brother. "What will it do to our parents if you tell the world this shame?"

The chair which had fallen over was not blocking the doorway. Rather, it lay half shattered against the wall, where it must have been thrown by Yusuf, because Elias's hand was otherwise occupied. He held a long, serrated knife with the point only a few inches from his brother's chest.

Rania stood, transfixed. She had never been in this situation. They had gone over it in police training, of course, but she had never had to put that training into practice. She could not even remember, now that it was relevant, what they had said. Keep them talking, was one piece of advice that rang in her head.

"Elias," she said. "Put down the knife. Talk to me."

He rewarded her by swinging toward her, brandishing his knife in her direction. At least she had gotten him to stop threatening his brother, but that was little comfort. As if he knew her secret, he was pointing the knife directly at her belly.

If he wouldn't talk, maybe it would help to talk to someone else.

"How did you get the soldier's gun?" she asked Yusuf, careful to keep her voice conversational. He looked at her as if he had just noticed she was in the room.

"Issa gave it to me," he said. "He found it in the house. He threatened Daoud with it, but he could not use it. He said to give it to Abdelhakim for the fighters in Nablus. I heard the soldier had fought with Daoud over it that day in the village. I called and told him to meet me before the party and I would give it to him."

Rania knew she should stay focused on the danger in front of her, but her detective's mind was trying to piece the events of the fatal day together. Daoud had been threatened three times that day and then had made a threat of his own. Yusuf had promised to kill him, yet Daoud had gone to receive a weapon from his hands? Perhaps Yusuf was right, and death really was his wish. Or, more likely, he could not believe Yusuf would harm him, just as she could not believe Elias meant to harm her now.

"Daoud was right." Elias said. His voice had gone down a notch, but it was still deafening in Rania's ears. That could have been the echo in her head, though.

"He wanted me to emigrate with him, to Europe or America. He said it would be too hard to be together here. I said no, I would not leave my country. But he was right."

"I do not believe that," Rania said. "There is a place for you here. It will take time; that is all."

"You know nothing about it," he said. He turned back toward his brother and took a step closer. The knife was touching Yusuf's shirt.

"I loved him," Elias screamed. "You took away my happiness."

"You could not have been happy in an unnatural relationship," Yusuf said.

"Be quiet," Rania croaked, just as Elias raised his arm. She did not think about what she was doing. She felt Chloe push past her, trying to get there first. Naturally, the American would see herself as everyone's protector. But she wasn't. Rania's job was to protect her people, and these were her people.

Rania jumped in front of Yusuf just as Elias swung the knife. She heard it slice the polyester of her jilbab and felt it plunge into her right shoulder. It didn't hurt, really. She reached out with her left hand and grabbed Elias's wrist with all her strength. Which was waning rapidly. She felt him being pulled off of her and saw Chloe wrestling him to the side. She heard the knife clatter to the floor.

"Relax," she heard Chloe say in English. That was it: that's what Rania had learned in training. Be calm. Get them to relax. She hoped Elias knew the English word.

Yusuf bent over her, tying something around her shoulder. She was wet and cold, and, somewhere in her consciousness, she understood that it was her blood which was soaking her clothes and making her so cold.

"Go get a taxi," Chloe was saying to Elias in English. Rania understood that her friend's Arabic had deserted her. "Hurry. We need to get her to the hospital."

That was the last Rania heard before she lost consciousness.

✶ ✶ ✶

"There's someone here to see you," the nurse said.

Rania's eyes fluttered open. She was pale, but her black eyes sparkled. She was not wearing her glasses, and, without the raccoonish effect they created, her face was beautiful, already a little fuller than usual. Chloe made a mental note to talk to her about contacts, or at least some more flattering glasses. She remembered hearing pregnant friends say that they could not tolerate contacts. But new glasses were a must.

Bassam entered the bright little room, holding Khaled by the hand. They approached Rania's bedside. She reached for her son, and Bassam lifted him up and over the guardrail so he could cuddle on his mother's good side, the side not bandaged with bulky armor of cotton and gauze.

"Who did this to you?" the child asked. Rania kissed his cheek and forehead, over and over.

"Someone who was very upset," she said.

"Did you take him to jail?" Khaled asked.

"No," she said. She looked at Bassam. Rania would have no way of knowing what might have happened to Elias or Yusuf after she passed out.

"The police questioned him," Bassam said. "But then they let him go."

"He didn't mean to hurt me," Rania explained to Khaled. She turned her eyes back to Bassam. "What about Yusuf?"

"Him also. They seem to have concluded that he only meant to scare Daoud, and the killing was an accident."

"That's not true," Chloe said.

"Truth is not always the most important thing," Bassam said.

Chloe contemplated that. She did not believe in prisons, and it seemed unlikely that Yusuf would kill anyone else. But Daoud had died because he did think truth was important. If his killer was not punished, would that mean he had died for nothing?

Rania motioned to her husband to come close. He obliged.

"What about the baby?" Chloe heard her murmur.

"Baby?" Bassam looked quizzically at his wife. Rania blushed as a big, lopsided smile spread over her husband's face. "You're going to be a big brother," he said, reaching over his wife to tousle his son's hair.

"I'll see you later," Chloe said from the doorway.

"You do not need to go," Bassam said. He was still smiling broadly.

"You are very polite," Chloe said with a small laugh. "But I will leave you alone now and see you all tomorrow. Salamtik," to your health, she added in Rania's direction.

"Chloe," Rania said as she opened the door. Chloe turned her head toward her friend. "Thank you for everything."

"For nothing," Chloe said. She closed the door behind her and went to the chair where Tina sat reading. Chloe turned the book over in her hands to read the title.

"*The Da Vinci Code*," she said. "Don't waste your time. It's terrible."

"You left it lying around the apartment," Tina said. "I was bored."

Bored. Does that mean you haven't been spending all your time in heart-to-hearts with Yasmina? Chloe would not let herself say it. She was going to be the person she should be, not the person she usually was.

"Rania's going to be okay," Chloe said. "She lost a lot of blood, but there is no damage to the tendons, and the knife missed her lung."

She couldn't say "he missed." She couldn't see Elias as a killer, even though he had tried to kill. She couldn't even see Yusuf as a killer, though he had killed. It was easier to see Ron as a killer, and, as far as she knew, he had never killed anyone. Life here was so much more complicated than it was at home. That's why she loved it.

"Let's go home," Tina said. She stood up and put the book in her backpack.

"Can we get a bottle of wine on the way?" Chloe said.

"I already got one," Tina said, twining her fingers with Chloe's. A current of warmth ran up Chloe's arm and down through her throat to fill her rib cage.

"Adloyada after dinner?"

"Maybe tomorrow," Tina said. "I had some other ideas for tonight."

Chapter 52

Abu Suleiman wore a long, billowing white robe and sandals. Sweat glistened on his bronze face as he knocked on Jamal al-Khader's door.

"That's the guy?" Chloe whispered to Tina. "He looks so…regular."

They stood a short distance away from the procession of twenty men and one woman arranging themselves in a line along the driveway.

"Abu Suleiman is the best *sulha* mediator in Palestine," Tina replied. "He did a workshop for the Women's Center. He seemed very sharp."

"I hope it works," Chloe said. Jamal emerged from the house, followed by Issa and his two younger brothers. Um Issa and her daughters were nowhere to be seen, but, at the last minute, Hanan strode out and took her place next to Issa. He turned and said something to her and she shook her head, her uncovered ringlets bobbing around her shoulders. Issa shrugged and followed his father down the line of men, shaking hands with each. He and his father shook Rania's hand too. Hanan offered each man her hand as well. Most shook it; a few did not.

The man at the head of the reception line stepped forward and presented Jamal with a long pole from which a white sheet fluttered.

"That's Abu Ziyad, the DCL," Chloe whispered to Tina. "Rania hates him."

Abu Suleiman stood next to Jamal and guided his hands as he tied the fabric into a knot. Issa then copied his father. When Hanan tried to move forward, Rania shook her head almost imperceptibly, and the girl stepped back. Rania had an intuitive understanding of how far she could push things that Hanan was going to need to learn.

"Poor Hanan," Chloe said. "She's lost two finacés in three weeks."

"From what I can see, she will be okay," Tina whispered back.

The men were piling into waiting cars now. Chloe and Tina climbed into the back of the BMW where Bassam waited behind the wheel. Khaled sat in the back, playing a handheld video game. Chloe took him on her lap so Hanan could squeeze in next to them, as Rania settled herself in front.

"What game are you playing?" Chloe asked Khaled in Arabic.

He tilted the screen so she could see. Gears of War. Two heavily armed hulks were locked in mortal combat against a fiery backdrop.

"His grandmother gave it to him," Rania said, twisting around to face them. "He loves to kill."

Proving her point, Khaled pressed a button and set off a burst of machine gun fire.

"What happens now?" Chloe asked, as they jounced over the rocky road.

"They will take the truce flag to Yusuf and his family, so that they can travel under its protection," Bassam explained. "Then, we will come back here to the town hall and the Jaha—the sulha committee—will hear from all the parties. At the end, the truce agreement will be signed, and the blood money will be presented to Daoud's family."

"So, the family will receive compensation for the loss of their son after all," Chloe said. "How much will they pay?"

"I am not sure of the exact sum that has been agreed on, but it is often around two hundred and fifty thousand shekels."

"But that's more than fifty thousand dollars!" Chloe exclaimed. "Yusuf's family is not that wealthy, are they? How can they ever pay that much?"

"It needs to be a significant amount," Rania said. They were passing the quarry now, almost to their destination. "But I believe the al-Khaders plan to return some of the money."

Bassam pulled up behind the line of parked cars. He and Khaled stayed in the car while the others clambered out to join the small crowd from the village who had gathered to watch the proceedings.

Yusuf and his brothers exited the house. Abdelhakim and Kareem were with him, Chloe noted. Elias was not. Then, she noticed a figure approaching from the opposite direction. Elias. He did not join the men from his family. Instead, he came to stand with her and Tina.

"How are you?" Chloe asked him.

"I am not sure," he said with a little laugh.

"You are not going to participate in the sulha?"

"I would not know where to stand," he said. "My brother and I will have to make our own sulha."

"Mwaffak," good luck, Chloe said.

* * *

Tina and Chloe did not stay for the communal meal following the signing of the truce. They were not part of the community, after all. Instead, they celebrated the resolution with their own meal at Enrico's. It seemed appropriate to Chloe, to be back at the place where she had met Daoud and Elias.

"I still don't get why Benny got Rania out of prison," Tina said, twirling long strands of fettuccine con gorgonzola around her fork. "Or why the military guys agreed."

"I think Benny knew all along what had happened," Chloe said, nibbling her calzone slowly. "Daoud was pretty open, after all. I'm sure the Israeli police have spies at Adloyada. And Palestinians who go out of the country are investigated quite thoroughly."

"So, you think he wanted Rania to expose Daoud and Elias?"

"The Israelis want as much division in Palestinian communities as possible right now. Benny knew Rania wouldn't stop searching for the truth even when it was clear that everyone would prefer it to remain hidden. I think he hoped she would reveal the truth and that would intensify the conflict between the Islamist and secular factions."

"But she said she wouldn't help with the investigation." Tina sopped up the last of her cream sauce with a crust of garlic bread.

"He knows her," Chloe said. "Probably, he spread enough rumors to make sure she couldn't go back to work. She wouldn't sit around and make embroidered crafts. It was the only investigation she could take on, so he knew she would do it."

Tina shivered a little, though the night was warm. "It gives me the creeps," she said. "Like one of those John LeCarre novels where everyone's a triple agent."

"Or *The Da Vinci Code*," Chloe said. They both laughed. Tina had read the book in two days. Chloe had never finished it, but she got Tina to tell her how it ended.

"Why would the army guys agree?" Tina asked.

"They would've had to let her out eventually," Chloe said. She wiped her mouth with the cloth napkin and frowned at the tomato stain it left. "Probably, Benny convinced them that this would undermine her credibility, and that would neutralize her more effectively than locking her up."

"You think it will work?" Tina stopped abruptly as the waiter came to offer them dessert menus.

"No. Rania's smarter than they are. She'll come out of this stronger; you'll see. Want to split a piece of cheesecake?"

"Cheesecake and cannoli. We're celebrating."

✳ ✳ ✳

The bus driver checked the road twice before pulling over at the intersection of Emek Refaim and Bethlehem Road.

"Hurry, hurry," he said. "I cannot be seen stopping here."

Samia scrambled down the stairs of the bus. When the bus had pulled away, she looked both ways three times to make sure that no border police were hanging about. She stepped into the crowd of shoppers and people hurrying home from work. She paid no attention to which direction she was going but just walked for a block or two to get used to being in West Jerusalem. She had not been there since before her arrest in 1991. Eventually, she stopped and checked a street number, then turned and walked back the other way.

She remembered the address, because she had looked at it twelve times since this morning, but she extracted the piece of paper Rania had given her once again. This was the building, but the door was locked and no one answered her ring. She was early. She walked down the street and found a café. She did not see any soldiers drinking coffee inside, so she went in. She felt like everyone in the café turned to look at her while she ordered a cappuccino. She caught snatches of Hebrew conversation as she moved to a table in the back, far away from the plate-glass windows. She had not spoken Hebrew since prison, but she understood what she heard perfectly. She did not think anyone was talking about her.

She had not brought anything to read, so she thought about what she was doing while she nursed her coffee. Was it a huge mistake? She could not imagine what these women would be like. But it seemed worth finding out. If they were weird, she would not come back again. She checked her watch. Five twenty-five. Maybe they would be a few minutes early too. She left the coffee shop and made her way back to the nondescript office building. She rang the buzzer again and again; nothing happened. But, when she turned to walk back down the stairs, two women were coming up. One had short, brown hair that stood up in jagged spikes and a tattoo showing on her bare left arm. Samia peered closely at the image. Handala, the little cartoon character representing the refugees' right to return. This Handala carried a little flag in all the colors of the rainbow. She wondered what that meant.

The other woman, the one with the long, dark curls and green eyes, smiled at Samia and stuck her hand out.

"Marhaba," greetings, "are you Samia?"

"Yes," Samia replied, shaking the woman's outstretched hand. The woman's Arabic was tinged with something she couldn't quite place.

"Ahlan w sahlan, yaa achti," welcome, my sister, the pretty woman said. "I am Tina, Rania's friend. This is Rihab," she indicated the woman who was opening the door with a key.

"It's a pleasure," said Rihab, ushering her into a bright, peaceful room covered in rainbows. Rainbow flags on the mantel, rainbow stickers on the wall, a rainbow umbrella in the corner, and, on the coffee table, a little Palestinian flag with a rainbow triangle instead of a red one.

"What is the meaning of the rainbow?" Samia asked. Both of the other women smiled.

"We can discuss that, and many other things," Tina said.

✷ ✷ ✷

Benny's office door was shut when Rania arrived. She planned to burst in without knocking, as she usually did, but, when she tried the knob, it did not turn. It had never occurred to her that Benny wouldn't be there. She turned to go, not relishing the smug satisfaction on the receptionist's face when she asked if he was scheduled to return today.

She was nearly to the stairs when she heard his inimitable voice behind her, saying goodbye to someone. She turned to see a huge man with toned muscles shaking hands with Benny. Before she recognized his face, she recognized his tattoos. Green snakes with red tongues wound their way up one arm and down the other. He had once threatened to torture her because she spoke to a prisoner without his permission. He was part of the dreaded SHABAK, the Israeli secret police. Seeing Benny shake his hand made her teeth chatter.

"You must release Ron Binyamin," she said without preface, once she had dumped his files on the floor and seated herself opposite Benny's desk.

"Why should I?" he countered.

"He did not kill Daoud al-Khader."

"Who did?" he asked, oozing wide-eyed innocence.

"Either you already knew that the day you visited me in prison, or you figured it out because your spies in the villages told you every person I spoke to and every question I asked." He gave her a hurt look that said, How can you suggest I would spy on you? It only confirmed her belief. "And, if you did not, your Snake Tattoo friend did. I do not need to know which. It is enough to say that it is an internal Palestinian matter, and we will handle it in the way we feel is best."

For a minute, she thought he was going to argue with her. Then, he set the legs of his chair down and scribbled in Hebrew on his yellow notepad. She waited for him to look up at her. She waited a long time. Finally, she stood up to go.

"You are going to release him?" she asked.

"It's an internal Israeli matter," he said, not looking up from his writing. Slamming the door on her way out didn't satisfy her as much as it usually did.

Her next stop was the police station in Salfit, where her first task was the hardest. Abdelhakim was standing right near the front door, doing the religious man's version of flirting with the receptionist. The young woman gave Rania an unappreciative stare when she asked if she could speak with him privately for a moment. He followed her into the little, empty office where they kept stacks of pads for note taking and sponges for the little kitchenette. She pulled the door nearly shut, leaving it open a few inches as propriety required.

"I wanted to say thank you," she said. "I know it was you who convinced Yusuf to free my son."

"It was Kareem, actually," he said. "But thank you for your thank you."

"I am curious about one thing," she said. "When did you put the gun in the Palestinian American's house?" She chose to read his surprised expression as grudging respect.

"While you were upstairs," he said. "We went to place it in the house before the soldiers got there. But then you arrived. We hid in the groves and watched through the windows. When we heard the jeeps coming, we snuck in and left it in the front room."

"Thank you again," she said and started to leave.

"We thought he was protecting his brother," he said. She turned back to face him. "He told us Daoud made improper advances to Elias, and Elias killed him in self-defense."

"Yusuf also thought he was protecting his brother," she said. "But his brother did not want his protection. I hope Khaled will love his little sister or brother as much, but more wisely." A phrase from a long-forgotten English play she had read in college popped into her mind: "One that loved not wisely but too well."

Captain Mustafa was at his desk. He welcomed Rania by pushing his eyeglasses down onto the flat of his nose and peering at her over the lenses. She sat in the chair opposite his desk, as she had so many times, usually being bawled out over some breach of protocol caused by her impulsiveness during an investigation.

"I finished investigating Daoud al-Khader's death," she said.

He looked like he knew that, and doubtless he did. "Did you write a report?" he asked. He half-reached out his hand for it, though she clearly did not have any papers in hers.

"I thought it would be better to discuss it," she said. She did not point out that, since he had not assigned her the case, she had no reason to write a report for him.

"Daoud was very close with Elias Horani." He blinked his eyelids once, his version of a nod. "Yusuf Horani killed Daoud because he felt he was a bad influence on his brother." Another blink.

"The families have signed a sulha agreement," she said.

"Did the mediator bring up homosexuality?" asked the captain.

"No. Part of the agreement between the families was that no one would speak of the reasons for the crime. But Elias Horani has asked his brother to attend a workshop on the issue with him, at Wahat as-Salaam. I hoped you would talk to Abu Ziyad about getting them the permits to go into Israel." He closed his lids for a second longer than a blink, but, when he opened them again, she took it as an assent.

"I want to come back to work," she said.

"For the women's force?" he asked. Their eyes locked.

"No. The girls are intelligent and, if you can hire them, I will be glad to help train them. But I am a very good detective, and I want to be a detective." She cocked her chin up and made her expression as defiant as she could muster.

His mustache curved up just slightly. "I will speak to Abu Ziyad," he said. "I believe it is possible."

Rania was surprised that he gave in so quickly. Maybe she had not been forceful enough before. More likely, he now felt confident that she had not become a collaborator.

"And one more thing," she said. He was already looking down at the reports he had been reading when she walked in. He looked up and adjusted his glasses once more.

"In six months or so, I will need some time off," she said.

Afterword

Murder *Under the Fig Tree* is fiction. While some of the characters are inspired by people I met in Palestine and Israel, they are all composites and products of my imagination. None of the major story lines are based on actual events, although the election of the Hamas-led government, the subsequent Israeli raids and arrests, and the freezing of Palestinian funds by the United States and Israel are historical facts.

This is a snapshot in time, set in the spring of 2006. Much has changed in Palestine since that period, much of it for the worse and most of it driven by Israeli actions and policies (more walls, more killings, more collective punishment, more economic devastation). At the same time, organizing among Palestinian LGBTQ people has been vibrant and created needed institutions for support and liberation. While the lesbian group in this book is fictional, Palestinian queer organizations do provide hotlines, clubs, support groups, and workshops throughout their country. Palestinian queer leaders have also played an active role in the international LGBT community, consistently demanding that their liberation struggles be placed in the context of the Palestinian national struggle for land, recognition, refugee return, civil and political rights, and an end to occupation. They have joined the call by Palestinian civil society for boycott, divestment and sanctions to pressure Israel to honor its responsibilities under international law.

I hope this book has inspired you to want to learn more about the situation of Palestinian queers as well as everyone living in the area. Check out alQaws for Sexual & Gender Diversity in Palestinian Society (www.alqaws.org), Aswat Palestinian Gay Women (http://www.aswatgroup.org/

en), B'Tselem—The Israeli Information Center for Human Rights in the Occupied Territories (http://www.btselem.org/), or Palestine Monitor, (http://www.palestinemonitor.org/) for further reading.

Huge thanks to everyone who read *Murder Under the Bridge* and immediately began asking, "When is the next one coming out?" You are the reason I managed to finish this book.

Thanks also to everyone who offered critiques and feedback on part or all of this manuscript, including Amanda Bloom, Andrew Eddy, Blue Murov, Caryn Riswold, Dan Berger, Elaine Beale, Erica Marcus, Fern Feldman, Janice O'Mahoney, Jennifer Beach, Jennifer Worrell, JoAnn Smith Ainsworth, Julie Starobin, Kristina Eschmeyer, Laura Petracek, Lindy Gligorijevic, Michelle Byrd, Miranda Bergman, Miranda Weingartner, Nancy Ferreyra, Radhika Sainath, Richard Friedman, Sasha Wright, Stephanie Carroll, Steve Masover, and Steven Long. Special thanks to Jean Tepperman for your unflagging support, and to Naomi Azriel and Zacariah Barghouti for help with language and culture. Needless to say, any mistakes are mine alone.

I could not have done it without my fabulous editors, Elana Dykewomon and Mary DeDanan, the organizational brilliance of Brooke Warner, Cait Levin, and the rest of the She Writes team, and the artistic wizardry of cover designer Julie Metz. Thanks also to publicists Lorna Garano and David Ivester.

I will be eternally grateful to Hedgebrook for the most nurturing experience of my life.

To all the incredible friends who have supported me in every crazy thing I did, from getting arrested in foreign countries to publishing these books, I love you so much.

It was the late Marilyn Buck who sent me a New York Times article about the formation of a separate women's police force in Gaza. This book is dedicated to her, who never compromised in the struggle for truth and justice.

About the Author

© Jane Philomen Cleland

Kate Raphael is a San Francisco Bay Area writer, feminist and queer activist and radio journalist, who makes her living as a law firm word processor. She lived in Palestine for eighteen months as a member of the International Women's Peace Service. She spent over a month in Israeli prison and was eventually deported because of her activism. She has won a residency at Hedgebrook and been a grand marshal of the San Francisco LGBT Pride Parade. She produces the weekly radio show, Women's Magazine, on Pacifica's KPFA, which is heard throughout Northern and Central California. Her debut Palestine mystery, *Murder Under the Bridge*, won the 2016 International Publisher Book Awards (IPPY) Silver Medal for Mystery.

Connect with her at www.kateraphael.com

Glossary

Abbreviations:

Ar. = Arabic

Heb. = Hebrew

fem. = feminine   m. = masculine

lit. = literal

abu abui (Ar.) my father's father

abu imik (Ar.) your mother's father

achar kach (Heb.) after

achshav (Heb.) now

Adloyada (Heb.) a carnival held for the Jewish holiday of Purim; lit. "until you did not know"

ahlan w sahlan (Ar.) welcome; **ahlan fiik/fiiki** Welcome to you, too.

ahleen (Ar.) hello

ahsan (Ar.) better

Aish hon? (Ar.) Does he live here?

aiwa (Ar.) yes

Al Aqsa (Ar.) the mosque on the Temple Mount in Jerusalem's Old City

Al Haq Palestinian human rights group

Al Hayat Palestinian newspaper (lit. The Life)

aliyah (Heb.) Jewish immigration to Israel (lit. going up)

Al-Khalil (Ar.) Hebron

Allah yirhamo (Ar.) God have mercy on his soul

Allah ysalmak (Ar.) May God grant you peace. (response to al-Hamdullilah assalaam)

Al Quds (Ar.) Jerusalem

ana (Ar.) I, I am

Ana bidish ahki inglisi (Ar.) I don't want to speak English

ani (Heb.) I, I am

Ani lo reavah (Heb.) (fem.) I am not hungry

anjad (Ar.) definitely

argila (Ar.) flavored tobacco (also **sheesha**)

asfi (Ar.) (fem.) sorry

ashara bil miyya (Ar.) ten percent

asirah (Heb.) prisoner

At lo rotzah ochel? (Heb.) You don't want food?

At re'evah? (Heb.) Are you hungry?

Austrian Hospice A Pilgrim's guesthouse in on the Via Dolorosa in the Old City of Jerusalem. ("Hospice" is from "hospitality".)

Awal marra hon? (Ar.) Is it your first time here?

Bab el-Amud (Ar.) Damascus Gate (lit. Gate of the Column)

baba (Ar.) papa

badeen (Ar.) later

bamiya (Ar.) okra

bandura (Ar.) tomatoes

bekafi (Ar.) enough

Bidi atalam Arabi (Ar.) I want to learn Arabic

Birzeit Palestinian university near Ramallah

bissa (Ar.) cat

boi (Heb.) (fem.) come

boi heyna (Heb.) (fem.) come here

b'seder (Heb.) okay

Btselem Israeli human rights organization

chamesh esrei (Heb.) fifteen

dabka a Palestinian folk dance

Dafaween (Ar.) West Bankers

Edward Said Conservatory music school, named for Palestinian intellectual Edward Said, with branches in Ramallah, Jerusalem, Bethlehem, Nablus and Gaza

esrim shekel (Heb.) twenty shekels

Fanoun (Ar.) artist

Fatah (Ar.) Palestinian political party, cofounded by Yasir Arafat, late president of the Palestinian Authority

filfil (Ar.) pepper

First Intifada Palestinian civil society uprising which lasted from 1987–93

Forty-Eight the territory held by Israel at the end of the 1947–48 war; many Palestinian nationalists refer to Israel as '48

ful (Ar.) a fava bean dish

habibi (m.)/**habibti** (fem.) (Ar.) dear one

Hai hawiyyatik? (Ar.) Is that your ID?

haj (m.)/**haji** (fem.) (Ar.) term of respect for an older person; lit. someone who has made pilgrimage to Mecca

Hakol b'seder? (Heb.) Is everything okay?

hamam (Ar.) bathroom

Hamas Palestinian political movement formed in 1987, during the First Intifada; acronym for **Harakat al-Muqāwamah al-Islāmiyyah,** Islamic Resistance Movement

Hamdullilah or **al-Hamdullilah** (Ar.) lit. All praise is due to God alone; polite response to How are you?, or a way of indicating you are done eating.

Hamdullilah assalaam (Ar.) greeting for one who has returned safely from a trip, from prison, or survived an injury or illness (reply: Allah ysalmak/ysalmik)

haram (Ar.) for shame

harbaan (Ar.) damaged; out of order

Hasidic a Jewish fundamentalist sect

hawiyya Palestinian ID card issued by Israeli authorities

Hek willa hek? (Ar.) Like this or like that?

Hezb i-Shab Palestinian People's Party, formerly the Palestinian Communist Party

hijab (Ar.) head covering worn by many Muslim women

Hinei he (Heb.) Here she is

hon (Ar.) here

Iftah, lo samaht (Ar.) Open the door please

Il Ra'is (Ar.) the President

Btihki Inglizi mnih, sah? (Ar.) You speak English well, right?

Andik camera? (Ar.) Do you have a camera?

insh'alla (Ar.) God willing

Inti mitjawzi? (Ar.) Are you married?

Intifada il Uwle (Ar.) First Intifada

Ismo Bassam (Ar.) His name is Bassam.

Israelien (Palestinian English) Israeli

Itsharafna (or **tasharafna**) (Ar.) Honored to meet you

jahez (Ar.) (m.)/**jaheza** (fem.) ready

Jamia i-Shabia Popular Front
for the Liberation of Palestine
(Palestinian political party)

jamil (Ar.) beautiful

Jawwal (Ar.) Palestinian mobile
phone carrier; lit. walking
around

jesh (Ar.) (Israeli) army

jid (Ar.) grandfather

jidi (Ar.) goat

jilbab (Ar.) a long coat worn by
many Palestinian women

joz (Ar.) husband

kalb (Ar.) dog

Kama? (Heb.) How much?

kamaan wahad (Ar.) one more

keffiyeh (Ar.) a traditional Arab
scarf or headcovering

ken (Heb.) yes

khalas (Ar.) finished; stop; enough

Kiif halik? (Ar.) How are you?

knaffe a Palestinian dessert made
with cheese, especially common
in Nablus

kousa (Ar.) squash

k'tzat (Heb.) a little

kundera (Ar.) shoes

laa (Ar.) no

labneh (Ar.) yogurt

L'an? (Heb.) Where are you going?

Lekhasot (Heb.) to cover

Lo, ani lo reavah. (Heb.) No, I'm
not hungry.

Lo bseder (Heb.) Not okay

Lo mevinah (Heb.) I don't
understand

Lo yodaat (Heb.) I don't know

luuti (Ar.) homosexual
(derogatory)

Maat (Ar.) He died

mabrouk (Ar.) congratulations

Machsom (Heb.) checkpoint
Machsom Watch Israeli wom-
en's organization that monitors
checkpoints in the West Bank

Ma habe'ayah? (Heb.) What's the
problem?

Ma koreh? (Heb.) What's going on?

mahsheesh (Ar.) stuffed vegetables

**Mah yesh lachem b'Sha'ar
Shchem?** (Heb.) Why do you
want to go to Damascus Gate?

makluube (Ar.) a Palestinian dish
made with rice, vegetables,
silver noodles, and chicken

ma'lesh (Ar.) never mind

mamnuah (Ar.) forbidden

Manara Square the center of
Ramallah

mansaf (Ar.) lamb stew

maramiya (Ar.) sage

marhaba (Ar.) greetings

mashalla (Ar.) a blessing, lit. It's God's will.

matbach (Ar.) kitchen

Me atem? (Heb.) Who are you?

Meayfo? (Heb.) From where?

miin? (Ar.) who?

Miit marhaba (Ar.) A hundred greetings

min Gaza (Ar.) from Gaza

Min weyn inta? (Ar.) Where are you from?

mish mushqele (Ar.) no problem

mithli (m.) /**mithliya** (fem.) (Ar.) gay; lit. like; same; homo

mujaddara (Ar.) Palestinian dish of lentils and rice

molochia (Ar.) soup made from Egyptian spinach

mnih (Ar.) fine

mqabala (Ar.) dialogue, normalization

muhabarat (Ar.) secret police

mujaddara (Ar.) a Palestinian dish of lentils and rice

mulsaqaat (Ar.) stickers

mumkin (Ar.) could be; possible

Mumkin ahki maa... (Ar.) May I speak with...

mwaffak (Ar.) good luck

naam (Ar.) yes

naami andna (Ar.) sleep at our house

Nakab (Ar.) the desert in southern Israel (Heb. **Negev**)

nana (Ar.) mint

Neve Tirzah Israeli women's prison in Ramle

Nimti kwa'is? (Ar.) Did you sleep well?

niqab (Ar.) face-covering veil

N'okel (Ar.) Let's eat

Olim (Heb.) Jews immigrating to Israel ("making aliyah")

PASSIA Palestinian Academic Society for the Study of International Affairs, publishes an annual datebook and directory of Palestinian, Israeli and international governmental and nongovernmental organizations

Pesach (Heb.) Passover

Qaddeesh umrik? (Ar.) How old are you?

raqabe (Ar.) neck

Red Crescent The Palestine Red Crescent Society (PRCS), a national humanitarian organization which runs ambulances, hospitals, medics and dispenses emergency relief

Red Cross The International Committee of the Red Cross (ICRC), an international humanitarian organization with quasi-governmental status; functions include oversight of prison conditions and monitoring of weapons used against civilians

rotzah (Heb.) (fem.) want

sabah al-kheir (Ar.) morning of joy

sabah an-noor(Ar.) morning of light (response to sabah al kheir)

sabah sneen (Ar.) seven years

sah (Ar.) true

sahibtik (Ar.) (fem.) your friend

Salamtik (Ar.) (fem.) your health (said to someone who is recovering; also when someone sneezes)

Sawrini (Ar.) Take my picture

servees (Ar.) service taxi

settlement an Israeli colony in the West Bank or East Jerusalem for Jews only

Sha'ar Shchem (Heb.) Damascus Gate

shabab (Ar.) youth

SHABAK Israeli secret police, also called Shin Bet

shater/shatra (Ar.) clever boy/girl

shawarma (Ar.) a sandwich of grilled chicken or lamb, served with salad

shelach (Heb.) yours

sherut (Heb.) shared taxi

Shu akhbarik? (Ar.) (fem.) How are things? (lit. What's your news?)

Shu hada? (Ar.) What's this?

Shu ismik? (Ar.) (fem.) What's your name?

shukran (Ar.) thank you

sitti (Ar.) my grandmother

snaan (Ar.) teeth

suhaqqiyya (Ar.) lesbian (derogatory), plural **suhaqqiyyaat**

sulha (Ar.) a traditional Palestinian form of conflict resolution

sulta (Ar.) authority; Palestinian authority

suq (Ar.) market

ta'al/ta'ali (Ar.) come

taba'an (Ar.) of course

tachtonim underpants

tamam (Ar.) okay

tasrih (Ar.) permit

tawjihi (Ar.) college entrance exam

Taybeh Palestinian beer (manufactured in Taybeh village, in the Ramallah area)

tayeb (Ar.) good

Tekhase et ha'einayim shela (Heb.)
Cover her eyes

T'faddal/t'faddali/t'faddalu (Ar.)
(masc./fem./plural) Come in;
join me

**Tash'iri et ha'einayim shelakh
mekhusot l'od khamesh dakot!**
(Heb.) Keep your eyes covered
for five more minutes!

tjawaz (Ar.) to marry

Tsharafna or **itsharafna (Ar.)** Nice
to meet you

ustaz (Ar.) teacher (also general
term of respect)

wajib (Ar.) duty; homework

Waqf (Ar.) the Islamic trust with
authority over the Muslim holy
sites in Jerusalem, including the
Al-Aqsa Mosque

Weyn? (Ar.) where?

Weyn bakeeti? (Ar.; *colloquial*)
(fem.) Where have you been?

Weyn imik? (Ar.) Where is your
mother?

yaa achti (Ar.) my sister

yaa akh (Ar.) my brother

yaa binti (Ar.) my daughter

ya'anni (Ar.) I mean, like… (lit. it
means)

yaa walad (Ar.) young man

Yahudi (Ar.) (m.) Jew; Israeli

yalla (Ar.) Let's go!

yesh (Heb.) there is/is there

Yesh lach teudot? (Heb.) Do you
have papers?

Yesh po mishehu (Heb.) Someone
is here

Yom il Ahad (Ar.) Sunday

Yom il Jumaa (Ar.) Friday

za'atar (Ar.) a Palestinian blend
of oregano, thyme, and other
herbs, usually mixed with
sesame, salt, and sumac; also a
wild herb, similar to oregano or
thyme, indigenous to the Levant
countries

zai hek (Ar.) like this

zaki (Ar.) delicious

zar/bizur (Ar.) visited/visiting

SELECTED TITLES FROM SHE WRITES PRESS

She Writes Press is an independent publishing company
founded to serve women writers everywhere.
Visit us at www.shewritespress.com.

Murder Under The Bridge: A Palestine Mystery by Kate Raphael
$16.95, 978-1-63152-960-3

Rania, a Palestinian police detective with a young son, meets cheeky Jewish-American feminist Chloe at an Israeli checkpoint—and soon becomes embroiled in a murder case that implicates the highest echelons of the Israeli military.

In the Shadow of Lies: A Mystery Novel by M. A. Adler
$16.95, 978-1-938314-82-7

As World War II comes to a close, homicide detective Oliver Wright returns home—only to find himself caught up in the investigation of a complicated murder case rife with racial tensions.

The Wiregrass by Pam Webber
$16.95, 978-1-63152-943-6

A story about a summer of discontent, change, and dangerous mysteries in a small Southern Wiregrass town.

Water On the Moon by Jean P. Moore
$16.95, 978-1-938314-61-2

When her home is destroyed in a freak accident, Lidia Raven, a divorced mother of two, is plunged into a mystery that involves her entire family.

Glass Shatters by Michelle Meyers
$16.95, 978-1-63152-018-1

Following the mysterious disappearance of his wife and daughter, scientist Charles Lang goes to desperate lengths to escape his past and reinvent himself.

A Girl Like You: A Henrietta and Inspector Howard Novel by Michelle Cox
$16.95, 978-1-63152-016-7

When the floor matron at the dance hall where Henrietta works as a taxi dancer turns up dead, aloof Inspector Clive Howard appears on the scene—and convinces Henrietta to go undercover for him, plunging her into Chicago's gritty underworld.